Too Far North

Musical Scenes from the North East

Ian Fawdon

© Ian Fawdon 2024

ISBN: 978-1-7392233-4-2

All rights reserved. No part of this book may be reproduced, stored or introduced into a retrieval system or transmitted in any way or by any means (electronic, mechanical, photocopying, recording or otherwise) without the prior permission of the publishers.

The opinions expressed in this book are those of the author.

Published by:

City of Newcastle Upon Tyne
Newcastle Libraries
Tyne Bridge Publishing, 2024
unless otherwise indicated

Front cover: Lindisfarne playing one of their famous Christmas concerts at Newcastle City Hall.
Photo credit: Stuart Outterside.

Back cover: This Aint Vegas at the Royalty Pub, Sunderland c2001.
Photo credit: Steven Landles

Contents

Introduction 7

1. The Animals and the 1960s 13
John Steel - The Junco Partners - The Elcort - Mick Gallagher - Johnny Turnbull

2. Folk Music 59
Lindisfarne - Prelude - The High Level Ranters - The Unthanks - Kathryn Williams - Richard Dawson - The Young'uns

3. Punk Rock 143
Penetration - Punishment of Luxury - Angelic Upstarts - The Carpettes - Neon - The Toy Dolls - White Heat - Showbiz Kids

4. New Wave of British Heavy Metal .. 222
Raven - Venom/Venom Inc - Tygers of Pan Tang - Steve Thompson - Fist - Mythra

5. Kitchenware Records 287
Keith Armstrong and Kitchenware Records - Martin Stephenson and the Daintees - The Kane Gang - Hurrah!

6. Sunderland Scene 332
The Futureheads - Maximo Park - This Aint Vegas - Field Music - Frankie & The Heartstrings - Nadine Shah

Conclusion 399

Introduction

In 1964 The Animals, from Newcastle, had a number one hit with "House of the Rising Sun" in both the UK and the American singles chart. It catapulted them into the epicentre of the 'British Invasion' that conquered the US along with the Beatles and the Rolling Stones. They appeared on *The Ed Sullivan show* in the US in October 1964 just as the Beatles had done so famously only eight months earlier. They quickly moved to London and, in a sense, never returned to their North East roots. They showed themselves comfortable in the pop world of London where they would hang out with Lennon and McCartney in the capital's trendy nightspots. However, after they made their move the music scene from which they emerged in 1960s Newcastle remained a busy one. They left behind lots of great bands, great clubs for the bands to play and a large, receptive audience of loyal fans. Despite all this, A&R men weren't beating a path up to Newcastle to find 'the next Animals'.

Meanwhile, the Liverpool music scene dominated the UK charts for a number of years following the emergence of the Beatles. This scene became known as the Merseybeat and included Gerry and the Pacemakers and Cilla Black, who had number ones around the world. Other acts from Liverpool that went on to have national hits included Billy Fury, The Merseybeats, The Swinging Blue Jeans, Billy J Kramer and the Dakotas, The Fourmost and The Searchers. Some were great, some less so. The equivalent success from the North East was scant, in fact it was almost non-existent. People who were involved in the North East scene will argue, with some justification, that the top bands from the North East at the time, The Junco Partners, The Elcort, The Sect and others were certainly as good as some of the lesser Merseybeat bands if not better. Why, then, did they not repeat the Liverpool bands' success? The reasons may be manifold and will be discussed on these pages but one reason may be that we are just too far north.

In subsequent years there have been many so-called music scenes attached to different geographies in the UK. There have been scenes from Manchester with Factory Records and then the 'Madchester scene' of the Happy Mondays and the Stone Roses. There has been the Glasgow Scene around Postcard Records and an electronica scene around Heaven 17, The Human League and Cabaret Voltaire in Sheffield. In the 1980s and 90s in Bristol there was a Trip Hop scene that included Massive Attack, Tricky, Portishead and even the graffiti artist Banksy. There has been no equivalent scene in the North East. Why this is so is one of the questions that this book will attempt to address.

So, what makes a music scene in the first place? Certainly a scene needs bands who have similar tastes and similar attitudes coming into being at the same time. However, we will see in the Kitchenware Records period in the 1980s, there were four bands from the North East, in Prefab Sprout, the Kane Gang, Martin Stephenson and the Daintees and Hurrah! who were successful at the same time and shared the Kitchenware label but had completely diverse musical influences. So, although they may have shared attitudes, particularly a belief that you did not need to move to London to succeed, there was never a definable 'Kitchenware sound'. Indeed there has never been a period where there has been a 'Newcastle sound' or a 'North East sound' and this may be one of the reasons why no scene has been nationally acknowledged.

Other elements required to have a coherent scene are musical venues that are willing to put these types of acts on, and an audience that will turn out to support them. You also need recording studios, good music managers, music journalists who will champion the bands of the scene and record labels, ideally in the area, or alternatively record label A&R staff drawn to the area. Not all these elements exist effectively at the same time in any of the periods I will look at and that may contribute to why there has been no nationally recognised scenes.

To try to answer some of the questions posed above I set out to hear stories from the horses' mouths. I have identified six different periods of time when so-called scenes existed and have talked to people who were at the centre of those movements. It starts with the Animals in the 1960s, then moves on to Lindisfarne and the folk scene, then punk, The New Wave of Heavy Metal and then Kitchenware Records of the '80s and '90s. The book finishes with what may be the most coherent of all scenes now based in Sunderland with bands like the Futureheads and Field Music along with Maximo Park who, though not from Sunderland, were very much part of that explosion that began in the early 2000s. The reason why I say that it may be the most coherent is because 20 years after it began its protagonists are still going and are opening venues and studios in the city, they are helping to drive cultural change in their city and usher in the next generation of talent.

In talking to this musically diverse bunch of weird and wonderful people I got some answers to my questions but more importantly I got viscerally human stories of amazing highs and crushing disappointments. I got a glimpse of why some people rise to prominence and why some fall by the wayside. Sometimes I got hints of a wider North Eastern trait of the brash, loud and assertive exterior masking an inner lack of self-confidence. As you would guess, I consistently got a passion for music, that in some cases is still taking them round the world 40 years after picking up their instruments or singing their first song. It also became apparent that I was getting firsthand accounts that may vary from the recollections of others who were involved at the time. I have therefore subtitled each sections as that person's story in recognition that had I talked to another member of said band I may have got a wildly different account. Such is the vagaries of the human memory.

If the above sets out what this book is generally about it is important to state what the book is not. It is not an attempt to write an exhaustive history of popular music of the North East. If I have missed out your favourite band or singer I apologise as I am sure there will be readers who will scream the name of the band I have omitted. I could have done a section, for example, on the great 1970s rock bands such as Beckett, Brass Alley and Fogg. Equally, there have been many great punk bands in the region after the initial explosion such as Leatherface from Sunderland, China Drum from Ovingham, Crane from Newcastle and currently one of the best bands in the regions, Martha from Pity Me in Durham. However, any book needs to not out stay its welcome. I have chosen, rightly or wrongly, to stick to the six periods identified above.

It also needs to be acknowledged that although I have included a number of fantastic female artists they are massively outweighed by their male counterparts. I did approach a number of females who were either unwilling or unable to contribute but there has been a general lack of female artists that have risen to prominence in this area of the country. It is, therefore, encouraging that things appear to be changing on that front with Keith Armstrong's Soul Kitchen Recordings championing a lot of female talent and great acts coming through such as the late Faye Fantarrow and Bigfatbig. Hopefully this trend continues.

When interviewing Ray Laidlaw of Lindisfarne, he mentioned Mark Knopfler, who he had known prior to Mark's move down south. He asked me if I thought Dire Straits were a North East band to which I replied, 'No, they are not.' Although Mark and his brother Dave grew up in Gosforth and their keyboard player, Alan Clark, was born in Chester le Street, they were formed in London and that's where they remained. The same can be said with Bryan Ferry and Roxy Music, Sting and the Police and Dave Stewart and the Eurythmics. They may have cut their teeth with bands like The Gas Board, Last Exit and

Longdancer but their careers took off in London. They are associated with multi-selling bands that are definitively not North East bands.

Whether this book answers the question as to why there haven't been nationally recognised music scenes from here in the North East will be decided by you the reader. Whether it is even an important question is also worth considering. However, what the book does do, is give a voice to many musicians who have had various levels of success but all seem to have the same passion for music and the same pride in the regions in which they were born and grew up in. They will tell tales of success, failure, pride and disappointment. They will also tell of periods of great excitement that produced fantastic music and fantastic memories for those who created this music and those who were in the audience. If it does nothing else I hope that it may get you to seek out some musicians and singers that you may not have come across before and you may find your new favourite band, even if its 40 years too late.

Ian Fawdon

1. The Animals and the 1960s

The 1960s were a vibrant time for the UK and for British music it was the most vibrant time. This decade has been given the epithet The Swinging Sixties and one particular year, 1967, The Summer of Love. It was a period of optimism and opportunity. The biggest single reason for this was the end of post-war austerity. Rationing had ended in 1954 and by the early '60s there was an economic boom in the UK and an extended period of full employment. People had money in their pockets and, coming out of a grey, dreary time, a desire to have fun and spend their hard-earned money on being entertained.

Three particular phenomena contributed to the fuel that fed the music boom of the '60s. Firstly, National Service ended in 1960. This was a system of peace-time conscription whereby young men from the age of 18 had to serve two years in one of the armed services. For some this was a chance to travel the world but for others it was a dark cloud that was to be dreaded and then endured. For the members of the Beatles, The Kinks, The Rolling Stones, The Who and The Animals it was like the lifting of a veil. It said to them you decide your future not the state. And subconsciously all those people and thousands of others determined to make the most of the two years of their life that they had been given back.

The second major contributing factor to the mushrooming of the music scene was the existence of skiffle music. This was a do-it-yourself musical movement that used acoustic guitars along with readily available household objects like washboards for percussion and tea chests to make rudimentary bass instruments. Lonnie Donegan took this style of music to the top of the charts but it was the first time that young people could truly see that making the music of their heroes was actually accessible. This was repeated 20 years later with the punk rock movement but the effect of skiffle was greater and more widespread than its punk successor. It has been said that at its height in 1957, there were 50,000 skiffle bands in Great Britain including, most famously The Quarry Men, the first band of John Lennon and Paul McCartney.

Thirdly, was the rise of the teenager. The term teenager, although first used in the 1890s, really came to prominence in the 1950s. Prior to this, children between the ages of 13 and 19 were to 'be seen and not heard'. In the late 1950s and the 1960s teenagers began to question authority and ask whether, in fact, their parents' generation had all the answers. The outpourings of emotion and hysteria that was evident in Beatlemania was seen as a threat to the norms of society but was perhaps young people expressing, very loudly, that this new music was something they were passionate about and something that was uniquely for them.

There were other contributing factors in the rise of teenage music, such as the proliferation of Arts Colleges and the idea that one could leave school and join an Arts College to develop a career in some part of the arts but perhaps more importantly hang around with other creative souls and find yourself. Both Eric Burdon and John Steele of the Animals went to Art School in Newcastle which is where they met and started their musical career. This was replicated by John Lennon, Pete Townsend, Keith Richards, Ray Davies and many others.

A further factor in the music explosion of the '60s was the

existence of pirate radio stations. Prior to their rise people would listen to a rather staid and middle-aged BBC which favoured big bands and balladeers. Radio stations such as Radio Caroline and Radio London broadcast on the medium wave from offshore locations such as ships or disused sea forts. For the first time rock and roll music by people such as Elvis Presley, Buddy Holly and Little Richard could be heard by the youth of Great Britain and created a template for them to follow.

So, in 1964 all the factors were in place for the Animals to be ready to make their move for global stardom. The North East was full of clubs that would put bands on that catered for the demands of the youth market. Most famously there was the Club a'Gogo in Newcastle, which put on all the top acts of the day such as the Rolling Stones but also top blues stars from the US such as Howlin' Wolf and Muddy Waters. The Club a'Gogo had the Animals as their resident band, later followed by the Junco Partners. However, there were many other equally bouncing clubs such as El Cubana in Sunderland, the Majestic Ballroom in Newcastle, the Manhole in Wallsend, the Quay Club in Newcastle, the Mayfair Ballroom in Newcastle, the Cellar Club in South Shields. Full employment meant that there was a surfeit of disposable income that could ensure that such clubs could be full whenever opened and enough great bands to mean that there were gigs to attend sometimes six nights a week.

The Animals scored their first number One hit "The House of the Rising Sun" in July 1964 and were then pretty much lost to the North East. The scene they left behind remained a lively one, probably up until 1968, but no other band followed the ascent of the Animals. The reasons that the Animals achieved such dizzying success can be explained by a number of factors. They were the North East's undisputed top band. The gritty, soulful and powerful singing of Eric Burdon was a key standout. So was the Vox Continental organ sound of Alan Price, along with the musical strength of the rest of the band. They had a pushy and sometimes aggressive manager in Mike Jeffrey and their choice of songs to record was pretty inspired. Their early big hits, with the exception of "I'm Crying" were cover versions of songs by other artists.

Why, then, did no other bands repeat the success of the Animals? As will be discussed, the bands didn't tend to write their own songs. They had seen the Animals score a transatlantic number one with a song first played in the pop and rock market by Bob Dylan. Why bother writing your own songs when there were any number of obscure R&B songs recorded unsuccessfully by other artists? By 1964 the British Invasion of the US was in full swing and most of the bands involved had started successfully writing their own songs. This failure to recognise the importance of writing original material may be the biggest factor in why there was so little follow-on success for the region.

It may also be that there weren't enough good managers about to exploit the boom. Equally, the national reputation of the region's music may have been affected by the lack of journalists promoting the bands in the area, as Bill Harry had done with his fledgling pop magazine in Liverpool in 1961 *The Mersey Beat*.

Whatever the reasons were, there is undoubtedly a little sadness that we didn't get to hear much recorded material from the likes of the Junco Partners, The Elcort, The Sect, The Kylastrons and others. Go on YouTube and listen to "Take This Hammer" by The Junco Partners and you will hear some great music and great singers and musicians. That there were so few bands signed and recorded from that period is something to regret. However, talk to musicians from the time and you will hear little regret. You will hear musicians who feel lucky to have been about and at the centre of probably the most exciting musical scene ever in the North East of England.

The Animals

John Steel's Story

On July 11th 1964 the Animals went to number one in the UK charts with their second single, "The House of the Rising Sun". This single also topped the US charts that same year. Their first single, "Baby Let me Take you Home", had been released in March of 1964 and rose to a very respectable 21 in the UK charts.

The Animals story began, however, in 1956 when 15-year-old Eric Burdon met 15-year-old John Steel at the Newcastle College of Art and Industrial Design. Their first band was called the Pagans. Various groups coalesced into the Alan Price Rhythm and Blues Combo between 1962 and 1963. This was the group that contained the five members of the first, definitive group known as the Animals – Eric Burdon, Alan Price, Hilton Valentine, John Steel and Chas Chandler. The band moved to London in January 1964, leaving behind a scattered group of musicians and groups but no discernible scene.

Eric Burdon was born on May 11th 1941 in Walker, a small suburb nestled just to the east of Newcastle upon Tyne. Like so many places in the North East of England, Walker's history is tied up with the twin industries of coal mining and shipbuilding. Wherever it came from, Burdon turned out to possess one of the most distinctive and powerful voices in rock and roll.

Alan Price was born in Fatfield, County Durham on April 19th 1942. Fatfield, now part of the City of Sunderland, is a pit village and is nearly 12 miles from Newcastle. Alan was a self-taught musician. He later studied at Jarrow Grammar School. He was a naturally talented musician playing both keyboards and guitar. And like Eric and John he was inspired by Skiffle. As he moved on to rock and roll, and most notably with a fascination in Jerry Lee Lewis he began to get a reputation in the North East as a musician that was going places.

Burdon, Steel and Price played together as the Pagans and the Kansas City Five (and Seven). Failing to turn up for a gig, the rest of the band discovered that Price had been poached by the Kon-Tors without telling the remaining Kansas boys. It turned out that the bass player of the Kon-Tors was a burly 6ft 4 inch Bryan 'Chas' Chandler. A few years older, Chas was born in Heaton, another suburb of Newcastle, in 1938. Chandler was far more a pop fan than the more obscure R&B/Jazz tastes of Burdon and Steel. He was a Beatles fanatic. He was a happy-go-lucky gent who loved a pint and a night in the pub.

Completing the classic Animals line up was guitarist Hilton Valentine. Hilton was born in to 1943 in North Shields, just down the road from Burdon's birthplace of Walker.

The Animals were Newcastle's equivalent of the Beatles. They had a string of hits including the aforementioned number one "The House of the Rising Sun", "Don't Let Me Be Misunderstood," which got to number two in the UK charts and "We Gotta Get Out of This Place," which got to number three. They were also part of the 'British Invasion' of the US along with the Beatles, The Rolling Stones and The Who. They first played in the US in October 1964 and featured on the *Ed Sullivan Show* as the Beatles had, so famously, done just eight months earlier.

Although I have had fruitful correspondence with John Steel, my friend and broadcaster/writer, Neil Saint, had recently interviewed John for his Retropopic Radio show and kindly let me reproduce the interview for this book. Thanks Neil!

NS: What are your childhood memories growing up in Gateshead?

John Steel: I've got happy memories. The part of Gateshead I grew up in was high up and looked out over Newcastle and over to the coast. So it was a nice view. You could see 'the big city' but a lot of Tyneside at the time was black and dirty with coal mining and heavy industry. Where I lived it was almost a village on the fringe of Gateshead, so I had a very happy childhood.

NS: How did you listen to music in those days?

John Steel: We always had a record player at home. I was the youngest of four children and my elder brother was into some good stuff really. He tended towards jazz and he had things like Fats Waller and that interested me. My two sisters were into show tunes so there was always music going on. We started off with 78 rpm shellac records when I was a kid. The first single I bought in something like 1954/5 was a Bill Haley single, "Shake Rattle and Roll". It was a good number. Me and my mates were 15 and we were exploring rock and roll and discovered that this song was originally a hardcore rhythm and blues song by Big Mama Thornton. From that we started to discover that a lot of pop hits were actually covers of black artists' rock and roll and rhythm and blues songs. It was really exciting at the time to be a teenager.

NS: Can you tell me about those early days of your friendship with Eric Burdon?

John Steel: It was at the Newcastle College of Art and Industrial Design and on the first day, actually, while we were enrolling, I turned round and shouted, 'Does any else here love jazz?' Eric piped up 'yeah' and we hit it off on that very first day. We discovered that we both liked the same things, jazz, rock and roll, American movies. Just about anything that inspired us then came from America. This was 1956 and England was struggling to get out of the war years and things like rationing and austerity and America seemed to be this magical new planet from across the water. So it was a great time to be a teenager and Eric and me had the same outlook on things. We became great chums and within months we formed a band.

NS: Your first love was trad jazz. What turned you away from that and onto rhythm and blues?

John Steel: Until about 1956 when rock and roll took over, the music for young people was trad jazz and that was what was played at things like the college hops. And suddenly it all changed in 1956 with Elvis Presley and "Heartbreak Hotel" and then with Lonnie Donegan starting the Skiffle craze with "Rock Island Line" [1]. After Lonnie had his hit, everyone was listening to it and thinking well, I could do that, it's only three chords. All you needed was a cheap guitar. This was the new music and suddenly trad jazz was old hat.

NS: What drew you towards the drums?

John Steel: We started off as a four-piece dixieland jazz outfit. I was getting by on trumpet but Eric was struggling on trombone. We had a lad called Jimmy on banjo and a lad called Alan with a snare drum and a hi-hat and that was his kit. There was just this moment when we knew we were wasting our time. Eric said, 'I don't want to play trombone, I want to sing rock and roll.' He just knew he wanted to sing. At that age you're so open minded so Jimmy said, 'Ok, I'll sell me banjo and get a guitar.' Alan, who had the snare drum said, 'I want to get one of these new things, the bass guitar.' I said, 'Ok, well I'll play drums then.' So we became the Pagans rather than the Pagan Jazz Men and started playing rock and pop covers. Simple as that!

NS: Tell me how you met Alan Price and encouraged him to take up the keyboard?

John Steel: We had a gig in a church hall in Byker, a rough area near Newcastle and there was another band playing and the leader of this band played the Jerry Lee Lewis piano. There was another kid playing rhythm guitar and he strolled over to us while we were doing our set and asked if he could sit in. There was an upright, church hall piano, probably out of tune and he sat at this piano and knocked seven bells out of it. He was great, he had a really strong 'boogie' left hand. And that was Alan Price. It was a collective decision, *we've got to have him*. Alan knew he was a better player than the leader of his current band so he was ready for a move and we just poached him and that became the nucleus of what became the Animals, Eric, Alan and me.

NS: How did it progress from there?

John Steel: Well we all needed jobs. Eric became a window dresser, Alan worked in the Tax Office and I got a job in an aircraft factory in Hertfordshire doing technical drawings as the college we'd been to had been more industrial than fine art. So the band split up for a while. Eric never got what I'd call a 'proper job'. I think he always knew he'd be a musician of some sort. He got some work doing the interior design for a jazz and blues club called the Club a'Gogo in Newcastle and that kept him going with pocket money. I did four months in the drawing office down south and I thought I'm in the wrong place here so I headed back to Newcastle and got a job in a department store. I got back with Alan and Eric and we played around with a whole bunch of guys and had different line ups but we called ourselves the Kansas City Five. The whole inspiration for the band was an album by Joe Turner called *Boss of the Blues* which featured the Count Basie rhythm section who were from Kansas City. We got a couple of guys from Ghana who played alto-sax and trumpet and we became the Kansas City Seven.

NS: I get the impression you were just absorbing music in the Newcastle club scene. Is that what is was like?

John Steel: It was, we had some great things going on. There was a world class jazz outfit called the EmCee Five with Ian Carr and his brother Mike Carr and plenty of other people who we could watch and learn from. We had lots of gigs and one day Alan Price just didn't turn up. He'd been poached by another band called the Kon-Tors who were a good covers band. The guy who poached him was their bass player called Chas Chandler, who eventually became the bass player of the Animals. That move took the heart out of the Kansas City Seven and it just fell apart. I got a job in a night club wearing a tuxedo, playing the brushes on stuff like "Fly Me to the Moon" and "Girl From Ipanema" backing cabaret singers. Because I was playing in nightclubs between sort of eight till two in the morning for about a year I was out of touch with what was going on. Anyway I was walking down the street in Newcastle and I bumped into Chas who said, 'Johnny, we've been looking for you, we've got this band together with Eric and Alan and the drummer is driving us up the wall. Would you come and join us?' And I said 'I can't afford to do that Chas, I'm on £15 a week.' So Chas said, 'Hell man, I think I guarantee you £14 a week and you'd be playing good stuff'. So I said, 'Ok, you're on.' Anyway I had to work my notice so I had no time to rehearse and we had a gig at the Downbeat Club for an all-nighter - 12 till three in the morning. I turned up and there was Alan, Eric, Chas and a new guitarist, Hilton Valentine and we were called The Alan Price Rhythm and Blues Combo.

NS: Who came up with the name the Animals?

John Steel: This was a guy called Graham Bond [2] who had a great band with Ginger Baker on drums and bass player, Jack Bruce, both of whom formed Cream with Eric Clapton. At this time we were the house band at the Club a'Gogo and Graham was a star turn there. One night Graham got up and jammed with us on our second slot and he loved it. He said to us 'You've got to get down to London, you guys'. It was 1963 and the Beatles were already showing the way to go. So the manager of the club, Mike Jeffrey, immediately saw pound signs. He got us to sign a management deal and went off to meet some people down London that Graham had put him in touch with. He met up with a gentleman called Rohan O'Rahilly who ran a club in the heart of London called The Scene Club. Mike came back to

Newcastle in November/December 1963 and said, 'We've got a deal. We're going to swap gigs with the Yardbirds[3]. They're coming up here and you're going down to London.' And he said, 'By the way Graham Bond came up with this great name for you. You're going to be called the Animals. Graham said you've got to get rid of that big clunky name and get something more snappy like the Beatles.' The only guy who didn't like it was Alan Price.

NS: You recorded your first single down in London, "Baby Let me Take you Home" which was a retitled and rocky version of Bob Dylan's "Baby Let me Follow you Down". It was a top 30 hit. How did it feel entering the charts with your first record?

John Steel: It was really exciting. While we were playing these gigs down in London two key people came up to us. One was Mickie Most, who was a top independent record producer. The other was Peter Grant, who later managed Led Zeppelin. At the time Peter was a booker working on the phone for the Don Arden Agency[4]. So, through Peter, we were invited to meet Don Arden at his Mayfair office. Peter and Mickie were there. Don told us, from behind a massive desk, that he was bringing over Chuck Berry from the US for his first ever UK tour and he wanted us to tour with him for three weeks. We thought wow because Chuck Berry was one of our gods. So within weeks of leaving Newcastle we had a hit record with Mickie Most and a tour with Chuck Berry.

We were out on the tour with Chuck and we had a respectable hit with "Baby Let me Take you Home" but the song that we were playing that really caused a stir when we played it live was "House of the Rising Sun". We realised we had to record it.

NS: How did you put "House of the Rising Sun" together?'

John Steel: We lifted it from Bob Dylan's first album which was acoustic. We just played it in our style but Hilton had come up with that distinctive guitar arpeggio. Funnily enough Alan didn't like that intro and was a bit sniffy about it and he went off in a huff. When he came back he heard us play it and then dropped in this great organ solo in the middle which took it up a level. Mickie had booked a session for the show *Ready Steady Go* and we were asked to do something. We said, 'While we're there let's get "Rising Sun" in the can.' We played Liverpool with Chuck Berry and having played our set we drove down to London to this tiny one-track studio to do the recording. We set up, played a few bars to get the sound levels right and then went for a take. We played it once all the way through and Mickie said, 'Come and have a listen to this.' We trooped in and listened and Mickie said, 'That's it we've got it in the can and that's a hit record.' So what went to number one was a one take, live recording with no overdubs.

NS: You had three hits in a row all featuring Eric's distinctive voice. How did success affect your art school mate?

John Steel: We were still very much a co-operative five piece and we all accepted Eric was the front man. We also accepted that we each had a part in the distinctive sound so there was never any conflict in that and no ego trips from Eric.

NS: By 1966 you'd had five top 10 hits in the UK and "The House of the Rising Sun" had been number one in both the UK and the US. So why did you leave the Animals?

John Steel: Basically it was down to bad management. Mike Jeffrey, our manager, had never managed anyone before. We were on a weekly retainer and I'd just got married. We were on the same money we'd been on since 1964. We'd been promised record royalties but they had been going into an offshore account in the Bahamas and not to us so, we were basically ripped off. And by 1966 I thought what am I doing here. It was like a treadmill. You hardly got a day off playing and if you did get a day off you would have to do photo shoots or interviews. And by this time there were already cracks in the band. The band got a replacement for me but completely broke up three or four months later.

•••••••••••••••••

Eric Burdon and John Steel were art school boys at around the same time as future rock and rollers John Lennon, Pete Townsend, Keith Richards and Ray Davies. Art schools in the '50s and '60s were free thinking places where young people with a creative bent but no fixed career ambitions could go to 'find themselves' and be inspired by the fellow creatives they met there. Such institutions barely exist now. However, equally importantly all the Animals would cite the Skiffle movement and Lonnie Donegan and the DIY ethic that it espoused as what set them on the road to stardom. Read any book by or about the Beatles, the Who, the Rolling Stones or the Kinks and they were also all set on their way by Skiffle. It is not that much a stretch to say that the DIY ethic that Skiffle engendered was the same as what fired the punk rock movement 20 years later or even the home recording culture that exists today. What we can say is that the 'British Invasion' groups were the first wave after Skiffle (and Elvis Presley) and every wave that has come since has been part of this continuum.

Another one of the Animals 1960s acolytes, the non-art school attending Paul McCartney, headlined Glastonbury at the splendid age of 80. John Steel mentions to me in our correspondence that he is off to Port Talbot that day to do a gig with his current incarnation of the Animals. That may not be on the scale of Glastonbury but it is impressive nonetheless. When their bands started off it was felt that musicians who reached the age of 30 were past it and ready for retirement. Yet here we are 60 years later and the people who started rock and roll in the UK are still leading the way. And so the wave continues.

1. "Rock Island Line" was the first UK skiffle hit for the singer Lonnie Donegan in 1956. It was a re-working of a song by the blues singer, Lead Belly. George Harrison is credited as saying 'No Lead Belly, no Beatles'. And in doing so he is identifying the key influence of Skiffle on the Beatles.

2. Graham Bond was a blues and rock singer considered to be a founding father of the British R&B scene of the 1960s.

3. The Yardbirds were a British rock band in the 1960s who, at various times, had as their guitarist Eric Clapton, Jeff Beck and Jimmy Page. They had a string of hits in the 1960s including 'For Your Love'.

4. Don Arden was a tough-guy music manager who managed amongst others Jerry Lee Lewis, Black Sabbath and ELO. His aggressive and sometimes illegal approach to management earned him a number of monikers including 'the Al Capone of Pop'. He was the father of Sharon Osborne, who married and managed Ozzy Osborne.

Junco Partners

Ron Barker's Story

The Junco Partners were the next band after the Animals touted to make it big when the Animals left for London in 1964. Legend has it that the Junco Partners replaced the Animals as the resident band at the Club a'Gogo in Newcastle. While this may not be strictly true, it can be said with certainty that they were massively popular with North East audiences and there was a certain expectation that national fame awaited them. They were signed up by the music mogul, Robert Stigwood, a man who is famous for managing the Bee Gees but was also suggested as one of the people who was considered to replace Brian Epstein after he died. They released one single in 1965 on Columbia records, "As Long as I Have you", which unfortunately sank everywhere but the North East. It is, as their singer Ron Barker readily admits, a rather pedestrian choice of song. However, if you listen to the B-side, a cover of the Lead Belly song, "Take this Hammer" you get more of a feel of what made the band stars in their native area. With its stirring harmonica introduction, its fantastic wailing dual vocals and its R&B stomp it gives you some idea of the energy that gave them their reputation. It has a feel of both the early Who and the Rolling Stones. However, it wasn't to be and their singers, Ron Barker and John Anderson left in 1968. The band then morphed into a psych-rock sound and released one album and famously sat in as the house band for blues legend Howlin' Wolf before finally calling it a day in 1971.

Then in 1977, inspired by the energy of punk rock, they got back together to play to appreciative audiences around the region. Amazingly they played for another 37 years until eventually succumbing to the march of time in 2017. Like no other act in this region, they justifiably secured legendary status and yet outside the narrow confines of this area they are almost completely unknown. Their story, in some ways, epitomises the whole premise of this book.

It is apt that I meet singer Ron Barker for a couple of pints and a good old chin wag in the Gosforth Hotel on Gosforth High Street on a sunny June day. This pub has played host to many memorable nights of music and is a place where Ron himself has often sung. Ron is fantastically entertaining company but expresses some surprise that there should still be interest in his band after all these years. Not so, I tell him, before settling back to hear his tale of rubbing shoulders with everyone from Little Richard to Chuck Berry and Jimi Hendrix.

IF: What inspired you to get into music?

Ron Barker: I always sang from being a kid. My uncle sang and my mother sang and it was a musical family. There was Cliff and Bobby Vee and things like that going on and that was okay but really we liked black music such as Chuck Berry and Little Richard. That was what excited me and my mates. Me and John (Anderson, Ron's co-singer in the Junco Partners) used to go to a jazz club and we'd hear things like Lead Belly. This led onto other music like Big Bill Broonzy and Sonny Terry and Brownie McGhee. It quite fired us up.

When I'd just turned 18 I went to the Majestic in Newcastle (which later became the O2 Academy) to see the Beatles. It was their first time in Newcastle. I'd liked their first record, "Love Me Do", and then when "Please, Please Me" came out that was really different, with McCartney's harmonies really standing out.

It was late January 1963. There was a big queue when I got there and I was not too keen to stand in that. But, anyway, I did queue and when they came on, I'd never seen anything like them. I was mesmerised by McCartney with his singing while he was playing the bass. It was incredible. Again, this fired me up another notch. Anyway, I had a pal called Dave Sproat and he was in a band called the Dynamic Orients and they were looking for a singer. They played The Shadows stuff but they needed a singer. Also, I could play the harmonica part from "Love Me Do". So, I was in. I wasn't a bad singer.

Our first booking was autumn '63. We'd play in places like the Snakepit in Blaydon for £5 on a Sunday and that was a real rough house. We'd basically play the Beatles first LP plus a few other songs. Slowly the R&B sounds started coming in. We then started rehearsing with some lads across at Lobley Hill in Gateshead and this developed into what was the Junco Partners. It was me and John singing, with Charlie Harcourt on guitar, John Woods, who was a mate, on drums, and Dave Sproat on bass. We thought we needed an organist because we knew what the Animals were like and we saw Peter Wallis playing in a local social club and we persuaded him to join.

We used to go the Club a'Gogo to see bands. So, we started to practise there and then started playing there after the Animals had had their big hit and moved to London. We used to play the 'Gogo loads.

IF: How serious were you?

Ron Barker: Well, it started as fun but then we got really popular. And, of course, I hated my job at the Ministry, we all hated our jobs! We got the offer to go to Germany to play but Charlie was only 17 so he couldn't go and so we all didn't go. But after a while we thought we would give up our jobs and give it a whirl at being professional musicians.

IF: What other places did you play?

Ron Barker: The Newcastle 'Gogo was the prime place and we'd play there two or three times a week. The Downbeat Club was in Carliol Square in Newcastle, which is where Alan Price used to play early on and we'd play there. There was another Club a'Gogo in Whitley Bay where we'd play. We played a lot in Sunderland at the El Cubana. They were all just little pokey rooms but you could fill them out on a nightly basis. We could be playing up to five nights in a week.

Our reputation also went beyond the North East so we would play in places like Carlisle, Sheffield and Leeds. There were R&B clubs round the country so there was a circuit to play. We would play with people like Rod Stewart, Chris Farlowe and Long John Baldry. I guess we were part of the R&B boom in the mid '60s.

IF: Who were your competition at the time?

Ron Barker: The Gasboard with Bryan Ferry, were quite good for a while. The Elcort were good. There was also the Invaders. We didn't think of them as competition as we were quite arrogant and thought we were the best. We had two singers, which was different and that was purely because John was my mate, it was just fortuitous. John wasn't the greatest singer but he was a natural when on stage and we got on well together.

IF: Were the Animals viewed as the top dogs?

Ron Barker: No, not really. They were known as the Alan Price Set and they didn't really stand out. I remember when they announced at the 'Gogo that they were now called the Animals and they were going down to London. After that they didn't play much up here. The Gamblers[1] were far more popular in Newcastle than the Animals. And we weren't too impressed with their new name!

IF: How did you get your record deal with Columbia Records?

Ron Barker: Well, that was with Robert Stigwood and, to be honest, it was a bit of a mistake. The single we did with him was called "As Long as I Have You" and I hated it. He picked us up just before he got the Bee Gees. Somehow we got to audition for him at the Marquee Club in London. That went well but we recorded the wrong song in my opinion. We recorded it down in a studio in London off Wardour Street where the Rolling Stones had recorded. I think that Stigwood chose the song. The song on the B Side "Take this Hammer", an old Lead Belly song, is better. That should have been the A Side and might have had half a chance. Unfortunately, it didn't get anywhere. We came back home and Peter Wallis left to play with Billy Fury's band The Gamblers and Bob Sargeant came in. This was about 1967.

IF: Did you still have ambitions to get on *Top of the Pops*?

Ron Barker: Sort of but I was married by now and, to be honest, we started to play more progressive music with long solos in it and I hated that sort of music, so it became time for me to leave the band. That was the music of the time. They went to London but I didn't want to go. They went on to be the house band for Howlin' Wolf and people like that. They remained a great band.

Really, we were big in the North East but nowt outside of it. What you needed to do was write your own songs. If the Beatles had just done covers they would have sank eventually, no matter how good a band they were. There was nobody in the North East writing their own stuff except Alan Hull with the Chosen Few. We should have tried and that's the one thing I regret but you don't really know if its in you. We did have a song written by Dick Heckstall-Smith, the jazz musician (Ron sings a few bars of the song), especially for us but I'm afraid we thought it was rubbish.

IF: What led to you reforming in 1977?

Ron Barker: Possibly the punky thing. I quite liked some of the punk music. I liked the energy of it. I was sat in a club watching a band and I thought Christ, I can do better than that. So, that was it and we got all fired up again. My brother, Kenny, who was 16, joined the band on the guitar, which was great. We made a couple of records but it was really just a bit of fun. We were probably too old by then anyway.

IF: How did you end up on the telly?

Ron Barker: We had reformed and we played on a TV programme called *Alright Now* which was fronted by Den Hegarty, who was singer from the band Darts. And then after that they shipped Eric Burdon across from America to sing with us, which was a total surprise for us. We went back to the old Club a'Gogo which was no longer in use. Eric was great with us.

IF: What was the difference for you between the '60s and the '70s for you?

Ron Barker: Well, we were more organised in the '70s. We didn't play the social clubs as the R&B we played went down like a lead balloon in those places. So, we liked to get our own places to play like the Tyne Theatre and we could guarantee a crowd there. Often the audience was those who had followed us in the '60s. Eventually we got too old but I have no regrets.

IF: Looking back what were your most memorable moments?

Ron Barker: Supporting Little Richard at Newcastle City Hall was one in the mid '60s. He was not that little but he was powerfully built. He was great and a nice fella. I also sang with people like Rod Stewart, which was just great. I had a great a time and, really, wouldn't change a thing.

•••••••••••••••••

Ron has a tendency to underplay his band and his career and that is maybe an example of people from the North East not wanting to boast. However, their story is one that needs to be told. It is part of the social history of the North East in the 1960s where people wanted to break out of the post-war shadow that seemed to loom throughout the previous decade. It's great to hear about all of these amazing clubs that would be packed with lively bands and equally lively punters. This was an incredibly vibrant period in the UK and in the North East and the Junco Partners were a big a part of that story. When you consider that Ron started singing in 1963 and didn't put his microphone down until 2014, I can't help feeling that I haven't done his story justice.

1. The Gamblers were a Newcastle based band in the early 1960s. They were signed by Decca Records and went on to be the singer Billy Fury's backing band.

The Elcort

Paul Nichols' and Dave Eckhard's Story

If you research the North East music scene in the mid-1960s, a common consensus is that after the Animals moved to London there were three top bands doing the circuit who were 'the most likely to succeed'. They were The Junco Partners, The Sect and the Elcort. It is for that reason that I am at the Bridge Hotel in Newcastle on a quiet midweek afternoon with Paul Nichols, drummer of the Elcort, Dave Eckhard, bassist, and their friend Christine who was an audience member when they were playing the clubs and who is invaluable for keeping them both right. Both gents have rock star hair despite their age (Dave tells me he is approaching his 77th birthday) and both look good. Dave also tells me that he is currently in three bands, a jazz band, a rockabilly band and a rock band. Paul's post-Elcort career is the more stellar of the two. After the Elcort he played in Lindisfarne, Skip Bifferty, who enjoyed success in the 70s and was part of a 1970s supergroup called Widowmaker. Widowmaker featured members of Mott the Hoople, Hawkwind and a later member of Rainbow. They toured the US supporting ELO and a rather 'out of it' Aerosmith. Paul also later toured with John Cale, ex of Velvet Underground.

Paul and Dave bicker like an old married couple or maybe Waldorf and Statler from the Muppets but they are fantastic company with Paul often reducing me to tears of laughter with his dry wit. They tell of an incredibly vibrant North East music scene and I leave with a feeling that maybe the North East has never had it better than that period from 1963 to 1968. A pint of Amstel for me, a red wine for Paul and an orange and soda for Dave and we're off.

IF: How did the Elcort start?

Paul Nichols: It really started for me when myself and Kenny Craddock[1] joined in Christmas 1965. We were both only 15 and still at school. So there was me on drums, Derek Rootham on guitar, Rob Turner on vocals, Dave on bass and Kenny on Hammond organ. We decided to get in a second vocalist, Glyn Sadler and that helped make us stand out. Glyn had been in a band with Kenny called the Heatwaves.

IF: What were you like?

Dave Eckhard: We were the only band up here to do Tamla Motown songs. We played songs people had never heard of.

Paul Nichols: When you listen to the single we put out it didn't really represent what we were about. We were almost like a soul band. We were a really great live band. We were the loudest band around, really powerful.

Dave Eckhard: When we first played with Paul on drums he virtually destroyed the kit he was so powerful. We played things like "Heatwave" by Martha and the Vandellas and the way Paul played was like a mad version of Keith Moon.

Paul Nichols: I was always very sure of myself.

IF: Where did you play?

Paul Nichols: We played all over. We played the YMCA in Gateshead. We played a club in Wallsend called the North East Marine. We would play the Mayfair in Newcastle. We would play the Locarno Ballroom in Sunderland along with the El Cubana in Sunderland which was a really jumping, lively club. We played the Quay Club on Dean Street in Newcastle, opposite where the Crown Posada pub is. We played the Cellar Club in Shields. They would all be packed out and jumping. There were just so many great clubs to play. We could play four or five times a week and each night would be full.

Dave Eckhard: It was often mayhem when we played. There was about 3,000 people there when we played the Locarno. We also played the Cavern Club in Liverpool. We had done a mini tour round England at places like Manchester and the last date was Liverpool. We went on in the Cavern at 5:00 in the morning and the place was packed. The Coasters were headlining.

Paul Nichols: The Cavern was great. The atmosphere was amazing. It was packed, sweaty and noisy and we had to carry our Hammond organ down a few flights of steps to then get it onto the stage. It was fantastic. We were so high on the vibe of the place, not on drugs or drink but just the atmosphere of the place. We didn't know about drugs and we didn't really drink although I seem to remember that the Coasters who came on after us were completely out of it and pretty rubbish.

We got invited by a young lass from Anfield in Liverpool back to her mam and dad's for breakfast. So that's what we did. We had a bit of sleep then got up and her Mam made us a massive breakfast. It was like something out of a book.

IF: Did you have a manager?

Paul Nichols: There was a guy called Derek Balmer who ran the record department in T&G Allans and he said he could get us a record deal and later said he was getting us on *Top of the Pops*. He was a lot older than us and unfortunately we believed him. But he did get us an audition with EMI.

Dave Eckhard: He told us he had managed the Migil Five, the Pretty Things and Manfred Mann. I think in reality he may have been a roadie. He was a big lad, a wrestler who drank milk shakes but no alcohol. He did know someone at EMI though and we ended up recording the single at Abbey Road with Norman Smith who did the Beatles' engineering.

Paul Nichols: We had done a demo of the song "Tammy" at Morton Sound in Newcastle, which used to be on Worswick

Street but is long gone now. So that led to going into Abbey Road studios on 9th April 1966. We recorded two songs "Tammy" and "Searching". The Beatles were in there at the time and they were doing *Revolver*. I pinched one of Ringo's drumsticks.

To be honest we were very confident in our own ability, even though Kenny and I were still only about 15. While we were down in London recording, we played a string of dates including The Sibyla Club, which was part owned by George Harrison. While we were playing there Brian Jones of the Rolling Stones was sat there at the front with his stripey suit on.

Dave Eckhard: Yes, and Brian Jones thought it would be funny to pull out the power cable from my amp so my bass went off. I didn't know who he was, so I chased him up the stairs ready to give him a right clout and only stopped when the bouncer told me who he was. We were down there probably for about ten weeks in total and it was full of high jinks. It was a great time.

Eventually, though we got sick of slumming it and me and Derek decided to go back home, which was probably a mistake. The last gig was at John Gregson's, the actor's house in Kent. It was that sort of surreal time when things like that happened.

IF: What happened with the single?

Dave Eckhard: Well, it sold well in Newcastle and made us stars up here but really flopped nationwide. EMI seemed more bothered about pushing other bands rather than us. At the time, with the Animals gone, we were the biggest band in the North East but that didn't count for much with EMI. We were supposed to do a second record but there were no songwriters in the band and that was a problem.

IF: Why didn't you try write your own songs?

Paul Nichols: Well, no one did back then. Kenny Craddock later became a really good song writer but we just didn't really try. There were so many good songs out there for us to play. And to be honest the Animals didn't write their own songs and they were doing great. In hindsight not writing our own songs held us back but at the time that didn't occur to us.

Dave Eckhard: The covers we did were so obscure, Northern Soul and Tamla, and it didn't really cross our mind to write songs. The audience loved what we were doing and our set list was varied and interesting and we kept it fresh.

IF: Because the Animals were doing well was there a lot of interest from the music industry in the North East in the mid-60s?

Paul Nichols: No, I don't think there was. The Juncos had a record out and the Chosen Few had a couple of records out because Alan Hull was a prolific song writer but there wasn't that much interest from the London record labels.

IF: Who were the best band on the circuit in the North East when you were playing?

Paul Nichols: The Sect were very good. They were a standard pop band. The Downbeats were another great band and they were great players. They were from Spennymoor in County Durham. Their drummer was a young Alan White who went on to play with John Lennon and Yes for many years. Their mastermind was Kenny Potts, who has just died, and he was like Brian Wilson, a real talent. He was brilliant at working out harmonies.

Dave Eckhard: The Junco Partners were very good. They were quite simple in their approach, but they had a huge following. They were quite low key.

Paul Nichols: There was a band called the Kylastrons and they had a guitarist called Malcolm Longstaff and he was way ahead of his time. He went on to play with Screaming Lord Sutch and later with Keith Emmerson in the Nice. He used to use an echo chamber and would wear leather pants as early as 1962. They later played in Hamburg. They were great and really pulled in the crowds.

Dave Eckhard: When I saw Malcolm play he would be so fast in his playing that I thought he was miming. He was quite a character.

Paul Nichols: There was a great band that used to play the

Club a'Gogo called the Invaders. They were earlier than us, maybe '62 or '63 and they had a residency at the 'Gogo. They had a sax player and they were popular with the youngsters at the Young Set at the Club a'Gogo. The Young Set was a separate room where under-18s were allowed in to watch bands. Under-18s wouldn't have been allowed in the Club a'Gogo main room. The Invaders would pack the place out.

IF: Was it a competitive scene?

Paul Nichols: No, we were all friends. We would help each other.

IF: Was this a vibrant period for the North East?

Paul Nichols: The was a music shop called Barratt's in Newcastle and on any Saturday it full of local musicians on the scene. There were so many bands about and we all knew each other. It was a fantastic time to be a musician in the North East. It really was a high spot for music in this region. It was so exciting and there was a real vibe to the clubs we played. There were new guys coming through all the time.

Dave Eckhard: It was a great time to be in a band. I don't think it's been matched in this region since.

IF: Did you expect to have a career in music?

Paul Nichols: Well for me I was really young but I just believed that this would be what I would do and I would just keep moving up and up. And, I guess, that's what I did but with the Elcort it was just about enjoying the moment.

IF: Why did the Elcort end?

Paul Nichols: I think me and Kenny wanted to move up and the Elcort was going nowhere. We went on to form a band called the New Religion with Brian Short who was the singer of the Sect. That was a good band. Then I was offered £30 a week by the Gas Board, which was Bryan Ferry's old band and had Mike Figgis, the film director, playing trumpet. We played at 'The Love-In'[2] in 1967 in the Handyside Arcade. I then got an offer from London with a band called The Entire Sioux Nation with Larry Wallis and from there it was Skip Bifferty and so on.

Dave Eckhard: I went with Rob the singer and formed the Funny Farm. Rob went on to sing with the great band Beckett and later tragically died young in car accident. Also Rob and I joined the Pleasure Machine who weren't great but were very popular.

I think the problem with the Elcort is that we were a big fish in a small pond up here. We escaped to London and then came back to the small pond and that was a mistake. Kenny and Paul wanted to get back on the up so that was the parting of the ways. But what great days!

•••••••••••••••••

The Elcort existed for not quite two years. They released one single on EMI called "Tammy" backed up by 'Searching'. However, they were very representative of a flourishing music scene in the North East where band members all knew each other and often moved from band to band. It is nearly 60 years on but the excitement of the time is strongly conveyed when I meet Paul and Dave and their enthusiasm is infectious. Like most of the people I have talked to for this book Paul soon left for London as that was the only route to a professional career and went on to have a great career as a respected musician. Despite their bickering, Paul and Dave are clearly happy to be in each other's company and if Paul's taxi had not arrived, I think I could have been regaled with another two hours of rock and roll tales in what would have been quite a boozy afternoon.

---

1. Kenny Craddock was a highly successful musician and composer from Gateshead who went on to play with George Harrison, Ringo Starr, Van Morrison, Lindisfarne and Billy Bragg. Tragically, he died in 2002 aged 52 in a car accident in Portugal.

2. 'The Love In' was a concert held in the Handyside Arcade in Newcastle in 1967 to reflect Newcastle's contribution to the 'Summer of Love'. You can see a short film on the BFI's website on the concert and actually see Paul Nichols drumming in the band The New Religion. Bryan Ferry's The Gas Board also played at the concert.

Mick Gallagher

The Chosen Few/The Animals/Skip Bifferty

The Chosen Few were formed in 1962 by Alan Hull and Mick Gallagher. By many they were recognised as, after the Animals, the best band in the North East along with the Junco Partners. It may not have been recognised at the time but what made them different was the fact that their set was made up of R&B covers along with original compositions from the immensely talented Alan Hull. Alan would later take that ability to Lindisfarne and help cement their position as one of the most successful bands of the early 1970s. Alan was a wandering soul who was searching for artistic contentment and vindication throughout his life. Gallagher, the band's keyboard player was possibly an equal but different type of talent. He was and is adaptable, reliable, likeable and a keyboard maestro. This was recognised by the Animals who took him on tour with them in 1965 to replace the errant Alan Price. That is, however, getting ahead of ourselves in this tale and it is the Chosen Few we start with. You can listen to their two singles released on Pye Records in 1965 and, although Mick will say that the songs, written by Alan Hull, show the seeds of what later flourished in Lindisfarne, to my mind I can hear more the influence of the Beatles and the Kinks.

As with Mick's pal and fellow Chosen Few member, Johnny Turnbull, he left the North East in the late 1960s and never really returned. By the strict definition of this book the story should end there. However, if you chat to someone whose musical life includes playing with Peter Frampton, Ian Dury and the Blockheads, the Clash, Paul McCartney and Robbie Williams, it is simply not credible to end this story in 1967. So, over to you Mick.

IF: How did you start in music?

Mick Gallagher: I was sent to piano lessons when I was nine or ten but I hated that and used to play truant from them. When my mam found out she realised it wasn't for me. At about 14 or 15, round about 1960, I joined the Methodist youth club. We were Catholics so I was stepping over the line. When I was there I saw a lad banging out some rock and roll on the piano and he was getting all the attention and I thought *I can do that*. I could slowly read music, so I got some music - "Nut Rock" by B. Bumble and the Stingers and something by Floyd Cramer. I would then go to the youth club and play those things and sure enough I got attention. It was a way to be popular and I was hooked. I joined a local band at the youth club called the Wayfarers. My mam sewed a capital 'W' on to each of our shirts for when we did shows. She was a big fan!

From there you start to meet people while you're out playing and, luckily for me, I met Alan Hull very quickly through a bass player I knew.

IF: What was Alan Hull like?

Mick Gallagher: Oh, Alan was great. He was so inspiring. He was about 17 or 18 when I joined up with him and he'd written all these brilliant songs. It was all really original stuff.

IF: What sort of music was he writing? Was it like the R&B that was so prevalent at the time?

Mick Gallagher: To be honest all the elements that you saw later with Lindisfarne were already there. He had many of the songs that he did later on already written. Pretty quickly we formed a band together called the Chosen Few.

IF: Did this original music differentiate the Chosen Few on the Newcastle scene? I am guessing the other bands were primarily covering pop or R&B songs.

Mick Gallagher: We would throw in a couple of crowd pleaser covers but we had all this great original music and we thought let's concentrate on that. We thought we were following in the footsteps of the Beatles who had broken the monopoly of the tin pan alley type of writers' scene. They were writing for themselves, so why shouldn't we. So, right from the start that was the plan and, yes, it did make us a bit different.

IF: Did you think at the age of 17 or 18, that this may be the start of career in music?

Mick Gallagher: You don't really think that deeply at that age. I'd spent a year working at the Ministry for Pensions and National Insurance but I didn't take to that so I packed it in. This didn't go down well with my mam and dad and they said I'd have to fend for myself so I started hanging around the clubs. Bill Keith, who was the manager of the Chosen Few, had The Manhole Club in Wallsend and he gave me a room above there and I was a bit of caretaker. So, I really was up to my neck in that scene.

IF: Where did the Chosen Few play?

Mick Gallagher: Well, the Club a'Gogo was a special place. It was a cut above but the usual places for us were the working men's clubs around the North East. They were the bread and butter. We'd have to play a mix of covers and originals in those places to fit in and earn the coin.

IF: What were the audiences like? Were they up and dancing?

Mick Gallagher: Not really, you were more like a turn in the corner of the room with your name written on the drums. It was all quite low key. There were no great aspirations. It was just something to do with our time that was productive.

To be honest, it didn't really progress very far. There was little happening up in the North East. We had to go out of Newcastle. There wasn't really the facilities in Newcastle to get records done and Tyne Tees TV weren't really interested. So the scene was really restricted to the clubs like the Manhole in Wallsend and the Quay Club in Newcastle. This provided some work but just not enough.

IF: How did you join the Animals?

Mick Gallagher: I was playing the Club a'Gogo one night in May 1965 with the Chosen Few and it was the night that Alan Price didn't turn up and they were about to go on tour so they were all panicking. They tried to find Alan to persuade him but couldn't find him. So they rang Myer Thomas, manager of the Club a'Gogo, to see if he had any ideas. He said, 'Well, we had a band on tonight and they had a competent keyboardist, I think he could do it.' So, I was in the right place and the right time for that to happen.

IF: Was it daunting to join the Animals who had had number one hits both sides of the Atlantic at this point?

Mick Gallagher: If I hadn't been so young, I was only about 20, I would have been more scared. At that time, being so young, I thought I was invincible. Looking back I can see the onus that was on me but at the time I thought *oh well*, it's just playing the piano. I was with them for the best part of a year but really they wanted a gent called Dave Rowberry, who was their school mate. However, Dave was contracted for six or nine months to the Mike Cotton Sound[1] so wasn't immediately available. When he was available I left. We toured mainly round Scandinavia, Denmark and Sweden, then round England. It was great and quite exciting but I knew it was only temporary. With the success of that it gave me some fresh impetus and with the money I made I bought the Chosen Few a load of new amplifiers and stage clothes and smartened the whole thing up. This is when we got our deal with Radio Luxembourg.

Through Bill Keith we got an arrangement with Cyril Stapelton[2] from Radio Luxembourg to go down to London and record a number of sessions for the radio and that led to recording a couple of singles for Pye. If you listen to them you can hear that they were like the stuff he later did with Lindisfarne. Anyway, we went down there in a battered Ford Transit van with a brown ale beer mat for a tax disc, all rough and ready. We recorded a couple of Alan's songs "I Won't be Around Anymore" and "Today, Tonight and Tomorrow". They gave us a 15-minute slot every Saturday night for Radio Luxembourg called 'Meet the Chosen Few'. We did five or six weekends and we thought we'd hit the big time. We got a sponsorship through Hohner for some gear and had an advert in the *NME*. So, I could say to my mam, 'Look I'm in the papers,' but really that was about it. There was no such thing as royalties and the returns were pretty meagre. It was all hand to mouth but when you are young you don't worry about that.

As it wasn't going anywhere, Alan Hull and the bass player Bumper Brown decided to leave and do something else. At the time I was living at the Quay Club, where we were based, and I put together a new band, still called the Chosen Few, and brought in Johnny Turnbull and Colin Gibson and continued as a local band. I'm not sure how we met but we got together with a singer from Blyth called Graham Bell and soon morphed into Skip Bifferty. But because Graham had contacts in London we decided to give it a go down there. This was about the time when 'Flower Power' and all that hippy stuff was coming in so that was our direction and we managed to get a deal with the tyrannical Don Arden[3] (Note: this episode will be covered in more detail in the next section with Johnny Turnbull). He got us a house down in London, got us gigs, and got us a record contract. Nothing was happening for us up in Newcastle so this was so exciting. To take the next step you simply had to move to London. When we were in Newcastle we called 'semi-professional' so I suppose when we moved to London we could call ourselves 'professional musicians'. But that turned pretty nasty pretty quickly due to Don's less than above board business practices so we had to scarper. From there my life has taken so many twists and turns of which I can give you a potted tour.

Peter Frampton

Mick Gallagher: I went off to America with Peter Frampton but I didn't really enjoy that experience too much. It was from the frying pan into the fire. I had been with Don Arden in London. Once I escaped him, I was in the US with Frampton and that got us involved with a chap called Dee Anthony[4] who was an Italian version of Don Arden, if you get my drift. There was all manner of sinister and shady deals going on. This lasted, on and off, for a couple of years but I didn't want to move there. We did a few recordings and we'd written a few songs that went on to *Frampton Comes Alive* and his massive success but I left just before that.

Loving Awareness

Mick Gallagher: Ronan O'Rahilly[5], who was a big figure in the London music scene, had this mission called 'Loving Awareness', which was like a far eastern love and peace type philosophy that Ronan was into and he used Radio Caroline to push it. So, me, Johnny Turnbull, Norman Watt-Roy and Charley Charles put a band together to help with that and put a few jingles together. This was about 1976 and we released an album under this name recorded in the US to promote this philosophy. We did some really good stuff.

Ian Dury and the Blockheads[6]

Mick Gallagher: When we came back from recording the Loving Awareness record we switched on the telly and saw Johnny Rotten, swearing on some TV programme and punk had arrived. We thought *well, we're right out of step here singing about love* *and peace*. We realised straight away we weren't going to get gigs as we were and so we all just went out separately and started playing the session musician circuit and one of the sessions that Charley, the drummer, and Norman, our bass player got was with Ian Dury to record the *New Boots and Panties* album. Listening to that we thought *well, this is something different and it's really great*. We knew of Ian as singer of Kilburn and the High Roads who were on the pub rock circuit, but he had now sprang out on his own. So, when he needed to take the album out on the road he needed a band and Norman and Charley said, 'Well, we're in a band' so that was that and we joined him for the Stiff Tour.

IF: What was Ian like?

Mick Gallagher: He was very creative and artistic in his approach to life. He was trained as an artist and knew the likes of Peter Blake. So he brought all that arty background with him and the pretensions that go with it. He wasn't a musician but used bongos to allow him to write his lyrics. It was immediately obvious that he was a genius. And also, as soon as I met him I felt that I'd known him all my life. I also got that with Charley our drummer. But it all worked very organically. It had its amazing ups and also downs. It was exciting, it was rock and roll.

IF: Did you feel an affinity with punk, which Ian Dury was attached to, as it was at odds with what you had done before?

Mick Gallagher: I understood it as an artistic expression, but I didn't understand it as an ideology. It was just a bit of fun for me. We were musicians first and foremost. Ian was our punk and we were the funk.

The Clash

Mick Gallagher: The Clash were managed by the same people as Ian, after Bernie Rhodes[7] went out of favour. Anyway, our publicist, Kosmo Vinyl, was in with the Clash and he asked if I'd be up for recording with them. And I said, 'Yeah, great'. So, I did *London Calling*[8] with them. I'd jammed with them before and I'd thought *My God after the Blockheads this is hell on earth*, it was just a cacophony. The energy was great, and probably the musicianship was there underneath the noise but it was just all so hectic. However, by the time I went to do *London Calling* they had been through an epiphany. When I'd jammed with them six months previously it was everything before the Clash is rubbish. Then suddenly they were listening to soul and blues and lots of different types of music and taking inspiration from those songs and I thought wow, this is just great. And *London Calling* was great and a real step up for them

I then did a couple of US tours with them and recorded *Sandinista* after that. They had a road crew that didn't like keyboards and so kept turning it down but after I sorted that it was great. The audiences in America were just going insane and it was a massive rush for us. They were very much flavour of the month. To promote *London Calling* we went right across America, east to west, in ten days. That really broke them in the US and they went stellar. For me, though, I was part of the band for tours but wasn't part of the band when it came to business. That became a bit of a problem.

They certainly were a special band, especially when their sound diversified. Topper Headon, their drummer, was a big part of that change and growth. Topper appreciated the history of the music whereas the others were pretty blasé about the past. His influence made them more musical than they probably intended to be in the first place. I later did some stuff with Topper when the Clash went on hiatus and went on the road with his band.

Paul McCartney

Mick Gallagher: I played on Paul's Russian album called *CHOBA B CCCP* which was released in Russia in 1988. This was an album of rock and roll standards in response to an earlier John Lennon rock and roll album. The experience for me was really good. We had done a TV programme where Paul had put a band together to play some rock and roll and I had been asked by his management to do it and that went well. So, after that the album followed on. He liked what I did. So, I went down to his studio on the south coast and hung out with him and Linda and that was great. And doing the album was great fun, although I would have loved to do some of his own songs with him.

IF: Was working with Paul McCartney daunting or nerve racking?

Mick Gallagher: No, because they were nice people. I have had nerve racking moments with so-called famous people who make it awkward for you and not pleasant but working with people like Paul McCartney and later with Robbie Williams they were just nice, humble people

We did a tribute album to Ian Dury, called *Brand New Boots and Panties* with various people like Robbie, Shane McGowan, Sinead O'Connor and Paul McCartney. Robbie did a version of "Sweet Gene Vincent" which was great.

IF: Where did it come from this idea that you can just sit in with anyone and add to the sound?

Mick Gallagher: I guess I am a chameleon-type person. When I was a session musician, they tended to want me rather than just a keyboard. So I must have been bringing something to it. I wasn't necessarily the most proficient but, for some reason, they liked me.

IF: What makes you carry on?

Mick Gallagher: Well, to stave off boredom really. When the pandemic came, my career as a live musician completely went down the pan. So I got into home recording and got approached by the actor Jane Horrocks, who had been a girlfriend of Ian Dury's. She had all these letters from Ian and some were quite poetic and she wanted me to put music to them, so we did that. Some of the songs didn't make it as Ian's language in the letters was just too fruity for the radio. It was certainly an interesting experience writing this stuff, with Ian, who died in 2000, looking over my shoulder. Jane wanted to do an installation (Mick does a recognisable Lancashire accent to approximate what she said) and then it moved on to a play and that turned into a Radio 4 play. So, as you can see, things happen. And now we've got the Blockheads back on the road.

IF: Looking back, you have had an incredible career. Why did you succeed where others may fall?

Mick Gallagher: Well, firstly, I've been so lucky. Also, maybe it's my demeanour. I get on with people and they like me for what I do. I'm no problem. I'm reliable, I turn up on time. It has never been massively lucrative and I've always lived hand to mouth, some times better than others but it has been a creatively rich life. I've no complaints.

....

Mick is a pleasure to chat to. He is probably a tad overly modest about his musical abilities but I fully believe that he has had all these incredible experiences in part due to his likeability and his warm personality. Mick has had an incredibly varied career from starting with Alan Hull, joining one of the original 'British Invasion' bands in the Animals, rubbing shoulders with Cyril Stapelton, a 40s and 50s jazz bandleader, playing and recording with new wave legends Ian Dury and then the Clash and then playing with rock royalty in Paul McCartney and Peter Frampton. Whatever it may look like on the page there is no element of name dropping. Mick is the sort of bloke you could listen to all day. Thanks, Mick!

1. The Mike Cotton Sound were a jazz/pop band of the 1950s and 1960s who had a UK hit with "Swing that Hammer" in 1962.

2. Cyril Stapelton was a jazz bandleader who had a career that stretched from the 1930s to the 1970s.

3. Don Arden was an English music manager who managed acts from Little Richard to Black Sabbath and the Move to ELO.

4. Dee Anthony was an American music manager who managed acts such as Humble Pie, King Crimson, Traffic and Peter Frampton. Like, Arden, he had a reputation for dubious practices. Steve Marriott, singer from Humble Pie, tells the story of a dispute they had with Anthony that was resolved in a social club in New York that belonged to the Gambino crime family and in the presence of John Gotti.

5. Ronan O'Rahilly was an Irish businessman who was active in the London music scene from the early 60s. He was most famous for launching the offshore radio station, Radio Caroline.

6. Ian Dury and the Blockheads had a number one hit in the UK with "Hit me With Your Rhythm Stick' in 1978 and a number three hit with "Reasons to Be Cheerful" in 1979. The Blockheads were recognised as the most proficient musicians of the new wave movement of the late 70s and early 80s.

7. Bernie Rhodes was the Clash's first manager and rival to the Sex Pistol's Malcolm McLaren.

8. *London Calling* was the Clash's third album, released in 1979. Rather erroneously it was voted by Rolling Stone magazine the best album of the 1980s. In 2010, it was one of ten classic album covers from British artists commemorated on a UK postage stamp issued by the Royal Mail.

Johnny Turnbull

The Chosen Few/Skip Bifferty

You may or may not have heard of Johnny Turnbull. You will, however, have heard of the people he has gone on to play with. From Ian Dury and the Blockheads to the Eurhythmics and Bob Geldof he's has played with the cream of British rock and pop. He played at the iconic Live Aid concert in 1985 as well as singing on the soundtrack of the almost equally iconic film *Get Carter*. In 1965, at the age of 15, he began as a semi-professional guitarist with Alan Hull's ex-band The Chosen Few in Newcastle. He pretty much hasn't put the guitar down in the intervening 50 plus years. It's a meandering tale of fame, rock and roll and gangsters. Sometimes you may think Johnny is name dropping. However, since he has played and rubbed shoulders with the very best of British music it is impossible for him to do otherwise. A few pages in this book cannot do Johnny's career justice and so I ultimately end our chat firing names at Johnny and he gives me a snapshot of each musical relationship.

IF: Where did you grow up?
Johnny Turnbull: I was born in Walker in 1950 but grew up in Benton, Newcastle. I was about 12 when I started a band with Colin Gibson, who I had known since I was five. We were called

the Primitives, which became the Primitive Sect. My Dad used to get us gigs at 'go-as-you-please' nights or people's 21st birthday parties. And from there we met people like Kenny Craddock, who later played with Lindisfarne, Pete Kirtley and Alan White, who drummed in Yes and played on John Lennon's early albums, through playing around the circuit. Kenny was in a great sixties Newcastle band called The Elcort, massive on the Newcastle scene but maybe not known outside of our region. That was very much a feature of the scene in Newcastle in the mid-1960s. We had so much talent about and a really happening scene but there wasn't that much interest from the London-based record labels.

IF: Who inspired you to pick up the guitar?

Johnny Turnbull: Well not to pick up the guitar but my big sister, Ann, inspired me to get into music. She was older and she used to buy records. She would bring in fantastic singles like "Lucille" by Little Richard and Chuck Berry records. She exposed me to all the basics of rock and roll through Elvis, Gene Vincent and Little Richard. It fired me up and contrasted to the radio with light music shows like *Friday Night is Music Night* on the BBC. We used to go the annual Hoppings Fair on the Town Moor in Newcastle and they had big Wurlitzer jukeboxes and all the teddy boys would be strutting around them. It was great at the fair with music being blasted out and being surrounded by teenagers.

I started off by playing an egg slicer using one of my mam's knitting needles to plink plonk away. My auntie then bought me what was effectively a ukelele called an Elvis Presley Teen Time Guitar from Woolworths for about 17 shillings and sixpence. It had four strings but I learnt "Peggy Sue" by Buddy Holly just by trial and error. I played it to the adults and my Auntie Cissy said to my Mam, 'Eeh, Lily you'll have to get him a proper one.' So she got me a 'proper' one on HP. I was self-taught until I met my girlfriend's dad, Bill Fisher, who was a music teacher. He said, 'What you are playing there is 'C' and if you put your little finger there it's C7', and that gave me a whole new window of opportunity and off I went. Years later, when I did the demos for Alan Hull's solo album, Alan told me to take a finger off the C chords and that would make Cmaj7 and that, again, was a whole new sound.

IF: How did you move from a band with your mates to playing with the well touted Chosen Few?

Johnny Turnbull: Well, it was through Mickey Gallagher who had seen me and Colin playing and with Alan Hull and a lad called Bumper Brown leaving, Mickey needed some new blood to keep the Chosen Few going as they had contracts to fulfil etc. So he got Colin to play the bass and he needed guitar and vocals and so he got me in. And I am still playing with Mickey 50 years later in the Blockheads. We were playing a lot of Alan Hull's original stuff but this was much more rhythm and blues than the stuff he did later. We would be going to the Club a'Gogo to see people like Geno Washington and we thought we'd better do more rhythm and blues dancey type stuff. I was only 15 at the time and I'd started a job at Jackson the Tailor's in Newcastle.

The band had a good reputation and gigs were getting further afield. On one occasion Mickey got us a gig in Spennymoor, 30 miles or so down the road, and he said we'd have to set off early. To get me off work early, Mickey said eat a bar of soap and pretend to be ill. So, I ate half a bar of soap at lunchtime and pretty soon turned green at the gills and started throwing up. So the boss said 'You'd better get yourself off home son.' So off we went to Spennymoor for the gig.

IF: You later played on Alan Hull's solo album. How did that come about?

Johnny Turnbull: Well, when I met up with Mickey and joined the Chosen Few, Alan had left but we still hung about with him. So he asked me and Mickey to do the demos of some new songs he had including the first version of "Lady Eleanor". I was 15 at the time so it was pretty daunting. He asked me if I wanted to join him in what he was going to do but I said, 'Well, I've said yes to Mickey now so I can't really leave him.' So, it's conceivable that I could have been in Lindisfarne. But anyway later, when he was on a break from Lindisfarne, we recorded Alan's solo album, *Pipedream*, at Trident Studios in London, which was an amazing experience. That was again with people I'd grown up with in Newcastle, Colin Gibson and Kenny Craddock. It was great songs and great camaraderie.

I was in the Chosen Few from the end of 1965 till sometime in 1966 when our singer, Rod Hudd, packed it in and we got a new singer in called Graham Bell. Through Graham, who was from Blyth in Northumberland but had been living in London, we met a gentleman called Alan Eisenberg who was a friend of Brian Epstein. Through that connection we got a gig at the Marquee and pretty soon it was clear that we had to pack in our jobs and get down to London.

We changed the name to Skip Bifferty and got signed by Don Arden for his management company. He got us a record deal with RCA and things were really looking up.

IF: Where did the name come from?

Johnny Turnbull: It was a funny little character in the books that Colin used to write. In Newcastle a 'biff' was a fart. People thought we were from somewhere like Louisiana and used to ask 'who is Skip?' when we were just named after this character named after a fart.

It was a very exciting time, but we were very green. We were five wide-eyed lads from Newcastle in this big, ugly world of the music industry. Some of our early records were produced by Steve Marriott and Ronnie Lane, of the Small Faces. They became our mates and they gave us the low down on Don Arden, who was known as somewhat of a gangster. We found we were pretty much on our own and after releasing an album we were still penniless. Apparently, we had got an advance of £45K from RCA but never saw any of it. We were paid a small wage to keep going but that was it. In those days you couldn't really get a lawyer to go and ask Don things like 'where are the royalties from RCA?' Let's just say we fell foul of Don Arden and had to run away and hide out on the Isle of Wight. We had been visited by one of Don's heavies who said 'Don's not very happy with you.' It was heavy stuff. It was like something out of a bad gangster movie. To get away we changed our name to Heavy Jelly and we were helped out by Chris Blackwell who released a single by us on his new Island Records label.

IF: How did you get involved in the *Get Carter* soundtrack.

Johnny Turnbull: Me and Mickey used to get involved in sessions with Alan Holmes at Robins EMI publishing. He was mates with the producer, Jack Baverstock, and he was doing the film. I'm not sure whether it was the Geordie connection but we were in the Olympic Studio recording something and we sang the song that follows Michael Caine on the train and then getting off in Newcastle and going to the pub. We recorded the song with the actual pictures playing. The studio had a massive screen and we were recording next to these massive shots of Michael Caine, which was some experience.

IF: How did that progress on to the Blockheads?

Johnny Turnbull: When it all came crashing down, I ended up back in Newcastle with Colin. Mickey stayed down in London, sleeping on John Peel's floor. Eventually me and Mickey tried again through Robins EMI. To be honest that time from 1967 to 1977 was a bit of a mish mash. I went with a band called Glencoe with a bassist called Norman Watt-Roy and Mickey went with Peter Frampton. I lived with Errol Brown from Hot Chocolate for a time and knocked about with Stewart Copeland.

Anyway, eventually Mickey joined us in Glencoe and through a kind gentleman called Ronan O'Rahilly we started writing jingles for Radio Caroline, a famous pirate radio station that Ronan had started. Ronan changed our name to Loving Awareness and wanted to use us to promote the radio station. We started to do sessions for people like Lulu. Norman and our drummer, Charley Charles, got offered the session with Ian Dury to play on his album *New Boots and Panties*. Ian then said, 'Dave Robinson wants us to go on the first Stiff Records tour (in 1977) and we need a band' and Norman said, 'Well, I've already got a band called Loving Awareness.' So we drifted in to it and because of our past we could play rock and roll, a bit of jazz, a bit of funk and that seemed to fit the bill for Ian. We managed to pull it off and on the Stiff Tour we shone. We would share the bill with Elvis Costello, taking turns to go on last. It became apparent that our song "Sex and Drugs and Rock and Roll" was the tour anthem. We would end the whole show with everyone from Nick Lowe, Wreckless Eric and Dave Edmunds to Elvis Costello joining us on stage to do that one. I think ending the show with this song put Elvis' nose out of joint.

IF: What is the secret of your success?

Johnny Turnbull: We were so lucky that we started when it was all opening up. We were all working-class kids from Newcastle or Gateshead, but we had no fear. We knew it was our time. If you had a bit of talent the doors would open. So, I think there was a lot of luck and perseverance. I wasn't very good at Jackson's the Tailors so I couldn't really do anything else. I am a guitar player and I have been pretty much since I was 11 or 12. I am certainly versatile. I can play on ballads or jazzy things or rock and roll. I was brought up playing Chuck Berry at 'Go-as-you-please' nights, so I go back to the roots of rock and roll.

(At this point I ask if I can fire some of the names that Johnny has played with at him to get a quick response)

Ian Dury

Johnny Turnbull: He was crackers, but he was a genius. Some of the funniest but most irreverent lyrics I've heard in my life. If you read his stuff now you don't need a tune its pure poetry. He was a handful and we had some merry times and some tough times but I'm glad I met him. He was very charismatic but could be challenging.

I looked like something from the Bee Gees with long hair and a beard. One night Ian said 'lose the tache' so I got all my hair, facial and on my head, cut off and Ian said 'that's better.' Keeping Ian happy was the only thing to do for your own sanity.

Paul Young

Johnny Turnbull: Well, I was rehearsing with Banararama but I wasn't enjoying it. I would be asking them who would do the harmony lines and they would say they would all be doing the same lead lines, leaving the harmonies for me. Anyway, the phone rang and it was Paul Young who was putting his band together. He asked me to play guitar and I absolutely jumped at the chance. I did that album with Paul and it was great. I used a sitar guitar that I'd used on "What a Waste". You can hear that on "Every Time you go Away" which got to number four in the UK and was top ten in the US. We did Live Aid in 1985 with Paul and Alison Moyet.

Talk Talk

As the time with Paul was ending, I got another phone call and it was Talk Talk, so I was truly blessed. They needed a guitar player and so I was in. They were an incredible band and though Mark (Hollis) was the quiet one he had this incredible presence on stage. You wouldn't think it to look at him, he looked like a Mod. They were, at that point, one of the top bands around. The gigs were fantastic and it was great to be a part of.

Bob Geldof/Karl Wallinger

Dave Stewart, of the Eurythmics, was having a party for Bob Dylan at his studio in Crouch End. I didn't want to go but the wife told me to get my arse down there and take the harmonica in case Bob wanted to jam. I was stood chatting to Bob Geldof and Karl Wallinger, of World Party and previously the Waterboys. Karl went off to talk to Eric Idle and while he was gone Bob (Geldof) asked me if I wanted to play guitar for him on a US and Canada tour in the October. So I said 'yes, great.' Karl came back and said 'Do you want to come and play guitar for me in Europe.' I said 'well, when?' He said 'November,

December.' And I said, 'Yes, I'll do that after Bob's tour.' So, after not wanting to go to a party I got two gigs that I am still doing 25 years later.

Karl was an amazing song writer. I would put him up with Alan Hull. Karl was a big Alan Hull fan.

Dave Stewart

He's another absolute firecracker. He has so many ideas. He was a folk singer when I met him but he wanted to do everything from being a film director to doing the lighting. I remember one Christmas just after him and Annie split up and they were living in two separate flats just down the road from me. Dave became scarce. We had always been hanging out and jamming the guitars together. Then he re-appeared with a little synth playing 'dugga-dugga-dugga-dugga' (Johnny approximates the opening riff from "Sweet Dreams"). He swapped a guitar for the synth and this changed the way they wrote. I ended up being one of the Spiritual Cowboys in Dave Stewart and the Spiritual Cowboys and as well as playing with Annie and Dave in the Eurythmics.

·················

Johnny clearly hasn't finished yet. As he stated he began playing in bands at the age of 12 in 1962 and literally 60 years later he is still playing with the Blockheads, with Bob Geldof. It may be a stretch to include all his career highlights in this book as from 1967 or 1968 he was outside the north east. However, his background and grounding was from the same scene that spawned the Animals and Lindisfarne and there has always been a Geordie hue to what is doing. This is especially so as he started with his pal from Fenham, Newcastle, Mickey Gallagher and plays with him to this day in the Blockheads. He is a son of the north east but in his native land his story is not really known. Hopefully, this summary goes someway to rectify that.

2. Folk Music

The Irish folk singer Lisa O'Neil was recently quoted in *Mojo*, the music magazine, saying this: 'I think all music is folk music. If anything has a story in it and mirrors society, it is folk.' This very much echoes what Alastair Anderson, North East folk musician, said in my chat for this book. It is probably also fair to say that outsiders are more bothered about what is and what isn't folk music than those who make it. That is not to say there hasn't been a whiff of snobbery in the more traditional folk clubs when poppier elements are introduced.

Most of the scenes I have looked at have been broadly time bound. The Animals scene probably lasted from 1962 to 1968, punk in the North East was roughly 1977 to 1982, the Kitchenware bands were prominent from 1982 until the late '80s or early '90s and so on. If we were to put a timeline against folk music in this region we should really talk about Joe Wilson writing folk songs in his native Newcastle from about 1860 right up to releases by The Young 'Uns and the Unthanks today. For that reason I have been far broader in my definition and who I have included in this section. It is important, however, to acknowledge that the line from Joe Wilson to present day very much exists.

At its purest, folk continues to emanate from the plethora of folk clubs that continue to exist almost unnoticed by the majority of us. The singer songwriter scene that will be described by Kathryn Williams is quite different in its settings and intent (in that traditional songs passed from generation to generation is a key part of the folk club tradition) but it is, as Alastair Anderson may reflect, very much of and in the local community. That scene has spawned many fine singer songwriters such as Kathryn, Richard Dawson, Lake Poets and the less well known but revered Nev Clay. Whether it is folk music is pretty much a moot point.

Lindisfarne, as will be discussed, are by far the most successful of any folk band and it can very much be argued that they are, in fact, a blues band. In reality they began as a blues band but were very informed by the folk scene and the folk clubs as they developed.

The world of folk music is very much a melting pot. It is music that often sounds great on record but comes alive in rooms where the band or singer can commune with the audience and the audience can be as much part of the experience as the artist. The North East has the reputation in the folk world as being a hotbed of folk music. There is great folk music being played in a venue near you, be that a pub, a folk club or a concert hall, so go out and see it or it may not be there for the next generation.

Lindisfarne

Ray Laidlaw's and Rod Clements' Story

It is not difficult to make the argument that Lindisfarne, after the Animals, were the biggest band to come out of the North East and also the best. They sold records by the boatload. Their golden period between 1970 and 1973 saw three classic albums released in *Nicely out of Tune* (1970), *Fog on the Tyne* (1971) and *Dingly Dell* (1972). *Fog on the Tyne* got to number one on the UK album charts and the less critically well received *Dingly Dell*, as Ray Laidlaw, their drummer, says 'Only got to number 6'. They had top 10 hits with "Meet me on the Corner", "Lady Eleanor" and the later released "Run for Home", which also hit the US Top 40. Dire Straits may have sold more records but they were formed in London and despite Mark Knopfler growing up in Gosforth they could not be termed a North East Band. Lindisfarne reeked of the North East, they were Geordies to their bones.

Sometimes history looks at them as merely a folk band of their time. This is far too narrow a description. If you listen to their early albums you will hear stronger influences from the americana of The Band[1] and the three-minute pop sensibilities of Cat Stevens than the more faithful folk stylings of Fairport Convention or Steeleye Span. In fact the band, who were termed 'the 1970s Beatles,' were all fans of the Fab Four and had the same hunger for perfect melodies. They themselves saw Lindisfarne as primarily a blues band. Ray tells me that their first record producer, John Anthony, said they were 'folky but not too folky, rocky but not too rocky, poppy but not too poppy'.

What made the band unique, though, was something quite alchemic. They had three great singers who sang harmonies that may have had a hint of the West Coast sound of Crosby, Stills and Nash but that had a raw quality that reflected the personality of the band. They wrote great songs and had three songwriters and they played a variety of instruments that suited each song, unusual for the time. In Alan Hull, Ray Laidlaw, Rod Clements, Ray Jackson and Simon Cowe they had five strong characters who all played a key role in the band's sound and feel.

Ray tells me in our chat that maybe they were lucky in their timing and that if they had been two years sooner or two years later they may not have had the impact they did. Although he also caveated that with the comment 'Hully (Alan Hull) would have made it one way or other. He was such a talent'. However, when you listen to their story there is a feeling that the coming together of these five musicians had the same fateful element as the coming together of Lennon and McCartney ten years or so earlier.

I meet Ray Laidlaw in the fantastic Priory Café in Tynemouth, his 'local' and a nice combination of tea, ambience and good music. The next day I talk to Rod Clements (Bass, Violin) via Zoom from his Northumberland home in Rothbury. Both gentlemen are great company and both show an undimmed enthusiasm and clarity of memory for what were amazing days and an amazing band.

IF: How did music start for you? Was there music in the house and what did you listen to?

Ray Laidlaw: When I was a kid there was not a lot of exciting music on the radio. You'd hear on the BBC the *Light Programme* and the Joe Loss Orchestra and stuff like that.

Gradually though you would start to hear the odd Lonnie Donegan skiffle song on these programmes. I became aware of that and then the Shadows and Cliff and then Elvis.

My younger brother was a classically trained pianist. My mother was a dancer but never professional and my Granda was a pub singer. So there was always music around. So I formed a little band and I fancied being the drummer. It was my Granda who bought me a drum kit. We did about four gigs and we did mainly Shadows. Simon Cowe, who was in Lindisfarne later on, was in this band as he lived round the corner and he had a very wide taste in music. So we also did a couple of Paddy Roberts songs (Ray suggests I google him – he is a rather eccentric and amusing and very English balladeer). We just did instrumentals as we had no singer but it was great fun.

Later on when I was 14/15 I was in a band with Bob Sargeant (who will turn up later as a producer both of John Peel sessions and the Carpettes albums, as well as early Newcastle R&B band, the Junco Partners) called the Druids. We did covers again but this time influenced by the emerging Merseybeat sound. I did that for a year but in the meantime met Rod Clements. Rod was a public-school boy and posh, Simon was a public school boy and posh and I wasn't. Rod had been in a band called Downtown Faction at school or college and we decided to form a band and kept the name. We both liked the blues. We got into that through the Beatles and the Stones then moved to what had influenced them with the likes of Howlin' Wolf.

Rod Clements: My dad was a big classical music fan and would buy LPs of the great composers and he would get me to listen to it with him. Some I liked, some not so much. He would also take me to classical music concerts at Newcastle City Hall to hear orchestral music. So very early on I had it impressed on me that music happened live as well as on record or the radio. My Dad also, somewhat surprisingly, got into the Shadows. He liked the tunes and the melodies and he got a couple of 45s such as "Wonderful Land" and "Apache". I cottoned on to this and so my interest was piqued.

Later, when I was away at boarding school, I would be hanging round with the guys who had guitars. I would borrow them and I was able to pick out Shadows' tunes and things like that in a primitive kind of way. This was '61 or '62 and then the Beatles exploded. The DIY of skiffle and Buddy Holly expanded into the Beatles music. At that time a lot of kids were prompted to pick up the guitar and have a go. Much to their surprise they found that they could actually do it

At school, Durham School, I had my first band called the Downtown Faction. We actually got quite good and we could sometimes do gigs outside of school. We had aspirations to be a kind of R&B or blues band.

When I left school I started another band but kept the name. I joined with Ray Laidlaw and a couple of others in North Shields where I lived. We progressed from the Shadows to the Beatles, then the Kinks, then the Stones. Via the Stones we discovered the original blues guys, where the Stones had taken their music from. I always feel the Rolling Stones should be given more credit for acknowledging their sources. People would say they were rip off musicians but if they hadn't said where they'd got their music from we wouldn't have heard of the likes of Muddy Waters, John Lee Hooker and Howlin' Wolf. Discovering that opened up a whole new world of music and gave us much wider horizons culturally. We found out about the social background of the blues, which had significance beyond music itself. The Animals certainly reflected that as well and Eric Burdon was very well versed in the roots of American blues.

The Downtown Faction became quite a hardline Chicago blues band or that's what we tried to do. We were influenced by the likes of the Paul Butterfield Band and John Mayall's Bluesbreakers. We also did a few Bob Dylan songs from his electric period.

We were a fluid line up. We had Ray Laidlaw on drums, myself on bass, a great guitarist called Jeff Sadler and a guitarist called Don Whitaker. Simon Cowe, who had gone to boarding school in Edinburgh, also was in the band for a period when he returned to live in North Shields. We had a few singers, some of whom didn't last long, until we landed on a singer called Ray Jackson, who had been in a band called Autumn States. We asked him to join us because he was a fantastic blues harmonica player, and still is. So the core of the Downtown Faction became myself, Simon Cowe, Ray Laidlaw and Ray Jackson

IF: How did you decide to pick up the bass, which was a less common instrument at the time.

Rod Clements: That was a bit funny and partially a misunderstanding on my part. As a teenager I was keen on twangy guitar instrumentals. I thought singing was a bit poncey. So I liked twangy guitar and I liked Duane Eddy who played on the bass strings on his guitar. I thought, wrongly, that that was a bass guitar and so picked it up. But I liked to listen to the bass parts on songs, the power behind the throne if you like. So I picked up the bass but kept up my guitar playing as well.

IF: How would you have found out about those original blues players?

Ray Laidlaw: It was probably through *Melody Maker*[2] and *NME*[2] but also we had a friend called Gus who had a great record collection. Rod also had a folk and blues compilation album. We realised that Lonnie Donegan's songs also went back to Lead Belly[3] and the blues. Then there's people like the Paul Butterfield Band from the US and early John Mayall's Bluesbreakers and also the Animals, who we loved. But it was all blues based. At the start there was just two of us. Me on the drums and Rod on bass. So it was a bit like Fleetwood Mac in that the rhythm section started the band and looked for other musicians. We had a flexible line up but we found a great guitarist called Jeff Sadler, who had the advantage of having a van. We were still playing the blues and mainly putting on our own gigs. Our big heroes were the Junco Partners from Newcastle and we used to see them every Wednesday and through them we learned how to be in a band. We'd see them at the Vic and the 45 in Whitley Bay and sometimes the Club a'Gogo in Newcastle. We learned from them that everyone had a job and everyone had to do that job well.

I then met Ray Jackson at college and he'd been in a few bands and he joined. Then Simon came back from London and he joined. And that morphed into Brethren. Rod and Simon began to write songs, mainly blues and Dylan influenced. We built up a big following. Sting used to come and see us. We could fill the Mayfair ballroom in Newcastle, which had a capacity of 1500. By then it was mainly originals with some more wacky covers like Frank Zappa or Moby Grape. This was about '67 or '68

IF: So you could fill the Mayfair, which is impressive. What were your aspirations at this point?

Ray Laidlaw: We were dead arrogant. From the very beginning we knew we had something a bit different. Rod and I were a traditional rock/blues rhythm section. Simon was different and quite wacky. He didn't play guitar like anyone else around at the time. He had all these different influences. He had a finger-picking style on both acoustic and electric but he was equally influenced by jazz and the likes of Stravinsky. He was the magic in the early days. Also, though, because we came up through the Beatles, we wanted strong melodies. Most of the songs we did were quite short but sometimes with odd or unusual instrumentation.

Rod Clements: This was about 1968 and our aspirations were to be a full-time band and 'make it'. We wanted to develop as a band and song writers and write and release albums.

IF: What was the scene like? Who were the other bands at the time?

Ray Laidlaw: Before Alan Hull joined us he was in a band called the Chosen Few for a while. Round about 1964 the two best bands in Newcastle were the Chosen Few and the Junco Partners. Later on there were loads of bands like Brian Johnson's band The Gobi Desert Canoe Club. There was the Urge who became the Hippy Urge who then became the Influence, which was John Miles's band. There were other blues bands about like One More Mile from South Shields. There were also some out and out pop band like The Sect who were great players and a bit like the Small Faces and had a big female following. There were loads of places to play and loads of bands.

Rod Clements: We used to play working men's clubs, weekend dances in towns and villages round the North East but also music clubs like the Club a'Gogo in Newcastle or the El Cubana in Sunderland or the 45 Club in Whitley Bay. There was also the colleges and the universities who put gigs on. We saw ourselves as counter cultural, alternative and left field. There was a big audience for this, politics with a small 'p'. You would see familiar faces as you went round and it was people with similar outlooks. It was definitely a scene as such.

Contemporaries of ours were the Junco Partners. They were a great band and had a great rhythm section in Dave Sproat and John Woods. Ray Laidlaw and I used to go along to watch them at the Vic at Whitley Bay on a Wednesday night and really study what the bass and drums were doing and attempt to emulate them. Both of us at separate times dept for the Juncos. It was a great privilege at the time to play with them.

IF: Did the venues stipulate you needed to play covers?

Ray Laidlaw: Well some did and many didn't. Sometimes, to make a bit of money, we would play social clubs and they would say 'Nee LP music, only *Top of the Pops*'. You would need a range of different sets. There were places like the Rex Ballroom in Blyth and the Locarno in Sunderland, which became known as the Fillmore North. We supported the Gas Board there, which was Bryan Ferry's band. All the pit villages in County Durham had somewhere to play.

IF: How did Alan join the band?

Ray Laidlaw: By this point we were called Brethren. He was always around but he was not in a band. We put on a free open-air show in Leazes Park in Newcastle. We went to the council and asked if we could do it. They said 'Yes, what are you going to do about power?'. Well, we'd never thought about that but they said 'Don't worry, we'll sort it'. When we got there it was a lamp post with cables hanging out and a 4-way adaptor to supply our power. No thought of Health and Safety but no one seemed to mind. We booked Hully to do that.

Around that time I got a call to go and do some session work at Impulse Studios in Wallsend. When I got there it turned out to be drumming for some demos Alan was doing. He was managed by Dave Wood, who owned Impulse. Alan didn't say much but I think he was checking me out for a band he wanted to start. I went back to Brethren and said we've got get him in the band and also be doing some of his songs. We needed a third voice. Alan was a bit arrogant and a bit bolshy and so he was struggling to find people to join him. I knew he'd fit us like a glove. We started going to each other's shows. This was often at folk clubs and it was then we discovered folk music. If we wanted to try things acoustically you could always get up at folk clubs and they were very welcoming. Then we started to do stuff together.

Rod Clements: By this time we'd made a few trips down to London to Morgan Studios to start recording an album as someone had taken a shine to us and offered us free recording time, normally in the morning. So we'd do a gig on Tyneside, drive down overnight, record in the morning and drive back home on the afternoon. Jeff Sadler recorded some of that with us but decided he didn't want to go full time. It was great shame as he was a great guitar player and still is a good friend. He was a great pal of Mark Knopfler as they went to Gosforth Grammar School together. I remember Mark Knopfler coming along to some of our rehearsals.

We were doing quite well as a blues band and we were starting to write our own songs but the gig market changed. It began to favour bands like Free, who were more rock blues or even pop rock. We didn't fancy going there but started to struggle for gigs. Largely through the influence of Ray Jackson's record collection we started to do more acoustic folk blues, doing tunes by the likes of Lead Belly. We could play these sorts of songs in the local folk clubs. We could stick to our principles musically but expand our playing opportunities and of course that's where we met Alan Hull. He liked what we did and we were a good fit for what he was doing. Being a blues band brought something to his music that he wouldn't have got otherwise. I actually saw it as a Dylan and the Band type of arrangement where we'd retain our separate entities but come together when it suited us but the music worked so well and the audience and the local media's response was so positive that we joined forces and the rest, as they say, is history.

When we got signed by Charisma it was because we had the songs. Alan arrived with a catalogue of 300 songs, most of which were good and some were fantastic. We also had a few of our own, some of which were pretty good. They picked up on Jacka's (Ray Jackson) harmonica and his mandolin, which was an unusual instrument at the time. I was a scraping a violin by this time. So we had a wider sound along with our repertoire of songs.

IF: So when did the harmonies come in?

Ray Laidlaw: From the beginning really. As soon as Rod started writing along with Simon we put in two-part harmonies. It was natural to us because we came through the Beatles. Despite all the blues influences, we liked good melodies and good sounds. We were always a song-based band.

IF: Did the change to a more folky sound come quickly?

Ray Laidlaw: No, gradually. The big change was when Jeff Sadler left. So we didn't have a main lead guitarist in the band and that changed the sound. Also, Ray Jackson was playing mandolin, which no one else was playing at the time, and this came more to the fore. So, it wasn't planned and it just happened naturally

IF: Did you have a manager by then?

Ray Laidlaw: A guy called Joe Robertson, who managed the Junco Partners, agreed to take us on. He is mainly known as the man who revolutionised bar life in Newcastle. He owned about 20 bars in the town. He had bars with no seats and music on which attracted the lasses, which in turn attracted the lads. As there was music on you couldn't hear too well so you drank faster. He was a good lad and he liked us.

We wanted to be an album band. We weren't interested in being pop stars. We wanted to be respected as song writers and players. By this time we were so busy playing all round the North East. At the Mayfair on a Tuesday there would be a local bands night which we'd play but then support 'name' bands on different nights of the week. I was told by the late North East music journalist Ian Penman that we played on the bill for Led Zeppelin's first ever UK gig at the Mayfair in Newcastle. They were called the New Yardbirds and changed their name the following week. We built a big audience and we could tell from the audience reaction that we had something special. And then we got Hully and that was the game changer. We then had access to all his songs. And also now had three fantastic singers.

Rod Clements: We had management in Newcastle. Alan was managed by Dave Wood, who owned Impulse Studio and we were managed by Joe Roberston. When we joined forces they joined forces too. It was costing twice as much money but we were getting bigger fees. When we did the Charisma deal they bought us out of the management deal with Joe and Dave. An inherent problem was that Charisma was our employer and our managers so it was a bit of a conflict. I wouldn't say they took advantage of us as much as they could have done.

IF: How did you get signed by Charisma?

Ray Laidlaw: Well there are two stories. Firstly, Charlie Harcourt had left the Junco Partners to join Jackson Heights, formed by Lee Jackson of the Nice. He asked Charlie to join. Joe Roberston saw an opportunity and went to see Charisma

Records to ask for compensation for losing his guitarist in the band he managed. Tony Stratton Smith, owner of Charisma Records, explained that this is not what happens in the music industry. So Joe said 'While I'm here will you listen to the tape of this other band, Brethren?'. Tony quite liked it and offered a support slot on a Charisma night in the Marquee in London. The other version is that when Jackson Heights were being formed they got all their amps built by Burman Amps in Newcastle. So in a conversation with Greg Burman, Tony asked 'what is happening in Newcastle?' and Greg said 'You've got to see this band Brethren'. So, Tony flew up and got Greg to take him to see the band play the Mayfair at their next gig. So, when Joe went down Tony Stratton Smith knew all about us and just played Joe, feigning lack of interest to be able to offer a poorer deal.

Rod Clements: The deal was done on the strength of the demos we'd done and a couple of shows we had done in London. Charisma used to have a showcase night on at the Marquee in London and they brought us down to have a look at us on that. We weren't just playing the North East then, we were playing all round the country as Brethren.

IF: So what was the deal?

Ray Laidlaw: Oh it was crap. It was maybe three years and three albums in that time. About a year later they licenced us to Elektra in the US and that led to a year's extension. I remember we got a cheque for £2,000, £200 each and I opened my first bank account with that.

They started getting us gigs. They had a house producer in John Anthony who had already produced Genesis and Van Der Graph Generator. We were rehearsing the songs in Rod's house in front of John Anthony. We knew we'd have to change our name because there was already a Brethren in the US. That night someone mentioned they had been up to Lindisfarne Island a few days before and John said 'That would be a great name.' For us it was like calling ourselves 'Seaton Carew', somewhere you might go. All a bit weird for a band name. John checked with the office and they loved it. We wanted something different. The metal bands were starting with the likes of Deep Purple and Black Sabbath and we didn't want to be a 'The' band.

IF: What was your image at the time you signed your deal?

Rod Clements: Well it's not something we thought about at the time but we saw ourselves very much as rather hairy non-conformists and this kind of went with the music. When we went to London both Charisma and the music press made something of that, we were billed as scruffy renegades from the North East and we were encouraged to play up to that, which we took great delight in doing.

IF: How did you feel about going down to London?

Rod Clements: Mixed feelings. Alan and I both had young families so that was a wrench. And it was also difficult to find somewhere to live given the small allowance that Charisma paid us. We managed it though. We were fish out of water to some extent. Mainly we had each other and we had the support of the record company. They kept us busy and there was a social scene around Charisma. There were only about 12 staff and we'd often go to the pub together after work with them to get a few free pints. It was a good social scene and we also did radio sessions and interviews as well as gigs so it was a busy time.

IF: Was the Charisma label a good fit for the band?

Rod Clements: It was a great fit. They were a maverick label and we always saw ourselves as outsiders so it suited us down to the ground. They had Genesis, who were wacky and out there at the time, Van Der Graaf Generator, Sir John Betjeman, the Monty Python team. So it was all quite an eclectic mix and quite out there compared to other labels.

Ray Laidlaw: Our deal with Charisma was both the strength and the weakness of the band. Tony Stratton Smith was our manager as well as label owner. We loved that it was all in house but really most bands have managers who protect the band's interests in negotiations with the label. Here there was no negotiation and we had to trust Tony. We never saw much money. We were on a wage but beyond that we didn't know anything about the finances. When he extended the deal he actually talked to himself saying 'Do you want to extend the deal? Yes, OK. Do you want any money? Yes. How about a grand? Yes, thanks very much.' Normally, a manager would fight your corner. But we loved that it was all in house and the company was full of characters. We let our hearts rule our heads. We were young and didn't think long term. We got the chance to make records and our crowds went from a hundred to thousands, so we were loving it.

IF: Did your life change?

Ray Laidlaw: Oh yes. We had all the songs and we made the album in Trident Studios in London in three days. A couple of us had moved down but it was tough for Alan and Rod who were married with kids. We'd been going down doing gigs anyway and so had pals who always had places where we could stay. For 18 months me, Alan and Jacka had a rotating set of pals who had beds or floors we could crash on. Eventually we all moved down. I moved with Jacka to Edgeware Road.

IF: How did you write what has become such an iconic song ("Meet me on the Corner")?

Rod Clements: It was written quite a while before this time. It was before Lindisfarne. I wrote it late '69 and I was living in a house in Tynemouth before we moved to London. The melody came out of my blues interest. I was finger picking a sort of rag time style and I thought it sounded nice. I wrote that in about 30 minutes and then put it to one side to feed the baby. The next day I thought I'd better write some words for it. So I picked up the guitar and I wrote all the words for it in about another 30 minutes. It kicked it around in that format for quite a while and the band tried it in various formats, even quite a rocky version. The version that everyone knows with the 12 string and harmonica was actually cooked up by me and Ray Jackson in some downtime while the others went to the pub and we stayed behind and worked on it and when they came back they said

'That's it' and we quickly recorded a demo.

IF: When you present such a song to the band does the band immediately respond with something like 'oh, that sounds special' or does it have a gestation period?

Rod Clements: Yes, I think 'a gestation period' is a good term for that. As I had written it as a solo acoustic piece the band didn't immediately know what to do with it. Unlike other songs like "Train in G Major". I wrote that acoustically but it was immediately obvious what the band could do with it. With "Meet me" I think the band recognised the quality but didn't immediately see what to do with it.

IF: Who chose the producer for the first album?

Rod Clements: Charisma did. John Anthony was their producer and he'd produced the early Genesis stuff and Van der Graaf Generator stuff. He was great and was actually from the North East although you wouldn't know it if you met him. He was very much a trendy Londoner in his speech, his dress and his general behaviour. He was really good and very encouraging and gave us lots of leeway. The first album, *Nicely Out of Tune*, has his fingerprints all over it. It's got so many different instruments and sounds on it. And I think the album's all the better for it. But then Charisma had a better offer for the next album to be produced by Bob Johnston, erstwhile producer of Bob Dylan. Tony Stratton Smith had contacts in New York and specifically Marty Machat, who was also Bob Johnston's lawyer. So Tony invited Bob over to the UK. John Anthony was ditched, which we felt a bit bad about it.

IF: What was the contrast between the two producers?

Ray Laidlaw: Chalk and cheese to be honest. Bob was great. A very entertaining and authoritative character and great company. He was, though, much more minimalist than John Anthony. The first day of the sessions we played all of our new songs to Bob and he threw nearly all of them out. So we had to dig back into the back catalogue to find stuff to play him. And these numbers tended not be rehearsed and played in a fairly stripped back style. Bob liked that and so the album, *Fog on the Tyne*, is much more stripped down and all the better for it. They are both good in their own ways. Bob gave us a breakthrough hit in "Meet Me On The Corner" after which everything changed.

IF: Did you ever feel starstruck or overawed meeting the likes of Bob Johnson?

Ray Laidlaw: No, not really. We knew he'd had success as he'd done three albums with Leonard Cohen, six with Bob Dylan, eight with Johnny Cash, a couple with Simon and Garfunkel. The only time we were a bit unsure was when we first met Bob Johnson before we did the recording. We went for a meal and we were all full of ourselves. Bob didn't say much and was a bit jet lagged and so buggered off to the hotel. So we said to Tony Stratton Smith 'You don't think he's changed his mind has he?' Tony said 'No, no he loves the songs'. We said 'Are you sure' and Tony said 'Well the only problem he had was that he couldn't understand a word you were saying.' To be honest he was just a great bloke. Because we were a five piece with five strong characters we needed someone to take charge and it worked a treat. The band were on top form.

IF: At the time did you know you were flying as a band?

Ray Laidlaw: We knew we were special and we knew if we went on stage with the three part harmony on "Clear White Light" we'd blow people apart. No one else in Britain was doing that. Simon worked out the harmonies, as he was the only one who could read music, and he would often put in a note that you weren't expecting. The difference between our harmonies and the Eagles was that theirs would be sweet and polished whereas ours would be anarchic. It was described as 'sweet and sour harmonies'.

We were like a band of brothers but there were big differences with two public school boys and three working class scruffs. For the North East it shouldn't have worked but it did.

IF: Did you do full tours of the US?

Ray Laidlaw: Yes, when *Fog on the Tyne* was climbing we went to the US in the spring of 1972 ostensibly for two weeks and ended up staying for six because the success of the album led to more and more dates being added. The opening night was at the Carnegie Hall supporting the Kinks, which was wonderful because we loved the Kinks. We had a great agency over there, Bill Graham[4] was involved. We went down to Texas and supported the Beach Boys, Don McLean and Tim Buckley. Getting to California was a dream. We flew into San Francisco and me and Rod roomed together. In the morning room service knocked on the door with breakfast. He asked if we wanted the drapes opening and we said 'yes.' It was floor to ceiling windows and there was the Golden Gate and the San Francisco Bay and I turned to Rod and said, 'Not bad for a couple of Geordie arseholes'. It was living the dream. People in the music press were saying that Hully was the best songwriter since Lennon and McCartney.

IF: Did you have any trepidation in playing such big stages, even if it is only metaphorically a big stage with the Troubadour[5]? Or playing with massive acts such as the Beach Boys?

Rod Clements: No, I think we felt it was our entitlement, we felt we'd earned it. We felt we were on our way and certainly the arrogance of youth played a part in it. It was all going very well until the wheel came off.

IF: You had a hit and then the album was a hit, was there a point where fame suddenly hit you?

Rod Clements: Yes, it was almost like you wake up one morning and you're famous. When "Meet me on the Corner" went top 10 we were actually in New York. Charisma had a tie-up deal with Elektra Records in the US and they were interested in us. So we went across to do some support gigs with the Kinks, Frank Zappa and the Beach Boys. We also did some club dates on our own in San Francisco and the Troubadour in LA. It was all quite low budget with low budget hotels. When we went top 10 it suddenly all changed with better hotels and limos picking us up. There was a lot more media interest and the US Tour was extended by two weeks.

Ray Laidlaw: Success was great but getting the records out was what we loved. The BBC loved us because we fitted so many genres. We could do folks shows, blues shows, John Peel, 'Whispering' Bob Harris. We were constantly in and out of Maida Vale Studios. We were always so busy and it was such good fun. We'd dreamt of this, not having to go to work. It was wonderful. The first album came out to great reviews but only sold OK.

For the second album, *Fog on the Tyne,* there was a real head of steam building up and so when it came out it was perfect timing and caught people's imagination. We really were quite different to anything else out at the time. It sold really well but took six months to get to number one. About three weeks after it got to number one we were rock stars, where we got recognised on the streets. That lasted about three weeks and then we got back to being a great band. I didn't really like that star stuff, none of us did.

IF: How was the recording of the third album *Dingly Dell*?

Ray Laidlaw: We shot ourselves in the foot with *Dingly Dell*. We were heavily into the ecological thing so we insisted on having a plain cardboard sleeve to make a point. We wrote a song about urban vandalism called "All Fall Down" which had a strange time signature and wasn't remotely commercial. Alan was insisting it would be the first single and we backed him up. There were two songs on that album that would have been number one if they'd been released, especially "Wake Up Little Sister". Noddy Holder told us on *Top of the Pops* he was delighted we didn't put "Wake Up Little Sister" out as it would have stolen the thunder from one of Slade's hits. Consequently, the album only got to number six and was perceived a failure.

IF: Did you feel disappointed?

Ray Laidlaw: Yes, a bit. We were a bit too much up ourselves. We should have been prepared that after *Fog on the Tyne* there would be a come down. Only the Simon and Garfunkel album *Bridge over Troubled Waters* sold more that year in the UK. After that we went back to the US and Alan was getting sick of it. He said he couldn't write on the road. We were keeping the record company afloat. So they pushed us to put the third album out quickly and Hully rebelled. To be fair those of us who didn't have kids wanted to tour and maybe didn't appreciate what it was like for those who did. So Alan fell out over it and basically quit.

IF: And why did the wheel come off?

Rod Clements: Alan decided he didn't want to be in the band anymore. By the time of the third album, *Dingly Dell*, we were running out of songs. Neither Alan or I were writing as much or as good as we had done before. Alan felt the reason for that was the constant touring and media work meaning a lack of downtime to enable us to write in peace and also missing out on the life experiences that inspired song writing. He either wanted out or he wanted changes in the band. Neither of those options we were happy with. Charisma came up with various solutions such as Alan could go off the road and we could get someone in to cover for him on stage. They also said 'If you do 60 more gigs you will never have to work again ever.' It's a pretty strange thing to be offered when you're only 22 or 23 and it wasn't an option anyone wanted. Alan just wanted out. With hindsight Genesis and Peter Gabriel were also at a crossroads. So Charisma, having seen what had happened to us, took them off the road for a year to allow them to write new material and sort themselves out. It paid off handsomely for them and with hindsight Charisma may well have wished they had done that for us.

Alan told the *Melody Maker* before it was announced and the next week it had the headline 'Lindisfarne split?'.

IF: How did you feel?

Rod Clements: I felt very let down and very disappointed. What happened next was quite strange from Alan in that he continued Lindisfarne with Ray Jackson and four others. Ray

Laidlaw, Si and I continued with Jack the Lad and recruited Billy Mitchell as our fourth member. This was really more like going back to the Downtown Faction. We all very positive about it. We continued to have the support of Charisma and recorded an album. After that I went freelance and worked with Ralph McTell (and played on the number One "Streets of London"), Michael Chapman and Bert Jansch. They were all musicians I admired for many years.

IF: Was that lower stress and a bit more freeing?

Rod Clements: Yes, it certainly was. Jack the Lad was great fun but with Lindisfarne it was a relief at the end to get away from it as it had turned quite sour. At that time I had more or less given up writing.

Ray Laidlaw: Actually within two weeks I was playing on Alan's solo record. Originally, Alan was going to come off the road and we would get a touring singer, like Brian Jones of the Beach Boys, which would be Billy Mitchell. Three days later it all changed and we split. Myself, Rod and Simon formed Jack the Lad and Alan and Jacka formed Lindisfarne Mark Two with some other lads and made another couple of albums. We still saw each other about.

IF: Were you bitter?

Ray Laidlaw: Simon took it the worst because Alan blamed Simon for the break up and everything that went wrong. The rest of us just got on with it. Jack the Lad was still with Charisma. We never sold many records but it was just as much fun. The gigs were fantastic. Rod only stayed a year and we got two lads from Hebburn from Hedgehog Pie. Then me and Alan had a band called Radiator. It was Van Morrison style. We played with two drummers.

It carried on for a year or so but then we had the Lindisfarne reunion back on. We had done a Lindisfarne reunion show and there were record companies sniffing about. We were older and wiser so we thought we could really make it work so we knocked Radiator on the head much to the upset of the other lads in the band.

IF: How did the Lindisfarne reunion come about?

Rod Clements: We had an offer to play at the Newcastle Festival in the Summer of 1976. Barry McKay was managing Ray Jackson in his solo career at that time and said, 'Don't do that. If you're going to get the band back together, do it properly and do it at Newcastle City Hall at Christmas.' He made us a generous offer and we agreed. It was sold out and an extra night was added. And it was a totally elating experience to be part of, especially due to the appreciation and warmth of the audience to see us back together. That created momentum for us to get back together permanently. Relations in the band were much better and for quite a long time until 1990 when Ray Jackson left.

IF: How did you feel coming back as Lindisfarne at the height of punk and new wave? Did you feel a different vibe in the air?

Ray Laidlaw: Well, we always thought we were punks. So we were a bit miffed when they lumped us with all the hippies like Gentle Giant. The music was a mile apart but I loved some of the punk music.

It was great to be back together again and we felt we'd come full circle. The things that had pissed us off about each other we now realised were strengths. And with help we formed our own management company, which gave us control. This really then carried on until 1995 when Alan died and then another eight years after that when we brought Billy Mitchell in. The spirit began to go towards the end around 2003 but we are all good now.

Rod Clements: It felt a lot different and in ways that I wasn't totally comfortable with. Barry McKay's belief was that in the first incarnation we hadn't got our due deserts and that we should, this time, be better rewarded and get the dues and treatment of rock stars. So, he made big demands from record companies and he got a big advance from Phonogram. A lot of that advance went on making the album, which was produced by Gus Dudgeon. He was a great producer but much glossier than Bob Johnston or John Anthony. What he said was what went. We had to be less scruffy, with higher quality photo sessions. One particular session made us look like the Eagles. It wasn't us. I felt we didn't have to live the five-star lifestyle.

IF: Can I turn the conversation to more reflective thoughts. Why have we not had a scene in the North East as Liverpool or Bristol have, which is one of the key questions in this book?

Ray Laidlaw: The infrastructure wasn't here. There were maybe two studios but they could only do demo-standard recordings. Liverpool was two hours to London whereas at the time it was five hours from up here. Also, North Easterners can be very idiosyncratic and different. But there was a great scene around Newcastle when we were coming up and some great bands. Maybe, due to geography this just wasn't recognised nationally.

Rod Clements: I think there are a number of reasons and remoteness has a lot to do with it. It certainly had in our time. In our time there was very little music on TV. The only opportunity to see music was to see bands live. I think musicians and bands up here were less prone to trend following as they may have been in London for instance. The music scene back then didn't tend to follow the fashions. You would see people on *Top of the Pops* wearing funny clothes and think *oh, no, that's not for me*. I think that distance and that reservation meant that trends took longer to catch on up here and that applied to music as well. In fact when Lindisfarne signed their first record contract with Charisma in 1970 it was a condition of the contract that we all move down to London. We did and they were absolutely right with hindsight as it meant we were onhand for radio sessions, interviews, photo shoots etc.

••••••••••••••••••

Lindisfarne are the quintessential North East band, even down to being named after a special and significant place in our local history, even if the choosing of the name was not really anything of great meaning. I talked to Ray about how a native North Easterner could possibly lack self-confidence, especially down south. Ray described a different experience where a group of Geordies together gave them a group strength, outsiders all together in the Big Smoke. He tells of times when they were bored in some top executive's company they would put on their thickest accents, which their company could never follow, and would then just slope off. He also says 'we were a product of our environment. We were quite brash and in your face. When you're in a band you have to have that self-confidence. In some ways we were a bit too Geordie, not in the songs but in our approach and off stage'.

Rod uses the example of Alan Hull to perfectly illustrate a common North East trait. His sometimes brash and almost aggressive exterior that shielded a more complex, introspective and insecure interior.

They are possibly the only band I talk about in this book whose regional character defined them but also made them a formidable force in their early days. To some, coming from this sometimes insular region holds them back, to Lindisfarne it was an identity that drove them forward. More than this, though, they were (and are) outstanding singers, musicians and song writers who created and recorded music that sounds as fresh today as when it was written and recorded over 50 years ago. And all of this is why they were so particularly loved in the North East. We talked about the legendary Newcastle City Hall Christmas gigs that started after their reunion. Quite remarkably they played 132 of those Christmas gigs. Some bands were loved nationally, some were loved and revered locally. Lindisfarne had the magic formula that they were loved particularly in their home region but for a time also throughout the land.

1. The Band were a US/Canadian rock band formed in 1967, who were credited with starting the 'Americana' style of music that is still prevalent today with the likes of Wilco and the Counting Crows. They later worked as the backing band for Bob Dylan and were highly influential with the likes of Elton John, George Harrison and Elvis Costello, as well as Lindisfarne, namechecking their importance.

2. *NME* and *Melody Maker* were musical weekly papers in the UK. In the 1970s through to the 1990s there were four weekly musical papers in the UK – The *New Musical Express (NME)*, *Sounds*, *Melody Maker* and *Record Mirror*. At their height sales of each of these papers could be up to an incredible 200,000 a week. Many artists I have talked to have cited one or all of these papers as their sources for finding out what was going on in the music scene.

3. Lead Belly was an American folk and blues singer who, though in and out of jail throughout his life, saw the height of his fame in the 1930s. He was a major influence on skiffle music and many acts that followed. George Harrison once said 'No Lead Belly, no Beatles'

4. Bill Graham was a legendary, tough and influential music promoter in the US, who, amongst other things, ran the music venues the Filmore West in San Francisco and the Filmore East in New York.

5. The Troubadour was music venue in Hollywood, LA, which was famous for launching the careers of singer songwriters such as James Taylor, Carol King and Linda Ronstadt. Elton John's legendary concerts, which cemented his fame in the US, were featured in his recent biopic Rocketman.

Prelude

Brian Hume's Story

Prelude are a three-part harmony band formed in 1970 by husband and wife Brian and Irene Hume and Brian's school friend Ian Vardy. They most notably had a hit with their acapella version of Neil Young's "After the Goldrush" which remained in the UK Top 30 for nine weeks in 1974. It reached number 22 in the US Top 30 and remained there for 13 weeks. They released records on major labels such as EMI and Pye. They are playing to this day and have had a life full of music. I talk to Brian on the phone, with Irene chipping in to keep him right. He tells me tales of being label mates with Max Bygraves and touring America, sometimes with a tinge of regret at missed opportunities.

IF: How did you get into music and how did you start playing?

Brian Hume: My mother was very musical. She could knock out a tune on the piano, every house seemed to have a piano in those days. She had a four-stringed guitar which got me interested. I picked out a few tunes on that. I used to listen to a transistor radio under the covers in my bed, listening to Radio Luxembourg[1]. That's when I heard things like Bill Haley, Elvis and the Everly Brothers.

I met Ian Vardy at school and we shared a mutual interest in music. We got some guitars and started to learn the Everly Brothers' songs. We found the Beatles a little more difficult to learn as they used more obscure chords. We were also enamoured with Paul Simon. So we started gigging doing Everly Brothers and Paul Simon songs. Coincidently later on we were signed to Paul Simon's publishing company and I think the guy who owned it, Alan Paramor, had an idea of us being the English version of Simon and Garfunkel, though it didn't quite work out that way. In fact, of the first four songs we recorded (under the name Carnival), two of them were Paul Simon songs.

IF: You were later famous for your harmonies. How did you learn to harmonise?

Brian Hume: When you listened to the Everlys you could pick out the two separate voices. Ian would do Phil's part as he had a higher voice than me and I would do the Don Everly part. It just fell into place. If you listen to Graham Nash's interviews it was the same for him and for Alan Clark of the Hollies, who were also blown away by the Everly Brothers' harmonies. It was the same all over the country where two guys would try and copy the Everlys' harmonising. I think it is quite a natural skill. I know some good singers who just can't harmonise but some people who think well, what's the mystery.

IF: Where did you kick off doing gigs?

Brian Hume: Well the folk scene at the time was massive. This was around 1965/6. We used to play at the Bridge Hotel in Newcastle, which at the time was a hub of Irish Republicanism. It was always jam packed there and there were some great performers on. You would learn your craft by watching the other performers. We would play other folk clubs as well and sometimes when we played a few Paul Simon songs we would tear the place apart and we thought wow, this is good.

There was something in the air. Young people at the time

were politically active, as we were. There was a feeling that something was happening and that society was going to get better, a more just and humane world. The songs reflected that, like early Paul Simon songs were all about civil rights. It was an optimistic time.

IF: Who were your contemporaries here in the North East?

Brian Hume: The Caffrey Brothers were in a band called Arbre and they were red hot. They should have had wider success because they were great singers and a great act. They had a deal but it didn't quite take off. They certainly took on the Crosby, Stills and Nash sound. There was also Pete Scott from Newcastle. He is in my mind a genius. He was a bit like Jake Thackray[2]. He was a genius with words and he's quite deadpan in his delivery but hilarious and actually quite deep, well worth checking out. There was Robbie Burns who had a single deal. He was great guy but rather troubled. Then there was Alan Hull and he just blew us away. We saw him in Tynemouth when he'd joined Brethren and he played a collection of songs including "Winter Song", "Lady Eleanor", "Clear White Light" and we were just amazed. He had an amazing voice as well as the songs.

IF: Was it your harmonising that made you stand out?

Brian Hume: Well, it did, but it wasn't until Irene joined and we started doing the three-part harmonies that we really started to stand out. We started spending a lot more time on this. When we got the first Crosby, Stills and Nash album and Ian and I were trying to work out the vocal parts. Irene was in the kitchen and she was, unbeknownst to her, singing the third harmony part. It happened purely by chance. We then started to polish that up, using things like Suite: Judy Blue Eyes[3]. Fortunately, we had a guitar player called Frank Usher who could play stuff like that well. He'd previously been in a band called Heavy Jelly[4]. We then moved on to social clubs playing the three-part harmonies. This would be around 1968. We had no plans, we just loved the sound we were making. We stood out from other acts due to our harmonies.

IF: How did you find your earliest experiences of going into a recording studio?

Brian Hume: Well, we'd made some demos in a recording studio in Newcastle called Morton Sound and we got an earlier deal with EMI and Alan Paramor and we had one single with them 'Big Bright Green Pleasure Machine', which was a Paul Simon song, one of his poor songs to be honest. This was before we became Prelude. We actually had quite a few false starts

We did a previous recording with Decca Records with a self-written song called "Edge of the Sea" which went nowhere. This is while we were called Carnival.

Carnival was me and Ian but we were originally going to called the Cobblers. Fortunately, we realised we could be subject to reviews such as 'what a load of Cobblers' so went for Carnival instead. We were then going to be Trilogy but there was a US band called Trilogy. Then we were Leaves of Grass for about three weeks but realised the drug connotations may be a problem, even though it was a quote from a Walt Whitman poem. We became Prelude when Irene joined. We then met our manager, George Carr, who got us our first record deal which led to our first record.

The deal was with Pye Records and their main act was Max Bygraves, the comedian, singer and family entertainer. To say they were behind the times was an understatement. Later on when we had a hit in the US with "After the Goldrush", we went to see Chris Blackwell of Island records, who had released it in the US, and the contrast was stark. Pye was full of typists and suits, Island was full of young people in jeans and t-shirts playing ping pong and so forth. Chris Blackwell was a very cool guy, very laid back. And we thought why aren't we with these lot? There were pictures of Free and Bob Marley on Island's walls and the top act at Pye was Max Bygraves. We were their token folk act and they didn't really know what to do with us.

Eventually then, after these twists and turns we we recorded the album for Pye at the famous Rockfield Studios in

Monmouth, Wales. Many big bands like Queen, Joan Armatrading and Dave Edmunds recorded there. It was a great experience.

We were there for a week recording the album. It was produced by Fritz Fryer, who used to be in a band called The Four Pennies, who had a number one with "Juliet" in 1964. Anyway, when we thought we'd finished, he asked if there was anything else we'd like to record before we wrap up. And Irene said why don't we do that song we sing at the bus stop, which was "After the Goldrush". I think we had been swimming so we didn't have guitars and just sang the song acapella. So, it all just came about by chance. We actually sang it with a more simplified chordal structure. We recorded it and he said, 'Oh, that sounds nice' but we just left it as an album track. It was Kenny Everett[5] on Capitol Radio, who picked it up. We'd never imagined in a million years it would be a success because it really was an afterthought.

The album was all self-written except for "After the Goldrush". The first single was "Out there" and the second one was Goldrush. It was only released due to all the radio play. And it got us in the charts and on *Top of the Pops*.

We then got a call from Ralph McTell's brother, who was his manager. He had heard "After the Goldrush" and asked us to do backing vocals for his re-recording of "Streets of London". Our record company was so backward that they refused to put our name on the record, so they used another name, 'The Goldrushers'. This got to number two in the UK Charts and, true to form, Pye failed to capitalise on it.

We did a big tour with Ralph McTell, including the Albert Hall. We then did a second album. Musically it was better than the first with people like Isaac Guillory on it and a few local musicians like Jim Hornsby. We had a lot of good musicians on it. Overall, we did four albums with Pye. None were really successful to be quite frank.

We then signed with After Hours, who were a subsidiary of

EMI, and had a couple of hits, firstly with a version of "Only the Lonely" and then with one of my songs "Platinum Blond", which we played on *Top of the Pops*.

Looking back because we didn't have a working band, we would use session musicians and so we didn't really develop a settled sound. I think it detracted from what should have been, a more acoustic, Americana sound, focusing on the vocals. After Hours were very good but the whole thing imploded when the record company fell foul of the Payola scandal[6]. That really marked the end of our time with major record labels. After that we generally self-recorded and sold them at gigs.

IF: Were you disappointed that this came to an end?

Brian Hume: Every band looks back on their career and thinks what could we have done better? I think Prelude always had potential that wasn't realised. We had a great sound with our vocals but, if I am honest I don't think we had the songs. Our self-written songs didn't connect with an audience the way that, say, "Streets of London" did. We seemed to lack avid fans. They may have liked our sound on certain records but we didn't get that following. People would buy anything released by Leonard Cohen or Kate Bush but it didn't happen with us.

However, some problems were our choice of label. We toured the US after Alan Hull had come back from touring with Lindisfarne. He said, 'Everywhere we went in America they were playing your bloody record', meaning "After the Goldrush". He said, 'Get your asses over there'. But because our record company was so backwards we didn't go across for another 18 months by which time the moment had passed. If we'd gone across when it was in the US charts we could have knocked it out of the park playing on prime time TV slots. However, we went across with nothing to sell. It was a great experience, playing with the likes of Jerry Garcia's band[7] and Don McLean but really for our career it was a waste of time. The single got to number 14 on the US Billboard chart and the album did fairly well but we didn't promote it at that time. Pye just didn't know what they had. It was almost criminal how badly we were handled by Pye. Equally we didn't have the savvy ourselves. We were quite young and naïve.

IF: How long were you in the US? Did you enjoy it?

Brian Hume: We were there about a month and it was great. We first played in San Francisco and played with a band called Bushwack and the Glass Backs who were a doo-wop band. Then we were in Berkeley with Jerry Garcia's band who had Nicky Hopkins[8] playing with them. Then we were over to New York where we played the Bottom Line[9]. It was great fun but ultimately a waste of time.

IF: I understand that there were mistakes but you can't have regrets.

Brian Hume: I actually regret a lot of things. I regret doing other people's songs. Someone should have sat us down and said, 'Your songs are OK but they are not great. Try harder.'

I was talking to Ian Matthews who was in Fairport Convention and had a hit with "Woodstock" with Matthews Southern Comfort. We were playing a gig to about three people and he told how he'd gone to the US and they had liked his sound and he'd got a career out of it, playing the West Coast style. In hindsight we should have gone to the US as our sound suited their tastes. We weren't folk but we weren't rock. It didn't quite connect at home.

•••••••••••••••••

Prelude are from Gateshead but produced a sound that suited California. Admittedly that is a little bit of an incongruous sentence but accurate nonetheless. Listening again to "After the Goldrush" the harmonies are without doubt pure West Coast. As mentioned they still play, often to sell-out crowds, albeit in small venues, as people love their harmonies.

What Brian also touched on was the scene that they came up through, which was both vibrant and politically charged. That scene, unlike, say, punk or heavy metal has no links or equivalence with the present day, which is a massive shame. Brian describes a time of optimism that demanded a more fair and caring world. It was also a time when the musicians believed they were part of the drive to change the world for the better. Whether they succeeded at all is the subject to many of a TV documentary.

There is, though, a melancholic regret within Brian's story. For those of us who can only dream of appearing on *Top of the Pops*, touring the US or singing backing vocals on an all-time great single in "Streets of London" this is hard to fathom. However, as is witnessed in many of the bands' stories in this book, there is a running theme of young, talented musicians let down by a record industry that is run by accountants and that treats their artists' careers and best interests as a low priority.

1. Radio Luxembourg is a commercial radio station which in the early 1960s, targeted the teenage market and was a great source for youngsters to hear the early rock and roll music of Elvis and Little Richard.

2. Jake Thackray was an English humorous singer, songwriter and poet, in later years often heard on Radio 4

3. Suite: Judy Blue Eyes is a song by Stephen Stills and performed by Crosby, Stills and Nash.

4. Heavy Jelly were a band predominantly from Newcastle who had previously been called Skip Bifferty. The reason for the change of name is explained in an earlier chapter of this book.

5. Kenny Everett was a humorous and very popular radio DJ who later branched out into TV comedy shows.

6. The Payola Scandal was about illegal methods of getting radio play in the '50s, '60s and '70s to enhance the popularity of songs and improve chart positions. It resulted in a US Congressional investigation, indictments and changes to radio play rules.

7. Jerry Garcia was songwriter, guitarist and singer for the US band The Grateful Dead. He later formed his own band as a side project.

8. Nicky Hopkins was a British keyboard player most famous for his work in the 60s and 70s with The Rolling Stones. He played with many other musicians including The Kinks and The Who.

9. The Bottom Line was a famous musical venue in Greenwich Village in New York.

The High Level Ranters

Alistair Anderson's Story

The wonderful music auditorium, the Sage Gateshead, is about to hold a concert to celebrate the 75th birthday of Alistair Anderson. They describe him as 'internationally recognised as a master of the English concertina and a leading performer on the Northumbrian pipes'. The English concertina could be described as a small accordion and the Northumbrian pipes are similar to the Scottish bagpipes but are perhaps a little quieter which means they are played in conjunction with other traditional folk instruments. Alistair has been playing these instruments in folk bands and on his own for nearly 60 years. He does indeed have world renown; he has toured the US no less than 37 times.

He has been recognised as innovative in his field but he has a desire to honour the folk musicians of the past as well as encourage new generations. He set up the highly acclaimed Folkworks organisation in the late 80s. This organisation took folk music into schools around the North and led on to the setting up of the Sage Gateshead. He also set up a BA Honours Degree in Folk and Traditional Music at Newcastle University.

He rose to prominence as part of The High Level Ranters, a legendary North East folk band who are highly respected in the folk world. And, if that wasn't enough, you can see him playing the English concertina with his arms draped around Kate Bush on the video of her singing "Rocket Man" by Elton John.

I meet Alistair, appropriately, at the café of Northern Stage on the Newcastle University campus. I begin by explaining that the section I am writing on folk music begins with Lindisfarne and that they may not fit a strict definition of folk music. Alistair is decidedly unperturbed by such debates.

IF: How would you define folk music?

Alistair Anderson: Well a lot of Lindisfarne's songs fit into that area and the structure of a lot of Alan Hull's songs reflect what people would call folk music from the British Isles and the US including songs from the Appalachian Mountains and the American coalfields. There are a lot of links and I'm not too worried by labels. There is a whole lot of music that I regard as folk music because it works with people. People in a room, dancing and singing and joining in. So, "When I'm 64" by the Beatles has been around for 60 years and been sang in pubs and if someone wants to call it folk music then that's fine by me. And there would be plenty of people who would disagree with that, I'm not too bothered about arguing that.

IF: So, is it the community or communal nature of the music that defines folk music?

Alistair Anderson: Yes, I would say so. It tends to be music that reflects people's lives and works in communities. I play a lot of music that is basically for dances and those dances have evolved through the hands, feet and bodies of people and communities over a long, long period. The musicians will make music to make people dance in a way that suits the people but also with melodies that grab their ears. Traditionally folk musicians will play at dances all night and if they're going to play all night the musicians want something reasonable to play.

Up until the Second World War an ordinary Friday night dance in this part of the world in the rural and mining communities would start at eight in the evening and finish at six in the morning. And then they would walk home and go straight to work. I was sceptical about this but the old musicians I used to play with in the 60s would say it was so and the guy who gave me the definitive answer was a fella called Gordon Cutty, who was a miner from North East Durham. He was a union man and also an early member of the Musicians' Union and he said, 'Oh, yes, a Friday Night Dance would be eight till six and if it went past six o'clock you'd get sixpence extra for each half hour.' He said that the longest he had played was on the day the First World War finished. He played from eight till eight and they wanted some more but Gordon said, 'I think you've had enough.'

IF: Did these dances involve drink?

Alistair Anderson: No, nearly all the dances were dry but outside in the rural areas there would be a series of earthenware drainage pipes stacked up in a triangle and that's where they would hide a whisky bottle. Periodically, people would pop out for a quick drink and then come back into the dance. They would stop for supper, then first breakfast at three and then second breakfast at five, then they would be able to go off to work.

For each village there may have been three or four of these folk dances a year. So maybe 80% of the village would turn up, some were shuffling and some were great at the dances and would be flung about. This tended to be a more rural thing whereas in the cities and major towns an equivalent may have been found in the Irish communities. It tended to be a mix of what you might call traditional folk dances along with more mainstream dances like the Valletta, which is a bit of a waltz. I remember going to a great folk dance in about 1977, local to where I lived, in an actual barn and in amongst all the traditional folk dances they did "The Birdy Song" because someone had learnt it on holiday in Spain and it was just a good dance. It was different and it had a groove that worked. It was about people taking something and making it work for themselves. Nobody was worrying about what was traditional, they were more bothered about having a good time. What you find is the bits that work for that community keep going and the bits that stop working gradually fall away.

IF: What drew you to folk music?

Alistair Anderson: The first thing that really grabbed me was hearing the Rolling Stones talking about the old blues masters in the early 60s. I really got into blues for a while but then someone mentioned a local folk club and asked if I would I be interested in going. There had been a little bit on the telly like the *Hootenanny Show* which showed people like Pete Seeger, which I thought looked quite lively. Anyway, this folk club was in Ponteland and they had a band on called The Reivers. That was a couple of guitars and singers and they had a fiddle player who played some tunes and I was impressed with that. I had done quite a bit of dancing as I had been part of the Rambler's Association who held dances every few months and they brought bands in. I loved it because it was lively and I could dance with ladies and twirl them around. So that was great but it was a drag going all the way up to Ponteland so I was told about one in Newcastle called the Bridge Hotel and I went there.

I'd probably picked up an instrument by then as my dad was Canadian and he had a mandolin so I picked out some tunes on that. I cycled to school at Wallsend Grammar School every day with a friend of mine and he was always late. While I waited for him I'd be asked to wait in his mam's front room. This room had a china cabinet and nestled in the corner was an English concertina. I asked what it was and it was his grandad's who had passed away. I asked if I could borrow it and then she agreed to sell it to me. And to this day, along with the Northumbrian pipes, that is my main instrument.

IF: Can you describe what the Bridge Hotel Folk Club was like when you started going in the mid-60s?

Alistair Anderson: Well, having been to the Ponteland club, which was such fun, the Bridge Hotel club was a bit formal by comparison. They sang big ballads which I soon got to love but everyone was very quiet as they intently listened and there was a certain amount of reverence about it. But in the interval a gentleman called Colin Ross got up and played the fiddle and I felt it loosened the proceedings up a bit.

IF: What instruments were being played?

Alistair Anderson: Johnny Handle played four-string guitar and melodeon and a bit of accordion but he was also singing and writing great songs. The club was actually set up by Johnny and Louisa Killen in 1956 and Johnny is still around. Tommy Gilfellon played guitar and sang. Ron Duke, who ran a fishing shop, was voice and guitar. A gentleman called Lawrie Charlton was quite often the MC and he would sing unaccompanied. A Scottish lady called Ray Fisher, who would marry Colin Ross, would pop down and play voice and guitar or sometimes unaccompanied voice.

The place would be full to bursting and there would be a stage with six to eight seats on for the resident singers who would sit there all the way through. Each would take it in turns to sing and then would invite audience members, who would be sat in rows of seats, to come up and sing throughout the night. You might say on the door, 'I'm happy to do a song tonight' and you may get on but generally everyone knew each other from the various folk clubs.

By the 1970s there would be visiting special guests booked and people would come to see them. This happens to this day in folk clubs most weeks but in the 70s there would be guest performers every three or four weeks so the resident singers had to have a big repertoire and they had to be good. 80 to 90% of the songs would be traditional songs but some people, like Johnny, were writing original songs. He had worked in the pits for a good while and he would write songs about that amongst other aspects of life. The singers also sang more modern songs by the likes of Ewan McColl or Peggy Seeger alongside the more traditional songs. There was a feeling, however, that some of the popular folk hits from the USA like Peter, Paul and Mary were swamping the scene so there was a need to get some English songs written. Some clubs would not allow these American hits to be played. So, the songs sung would tend to be dominated by English traditional songs, the great Border ballads, some Burns songs and also songs of Joe Wilson from Newcastle of the mid-19th century.

IF: How did you get a start performing at the Bridge?

Alistair Anderson: The Bridge was on a Thursday night but they started to put on a Tuesday night as well called a Ceilidh. At that time the word Ceilidh was unknown in England. It was quite a conscious decision of the people who ran the folk club to get the young people attending interested in folk dancing. That would be a mix of dancing and then stopping for people to sing songs. So, I went along to that and it was a lot less formal. This was 1964 or 65 while I was still at school. It was easier for us to get up and play there and me and my mate Dave got up and did a couple of songs. And then, as I was going more often than Dave (consequently he got better A levels than me), I started doing tunes on the concertina but without any singing. I find it physically difficult to sing while playing the concertina and actually have very little to offer as a singer.

I was inspired more by instrumentalists rather than singers. I was very lucky that there was a teacher at school whose husband made Northumbrian pipes, a Mrs Reed. They took me out to meet someone called Billy Pigg, from Corbridge, who played the Northumbrian Pipes and was a spectacular musician. I met him in 1964 and he died in 1968. John Peel from the BBC actually got quite heavily into folk music and what got him into it was an album of recordings people had made of Billy Pigg. Billy was very welcoming and supportive of me playing the pipes as an instrumentalist. I wasn't aware of the Northumbrian pipes until I was 16 when Colin Ross started playing a set that he had made. Most of the pipes had been made in the 19th century and then a gent called Hedley in Gateshead started making them in the 1930s but he was the only one making them. Colin learnt about making them from him. Nowadays, people are aware of them but in the 1950s and 60s they had almost died out.

IF: How did you learn to play these fairly obscure instruments?

Alistair Anderson: Well, I'd had some piano lessons as a youngster which I hated but it meant I could almost read music. I could get books of folk music but most of what I learned was through watching and playing with people like Billy Pigg and Colin Ross. John Doonan, the great piccolo player who was of Irish extraction but lived in Hebburn, was another one I learnt from. In fact he was in the High Level Ranters when it began. The whole environment was conducive to me learning my instruments.

When I started playing the Northumbrian pipes in the late 1960s it was still very hard to get a set. So, I went to see Forster Charlton, who was a founder member of the Ranters, and he had a lathe in his back bedroom so I started making a set but struggled a bit so Colin made me a set and that's the set I still play. By and large I am self-taught although Colin helped me a lot. I have lots of bad habits that a teacher would want to correct. I learned an awful lot of it through osmosis. Everyone was so supportive and encouraging. Some would say that the environment was too accepting of anyone at any standard and that maybe that didn't push people to improve but for me the environment was perfect to develop as a musician.

IF: How did you progress on to joining the High Level Ranters?

Alistair Anderson: The Ranters grew out of an informal band for the ceilidhs. It formed around Forster Charlton who played fiddle and the pipes, Johnny Handle on guitar and melodeon, Colin Ross on fiddle and pipes, Tom Gilfellon who sang and played guitar, John Doonan on piccolo and me on concertina. The idea was that we would play for dances and we could play as a concert band singing songs and doing instrumental pieces. At the time there were plenty of dance bands playing for English dances but they often came through the 40s and 50s and were a little on the formal side. We were younger guys with lots of energy and enthusiasm. So, we were quite different and we would get a lot of festival bookings. We played maybe the 2nd or 3rd Cambridge Festival and we were booked for a Ceilidh that would last from 12 noon till 12 midnight on the Saturday and 2 pm till midnight on the Sunday. To do this you take it turns to take a break. We'd get people we knew from the audience and get them to come up and do two or three songs and that would let you get a quick sandwich or cup of tea. We would have a big repertoire so we wouldn't repeat songs but maybe certain dances were repeated a few times. To do a dance may take quarter of an hour by the times you've got everyone up and sorted out.

IF: How did you get bookings?

Alistair Anderson: The scene was a very tight one so it was easy to get a reputation and the Bridge Hotel within the folk scene was well known. Until the 1970s I wasn't doing this professionally and the others, Johnny, Colin and Tommy, didn't wanted to do it full time. We were getting a good reputation though and getting bookings round the country. In about 72 or 73 we did a concert at the Newcastle City Hall for the Newcastle Folk Festival and we sold it out so it was a growing scene. So this brought up the question should we go full time? But the others didn't want to.

The reason I went full time was that I was teaching Maths and Science in a Middle School in Wallsend and there was a particular fortnight where we did Manchester, Leicester, Leeds and Wooler, travelling there and back in a night and I felt it wasn't fair on the kids I was teaching. It was ten gigs in a fortnight. I had started doing solo gigs. Johnny Handle did solo gigs and he asked me if I wanted to come along and do three or so solo instrumental numbers. He was just nudging me and giving me a platform to learn my craft. I'd met so many inspiring musicians up and down the country like Will Atkinson, the harmonica player, Joe Hutton, the piper player so they showed me what could be done.

At the same time I was so sad when Billy Pigg died. Not many people had heard him and the only way people could hear his stuff was if I went out and played it for them. So, I worked out how to be a solo player doing a 45-minute set of instrumental pieces that could hold an audience's attention with lots of chat in between and setting the songs in context. I'd been gigging while I was teaching and I'd put most of the gig money into the bank. So I had enough money to give up teaching for a year and not starve, so I decided to give it a go. The headmaster said, 'If you're going to do it now is the time and if it doesn't work then I'll give you a seriously good reference to get back into teaching.' So, I kept playing with the Ranters but started to build up the solo gigs. It was great because there were so many folk clubs about at the time, this was about 1972. As I rarely sang initially it was all pretty break-even but the next time you went you could charge a bit more. In places like Cheltenham I could play something like seven or eight nights within a fortnight.

IF: What were the key folk clubs in the North East?

Alistair Anderson: There was the Bridge, then there was the Birtley Club ran by the Elliott Family, the Marsden Inn at South Shields, which was always packed, there was a good one in Gosforth and Cullercoats on the coast and one at Felling. Johnny had come out of the pits and worked at ICI on Teesside so he started one at Stockton, which is still going now. There was a whole bunch along the Tees.

IF: How did you start recording?

Alistair Anderson: The main record label then was Topic, which was originally the Workers Music Association. It had decidedly left-wing beginnings. The first Ranters' record was done in Forster Charlton's house. Topic supplied an engineer called Bill Leader, who engineered a huge part of the folk recordings in the 1960s including Billy Connolly's first recordings with The Humblebums, early Barbara Dixon, Bert Jansch and early Waterstons recordings. He used a cross pair of microphones and then he worked out where each person would stand in relation to the mics and recorded us live. The folk scene was really taking off and Bill felt that Topic was a little stuck in the 50's and early 60s so he set up his own label called Leader and asked us to go with him for the next few LPs and my first solo LP. He used good mics and good equipment but we didn't tend to use proper studios. However, for my first solo album I used, a studio in Cecil Sharp House off Regents Park Road, which was run by Bill.

IF: Being on your own and being an instrumentalist did that give you more freedom to write and record your own tunes?

Alistair Anderson: Given that Billy Pigg, Will Atkinson and Will Taylor, three of my biggest heroes, all wrote their own tunes, meant that it was quite natural for me, despite folk musicians often focussing on traditional songs. With instrumental bands like the Ranters, you would have two players playing the tune with the guitar or other instruments behind acting as a rhythm section. I then heard some Swedish fiddle players playing harmonies. So, I started writing harmonies that worked as melodies. So I developed this style and on 1982's *Steel Skies* I had a five-piece band and everyone had a different tune to play. We would build the songs up separately and we had to really listen intently to get it all to fit together. It was quite different and caused a stir and was talked about as the way forward. It was a bit worrying as it really had be rehearsed very well to work, unlike playing in folk dance bands where people could come and go.

I did *Steel Skies* here in Newcastle, in this actual building (The Northern Stage), and the Purcell Rooms in London, which had only been a venue for classical music. The record had been well reviewed so I filled both nights. At the end of the London gig, I was approached by a gentleman who said (in posh accent), 'I say, that's frightfully interesting, could you do a week of this?' And I said, 'Yes, of course.' He ran the South Bank in London and he told me he had a festival called South Bank Summer Music. It had always been exclusively classical music but he wanted to know if I would I do a week. I had the freedom to do what I wanted and I did a Scottish night, an Irish night and a bagpipe nights would use different musicians each night. That ran for three years and by the end of it I put on "Brendan Voyage", which is an orchestral piece written by Shaun Davey and featuring Irish pipes, in the Festival Hall which sat 3,000 people. In an audience like that, half had never seen an orchestra before and half had never seen a set of Irish pipes. Over 25 to 30 concerts we sold out nearly every night. Then came Margaret Thatcher who disbanded the Greater London Council, which had been great at encouraging this sort of activity, and unfortunately that came to an end.

The Arts Council, fortunately had noticed this crazy guy from the North East coming down and putting on these diverse concerts in London and filling the place. A gent called Peter Stark, who is from Gateshead, came back north to be Director of Northern Arts and he offered me a spot as Folk Musician in Residence as part of Northern Arts. I said that what was needed was something with greater reach. My generation of folk musicians were getting older and we weren't getting replaced. By this time I'd toured the US quite a lot and had seen good engagement with schools. The idea I had, was getting various musicians to play art centres and then run workshops soon afterwards. The concerts would be held in schools in the afternoons and then the art centres in the evening. I could stand up after the concert and say, 'If you enjoyed this tonight then come back on Wednesday and we can teach you how to play the penny whistle or teach you Irish Dancing.' And that was the start of Folkworks, which was very influential for a while. We became part of the team that created the Sage Gateshead. What we were doing in schools by the late '90s was just spectacular.

IF: How is the health of the folk scene in the North East at the moment?

Alistair Anderson: The session scene, where people get together and play tunes, that is very strong in places, the sing around scene is also pretty strong. Some of the clubs are quite healthy. The Bridge is still doing ok, it's mainly the old gang. The Monster Ceilidh Band run some fairly lively ceilidhs, which has great potential. Festivals across the country are still pretty strong. We are all delighted to see young folk musicians coming through but sometimes I worry that the folk audience is too accepting and too supportive. Maybe the musicians should go to an open mic night where the people are expecting a soft rock band and the folk musicians have to work really hard to grab unsuspecting audience. That is the way to cut your teeth, put yourself out there. I was very fortunate to tour the US from 1974 onwards and US audiences let ou know very quickly what they think of you. That helps you get better and better, understanding your audience and adapting your act accordingly and turning on a sixpence. The English are too polite.

•••••••••••••••••

Folk music is an organic, living and breathing scene. Its musicians recognise that it's health is dependent on how much they give back. Alistair is a great example of what a folk musician is and should be. He very much honours the musicians and the music of the past but he is also an innovative, creative musician who can take the genre forward. He has taken Northumbrian music round the world and inspired generations of youngsters to pick up traditional instruments and get involved. Folk music, as Alistair explained, is all about community and what is apparent is that the folk music community in the North East of England is far healthier as a result of Alistair's efforts. More power to his elbow.

The Unthanks

Rachel Unthank's and Becky Unthank's Story

The Unthanks are a folk band made up of sisters, Rachel and Becky Unthank, musician and arranger, Adrian McNally, singer and violin player, Niopha Keegan and musician Chris Price. The Unthank sisters hail from Ryton in County Durham and come from a folk music family. Their music is often traditional and they are known for their ethereal, haunting vocals and beautiful arrangements. They challenge themselves to keep evolving and this has involved them playing with orchestras and some of the best brass bands in the world. They are also very aware that folk music is sometimes out of sight for the general public and they feel an onus to work hard to spread the word. Part of what they do to this end are their weekend singing retreats, where up to 60 people will join a residential activity to sing, eat and enjoy the Unthank community. They have been releasing records for nearly 20 years, have played round the world, been nominated for a Mercury Prize, played on *Later with Jools Holland* and, two days after I chat with them, are off to play Glastonbury with their 11-piece band.

IF: What was it like growing up in a musical household?
Rachel: Our dad is a Rapper Dancer[1] so we were in the

dance team when we were kids. We used to go to festivals and do club dancing. Our parents, George and Pat, are both folk enthusiasts. They got into folk music in the '60s. They were from Teesside originally but came up to Newcastle in the '60s and got involved in the folk club scene up here. So, because of that, we went to folk festivals and folk clubs as kids. We were influenced by floor singers in our local scene and by people like Alistair Anderson, who set up Folkworks. Me and Becky went to the Folkworks Summer School and met other young people who liked folk music. So, all of those things were a big influence on us.

Becky: I would say growing up in that world meant that everyone was a singer so it was just something we did naturally. We'd sing songs in the car, at parties and my mam has always been in a choir. And because we clog danced it was a way to get to folk festivals for free. Also, there was a community aspect to the music and the singing was very open and generous.

Rachel: Dad was actually in a group called the Keelers with other local singers, Jim Mageean, Alan Fitzsimmons and Peter Wood and they sang a lot of shanties and local folk songs.

IF: How did you start performing in front of audiences?

Rachel: We were encouraged to sing at the local folk clubs and then I might have been asked by friends to sing a song in their band. And also, as Becky said, we would clog dance at folk festivals and thought we could add in a few songs when doing that.

IF: How did you learn to harmonise?

Rachel: We learnt some of it at the Folkworks' Summer Schools but it mainly just listening, for example, when listening to my dad's group. We were surrounded by people harmonising. We loved the Wilsons from Teesside who were great harmonisers. And especially, as sisters, there was no embarrassment if we tried something and got it wrong. It was just trial and error.

Becky: We listened to a lot of unaccompanied harmony

singing groups so that was quite a normal thing for us to hear. We'd listen in the car and pick out parts and I always loved that. So, it wasn't a huge stretch for us to make up our own harmonies. It became part of our relationship as sisters to make up harmonies and it developed from there.

IF: How did you move on to having a band?

Rachel: It was quite a difficult transition. It was quite hard to make the move to say, 'right, I want to be a singer' because everyone in a folk club will sing a song. I think meeting Adrian McNally was a big part of it. He really encouraged us to get a bit more organised and think that maybe we were good enough to be in a band and that other musicians may want to play with us.

IF: How did you choose the songs to sing?

Becky: We started with songs that we knew. But that changed as we went on, especially with recording albums. The best way is to hear another singer sing it in a room. We are always on the lookout for songs by listening to records or going to gigs.

IF: Is it difficult to write your own songs to fit alongside more traditional songs?

Rachel: It was pretty painful at first. Initially there were so many songs available that I didn't need to tell a story of our own. But we had a go. Becky, you started writing earlier than me.

Becky: I have always written in books. I studied History of Art at Uni so I always had sketch books to draw and write in. Being a teenager in the '90s and 2000s, the popular music side of me wanted to write songs but the folk singer side of me didn't. I didn't feel there was a need to do that or that there was a hole that needed filling. We loved singing local songs, particularly women's songs. That was always the plan so I didn't feel the need to express myself in that way. But as the years went by it felt good to push ourselves and, as a band, reveal more of our selves by writing and collaborating more.

Rachel: We've always been like magpies when picking music. So, we could fit traditional songs next to songs we just liked and there was never any preciousness about it. Our dad writes songs so that made it more natural for us.

IF: The first album got great reviews and your second album was nominated for the Mercury Prize. Did it feel like a rapid rise? Was it at all daunting?

Becky: We've always sang and we always had the protection of being sisters and that helps us to feel comfortable. I think being nominated for the Mercury Prize took us from the folk world to the rest of the world. We weren't in a field anymore and had to put posh clothes on and would be in rooms with famous people. But, as we had each other, we weren't phased by it.

IF: Why did you change the name to The Unthanks?

Rachel: We always sang together but there is an age gap between us of 7½ years so, when we started, Becky was going to Uni. I wanted to give the band a go but Becky was unsure that she wanted to be a folk singer full time.

Becky: I enjoyed singing but not necessarily as a job. So, I didn't want to promise anything.

Rachel: So, we called the band Rachel Unthank and the Winterset so that Becky could be in the band but still decide that she may want to leave. But she didn't want to leave and we'd hear a song on the radio and they would say 'that was Rachel Unthank and the Winterset' when, actually, it was Becky singing. So, when Becky decided she wanted to do it full time we abridged the name to The Unthanks, which maybe we should have done from the start. At the time we were four female singers but changing the name also coincided with Adrian, who had always been involved creatively, joining us properly on piano.

IF: You work with orchestras and brass bands. How much rehearsal goes into those projects?

Rachel: There is a lot of rehearsal for us but not so much for them because they can read the music, and we don't really read music. Also, we would have to pay for them to rehearse, which is expensive. For us, it's an awful lot of preparation but it comes together surprisingly quickly when it gets to the larger band.

Becky: For us it's not that different to how we work now. So, going to Glastonbury we will have an 11-piece band. We have Adrian on piano, a string quartet, a trumpet player, a drummer and two bass and guitar players.

It starts with Rachel and I rehearsing our parts at home, then we get together. Then we'll get together with Adrian, then five of us and finally the 11 of us getting together. We love to practise a lot or otherwise we are rubbish!

IF: Is it nerve racking or does it get less over time?

Rachel: Oh, it's always nerve racking doing a new project. If you play with an orchestra, for example, if you miss a beat, whereas the band will cover for you, the orchestra just has to carry on and you have to find your way back in. So, it's nerve racking but also invigorating, which we like.

Becky: We are always learning and trying new things or new settings, which is really enriching for us. If we weren't nervous then we wouldn't care.

IF: How do you decide what the next project is going to be?

Rachel: We always have lots of ideas. We've got a list of long-term ideas that we may get to. Sometimes we get people coming to us with project ideas.

IF: In the past there have been fewer female voices in the North East pop and rock world. Is the folk world more welcoming towards women or more inclusive?

Rachel: I think the problem may be for music in general and not just the North East.

Becky: I think a lot of female folk musicians would still say there is an issue for them. For example at festivals the headliners are normally male. There are a lot of conversations going on now about why that is so and how do we encourage young kids to pick up instruments and to learn to sing and to have opportunities. It's also about having role models who are female as well.

Rachel: There are a lot of young female musicians coming through now, which is good. It is an important thing to address. We were certainly influenced by female singers growing up in the North East like Ray Fisher, a Scottish female folk singer, and Lal and Norma Waterson and then Eliza Carthy later on. And there are other female folk artists from round here that you may not have heard of such as Anni Fentiman. It is definitely more male dominated but we did have role models.

Becky: There is also Nancy Kerr and her mum, Sandra Kerr, who are not from the North East but have lived here a long time and have been quite integral in the folk scene up here.

IF: When you play abroad are the audience reactions different to the UK?

Rachel: We haven't been to America for a long time, but when we did they often thought we were Irish or Scottish or maybe Welsh but not English. In places like Norway and Sweden we have a lot of common dialect, so they seem to understand us better. In Australia we did quite well maybe due to the ex-pat sort of feeling that some have.

IF: Is the North East a hotbed of folk music?

Rachel: It's known as a hotbed from the '60s up to now. We have a strong sense of culture up here. Then there were things like Folkworks, which would have the summer schools or visiting acts going into schools. They had a clog bank, which meant people in schools could use them to teach traditional clog dances. We have the Northumbrian pipes, which are an instrument specific to this region. We have clog dancing and rapper dancing, which is a kind of sword dance, which comes out of the mining industry from the North East. People are proud to come from here and so songs that reflect our culture are popular.

Becky: I would agree with all that but folk is still a niche subculture that not everyone is aware of.

Rachel: There are not as many folk clubs anymore and Folkworks is not as big as it was, although a smaller summer school is coming up and my kids will go to that. So, people do feel there is more we could do to encourage the next generation and keep the tradition going. Although the dance teams are still quite strong.

IF: How does clog dancing fit into the show?

Becky: It's more rhythmically. We have many musicians on the stage when we play so we want to join in with the rhythm and that's how we can do it.

Rachel: There used to be a thriving dancing competition up here a long time ago but that's died a death. We learnt traditional steps and when we were young we'd make up our own steps. So coming into the band we just adapted the steps we knew to fit into some of our music, they added a percussion element. It's a bit about keeping the tradition going but it's also something we really enjoy. We are still in a team, the Kingsmen Clogs at the Cumberland Arms, Newcastle. When we go abroad people love the clog dancing we do. We think oh, it's not the 12 miserable songs we've just sang in harmony that you love? No, it's just the clog dancing. It's actually exciting. People think it's Irish dancing but it's actually our own version of dancing from the North East.

IF: Tell me about the musical weekends you run?

Rachel: Years ago before we had kids, me and Becky loved touring but we realised it was more difficult to sing in smaller environments with other people. So we came up with this idea of having musical weekends where people, maybe our audience, could come away and sing with us. It was an opportunity for other people to join in that experience of singing with others, which is something we know is really nourishing. On the weekend we might teach people how to do harmonies but also we go down on the beach and end up in the pub and sing songs that the attendees have learnt the choruses of. We do a concert at the end. We host it and we do the cooking, as Adrian is a frustrated chef. It would be anywhere between 30 and 60 people who come. We used to do them in Seahouses in a bunk house for 10 years. We ended up doing seven of these weekends a year. But after Covid we have brought them back and have done 10 so far this year. It is actually part of how we survive as a band

and works round our family life. We do one at Middleton Hall in Northumberland and we also do one in Summerhill Square in Newcastle. With that one we walk down to the river and then end up in a pub in Ouseburn where we can have a good sing. We love it and it seems that the people who attend love it as well so, hopefully, it will continue for some time yet.

IF: What is next for the Unthanks?

Rachel: Keep making music that is challenging to us as a band and keep doing the singing weekends. We think that is an important part of our calendar. It's been great getting out and playing live again after all the lockdown problems. We really are lucky.

••••••••••••••••••

Like a number of other acts in this book The Unthanks have worked out how to sustain a career in music in a world where streaming has replaced the need to buy physical product and where the income streaming provides is a pittance. Their voices are quite unmistakeable and that is a big part of their success but it's also their love and passion for the music they create that spills over into things like their weekend singing retreats. Folk music is a very accessible scene and it encourages the audience to be part of it and The Unthanks are great proponents of that approach. It is part of the reason why, as they acknowledge above, that the North East of England remains a hotbed for folk music.

Kathryn Williams

Kathryn Williams is a singer-songwriter, a songwriter for other artists, a podcaster, a painter, a novelist and a mam. She is unassuming company but she has been plagued by self-doubt, anxiety and an element of imposter syndrome. That her beautiful, honest and sometimes delicate music elicits great reviews, the respect of her peers and enduring fan support hasn't always been enough to get her over this lack of self-confidence. It certainly appears that everything she does is successful from her second album, *Little Black Numbers*, which was nominated for the Mercury Prize, to her recent debut novel, *The Ormering Tide*, which has been well reviewed. She is a true polymath! As someone whose life has been driven by the need to be creative she has interesting perspectives.

Kathryn was born in Liverpool and, despite living in Newcastle for the last 30 years, retains a soft scouse accent. She is lovely company and she is very open about her struggles with anxiety but her steely drive and great talent are unmistakeable. Like so many others I have met, her success and her ability to sustain a 30-year career is nothing to do with chance and all to do with talent.

IF: How did you get the confidence to start writing songs?

Kathryn Williams: Well confidence is a funny question because I am nearly 50 and I am still looking for that. Before I came up here to do an art degree, I lived in Liverpool. In my late teenage years I got really ill with glandular fever and was bed ridden for a long time, which mucked up my A-levels. With all that time on my own I would draw, read and write poems that were like lyrics.

I played piano at the time, not guitar, but when I went off to university my parents bought me a guitar and I moved on to write with that. I was exploring the guitar and finding out the chords and so I would write songs rather than playing other people's songs. I would play them very quietly on my own as I didn't have the confidence to play them to anyone else.

After finishing my degree I was living in Fenham, Newcastle, in a shared house. I was on the dole and then worked in a vegetarian restaurant called the Red Herring. I was just terrible at that. I remember thinking people had left and getting their plates and scraping them off only to find out they had gone to the toilet and hadn't finished. I mean, who goes to the toilet together in a restaurant? I was never good at that, so I got put in the shop next door.

So, I was in this shared house, 84 Sidney Grove, and I had a little Fostex 4-track recorder. It was an amazing time. I'd be lying on the floor, with the sun coming in the window, listening to Leonard Cohen. I'd write songs just for the joy of it, with no plans at all to do anything with the songs. There are actually a couple of those recordings on a recent box set that was released.

When I started singing in public there was a scene, like a songwriter's scene. My first public appearance was in the North Terrace pub in Spital Tongues, Newcastle. It was a singer-songwriter night. This where I saw Richard Dawson at one of his first ever gigs. We'd play probably three songs each and you might get £5 at the end of the night. It was a community of sorts. Before that I'd just played quietly in my bedroom and it was my friends who put me up to playing at these nights. There was one at the North Terrace, there was one at the Fighting Cocks and also a night at the Black Swan Arts Centre on Westgate Road. At the Black Swan I'd see Richard Dawson, Nev Clay, Beccy Owen, Dave Scott and it formed a real scene. Nev Clay was the Godfather of this world. He has been consistently amazing but never wanted to branch out. That was a genuine songwriter's scene and it was as very supportive. Only a few of those on that scene have gone beyond the North East.

BBC Radio Newcastle used to do sessions that would be recorded at their Newcastle studio. I did one of them.

I'd done a few of the singer-songwriter nights and then there was something like a Sound City weekend in Newcastle where they would put lots of showcases on. The *NME* were up reporting on it and they happened to attend one where I was playing and they wrote about me. They wrote that I said something like, 'Everyone in the music industry are a bunch of ****s.' I hadn't actually said that but it worked in my favour as they wrote it down and got me a bit of interest. They had said, 'You are a bit like Alanis Morrisette' and I'd said, 'Why because I've got tits?' I had no idea the *NME* were even in the crowd. My career is basically stumbling in the dark until the spotlight comes on. To get even a sentence in the *NME* at the time was a huge deal. Suddenly after that record labels started coming to my shows. It was really exciting and I started working with a management company based at Sam's Studio in Newcastle. They were called Bright Orange Biscuit Records.

Anyway, London Records said that they'd like to be involved in recording a record and they asked me what would I like. So, I said, 'I'd like four days in a studio with a producer. And I'd like the rights back for the recordings if I don't sign for you.' And they said, 'Fine.' So, I had four days in Sam's and that became *Dog Leap Stairs* and that's why it didn't really cost anything. It has been famously said it cost £80 to record but that is how it really happened. London brought in a producer called Head, who later worked with the likes of PJ Harvey, Yoko Ono and Thom Yorke. He was amazing and we had strings and other instruments that he brought in.

I was also getting help from someone called Danilo Moscardini and, with his help, we set up my own record label to release the record. It was called Caw Records. This was quite unusual for the time. It was the same with my agent, Nigel and my press officer, Jo. It was quite amazing that these people were on the look out for something they could believe in and they came to me. I had all these people helping me and the record got good reviews. So, I thought oh, maybe I'll do another record.

With the next record I got Head in again as I'd built up a relationship with him. He would teach me some of the recording techniques, so he was just great. It was funny because I was trying to master the business of running my own record label and learning as I went on. I would do things like trying to stagger payments for pressing so I could afford to pay for the next album. I even had a fax machine at the time. I had no knowledge but I just stumbled through.

IF: Being so young, was this overwhelming?

Kathryn Williams: The business side of it was manageable but the playing live side was a whole other story. I'd have to sit down to play because I would nearly black out due to nerves. Even for the singer songwriter nights I'd need all my willpower just to leave the house. When I did my shows I'd have this voice inside me saying *someone's going to find you out*. You're not qualified to do this. I'd be full of fear that people would hate me. Sometimes I'd only do two songs because I felt that I'd taken up too much of people's time. Looking back I'm not sure how I coped. When it jumped up from selling records from my bedroom to getting nominated for the Mercury Prize, I was still suffering. It has affected my career and my opportunities. For example, I'd be booked to play on *Later, with Jools Holland* or *This Morning* and they'd call and say, 'Where are you?' And I'd be like, 'Well, I got on the train but I had to get off at Peterborough and

I am just going to get the train back to Newcastle and go home.' I had really bad panic attacks, which I don't get now, but it really affected the opportunities that I got.

IF: How did it feel to get nominated for the Mercury Prize, for your second album, *Little Black Numbers*?

Kathryn Williams: Oh, it was amazing. I was working at the time at the Rising Sun Country Park in Newcastle selling tea and scones. I had a student rail card and got the train down and went to the Park Lane Hotel with my backpack and my jeans. They gave us a table, where normally record labels pay for a table, and they gave us a room which was so kind, as otherwise we wouldn't have been able to go.

IF: Did you feel intimidated by all the other nominees given your lack of self-confidence?

Kathryn Williams: No, everyone was lovely. I was up against Coldplay with *Parachutes*. Badly Drawn Boy won, and there was also Doves and Nitin Sawhney. I chatted to Chris Martin from Coldplay and I still cringe about that. I asked him how much his album cost to make and he said something like half a million and I said, 'Chris, let me give you a bit of advice', I had had a few drinks by this time, 'my record cost £3,000. You are never going to make any money spending that much on recording.' A few years later I was doing a session at the BBC and it was at the time of Coldplay's *XYY* album and Chris Martin came up to me with Gwyneth Paltrow, and I was thinking Oh, God and he put his hand on my shoulder and said, laughing, 'Hi Kath, thanks for the advice.'

At the time I really needed the money that came with the prize and I remember Badly Drawn Boy went up to collect the prize, took the cheque and ripped it to pieces. I felt so angry because I thought you just don't know how much I could have done with that money. He has talked about regretting doing it but at the time it was him being rock and roll.

But it was at the Mercury Awards that Christian Tattersfield, who was running East West Records, part of Warner Brothers, saw my performance and signed me.

IF: How did life change going on to a major label?

Kathryn Williams: Well, they took the album I had recorded but they wanted radio edits doing. I did a licensing deal so that I could get the rights back and it allowed me 100% creative control. It was amazing in that they would fly me to New York and I'd stay in a penthouse at the Four Seasons hotel and they spent £150K on one video shot in Prague. It was crazy with them spending all this money but what you don't realise is that its all going on your bill. Their plan was that I'd be the next David Gray after the success of his *White Ladder* album. Luckily for me I failed miserably at that. And that has been theme that has kept me happy all my life.

I was signed for three albums which were *Little White Numbers*, *Old Low Light* and *Relations*, which was a covers album. So, I fulfilled the contract and at the end of that they didn't want to renew. In the midst of that deal I got a management deal with Alan McGee[1] of Creation Records. I was managed by him for eight years. He was amazing. He'd call me up at all hours of the day or night to talk about football. And I'd just had a child and I'd be like, 'Alan, I don't like football.' But he really believed in me.

There has always been a struggle with the word folk and my music. It's been both a help and a hindrance. The folk world won't accept me as folk and the pop world says I'm folk and so I fall down the back of the sofa in a way. At the time there was a thing called The New Acoustic Movement under the banner 'Quiet is the New Loud', with people like Badly Drawn Boy, Kings of Convenience and Laura Viers and I was lumped in with that.

Alan said that he would manage me forever if I wanted and he saw me as an English Gillian Welch and he said (Kathryn does a great Glaswegian accent a la Alan McGee), 'You're not folk Kathryn, you're Nirvana unplugged.' He was great at helping with my nerves. He used to get me a little angry before I went on as he said it helped with my performance. I am still in touch with him and wouldn't have a word said against him but it got difficult being an artist at the level I was and having a manager who was more famous than me. He had so much going on and I needed someone who could just focus on me. But we parted amicably with an open door at the end. Maybe I should phone him up as I haven't got a manager at the moment.

IF: At this point did you go back to self-releasing albums?

Kathryn Williams: Yes, I did, but at this point my band kind of fell away. I had Laura Reid on cello, Dave Scott on guitar, Alex Tustin on drums and Jonny Bridgewood on double bass. Laura was sick of touring and wanted a normal job. Dave didn't want to lose his pension as a nurse and needed to go back to that for a few years. Alex had young kids and wanted to do drum workshops and Jonny was in London and worked with lots of other people. So, the band collapsed around me and that was really hard as I felt I couldn't do anything without them. I felt like they were the talent and I was just winging it. So I was really scared.

Luckily, I had done a really big show at the Barbican in London called The Daughters of Albion in about 2006 and I sang "The First Time Ever I Saw Your Face" by Ewan McColl and the guitarist was Neil McColl, who was Ewan's son. We got on really well and that resulted in Neil coming up to Newcastle and we wrote a whole album together. He brought session musicians up from London. This signalled a real transition for me because in the past I couldn't sing with anyone else in the studio and secondly, I started collaborating on songwriting, which I have done ever since.

IF: What is the process like when you write with others?

Kathryn Williams: Well I've collaborated with so many people over the years and I also write for other artists around the world and it's never the same. Sometimes I get music sent that I put lyrics to, sometimes I get music sent that I put lyrics and melody to. If I am in a room with someone and we are going to write three or four songs in a day we just talk and don't sing or play instruments. We just talk about what we want the songs to be about. Slowly you get trust and you get ideas and then piece it together. If it's writing for an artist, like I have done recently in Sweden, I am like a secretary and get them to talk and write down everything they say.

IF: If you are writing for other artists, do you get a brief from the company engaging you?

Kathryn Williams: You can get briefs. I have been places where they have different artists described on the wall and you pick one and it will say who they are, what they want to sound like, what they want the song to be about, whether it is to be up-tempo and so on.

I had a nice one early on in America. The brief was that the song was to be about Paris and the only other word was Doris Day. So, I had to think about a film with people walking down avenues. They had sent music and a bit of a melody and I had to piece it. I love doing it. I now tutor people in songwriting.

IF: Do you get the situation where you present the finished song and the artist doesn't like it?

Kathryn Williams: Yes, you do although not often with my songs (Kathryn laughs)! You just learn as you go along. When the song is not for you, you have to tailor it for them, for their voice and you have to work out the psychology of who they want to be. You have all the constraints of what the label tells you in terms of whether it will be a ballad or what tempo it is. It's a challenge but it's one I really enjoy.

There was a time where everyone wanted "Rolling in the Deep" by Adele or "Take me to the Church" by Hozier and the label may say, 'I want that.' What I will do with that sort of request is work backwards and listen to songs that have influenced the songs referenced.

I love the creative process and I love the output that comes from that process. I have written recently with Ed Harcourt and Peter Joback, who is a big star in Sweden, a bit like Elton John.

Maybe Ed and I do the bulk of the actual songwriting, but the ideas of what the song is about will come from Peter, so we always split the credit three ways. My rule is that whoever is in the room gets credit because even if a person only contributes one idea it could change the path of the song.

IF: How do your songwriting retreats work?

Kathryn Williams: I do a few different formats. We did some up in Scotland at Moniak Mhor where people pay to come. This may be people who have never written a song before or people who write songs for a living. At these workshops we often put people in groups together and that helps to build confidence.

I ran three retreats in Stroud for professional songwriters. We had people like Michelle and Romeo Stoddart from Magic Numbers there and I still work with them. We had Steve Nieve from Elvis Costello's band there. We had Graham Fellows, who was Jilted John, and Teddy Thompson. I would run the activities but we would put people together to get them to co-write. The ripples are still happening from these collaborations.

IF: You have written book. How different was that?

Kathryn Williams: It was really hard. It took me six years and I didn't tell anyone before it was complete. I didn't have a clue what I was doing but had an idea for a story. Then the characters in the book came alive and I felt like I was just watching them as the story developed. Eventually I had to edit out about 40,000 words out. I had to fit this round songwriting and picking the kids up from school, so it was hard. I have started another book and it is going slowly again.

IF: What inspires you to keep creating?

Kathryn Williams: It's not so much inspiration but that creativity is what I do. The challenge is to take an idea and make sense of it so someone else will understand it.

At the moment, I have just finished the third series of my podcast, *Before the Lights Go Out*. I love being a beginner and that is true of writing a book, doing a podcast, writing with others. I may not know what to do but I love giving it a go. It's the same with painting. I gave it a go and I now get commissions to do paintings, they may be portraits or portraits of people's pets. (Kathryn shows me some examples of her paintings, both portraits and abstract water colours and they are very impressive). To me it's what life is about, you've got to try to make something beautiful while you are here. The end product is what people see but the creative process is what is fulfilling. When I do songwriting courses, the best bits for me are when people say, 'I didn't think I could do that' or 'I've learned something about myself' rather then necessarily the songs themselves, as good as they may be.

I've just finished an album in Edinburgh with Dan Wilson from Withered Hand. I've just done an album with Matt Deighton and one with Michelle Stoddart and I am due to go in to do my next solo album with Neil McColl and Leo Abrahams. And I am about to start a tour with Polly Paulusma.

IF: Do you ever say to yourself, 'I'd like to take a month off and have a lie down?'

Kathryn Williams: Yeah, all the time. For me, though, I am quite low level. Lots of people don't know who I am but I have an amazingly loyal fanbase. It gets a bit harder as I get older as I now tour on my own. So, I will drive to the gig, will set up my equipment and then man the merchandise table. That's hard.

IF: You are from Liverpool but known as a North East artist. How supportive has the North East been for you?

Kathryn Williams: The North East has been everything to me. I came here when I was 19 for university but before that I would come up every year to visit my Great Auntie Winn, who lived in Cullercoats. So, when it came to doing my degree, Newcastle felt like home. It always felt like there was space and opportunities to be an artist and a musician. It was small enough to know people but big enough to be really cultural. My kids have grown up here, my husband has bakeries here and I can't see myself ever moving.

•••••••••••••••••

Kathryn is an inspiring force of nature. If she had to put her profession on her passport no doubt she would put creator as that is her raison d'etre, to be creative. Her amazing talent draws people to her and makes people want to collaborate with her. She is low key and under the radar but once you discover her music, podcast or book, you will certainly be hungry for more and be excited to find out what she does next.

---

1. Alan McGee was manager of the Jesus and Mary Chain and set up Creation Records where he most famously discovered Oasis and signed many bands such as Primal Scream, My Bloody Valentine and The House of Love. A noted bon viveur he has recently had a film made about him called Creation Stories.

Richard Dawson

Richard Dawson has been described as a progressive folk musician. Richard, rightly, takes issue with this description. He questions me as to whether he should actually be included in the folk music section of this book. He has a point. Why limit Richard's music to a two or three-word description? Richard actually has a quite unique sound that may fit more closely to the more avant-garde jazz rock acts Captain Beefheart or Frank Zappa than the folk sound of Fairport Convention. The question of what type of music he plays may be better answered by saying he plays Richard Dawson type music, as trite as that explanation maybe. He has recently released the third of a loose trilogy of albums looking at the past, the present and the future. They include songs reflecting our bucolic, agricultural past as well as songs describing the scene and the chatter when a dad watches his son play football. He is also part of the band Hen Ogledd. Their third album was recently released in 2020 to rapturous reviews. *Uncut Magazine* likened it to the Beatles *White Album* due to its confident eclectic nature. Richard's output is constant, challenging, inspiring and sprawling. In the North East he is somewhat of a hidden treasure but one you really need to check out if you don't currently know him.

IF: Tell me about how you got into music and how it inspired you?

Richard Dawson: I remember my dad's tape box in the car with things he'd recorded off the radio such as Mott the Hoople, Beatles, Hendrix, Captain Beefheart and Black Sabbath. We used to go to Cramlington Library and I'd get heavy metal cassettes like Iron Maiden and Halloween and play them in the car. Then I'd explore my sister's collection and she'd have the more glam metal like Poison and Motley Crue.

But getting to library's music section was a game changer. They obviously had someone there who was really into music as they had fantastic jazz and world music sections One of the first things I got out was Ali Farka Toure from Mali. I was about 15 at the time and I was initially intrigued by the cover of the album. When I listened to it I liked it because the songs sounded very samey whereas I'd been used to the razzmatazz of pop music with the juxtaposition of loud and quiet and fast and slow tracks. I couldn't really make head nor tail of this new music but I loved it. It took me years to unpick Ali Farka Toure's music.

Another one was Nusrat Fateh Ali Khan from Pakistan, which was more instant. It was still different from the normal song format I was used to but it made a lot of sense to me. It's a bit like jazz where you are hearing the sound first rather than the content or the song. I liked how cool they looked on the sleeve but also how all the players were listed and how that elevated the players. It was all so different to what I was used to. I did try all the typical indie bands of the time but once you've heard that straight drum beat once it's all a bit similar. I wanted to hear new things. I was drawn to jazz, and Indian, Pakistani and South American musicians. Listening to this music you would hear them using different scales and playing long pieces alongside shorter pieces. It was all really exciting.

IF: Were you discovering this on your own or did you have mates at school into the same stuff?

Richard Dawson: No, I think I was the only one into this sort of stuff. I did like stuff that my mates liked, like Nirvana or Jesus Lizard but I was also going down this other path on my own. I was also getting into experimental music particularly through the Tzadik Label which was John Zorn, the jazz composer's label. He released a couple of records by Mike Patton, of Faith No More, and that's how I got into that. Exploring that catalogue blew the whole thing out wide.

IF: Was music the be all for you to the exclusion of other things like football?

Richard Dawson: Yes, pretty much. I got my guitar when I was 12 or 13. Straight away I wanted to write songs. The day I got my guitar I said to my dad, 'Come on, let's write a song.' I always had the impulse to do that. From that point my performance at school went downhill sharply because I just wanted to write songs.

IF: Did you play these songs to others?

Richard Dawson: Well the first or second day at Gosforth High School I put a note up on the board saying 'Who wants to join a band, put your name and form class here.' A few people responded and we started playing in the music block. We had a great music teacher called Mr Howard and he was so accommodating and encouraging. Me and my mates, Neil Smedley and Amy Capes, and a couple of different drummers formed a band called Bean and we would do lunchtime concerts in the music block. We were probably awful but I was writing all the time, so we'd do my songs along with some covers. They would be a bit punky and a bit metally and it was a mess really but it was quite creative I suppose. When we would practice, Mr Howard would come through and make the odd positive comment like, 'Interesting time change there.' I didn't realise at the time but the only reason he was staying back till five was to allow us to practise, which I really appreciate now looking back.

We started doing gigs in Newcastle at places like the Black Swan Art Centre run by a fantastic man called Pete Ferry.

IF: When did you say to yourself, 'I want to do this for a career?'

Richard Dawson: Even before I got my guitar I was imagining doing big Iron Maiden concerts. I was just obsessed by this whole idea. Then I got into Tom Waits and started writing more ballad type songs and started playing some solo gigs at about 15 or 16. And I did this until I was about 23 or 24 but then I got down about it as it wasn't getting to where I wanted. I'd mucked up my A-Levels probably due to my music obsession. I'd started a music degree at Newcastle College but gave that up after a month as it wasn't for me. I had a year unemployed where I watched the entirety of the Showstopper Video's world cinema section, which was also quite inspiring for me.

IF: Did you get grief from your parents?

Richard Dawson: Yes, I think they were just worried about me and maybe disappointed. Then I started in the record shop Windows, where I was for four years, before I moved on to Alt Vinyl, another great record shop in Newcastle set up by Graham Thrower, where I was for six years. During that period I lost a bit of hope. I felt what I was doing wasn't very interesting and I wasn't going to make anything of it. I had two or three years thinking it wasn't going to happen. I had a little bit of time off work to allow me to contemplate what is the purpose of being a musician, why am I doing it. It helped me get focus and realise what I thought was important. So things like 'making it' doesn't matter and what I needed to focus on was all these ideas I had. I had to follow what I felt needed to be made rather than what I thought would help me be successful.

IF: Are you your biggest critic rather than the music media critics or your audience?

Richard Dawson: Well, looking back I was oblivious. I was probably quite ridiculed as I was doing very 'heart on your sleeve' and quite out-there music. I only got a sense of this in the past couple of years. I realised that you have to make the work you are doing good work if you're going to put it in front of people.

IF: How did you get your first album out?

Richard Dawson: Well, the first album was *Sings Songs and Plays Guitar* which I think is really quite bad, although it has one or two good kernals in there. Graham from Alt Vinyl released that and did a cracking job but I've sort of disowned it since then. So, the first one for me is *Magic Bridge*. I'd stopped working at the record shop as I realised I needed a completely fresh start in life. I changed jobs and moved house and was working on this album. I got a job at the Bodega pub on Westgate Road in Newcastle and with any spare moment I worked on the songs. I really felt that, with this album, I had something unique. I put the album out myself and made 500 or 1000 CDs. I recorded it at the John Marley Centre with someone called Phil Begg who was doing a music degree and made my record his project. I was dead lucky with that. I just dropped the CD into all the local shops. As I had played so much live, I had a generated a bit of a small local following. Then Matt Baty (now singer of Pigs x 7)[1] of Box Records said he liked it and wanted to put it out on vinyl. Then I got a bit of management. And so, I just started to get a little bit of momentum. I played a lot at places like The Star and Shadow and the Cumberland Arms. Then I released *The Glass Trunk* and that started to get some interest from labels.

IF: Are the people who have inspired your musical output the same ones who inspired you fifteen years previously as a 15-year-old?

Richard Dawson: Some of them. Certainly Nusrat and the spirit of his music. Certainly the Qawwali music, of which Nusrat was an ambassador. That is a form of Sufi devotional music. That influences what I do. Ali Farka Toure also opened a lot of doors for me. I learnt all about this stuff before the internet, you had to go and explore and take risks then. I have also always been inspired by Nev Clay who is a local singer and, in my books, the best ever North East songwriter, which I know is quite a claim.

IF: What inspires the next record?

Richard Dawson: It tends to be an impulse you follow.

When you put a melody with a lyric and the two things interact, it can be magic. Then songs on an album can interact with each other. I try to think of them not as individual songs but part of a pathway to some sort of expression. You have to follow where it leads. You are just part of it. Your character informs part of it. You may start with an initial idea or framework but as you go on that may completely change.

As to why I may do a new album I learned quite early on to follow what the music wants or what the songs want. I may be in an enviable position now but I wasn't when I did *Magic Bridge* but that was when I realised I had to follow that path. In 10 years' time I may not be in such a fortunate position but I would still have to follow whatever musical path I was on. With the last album I had the chance to add in extra instrumentation or spend a bit more on studio time but if I couldn't I'd just have to find another way. It may not be quite as good but if the intent is there then you'll achieve what you want to.

IF: You get great reviews from the likes of the *Guardian* and *Mojo*. How important are they?

Richard Dawson: It used to be important. When I put out *Nothing Important* in about 2014 I was waiting for the reviews but the novelty wears off quickly. When I sat down to write the next album, *Peasant*, I spent two months writing but I realised my mind was still on reviews or outside perceptions as I'd spent so much time doing interviews or gigs. So, I spent two months writing shit until I realised my focus was all wrong. I was second guessing how it might be received. So, I took a couple of months doing something totally different and then came back with the right focus. You need to go with what you think is good and take the risk with the audience and the critics.

IF: How much of the North East is in your music?

Richard Dawson: I used to say a lot but I've kind of backed off from that because when I was doing interviews there was a bit of a kudos attached to being from the North from the London centric press. And being a funny little tubby Northern man, I was treated as a bit of a novelty. The North East is obviously in there a lot but I don't want to be necessarily defined by it. I certainly feel blessed to come from this part of the world but, by the same token, we are citizens of the world so I don't feel that different to others.

I think sometimes people believe that some artists are entitled because of the wealth of their background but the advantage really comes from how they were brought up. For my generation up here there was a thing that being a musician wasn't viewed as a proper job. And so there comes a lot of shame from being a musician. You can become apologetic or not be as bold as you might be. Whereas someone from a different background, who has been told that a life in music is healthy and positive, can have such an advantage. All this can affect your confidence.

IF: When you collaborate with other people what draws you to them?

Richard Dawson: I am honestly not drawn to other people. Naturally I like working on my own but I realised that I was missing out. The first major collaboration I did was with Rhodri Davies and that was like ah, ok, that's how it works. I guess we were like minded. Then moving on to Hen Ogledd with my partner, Sally (Pilkington), Rhodri and Dawn Bothwell, I found that quite challenging because I am not the driving force with it and I had to take a different role, having been working on my own for 20 years. We are all really close but it can be challenging. For example, I may listen to a song and think oh, there should have been a key change there but it's not my song. And there was a bit where Rhodri was doing a solo and I loved it but he hated it, it was an ornate classical thing. So, when I listen back and it's not there I feel that there is something missing.

I also work with an incredible Finnish band called Circle and they are so inspiring and they say anything is possible and we can make it happen but it must be new. That really challenges me.

IF: Looking forward, what are your ambitions?

Richard Dawson: I don't know if I am ambitious by

outside perception. I have some albums in mind. So, I've got four things planned, two from me and two more collaborative. That's the next few years. But my ambition is probably to be an old man and still be able to play music and still connect with people.

IF: You have recently come back from a short tour of America. What was that like?

Richard Dawson: It was a mixed bag. I found it quite stressful because as I am visually impaired, so getting about was difficult. I am fine up here and in London but New York was a bit of a step up to get about. Everything is so much edgier there as I can't gauge people until I get up close but I didn't want to get too close to people in a strange city. So, it was pretty stressful but the gigs were really good. I did two solo shows in New York at Public Records and Union Pool and then I got the train to Boston to do three shows with Pigs x 7 covering Boston, Philadelphia and Washington DC. Then I did a solo show in LA, which was even edgier than New York.

IF: How did America take to your music, which is quite English?

Richard Dawson: They seemed to get my music. I have been building a bit of interest across there. There were people who travelled quite a way to see us. So, we sold out Union Pool, which was about 100 people and then sold out another show which was about 150 people, so that was really nice. People seemed really excited about it, which was great.

IF: Where does your music fit in? Would you say it was World Music?

Richard Dawson: I wouldn't put it anywhere, it's not for me to decide. I certainly take a lot of inspiration from some of the Indian classical musicians, not that I'm anywhere close to that, but that music is quite universally accessible.

To be honest I tend to be evasive when getting pinned down to where my music fits. It is often about blurriness so pinning it down is not really the point of it.

IF: Do you think what you do now is what the fifteen-year-old you would want to be doing?

Richard Dawson: (Laughing) I have no bloody idea. I can't remember. I think I was probably just a bit of a prick.

In the North East we just do what we are going to do. If there's money about to do stuff, great, but if there isn't we'll do it anyway. I've been very lucky with Domino Records because the focus has all been about what I want to do. The support is always there if I want it but I've always been 'here's the album'. They trust me and I trust them and, maybe, that could be quite rare. I really get given freedom to do what I want and I really appreciate that.

•••••••••••••••••

With that, Richard is off. He tells me about an art exhibition he had seen round the corner and, at his suggestion, I go and see it. It was great. He is off to get the train from Newcastle to Wylam where he will then have to walk a further mile to his house out in the wilds of the Tyne Valley. He is very much on his own path and he is a breath of fresh air both when you meet him and when you listen to his eclectic music. His new albums are treated by both the music press and his fans with excitement as you can't predict what direction he will take. I could try and describe some of the albums but I wouldn't do them justice. I would suggest, if you haven't already, that you listen to his albums on repeat and you will find your way into a new and endlessly fascinating musical journey.

The Young'uns

Sean Cooney's Story

Sean Cooney, Michael Hughes and David Eagle are three pals from Stockton on Tees who formed a folk band in 2007. They sang, initially, local traditional songs in an unaccompanied manner using natural harmonies and Teesside accents. The joyful sound they made quickly got them a reputation, then a career and then, via being named Folk Band of the Year twice in a row by BBC Radio 2, worldwide renown. Their tale is one of happenstance and luck on the one hand, and big-hearted passion on the other. Their latest album, *Tiny Notes*, their ninth, is one of the most emotionally affecting albums I've heard in a long time. In their rich, powerful and compassionate voices they tell modern tales of tragedy, redemption and hope and take the listener from the Troubles in Derry, Northern Ireland to a modern-day life saver in Sunderland. I talk to their principal songwriter, Sean Cooney, who tells me what is quite an unlikely tale.

IF: What music did you listen to when you were young?

Sean Cooney: Not too much really. I never considered myself into music as a kid. When I was in primary school, we had a teacher who taught us the basic chords on the guitar for stuff like the Beatles and Oasis. It inspired me a bit and I started changing the lyrics of famous songs and replacing them with songs about my favourite players at Middlesbrough Football Club. When I got to secondary school, the music department was a bit elitest and I struggled with music theory. I still can't read music, and that really put me off. But then I got into Bob Dylan. I had always heard Dylan's voice in the background from hearing my dad's records but at 16 or 17 something finally clicked and Dylan became really meaningful and transforming for me.

It was about that time that me and two friends, Michael Hughes and David Eagle, discovered the Stockton Folk Club. It was an incredible, life-changing discovery. We had no idea that there was this gathering of people who met weekly in a back room of a pub in Stockton, and had been doing so for 40 years. They met every Monday night and sang songs, mostly without instruments, and many about the North East. At that point I didn't know there were any songs written about the North East. I didn't know you could sing in a Teesside accent. It was such a revelation. What grabbed me was the honesty and accessibility of it. People would get up and sing a song and forget the words halfway through and no one was bothered. They would just join in to help them remember the rest of the words. It was all tied in with pub culture and it was boozy and funny and, in those days, it was smoky as well. It was warm and it was welcoming.

IF: How did you discover the existence of the Stockton Folk Club?

Sean Cooney: After getting into Dylan my dad just said, 'You'll have to go down to one of these folk clubs, I'm sure they still exist. I think there's one at the Sun Inn.' So, we went down and were just completely taken with it. We just kept going back week after week. We'd drag our mates down from Sixth Form College and they were just like *what the hell is this*? For us there was something really special about it. Particularly for me it was these Teesside songs.

People from Teesside are immensely proud of where they

come from. One of the main avenues for this pride is football, which is great but we didn't know there was a musical language as well. It seemed hidden far from the surface and, in many ways, it still is. We discovered that most of these local songs had been written by one incredible man called Graeme Miles. He wrote hundreds of songs in one prolific period between 1952 and 1972. He was compelled to write them because no one else was doing it. He realised that Teesside was changing, with industries declining and ways of life changing. He saw so much beauty and so much colour and so much solidarity and so many stories to be told. So, Graeme, inspired by people like Ewan MacColl[1] and others, looked at his history in Teesside and started writing about it. For me that was such an incredibly inspiring thing.

Eventually we got the confidence to actually contribute to these singing nights in Stockton. It took us a year to work out if we were allowed to get up and do it. We eventually got the confidence to sing a sea shanty. All we knew was the chorus so we got up and told the audience to sing the verses and we'd sing the chorus. It was such a transforming moment in our lives. Since then we've never wanted to do anything but sing these songs, really because of the way it made us feel. On good nights in folk clubs, you get that wall of sound that is so full of harmony and character. It never dawned on us that it would become a career. It was just something so wonderful to do in your spare time. We could drink the best beer in town and sing our hearts out. It was a beautiful couple of years.

IF: Did you try to put together harmonies between the three of you from day one?

Sean Cooney: I didn't know what harmony was. For me I loved the story telling but for Michael and David, who have more musical bones in them than me, it was like *oh these harmonies are brilliant*. And because its such a welcoming environment and you have that big wall of sound it means you can try out harmony lines and they certainly did.

IF: Were you the only young people attending the folk club?

Sean Cooney: Yes, absolutely and that's why we've got this ridiculous name which gets worse and worse with every year. It was literally what they called us at the club. We were known as 'The Young Ones' or 'The Young People'. So, when it came to us getting our first gig at the club, Ron Angel, who ran the club, and also wrote wonderful folk songs, asked us what we were going to be called as he had to write something on the poster. We said, 'Oh well, people call us the Young'uns so why not use that?' If we could go back in time we would have chosen a much better name. When I get asked what advice I'd give younger bands I say, 'Be very careful when choosing your band name.' It's a good story but to be defined by your age is not the best thing.

IF: Was it difficult transitioning to writing your own songs using your own stories? Was the folk club environment welcoming towards that or was there more of a demand for singing traditional songs?

Sean Cooney: When we first heard Graeme Miles' songs we just thought they were traditional songs as they sounded so timeless. One of his great strengths was that he could write songs that sounded like they were written centuries ago. We write songs that are new and are about things that are happening today but, because they are often unaccompanied, they can sound traditional. Our new album was recently album of the week on RTE in Ireland and every time they played it they said, 'We've got an album of traditional songs and sea shanties from the Young'uns.' And I thought no, they aren't, they are new songs about things that are happening now. But I guess that comes from the sound, which is very traditional. I think that is what endeared us to so many people in the North East folk scene because we were following in the tradition of unaccompanied folk singing in harmony, which went through the Wilson Family from Billingham, the Waterston Family from Robin Hood's Bay. They paved the way for groups like us. So, our sound and the tradition it came from helped as it could be quite contentious to write new songs in that environment.

IF: How did you build it up to a point where it would become your full-time career?

Sean Cooney: We started learning the songs and singing them in Stockton and a club in Wolviston in Billingham run by the Wilson family. The Wilsons are five brothers who sing with such power and they were very helpful and supportive of us. We tried to learn as many songs as possible and 20 years ago that was not easy as they weren't always online or in record shops. It was very much a case of going to the folk clubs, hearing a song and learning them. David would take a tape recorder for that purpose. Then we started to get noticed and started getting a few bookings in about 2005. Then we started playing a few festivals and it grew from there.

I'd moved to Hartlepool. My parents had a shed that I moved into. They said it was a log cabin but it was a shed. It was in the Headland of Hartlepool but I had no knowledge of Hartlepool and I fell in love with the place. We realised that there was no folk club in the Headland so we founded our own at a pub called the Pot House and we ran that for three or four years. At that point I was getting inspired by Hartlepool's history and, like Graeme Miles in the '50s, I was hearing stories and knew there weren't any songs about these events and so I started writing them. We got onto a sort of sea shanty scene right across Europe and we became known for singing North East songs, particularly about Hartlepool.

We then started to get booked at folk festivals around the UK. In the folk world you need to be seen first before someone will book you. There was one guy who ran a really big event and he didn't have an email address so everything had to be done by telephone and you'd be paid by cheque and this was 2007. But at the time we were one of the only young groups singing the old songs unaccompanied and it really got us some momentum and by 2013 were we thought we'd give it a go full time and we left the various jobs we had.

IF: Was that daunting?

Sean Cooney: I think it was daunting for Michael, who had the best job to give up as he was a teacher. For me and David we were self-employed, we went into schools for song-writing courses and so for us it was like a logical step. We were getting so many bookings and had started getting radio play on places like Radio Two. It had always been a dream. It got to the point where it would be too limiting if we could only gig at weekends.

IF: You were named best Folk Act on Radio Two for two years in a row and were getting great reviews for your records. How important is that sort of feedback for you?

Sean Cooney: Well writing an album can be pretty intense for me and, with the new album *Tiny Notes* some of the songs have taken two or three years to write. So feedback is important.

The Folk Awards were interesting because we'd been aware of and admired them from afar and we thought we'd never get to that level but fortunately we did and it meant a lot to us. I think the BBC stamp of approval meant something abroad and it allowed us to go and play in Canada, the US and Australia. We also got the Folk Album of the Year on the BBC for *Strangers* and that was a public vote so, again, that was special to us. That album was the first full conceptual piece that we'd done. Previous albums had been a mix of my songs, traditional songs and sea shanties with maybe a James Taylor song thrown in. Initially our albums would be a case of needing 12 songs to record and going out and finding them. From *Strangers* onwards it's been a case of having a theme and getting or writing songs to fit that theme.

IF: Tell me about *The Ballad of Johnny Longstaff*.

Sean Cooney: One night in May 2015 we were doing a show in Clevedon in Somerset and an old man approached us at the end of the set with an old photo of a scruffy teenage kid from the 1930s with a newspaper under his arm. He handed the photo over to us and said, 'That's my dad. His name was Johnny Longstaff and he came from Stockton and he died 20 years ago.' He handed us this other piece of paper that he'd prepared specially. It was a chronological list of the things his dad, Johnny, had seen and been involved in when he was a kid in the 1920s and 30s and ,40s and it was just incredible. It was like a checklist of some of the defining moments of working-class struggle. It included hunger marches, the fight against fascists on the streets of England, the right to roam, the Battle of Cable Street in 1936 in the East End of London against Oswald Mosely's fascist Black Shirts, the Spanish Civil War and the Second World War. At the end of this piece of paper it said, 'if you want to hear more go to the Imperial War Museum website where you can hear Johnny's story told by Johnny in his own words.' Johnny had recorded all his stories in 1986 in his own words. And when you listen to it you can hear this beautiful, old, funny, lovely Teesside accent. So, listening to those six hours of recordings, I knew straight away I'd like to try and write a piece of music about Johnny. Duncan, Johnny's son, had come along that night hoping we might write a song about his Dad but it ended up being 17 songs. I knew right from the start of listening to the tapes it would be a long piece.

Then a gentleman called Jeremy Davies from Roots Music helped us to put together a tour. It was such a beautiful thing to be part of because we were entrusted with it by Duncan and his family. The show is Johnny's voice telling his story and our songs weaving in and out of Johnny's story telling. We then, in partnership with Northern Stage and the Harbourfront Centre in Toronto, developed it as a stage theatre show. We staged it both in Newcastle and Canada. A lot of people came to see it not knowing too much about folk singing or having heard of us and that was the beautiful thing. It was not about us. It was about an incredible man from Stockton. And although it was a voice from the past, the war generation, it connected with people. The stories Johnny told were still so resonant with the rise of the far right, poverty and the right to roam, which are all current issues. It wasn't a didactic piece and we certainly weren't encouraging people to take to the streets but people naturally made the connection through the generations.

IF: What was the reaction from Duncan and his family when he saw the show?

Sean Cooney: One of the first times he saw it they all came to the Stockton Arc in Johnny's home town. At the end of the show we told the audience that the entire front row were members of Johnny's family and the place erupted and they all stood up for a standing ovation. Duncan has been such a supporter and has come to see it whenever he can. It's a beautiful relationship we have with him. Duncan was really involved with the whole process. He sent us loads of Johnny's books about things like the Spanish Civil War, often with Johnny's notes in the margins.

IF: How did some of the songs on your new album *Tiny Notes* come about, starting off with the title track?

Sean Cooney: Since 2015 I've been compelled to write folk songs about inspirational people of today. I guess you could say they are 21st Century folk songs. In the new album it starts off with one incredible story from Sunderland that struck me and moved me. I heard about this story in 2018 and it's taken me three years to get the song to the point where I thought it was worthy. It's a story about a young woman in her early 20s from Sunderland called Paige Hunter. She has suffered greatly with mental health problems. She decided that she would leave messages on the Wearmouth Bridge, a place where people had often taken their own lives. She wrote these notes, hundreds of them in felt tip pen and tied them to the railings, often with the number of the Samaritans on them. They were messages encouraging people to hold on to life rather than jumping off the bridge. In the time she had been doing that she realised she was responsible for saving the lives of at least 32 people. So, when I heard this story I was so incredibly moved and decided to write a song for Paige. It felt like it would be the most powerful song and it would direct the theme of the album.

Also, the idea of *Tiny Notes* is that people approach us with messages and that was the case with a man named Neil Airey, who we'd known for years from our singing workshops. We had no idea that he was the brother of Andy Airey, one of the 'Three Dads Walking'. That was Andy, Mike and Tim who are three dads who lost their daughters to suicide in a short space of time. They didn't know each other before their tragedies but they walk the length of the country to highlight suicide awareness. People are drawn to them, especially those who have suffered the loss of suicide. So, that request to write a song about them came from someone handing us a note.

Another example of someone asking us to write a song came from a lady called Rachel Robertson. She asked us to write about her brother who was killed in the Lockerbie bombing in 1988. That was an incredible email to receive. She said at the end of the email that she didn't see it as a sad song but as a love song. He was on the plane on the way to New York to spend Christmas with his girlfriend who was waiting for him. So, his life was filled with love. It was such an honour to be able to hold that story and that memory. Her trust gave us a huge sense of trepidation as to how we could do his memory justice.

With other songs I have chosen the subject and that gives me equal trepidation. I was determined to try and write a song about Jack Merritt, who lost his life in the London Bridge terror attack in 2019. There was no connection with the Merritt family or friends but I was compelled by the power of Jack's legacy that came through all the tributes. He had worked in prison rehabilitation and had changed so many lives through that. It was the first anniversary of his death in 2020 and people were talking about how inspirational he was. There was actually a hashtag #create with Jack encouraging people to create things in his honour. People were writing poems so I decided to write the song, which took about a year to complete. Of course, then you have the moment when you have to reach out to the family and the people connected and ask for their permission to put the song out. Thankfully the Merritts were completely moved by it.

So, we have developed really special relationships with the people involved and that makes it all the more emotional.

With the song about Richard Moore it was slightly different as it came from a friend of Richard's. She told me to read Richard's book called *Can I Give Him My Eyes* and it tells of how, as a 10-year-old in Derry he was shot and blinded by a rubber bullet fired by a British soldier and how later on, he met the soldier and forgave him. We had been doing a Radio 4 programme about our songwriting process and what the reactions of people are to the songs we write. So, we decided to do it differently by involving Richard from the start. We said to Richard, 'We want to write a song about you, do you want to be involved, how do you feel about that?' Deep down I knew that having read so much about Richard he'd be up for it and he'd be involved and he'd be great fun. This was at the start of Covid but we talked a lot on the phone. It helped having a deadline for the radio programme and, in the end, it came out fine. We ended up playing the finished song to Richard down the phone line and Lizzie, from the BBC, recorded his reaction on hearing it and it was just lovely.

IF: You must see emotional reactions in the audience when singing these affecting songs. Are they sometimes difficult to sing?

Sean Cooney: Yes, absolutely, and often. But I think it takes a lot of time to write and research them and get them right, so the majority of the emotion and tears comes out then. I'm still incredibly moved by them and you can sometimes hear the reaction from the audience. Coming from the folk club background it's always a good idea to tell the audience what the song is about before you sing it. On the recent tour we have been getting people coming up afterwards telling us of similar experiences in their lives. Andy Bell, who produced the record, said. 'Why don't you get an old suitcase and take it on tour and have luggage tags which people can then write their own tiny notes from which you can get ideas for songs.' So that's what we did and we've got over 250 of them. Some are so emotional, some are funny. That may be the next project *Songs from the Suitcase*. I'm just thinking of what we can do with all this trust people put in us. I guess, for some people, it's like lighting a candle for someone.

•••••••••••••••••

Sean is the sort of person you would happily chat to all afternoon. He is a natural storyteller and talks about the folk tradition and the subjects that he writes about with such passion. It may or may not be luck, but along with this passion the three lads are blessed with voices of such power and humanity that their songs can live in your memory long after you have listened to them. In doing this book I have discovered quite a few treasures that were, for whatever reason, hidden from me and the Young'uns are without doubt that, a North East treasure.

---

1. Ewan MacColl was a folk singer songwriter. He was most famous for writing the song "Dirty Old Town" which was written about life in Salford but later made famous by the Pogues as well as the song "The First Time Ever I Saw Your Face" which was a hit for Roberta Flack. He is also famous for being the father of the singer Kirsty MacColl.

3. Punk Rock

For anyone born after 1975 it is probably difficult to understand fully how shocking and threatening the rise of punk rock truly was. The safety pins, the unfortunate spitting, the violence and the raucous music frightened parents, politicians and broadcasters, but it exhilarated the youth. It was a threat to the roots of society from the Queen downwards. Looking back, the outrage may obscure what was a period of amazing music from the Sex Pistols, the Clash, the Jam, the Damned, X-Ray Specs and others. This is fantastic, life affirming music that has stood the test of time, even though punk really only lasted from 1976 to 1978. It probably ended on the 14th January 1978 when the Sex Pistols played their last gig in San Francisco with Johnny Rotten uttering the words, 'Ever get the feeling you've been cheated?'

Punk in those brief years was a snarling, technicolour threat that was designed to shock. It was an in-your-face scream aimed at upsetting the uptight 1970s. Britain at the time was grey, dull and in the midst of a decline that had us christened 'the sick man of Europe'. Punk had a pseudo-political philosophy that mixed Situationist sloganeering with the subversive fashions of Vivienne Westwood and Malcolm McLaren. Punk, they believed, was a wakeup call addressing our relentless fall from grace. Safe to say punks look otherworldly in the mid-1970s world of long hair and flares.

The early shows by the Sex Pistols inspired a generation of musicians, artists and writers. Their famous Manchester gigs at the Lesser Trade Hall in 1976 were attended by members of Joy Division, the Fall, Morrissey and Mick Hucknall, out of an audience of about 40. There was no equivalent epoch-defining event in the North East although in May 1976 the Pistols did play in Middlesbrough and Northallerton. These gigs were attended by Pauline Murray and other members of what was the North East's premier punk band, Penetration. Those gigs, however, were sparsely attended and did not set off an explosion as in Manchester. For the other bands from this region, they discovered what was going on via the weekly music papers and this led them to buy the records of the Ramones, the Clash, the Damned and the Sex Pistols. But the once-in-a-lifetime image that set them on the road was on July 21st 1977, when the Sex Pistols debuted on *Top of the Pops* to play "Pretty Vacant". The Sex Pistols looked great with the garish red hair of Johnny Rotten, looking cool in a Vivienne Westwood T-Shirt and boxy sunglasses. By this time, in reality, their decline had started, as the less-than-musically-competent Sid Vicious had joined the band on bass. That didn't matter as Sid looked great with an image that was archetypal punk, with spiked hair and leather biker jacket. Steve Jones and Paul Cook looked like the cheeky oiks they were, with Steve wearing a knotted handkerchief on his head to let everyone know that he was enjoying the ride at their expense. Beyond this startling image was the great music. Listen to *Never mind the Bollocks* now and you will hear driving rock music that is as fresh as it was in 1977.

So, for the nascent punk bands in the North East it was a TV appearance on *Top of the Pops* that drove them to embrace this new phenomena. It was the music and the look. It was not the newspaper headlines or the notorious appearance of the Sex Pistols on the *Bill Grundy Show* as the media was very regional in those days. No one up here would have seen or heard the swearing that so-shocked the nation.

What followed was suitably short, sharp and exciting. Penetration released two fantastic albums, as did the Carpettes. Punishment of Luxury released one critically acclaimed album on United Artists before imploding and Neon were cruelly dumped after two intriguing singles. The Angelic Upstarts had a longer run but, as their guitarist, Mond Cowie, will tell me, it was an exciting period that took them to the US and Abbey Road, but when it ended, that period of Mond's life was over, never to be returned to. There were a few notable aftershocks, which, although inspired by punk, fit more comfortably into the genre labelled New Wave with the likes of White Heat.

It is clear that there was lots of excitement, some violence and some amazing memories but in the North East punk rock was short lived, it involved a small cohort of players and probably didn't leave a mark on the region in the same way that the Animals or Lindisfarne had done but, boy, was it great fun for those in the thick of it.

Penetration

Gary Chaplin's Story

Britain in the 1970s was not a happy place. There had been a succession of unpopular and pretty ineffective governments. The Conservatives, led by Edward Hearth, ushered in the decade but were effectively brought down by the striking miners. They were replaced by an equally ineffective Labour government under Harold Wilson, who was later replaced by 'Sunny' Jim Callaghan. Unfortunately, there was little 'sunny' about life under his government. In that period the UK came to be known as 'The Sick Man of Europe' due to poor economic performance, high unemployment and crippling industrial strife. This culminated in what became 'The Winter of Discontent' in 1978/79 when there were widespread strikes from both private and public sector unions against a pay rise limit set by the Labour Government in an effort to combat inflation, which had peaked at an eye-watering 26%. The period was epitomised in the media by the strike by Liverpool's grave diggers. It was against this demoralising background that the divisive figure of Margaret Thatcher rose to power. Famously she used the advertisers Saatchi and Saatchi whose advert depicted people queuing up for jobs in a period of high unemployment, using the phrase 'Labour Isn't Working'.

If the youth of the country was disaffected by being let down by political parties of all sides, there was little for them in the musical scene of the time to offer them hope. Ten years earlier teenagers across the land were fired up by the DIY spirit of skiffle music. This spawned the Beatles, the Stones, the Kinks and the Who. By the mid 1970s the possibility of DIY music was gone. It had been replaced by the highly technical bombast of the prog or progressive rock of Yes, ELP (Emerson, Lake and Palmer) and Pink Floyd. This was the music of 'the Heads' or hippies with their long hair and flares. It was music to be revered rather than music that you could copy on instruments with your mates, it was just too difficult to play. It was music played by the middle classes for the middle classes. It was anything but protest music at a time when there was a whole heap to protest about.

However, bubbling under the surface was a raw seam of music that did speak to the youth and reflected their abandonment and despair. This music was found in what has since been termed 'proto punk' in groups like Iggy and the Stooges and the MC5 from Detroit or, closer to home, the art school rock of Roxy Music, Bee-Bop Deluxe and David Bowie or even the glam stomp of Marc Bolan or Slade. There were things happening that could catch the imagination of the more enquiring minds. There was no internet so you had to go out and search for it, but it was there. One of these enquiring minds was Gary Chaplin from the tiny mining village Ferryhill in County Durham. This is Gary's story. It's the story of how punk started for everyone outside of London.

IF: What were you listening to when you were young?

Gary Chaplin: I was an early adopter of lots of things and there was a small group of like-minded individuals where I grew up. I grew up in Ferryhill, a small mining village in County Durham. Music for me, when I got to 10, 11, 12 was the radio. I got interested in learning to play the guitar at about 11 so my mam and dad bought me possibly the worst guitar ever.

I was very aware of the likes of the Beatles and have vivid memories of seeing Jimi Hendrix on *Top of the Pops*, playing "Purple Haze". This all coincided with T-Rex becoming very big with "Ride a White Swan", seeing this weird guy with a mop of curly black hair was quite startling. I know it's difficult to shock now but it was quite easy in those days, in a very staid Britain. The record sounded strange compared to other records in the charts. Also, a bit earlier in 1969 there was David Bowie with "Space Oddity", another almost weird and different type of singer.

The rubbish guitar that my parents got me was a Spanish guitar that was virtually unplayable. I wanted to play "Get it On" by T Rex but none of those sounds would come out of a Spanish guitar. I struggled for two or three years but eventually managed to persuade my parents to buy me an electric guitar.

Even when we were 13 and 14 and first putting bands together, we always had original material. We always knew that, no matter how good, bad or indifferent you were you were never going to make it playing a version of "Alright Now"[1]. So we knew we had to write our own songs.

IF: Did you and your pals desire a career in music?

Gary Chaplin: We desired a career but never thought it would be possible. I had bands from a very young age but never bands that played anywhere. I had a network of people I played with. One was Alan Heatherington, whose father was my music teacher at school. He was the first bass player on the band that became Penetration. The other person was another school friend called Steve Jacobs who was a drummer.

IF: Who was influencing your early forays into music?

Gary Chaplin: Big influences were Bowie, T-Rex, Roxy Music, Cockney Rebel, who all indirectly played into punk rock. Another one was Bebop Deluxe, led by the charismatic Bill Nelson. I saw BeBop Deluxe at the Mayfair with Cockney Rebel and they were jaw dropping.

We had very catholic tastes. A big influence on us was a local lad called Peter Lloyd, who was Pauline Murray's first husband. Pauline, of course, became the singer of Penetration. Peter was the biggest influence on my musical life. He and I were record buying buddies. We were seekers. We were looking for something that was different. He was a bit older and had a job so had the capacity to purchase that something different. I suspect we'd be the first kids in the north east, never mind Ferryhill, who had certain records.

IF: How did you hear about the likes of Iggy, who is well known now but very obscure in the mid '70s?

Gary Chaplin: A lot would be to do with following the music press and then picking up on something the likes of David Bowie said in interview. In those days, way pre-internet, your education in music or art would come from chance mentions in the interview you happened to be reading. So if someone talked about William Burroughs you would think *oh, I must check that out*. There was scant information, more like glimpses, like the New York Dolls on the *Old Grey Whistle Test*.

IF: At what point did you say right we are going to be a punk band?

Gary Chaplin: It kind of happened sideways. I used to arrange bus trips up to Newcastle to see bands as there was no other way to get there and back from Ferryhill so I began seeing all these bands I've mentioned. At the same time Peter and I bought records by the likes of the Velvet Underground and Iggy and the Stooges, the pre-cursers of Punk.

We were searching for something and were the ready for Punk Rock. However, in the year before punk kicked off I'd seen Pink Floyd playing *Dark Side of the Moon*, which was boring! I saw Yes, but there was a thing with Yes as their drummer, Alan White, who has just died, was from Ferryhill. The band that blew our socks off were Genesis, *Selling England by the Pound*, and they were weird. You couldn't admit you had those records in the heyday of punk, but we did. Then there were other bands like

Can or Captain Beefheart who were making it through into punk. In reality Can and Pink Floyd were very similar but one was ostracised for being hippies and one was pronounced acceptable by the likes of John Lydon.

For me, a lot comes back to Peter Lloyd, who was seeking what was next and used to write letters and get them published in the *NME* about the subject. He had the most amazing and diverse record collection.

When punk came along we were in the right place, with the right influences and fortunately only rudimentary musical skills. Unless you were trained to a high level you would never have a hope of playing the guitar like Steve Howe of Yes or the piano like Rick Wakeman. Punk took away that necessity. The funny thing is that the only song I could play by Yes was called "You and I", and I stole the chord sequences for the introduction of the song called "Life's a Gamble", which became a hit for Penetration. But I was limited by my poor ability. Part of the reason we wrote our own songs is because we couldn't copy other bands' songs. I was in various bands such as the one with Steve and Alan, and sometimes Robert Blamire and then another one with Gary Smallman, who lived round the corner and ended up in Penetration.

IF: How did you get gigs?

Gary Chaplin: Well, we used to go to see bands at the Rock Garden in Middlesbrough. At that point we were doing gigs as The Points. Pauline Murray joined the band on my 18th birthday in August '76. We would play 50/50 originals and covers. At this time, I formed a good song writing partnership with Pauline. Gary then joined and then Robert as Alan didn't want to be in a punk band.

We befriended the guy who ran the Rock Garden, Les Allen, and we cheekily asked if we could have a gig and he let us play some gigs there in January 1977. There was also a group of guys at Newcastle Poly who had a thing called the Alternative Rock Society and they put gigs on at the Poly. We befriended them through Peter Lloyd and we did a support gig for the Vibrators. We did a few gigs like that and that led to the one gig that made a difference. I rang up Andy Czezowski, who had the Roxy Club[2] in London, and asked him for a gig. And amazingly he said, yes, you can support a band named Generation X. And we did that on the 9th April 1977. It may sound crazy, but it was a simple as getting the phone number and phoning up and then, all of a sudden, we were in the middle of all the mayhem that was punk.

From there everything went exceedingly fast. We were booked to do a gig then at the Bonham Hall with the Adverts, I think the next night. We went down to London but that gig didn't happen. However, gigs were still coming in Newcastle and the next month we did a gig with Cherry Vanilla[3] of Andy Warhol's Factory fame at Newcastle Polytechnic. It turned out that Cherry Vanilla's guitarist, bassist and drummer were the Police, Sting, Stewart Copeland and Henry Padovani. I think Sting liked us.

After this, two things happened. And I must apologise because it's quite a convoluted story. Firstly, Phil Sutcliffe of *Sounds* wrote a glowing review of us playing that gig. Secondly Sting and Stewart Copeland go back down to London and tell Stewart's brother, Miles Copeland[4] about us and tell him he needs to sign us. He then sends people back up to record us back in Ferryhill. In the meantime, Richard Branson read the review. In turn he rang up Andy Worrall, who was the manager of the Newcastle Virgin Record store and asked, 'Why haven't you told me about this band?' He wanted to hear a demo. So it became a competition to sign us between Virgin Records and Miles Copeland's label

We asked Phil Sutcliffe about Miles Copeland and he told us about the CIA links and we were not keen on him. So Miles Copeland rang me up in Ferryhill, much to my mam's consternation – 'Gary, there's been an American man ringing up while you were out. I told him you've already got a manager,' which we did in Peter Brent, who ran the Listen Ear shop in Newcastle. Then we had a call from Bernie Rhodes, who managed the Clash, but we blew him out. We didn't really want anything to do with people from down London. We were very green and naïve. Anyway, we did a demo for Virgin at our local youth club and played all the songs we had and sent it to Virgin. Virgin liked the songs and asked us to come down to re-record them in a studio in London. Sorry, I told you it was pretty convoluted!

At this stage we all still had jobs. I was an architect's assistant at the local council, Pauline worked in the Law Department at the local authority, Robert worked for his family's business and Gary was still at school. Shortly after that we got interest from a London management company, called Quarry, who also managed Status Quo and Rory Gallagher. This turned out to be our biggest mistake. We were impressed with their Wardour Street offices, but they were old school music management. They came in at the time that we got the record deal with Virgin records.

Virgin had only initially offered us just a singles deal. So we went down to a studio in Worthing and recorded "Don't Dictate". It was produced by Mike Howlett of Gong fame. The single was released and around this time we gave up our jobs. I'm hazy about the timeline but we certainly gave up our jobs too soon.

They released "Don't Dictate" and it got to about number 42. Virgin had underestimated the demand and had only pressed 25,000 copies, which sold out. That meant the single stalled at number 42 and so the chance of *Top of the Pops* went. It may have gone top 30 or more had they pressed more. The lead time for pressing was too long and momentum was lost. We were still constantly gigging, playing with the likes of the Stranglers, Elvis Costello, the Vibrators. It was really exciting but by 1978 the shine had worn off. We rushed into deals with Virgin and Quarry and maybe should have waited a bit longer. But none of us had that entrepreneurial nous.

IF: On YouTube there is a video of the band playing in the

Electric Circus in 1977. On it shows a fan repeatedly throwing beer at your singer Pauline. It is pretty awful to watch. Was this sort of behaviour common?

Gary Chaplin: No, that was the first time. Before that audiences were as respectful as you would expect. Things changed when the newspapers reported on punk fans spitting. After that, fans started doing that and it was pretty horrible.

The story of that gig was quite interesting though. We had played down in Manchester with the Buzzcocks and the opening act was a band called Stiff Kittens and it was their first gig. We were so impressed with them we invited them to play with us up here on Jubilee Day in 1977. By this time they were called Warsaw, and they later became Joy Division. They were great and nice fellas. Also, Tony Wilson, who started Factory Records with Joy Division, liked us when we played down there so later asked us to go down to be filmed for his music show on ITV called *So It Goes*, which is where the footage of the show you referred to was shown. Tony was great and we got a tour round Coronation Street. There were five songs recorded of us that night, which we were shown, but which have never been seen since. It's a real shame as they were great.

IF: Why did you leave the band?

Gary Chaplin: There were two or three things going on. Firstly, I didn't like the way we were being managed. Also, I thought it was my band and everyone else thought it wasn't. I also had a hand injury, where it used to cramp up. So I had to take some time out. I'd recorded the second single, "Firing Squad" and we then toured Italy in January 1978. I did the Rock Garden and then the Central London Poly and then my hand went and it turned out to be my last gig with them. I needed either an operation or steroid injections but would also need to lay off the guitar as well. They knew I was leaving but the plan was that I'd record the album but the injury occurred. I did think I would have a musical career after this and I did some things with Red Rhino that didn't really go anywhere. So after a couple of years kicking my heals I went to university. Walking away from it was hard but I think it was the right thing to do. I probably experienced the best bit of punk rock and got out at the right time.

IF: Looking back why did the North East not sustain a scene?

Gary Chaplin: I always felt that unlike the North East these other places, as well as having a pool of talent and great bands, also had a small cohort of campaigning music journalists who for their own benefit as much for their city, wanted to create the impression of a scene. Particularly in the seventies. These journalists, such as Paul Morley in Manchester, would big up the bands from their area, some of which were fantastic, some who were not so good. And this would be part of their campaign to become a journalistic personality. I don't think we really had that in the north east. Although you did have a small group of writers who coalesced around BBC Newcastle, such as the late Ian Penman and Phil Sutcliffe, who wrote later for *Sounds,* but maybe they had a smaller reach than the likes of Paul Morley. When you ask the question why do some bands make it and others don't, well, one of the reasons why we made it was Phil Sutcliffe. He wrote a review of us (Penetration) at exactly the right time.

IF: Where did your confidence come from? To pick up the phone and ask for a gig at the Roxy in London at the height of punk.

Gary Chaplin: My dad was an electrician at the pit but he was also a local politician. He instilled in me from an early age that 'you're as good as anyone and you can do anything you want to do'. I didn't do well at school. I couldn't concentrate, I went to Secondary Modern rather than the Grammar School. So I felt a little disadvantaged and so I felt more determined. I think I can thank my parents for that. They weren't punk but, in some way, they reflected the DIY ethic that drove punk.

•••••••••••••••••

Gary was there in the middle of the heady, sweaty and shocking days of punk sharing stages with Generation X, the Stranglers and the Vibrators. His stint in the limelight was, as it was punk, suitably short. After he left Penetration they released two great albums for Virgin Records and then split in 1979. They have actually reformed quite recently without Gary but with Pauline and Robert from their classic up line up. In 2015 they released another great album in *Resolution* and continue to gig to this day. For many the story of Penetration is Pauline Murray's. This is understandable as her amazing voice cut through the noise of the time and, as a woman in an aggressive world, she was an important figure. But this is Gary's story and its one he tells without a shred of bitterness. His rise and fall was sharp, exciting and swift and a perfect reflection of punk's ethos.

1. "Alright Now" was a number two hit in the UK charts for the rock band Free in 1970. It is quite easy to play on the guitar and, forever, has been a staple for club cover bands.

2. The Roxy Club was a punk venue in Covent Gardens, London started by Andy Czezowski, Susan Carrington and Barry Jones in December 1976. It put on early gigs by Generation X, Siouxsie and the Banshees and the Clash. Don Letts was resident DJ and his championing of reggae music was an influence on punks like the Clash and John Lydon.

3. Cherry Vanilla was initially known as a New York actress in Andy Warhol's play 'Pork'. She then moved on to David Bowie's company Main Man Ltd as a marketing person before starting as a singer in a band. In 1976 she was invited across to London by Miles Copeland and became part of the burgeoning punk rock scene.

4. Miles Copeland was one of the initial founders of the US intelligence agency, the CIA. He had a number of children, two of whom, Miles and Stewart forged careers in the music industry in London. Stewart became drummer of the Police and Miles founded a management company and later on a number of record labels. In 1979 he founded IRS Records who helped to launch, amongst others, REM, the Cramps, the Alarm and the Go-Go's. A third brother, Ian, was also involved in the music industry in the US as a successful promoter, particularly involved in the new wave movement supporting such artists as the B52's, the Cure and Simple Minds.

Punishment of Luxury

Brian Bond's Story

If you look on YouTube for Punishment of Luxury the first video you will see is that of Den Hegarty, previously of the mock fifties revivalists, Darts, introducing the band on the 1979 Tyne Tees Show *Alright Now*, which was a forerunner to *The Tube*. Den, in his theatrical style, explains that David Bowie studied mime under the legendary Lindsay Kemp (who actually grew up in South Shields). He says that another person who studied under Lindsay Kemp was Brian Bond, singer of Punishment of Luxury.

What follows is a performance of the band's first single "Puppet Life". It starts with some heavy breathing followed by some rather sinister talk-over voicing. Brian then appears moving in a jerky fashion, next some puppets, with Brian wearing an even more sinister crocheted balaclava mask. The rest of the band are also wearing such masks. With the benefit of 43 years it's easy to dismiss this as pretentious and dated. It's not. After spending a couple of hours with Brian you understand that this was a distillation of the band's many influences and experiences both musically and visually. Musically you may hear Devo, Sparks and Roxy Music. Visually you will see the aforementioned Lindsay Kemp mixed with David Lynch. They were a band with big ambitions without realising it. Or maybe we were just a bit more open minded musically in the 1970s.

I pitch up to Brian's house on a quiet street in South Gosforth. I am met by the deadpan Brian who greets me with a, 'Not today thanks'. This is followed by a big smile, a firm handshake and two hours of tea, nice biscuits and a tale that is similar to many bands whilst also being decidedly different. For many reasons Punishment of Luxury are a band you should check out.

IF: What were your influences when you were growing up?

Brian Bond: I grew up in the 50s and music was extremely dull for a long period with theatrical ballads dominating. It wasn't until I heard "Heartbreak Hotel" when I was six or seven that I got inspired. It was an utterly haunting sound, very riveting. My sister got me listening to "Hound Dog" and such like.

The first record I bought, I think, was "Jenny, Jenny" by Little Richard. I just could not believe what I was listening to. It was the manic energy of the song that got me and also because he ran out of breath towards the end of the song, and they didn't make him do it again (Brian proceeds to imitate Little Richard running out of breath – I later listened to it and Brian was indeed correct). I just thought *who is this man*. I also got "Great Balls of Fire" by Jerry Lee Lewis. There was suddenly this mass of energy which then subsided just as it had risen.

Around 1960 it got bland with Cliff Richards and his Elvis impersonation and singers became family entertainers. Then came the Beatles and the Stones and I got excited again. I listened obsessively to each record released by them. Again, there was that rush of energy. I think the Who, who I also loved, were, to me, Proto-Punks with their on-stage destruction of guitars and their power chords. I loved the music and the energy but I didn't think about getting into a school band as I was getting more into acting and plays at school. I went to a school in Berkshire but came from Staines in Middlesex.

IF: How did you become a performer rather than just a listener?

Brian Bond: I came to the North East to start a Drama group up here called Mad Bongo. I got into performing at university but when I came up here I was doing pub shows in places like the Scrogg Inn in Walker. I performed in pubs in Benwell and Elswick. We were doing short plays that involved acting and singing. We did a play called *A Fistful of Stotties*[1] which was a Western based around T Dan Smith[2]. We went to Cleator Moor in Cumbria and did a play called *Axe Me Another* about a boss who had cut lots of jobs, which in the 1970s was a big issue in society. The plays we performed would typically have been an hour or so long.

IF: Were you able hold their attention considering they would be busy pubs?

Brian Bond: In places like the Windmill in Cowgate you got all sorts of characters coming in, sometimes gangsterish people. In one pub in Elswick they had to hand their guns in to the ladylady when they came in. But they loved us, they certainly tolerated us, they were entertained. It was mid 70s and pubs were often full of all sorts of colourful characters and strangely we fitted in.

IF: Were people more open minded then?

Brian Bond: Yes, I think they probably were and we were doing quite well. We were funded by Northern Arts. By 1977 one of the co-founders got cancer and had to drop out and the funding started to dry up. So by that time I wanted to get into the music.

IF: What inspired you to move from acting to music?

Brian Bond: Well, we were starting to look at rock musicals and we always had music in the plays. And some of the people who later became Punishment of Luxury were performing in these plays – Steve the drummer and Nev Atkinson, who played bass at the time. I was getting more and more into performing music. It was the first time I'd performed with a band behind me and it got intoxicating. Then Phil Sutcliffe, the music journalist, wrote a musical called *Cop This Kidda* for us. So, in our early days Phil Sutcliffe gave us some great reviews. I was growing tired of performing for kids' shows and writing really bad plays. So I left, someone else took over the company. I started writing songs with Nev, who had moved on to guitar. Some of our songs such as "Puppet Life" were actually performed in *Cop this kidda*. There was no money in being in a band, so we all signed on the dole and spent the whole of 1978 trying to establish ourselves.

IF: Did the music of punk inspire you?

Brian Bond: Oh yes, definitely. Around 1977 when I was dropping the theatre and I was deciding to throw in my lot with music, I remember going to Nev's flat in Dunston and we watched *Top of the Pops* and we saw the Sex Pistols playing "Pretty Vacant" and it leapt out at us. We decided, yes, that's what we want to do, we wanted to generate that much energy too. So, as I said, we had songs from doing the drama so we did a demo at Impulse Studio in Wallsend with Dave Wood. We recorded three songs "Puppet Life", "The Demon" and "Blood of Love". With terrible timing we took a cassette of the demo down to London. It was December, the week before Christmas, and it turned out that nearly all the record companies were having their Christmas parties.

IF: How did you know where to go?

Brian Bond: We had no great plan. The only places we could get the tape listened to were firstly DJM, Dick James Music. Dick James[3] was not impressed at all. We just knocked on the door. It was like talking to a brick wall.

Luckily, we saw a chap called Arnold Frolows at Virgin and he listened to our tape. He said 'hold on' and played a record by a band called Devo, the song "Jocko Homo" and he said you sound a bit like this. I loved it. Arnold liked "Puppet Life" and "Demon". So he decided to come and see us up in Newcastle. We had a gig coming up at Spectro Arts Workshop on Pilgrim Street. My cousin joined the band as drummer but he was older than us and didn't quite fit in. The gig went well, Arnold Frolows came and Phil Sutcliffe gave us a great review in *Sounds*. Arnold was impressed and we got an offer from Virgin for a standard eight-album deal. We turned it down. I know that sounds strange but we just didn't feel settled or ready. The line-up wasn't steady.

IF: What was the scene like, where did you play?

Brian Bond: In 1977 the punk scene was really interesting and the top band of that scene was the Big G. We played with them in late 1977 but we just weren't well rehearsed. It was at Gatsby's in Whitley Bay and the Big G were great. They were full of energy and professionalism. We realised that we just couldn't muck it up like this again. It was time to get serious.

We did a lot of gigs. We then got a gig at the Guildhall with the Angelic Upstarts, Neon (from Durham) and ourselves. Neon were top of the bill and their audience were mainly bikers. They were a quirky band. The Upstarts had their fans from South Shields and there was quite a bit of restlessness in the crowd. The Upstarts were famous for having a pig's head on stage with a police helmet on it and they had a song about someone who had allegedly been killed by the police called *Who killed Liddle Towers*. We went on first and there was a can thrown. We were playing a song called "World War Four," which we never played again because it didn't really work. For some reason, don't ask me why, I was wearing a dressing gown. I think the can was nearly empty and I caught it, put it in my dressing gown pocket and carried on. There was no more unrest. The Upstarts came on with flashing lights and the pig's head being kicked about. I was in the bar away from the band. I was chatting to the manager of the Upstarts, Keith Bell[4]. I didn't know but while I was chatting to him there was a riot going on. Mensi, their singer, was rousing the fans and the Upstarts fans charged the Neon fans, the bikers, and there was blood everywhere. There were girls with their faces covered in blood. The police were called and when they arrived they got the Upstarts' fans to take their shoes off and walk home. They actually made them walk home in their socks. Could you imagine the police doing that today?

IF: Was there a camaraderie between the bands on the scene?

Brian Bond: Yes, there was in the early days. After 1980 there was less so. The Big G were very good but we pinched their guitarist, Mick Emmerson (aka Red Helmet) and that soured things a bit.

IF: After the Virgin offer what did you do?

Brian Bond: We looked for a single record deal. We looked at Rough Trade[5] and looked at Stiff Records[6] and they weren't interested. Then we saw Small Wonder Records[7] in Walthamstow. So we went across there and the owner, Pete Stennett, loved it. We felt we'd have control over the art work and the production. Small Wonder were perfect. They put us in a studio in London and the engineer was a bit bored so we just produced it ourselves. By now we had a settled line up with a reliable bassist in Jimi Giro, Red Helmet, Les, who was our original drummer, Nev and I. We were really happy with the recordings and Small Wonder released "Puppet Life" as our first single. It got a lovely review from Tony Visconti[8] in Sounds. I must admit It was dangerously close to a novelty record. However, it seemed to be well received and to sit in the Cooperage pub in Newcastle and listen to a transistor radio and hear John Peel play our single was like paradise.

We then got an agency in Asgard. We had set up a gig in the Elephant and Castle in London. There were about 12 people there but Richard Armitage from Asgard was in the audience and he liked it. We then started getting gigs and the fees started going up. We played from Plymouth right up to Aberdeen and Inverness and were generally headlining. We did a gig at the Lyceum in London along with Penetration and the Fall. My mum and dad even came to that one. My dad was amused that the band after us got canned off but we didn't. We were all on the dole and playing up and down the country and record companies started getting interested.

Two record companies mainly were interested – that was

United Artists (UA) and Charisma, both would be termed major record labels. Charisma dropped out and that left UA. They had an A&R man called Tim Chatsfield and he really liked us. So we got signed up for a number of albums. We were put on a wage. We played a gig at the Newcastle City Hall and they came to see us and gave us the contract at the end of the gig. This was the end of 1978. We also signed to EMI Publishing around that time.

For the first single we wanted "Jelly Fish" but they didn't like it. Maybe we should have held out for "Jelly Fish" but in the end they released "Engine of Excess". We recorded it with Mike Howlett[9] from Gong. It got bad reviews and it didn't do well. Vivienne Goldman from *Sounds* called it 'dinosaur cock rock'.

We had various managers throughout this period. Richard Armitage managed us for a while and he suggested we call the album *Gateshead Soup,* which we didn't go for. The publishers, EMI asked UA 'Why didn't you release Jelly Fish?' So, then UA deferred to the publishers and released it, but it was too late and it didn't do anything. We released "Secrets" as the next single, which got better reviews. Mike Howlett produced the album and he was great. He put up with all of our foibles and quirks. We stayed in a house in Ealing and life was pretty good.

We paid ourselves from our advance but that money gradually reduced as time went on. The album came out in September 1979 and got really good reviews. Things felt good. In early 1980 we went to record demos for our next record. It was a classic second album syndrome. For the first album we recorded songs we'd been touring with and they were battle hardened. Second time round they were new songs and the record company didn't like them. By that time EMI had taken over UA and Tim Chatsfield had left, so we had no one fighting our corner at the record company. EMI publishing still had us but EMI record label looked at our lack of sales and they didn't like the demos. Some of the songs were anti-military songs and EMI made weapon systems and so they weren't impressed with the demos, whether the two were linked I don't know. But they sacked us.

We were living up here and it was awful. It was a slap in the face and an utter rejection. Effectively they were cutting their losses as we hadn't earned enough to pay off the advance. The air went out of the balloon very quickly and we weren't too well equipped to deal with it.

IF: What were your plans then?

Brian Bond: Well, we still had tours organised. We had a tour of Holland, Belgium and Germany to do in February 1980. We were showcasing some of the new stuff. They went well but unlike now you couldn't really sustain a living just by playing live. It felt strange when we got back home with nothing to go back to.

We would have to start all over again and I think I went a bit crazy. There was a funny feeling within the band, something hanging in the air. Our tour manager, Rob, innocently said 'Have you got any surprises for us Brian?', prior to the last gig of the tour in Holland. In my feverish brain I thought, *surprises? Ok, I'll pull out a surprise*. Without telling the others I did the stupidest thing I've ever done in my life. I got a load of raw fish and for the encore, which was always the song "Jellyfish", I ran back, picked up the fish and threw it over the audience. It was the most ridiculous thing I could have done. There was raw fish on the lighting desk, the sound desk and the audience threw fish back so we became covered in fish. It was an insult to the audience and probably an insult to my fellow band members. I have apologised since. This soured things even more and we agreed to part ways. They carried on and I left.

I went into Newcastle Poly to write songs on the piano. I started a new band called Punching Holes and we got gigs in London and up here but we never got a record deal. I wanted to have another go but it didn't really happen. After that I had to get a real job.

IF: How did you get back together in 2007?

Brian Bond: I didn't see them for a while. Jimi (the bass player) and I were seeing each other and I was even his best man.

Back in 1983 there was a sort of reconciliation and there were mutual apologies. We did a gig in Brixton but they advertised the wrong night and not many people came. It was OK. It didn't quite work out then and we didn't see each other again until 2007. It was Jimi's 50th birthday party and I got a phone call asking if I'd play a gig for this. So, we did. I wasn't keen at first. I didn't put 100% into it as I was wary but it ended up being a really good gig. We've been playing ever since off and on. I really enjoy it now. We haven't played for three years partly due to the pandemic but we played the Westgarth Social Club in Middlesbrough and the Brudnell Social Club in Leeds both in December 2022.

IF: Why do you think you had success when some of your contemporaries in the North East didn't?

Brian Bond: We got confidence from performing music in pubs and Nev had travelled to places like Afghanistan and learned instruments there. Doing the musicals in Mad Bongo meant we had to be well rehearsed, professional, on time and when it came to the band we had that professionalism, which is important. We hardened our approach and we were determined. We took the demo down to London to get a result. We had aspirations.

IF: Do you regret anything?

Brian Bond: Well, I think the big regret is that for the second album the material wasn't as good or hadn't as much finesse as the material for the first album. We should have taken our time to come up with better songs but we were rushed by the record company. We did actually do a further EP in 2011 and that was pretty good. We had a hedge fund manager who was an old fan so he sponsored us to do that and it turned out quite well. When we play now we only really play from the first album and the EP but not the aborted record. And, most importantly, I still enjoy it.

••••••••••••••••••

Brian is such good company and has had what can be called an interesting life. When I ask him some further questions via Whatsapp, Brian tells me of performing in the play by Lindsay Kemp called *Flowers* in 1972 along with Kate Bush. He tells me of meeting Angie Bowie who was recruiting extras for Bowie's Ziggy Stardust. He also talks of seeing Jimi Hendrix and Frank Zappa in 1967 and the famous Rolling Stones show in Hyde Park in 1969, held immediately after the death of Brian Jones. He talks of busking around France in 1968. He is not even remotely name dropping but giving me more information on what his influences are.

It is apparent that Brian has a story to tell that warrants more than a paltry chapter in a book such as this. Punishment of Luxury only recorded one album with Brian. After Brian left when the band went under the name Punilux, and recorded one further album. It all seems such a shame. They were an avant garde band and this reflected the wide and varied experiences of Brian and Nev in particular. In hindsight, punk didn't have that much room for the avant garde and in many ways musically was a continuation from the Who and Glam Rock. Punk was, in reality, much more traditional musically than the outrage that accompanied it would have you believe. Conversely, Punishment of Luxury were quietly subversive and maybe this was too much for the record labels of the time.

1. Stottie Cake is a flat, round bread loaf that originated in the North East of England

2. T Dan Smith was a North East local politician who was leader of Newcastle Council in the 1960s and known as 'Mr Newcastle'. He was famous for the clearance of slums and their replacement by modern high-rise flats which unfortunately deteriorated quickly due to the use if substandard materials. He was later sent to prison for six years on corruption charges. The character Austin Donoghue, played by Alun Armstrong, in the BBC series *Our Friends in the North* was based on T Dan Smith.

3. Dick James was a music publisher most famous for setting up Northern Songs with Brian Epstein as the publisher of all of Lennon and McCartney's songs. Later on he signed Elton John and was portrayed by Stephen Graham in the film about Elton called *Rocketman*.

4. Keith Bell was a notorious local hard man who managed the Angelic Upstarts

5. Rough Trade Records is an independent record label that developed out of a record shop. They are most famous for the signing and success of bands such as the Smiths, the Libertines and the Strokes.

6. Stiff Records is an independent record label set up in 1976 by Jake Riviera and Dave Robinson. They had much success in the late 70's and early 80's with the likes of Elvis Costello, Ian Dury, Madness and their house producer Nick Lowe.

7. Small Wonder Records was an independent record label that operated out of a shop called Small Wonder Records in Walthamstow, London. They released early records by the Cure as well as Bauhaus, the Carpettes and the Angelic Upstarts.

8. Tony Visconti is a record producer who produced Marc Bolan and David Bowie.

9. Mike Howlett is an Australian record producer most famous for producing albums by OMD, Flock of Seagulls and Gang of Four. He had previously been a member of the UK prog rock band Gong and, for a very brief period, a member of a band called Strontium 90 with Sting, Stewart Copeland and Andy Summers around the time of the inception of the Police.

Angelic Upstarts

Mond Cowie's Story

Angelic Upstarts are a political punk band that was started in 1977 by a group of friends from the coastal town of South Shields. The friends were Thomas Mensforth, the loudmouth with a heart of gold known to everyone as Mensi, Derek 'Decca' Wade, their madcap drummer and the good looking one, Raymond 'Mond' Cowie. They were a band with contradictions. They were socialists who scored record deals with the major labels Polydor, Warner Brothers and EMI. They had an aggressive, in your face style, but with thoughtful and sometimes intelligent lyrics. They were left-wing in their politics but attracted the unwanted attention of right-wing skinhead thugs. They also had hit singles, hit albums and played *Top of the Pops*. Mond was with the band from 1977 until 1984. Mensi was with the band on and off until his tragic death due to Covid in 2021. The band continues to this day but with none of the original members.

I meet Mond in a pub in his home town of South Shields on a cold Wednesday afternoon in January. The town is deserted except for the pubs which are all pretty full of elderly drinkers. I am not sure whether this is so they can get warm as they are not switching their heating on due to the cost-of-living crisis or whether it's just that older people have more time to indulge in a north eastern favourite past time of drinking. I'm sure Mensi would have had an opinion either way.

IF: Were you all friends as kids?

Mond: We were all brought up on the Brockley Whins Estate in South Shields. That was me, Mensi and Decca along with Micky Byrne, who played a few gigs with us when we started and a few others. This is probably from the ages of five or six onwards and then all through our school years.

IF: What came first for you, punk or music and guitars?

Mond: No, not punk. I started playing guitar when I was about 13. I was listening to the likes of Deep Purple, Thin Lizzy and Free. I had started working in the shipyards but, like a lot of people in the yards, I played in club bands on Friday and Saturday nights, playing rock covers. That all changed when punk happened. Me and Mensi saw the Sex Pistols on *Top of the Pops* and Mensi stood up and said 'That's it, we're going to start a punk band. Mond, you're going to be the guitarist, Decca, you're going to be the drummer' and we said 'Great'.

IF: Was Mensi in your club band?

Mond: No, Mensi could never really sing. But, like Mensi, what I liked about punk was that it was fast and furious. When we were in the club bands we had to do chart stuff in the first set and maybe, when people had had a few drinks, you could do a bit of Deep Purple or Free in the second set. It was all very regimented. You were kept down in a sense. With punk you could play as loud and as fast as you want and whatever songs you wanted. So we loved it. Decca loved it because he was like Animal from the *Muppets*. It was just great fun.

IF: Were you writing songs from the start?

Mond: Yes, that was the first thing we did. Straight away Mensi started writing words and came out with songs like "Leave me Alone" and "Police Oppression". The first gig we did was at Percy Hudson Youth Club in South Shields where we used to rehearse. We only had six songs. We did them and the kids were screaming for more, so we did them all again. In about 1978 we went to Impulse Studio in Wallsend and recorded "Who killed Liddle Towers"[1]. That was when things changed. Our manager paid for it and we got 500 singles pressed.

Just before this we played what became a bit of an infamous gig at the Bolingbroke Hall in South Shields and lucky for us Phil Sutcliffe from the music paper *Sounds* was there. We were getting reported on for always having fights at our gigs so Phil decided to find out what we were about. At the time our gigs were quite theatrical. When we came on stage it would be all black and then we'd get blue police lights flashing on either side of the stage and then get a police siren blaring out of the PA. So when we walked on the crowd were a bit whipped up. Then we'd go into "Police Oppression" as the first song, so it was mad from the start. At the Bolinbroke gig we introduced the pig's head, which we put a police helmet on. We used to go to the butchers and get a pigs head. Then when we played "Who killed Liddle" our roadie used to come on with a fireman's axe and chop the pigs head up. To be honest he relished it a bit too much and more than once he chopped through a guitar lead. It was a bit too gory for me. Anyway, this all hit the newspapers and, to be honest, it really got us moving. Phil Sutcliffe had never seen such a thing in the North East, so he got us a centre page spread in *Sounds*. This was unheard of for a band who didn't have a record deal and had never played in London. So our rise all came through the music press.

IF: Where did the sentiments for "Police Oppression" and "Liddle Towers". come from?

Mond: We had always been against the police. Liddle Towers was very close to our hearts. Me and Mensi had had fights with the police all our lives. We would get chased by the police as kids. Then when we got motorbikes we'd get stopped by the police so we didn't like them. I remember being here in South Shields, about 20 of us out for a drink on a Friday night and we were causing no problems but the police were looking for trouble and it all kicked off and we got battered with truncheons. When we wrote "Liddle Towers" that got us notoriety with the police. From then on me and Mensi would even get followed. Mensi felt very strongly about Liddle Towers. How you can get arrested for drunk and disorderly and then end up dead the next morning at the hands of the police? The inquest called it justifiable homicide. So, he was murdered by the police but it was justified. Mensi wrote the song and considering how young we were, it was a really powerful and really fantastic song.

Garry Bushell[2] from *Sounds* took an interest and we started getting gigs in London at places like the Nashville Rooms and the Marquee. Bushell loved Mensi and loved us as a band.

IF: How did you get signed by a major record label?

Mond: Well, there was a guy from London who went to see Sham 69[3] and after the gig he had our single and he gave it to Jimmy Pursey, who was just forming a record label. From that he signed us. He loved us, he loved the lyrics. Jimmy's label was a subsidiary of Polydor and they gave us a £25K advance to do an album. Unfortunately, we were sacked by Polydor pretty soon after recording the album. What happened was that we were down at the Polydor offices and Jimmy was upstairs talking about releasing the album and we were outside acting like daft kids having a snowball fight. Anyway, the security guard took a dislike to us and started bawling us out and before you knew it, he and Mensi were rolling about in the snow having a scrap. Mensi could certainly handle himself. When the Polydor bosses heard the commotion and looked out the window, they decided it was time to part company. So we walked away with the £25K, a recorded album and walked into a deal with WEA (Warner Brothers) and another £25K advance. It was a win-win for us.

IF: From there you went on *Top of the Pops*. What was that like?

Mond: It was pretty horrible to be honest. It was cold and sterile in the TV studio and the audience were herded about like cattle. The guy before us was Joe Jackson with "Is She Really

Going Out With Him?". He was full of the flu and he kept mucking the song up and had to keep starting it again, maybe 10 or 11 times. We knew Joe from drinking in the same pub in London, in Wood Green where we lived at the time, so we were mates and we felt bad for him.

IF: How did it feel to have such a meteoric rise?

Mond: We were flying high then. It all happened so fast and we moved down to London quite quickly. We were meeting all sorts of people. We used to drink in a pub called the Ship off Wardour Street in London, right next to the Marquee. Our best mates were Stiff Little Fingers and them and the Starjets would do backing vocals on our recordings. They were fantastic singers. In the Ship we'd be meeting Lemmy, Phil Lynott and Pete Townsend. We'd meet up with the likes of Steve Jones and John Lydon from the Sex Pistols. All of these people were our heroes, so it was like we were in a dream.

Me and Mensi thought from the start, this is punk and we'll get two or three years out of it at best. So we enjoyed it for what it was, an amazing ride. For us punk was just a bunch of council estate kids having a daft laugh. Another milestone for us was touring all round America. We did two tours of America from Texas to New York, often headlining. We even played the Whisky a Go Go[4] where everyone had played, and we sold it out.

The audiences in the US were totally different to those in the UK. In the UK it was all working-class kids, sometimes looking for trouble. In the US punk was more of a fashion statement so often the audience looked like models. They would come to see us because we were punk and that was trendy, not because they knew us or were necessarily fans. They were like weekend punks. They loved us because we were in a band and especially because we had English accents. Our bass player didn't come back after the first tour he loved it so much. The gigs were generally fantastic and often sold out.

Amazingly our record company asked us if we wanted to record an album at Abbey Road Studios. We thought of course we do. We recorded the *Two Million Voices* album in Studio Two in Abbey Road, the same one that the Beatles used. A big regret of mine is we have no photos of us in Abbey Road but you don't stop to think. There was a restaurant downstairs and we thought it was all free food and drink. So we brought in our mates Stiff Little Fingers to do backing vocals and every day Jim Reilly, their drummer, would have a steak and ask to have one wrapped up to take home for his dog. His dog must have thought it was Christmas. We would have all our mates in all the time. Then our manager, Tony Gordon, got the bill for the studio time and for the food and drink. He said to us 'How can four people eat and drink that much in a month?' We didn't tell him about Jim's dog. We thought it was all included.

IF: Why did you move from Warners to EMI?

Mond: The first album did well but the second one, *We Gotta Get Out Of This Place* wasn't so good so we were dropped. We were just lucky to be picked up by EMI who we did three albums with. *We Gotta Get Out Of This Place* was quite weak, there were a lot of bum songs on it. We were falling apart a little bit at that time. Moving to EMI worked well for us and our first album for them had a much better vibe to it and was a stronger album. We were all a lot happier and we were on a good label. The songs were stronger. We then put out a live album on EMI, which was recorded at the City of London Poly, and that was our highest charting album getting to number 27, which meant big sales in those days. We hired the Rolling Stones mobile to record it. I was producing and mixing albums by then.

Our last album for EMI was *Still From The Heart* and that was a bit of a mistake. EMI had suggested a new novice producer called Steve Levine. He was sort of a soul producer and me and Mensi actually loved soul music so we said 'ok'. Steve came into the studio with a Linn drum machine. We had Decca in the band and we were a punk band so why would we need a drum machine? How he persuaded us to use that I just can't understand but he did. People think there are some good songs on that album but I'm not sure. Our manager, Tony Gordon, had just signed up another band, Culture Club, and asked Steve Levine if he wanted to produce them. So he said yes, produced "Do You Really Want To Hurt Me" and the rest is history. He practised on the Angelic Upstarts to get him ready to produce Culture Club, for which he won a BRIT award as Best Producer of the year.

IF: You were a very political band. At the time there was a problem with right-wing skinheads at gigs. Did that affect you?

Mond: We had more problems than most. We used to do things like Rock Against Racism gigs and left-wing anti-fascist stuff. It got us a lot of bother. I remember a gig in Wolverhampton where 17 people were taken to hospital, seven were stabbed including our manager. The National Front[5] were in the audience and from the first number there were glasses being chucked from the audience. We knew something was up and it was the National Front having a go at us because we were socialists.

IF: Were you frightened onstage?

Mond: We weren't frightened of anything. There were fights at every gig. Half the time we'd jump in and get stuck in or try to break them up, especially Mensi. He loved fighting and he could handle himself. He was a crackerjack. It only got scary at the Wolverhampton gig because there were that many glasses coming at us that we had to go back to the dressing room and barricade ourselves in. And they were trying to boot the door in. We thought we'd be okay until the police came but they didn't come. So our manager, who was a nutcase, said 'Right, we'll attack them and I'll lead the charge'. We said 'Aye, alright'. So he ran up the stairs, proceeded to get stabbed and then slid back down the stairs like something from a cartoon. So we grabbed him back in the dressing room and locked the door again. When the police finally arrived it was the first time I'd ever been happy to see them.

For us, if we had skinheads in the audience there was trouble, if we had punks in the audience it was fine. Eventually we had to come off the road and stop touring because there was just too much fighting. It was toxic. Every single time there were fights we'd have to stop playing and try and stop the fighting. It was very depressing because as a band we just wanted to gig.

IF: At what point did you leave the band?

Mond: It was 1983 and we'd left EMI and we did one album with Anagram called *Reason Why?* and it had some of the best songs we'd ever written like "Solidarity" about the trade union movement in Poland and "Woman in Disguise" about Margaret Thatcher. Mensi's lyrics were out of this world so I had to match that up with great music. "Solidarity" was the best song we ever wrote but it actually got us banned from playing a gig in Poland. We had Paul Thompson, who is from Jarrow, from Roxy Music drumming on some of the tracks. He was an unbelievable drummer and made us all up our game. Terry Slesser from Back Street Crawler did some singing on it and it was the first album I had fully produced. Unfortunately, after we left EMI we couldn't get an advance to record the album so we had to pay for it ourselves as Anagram were just a small label. We ended up having no money to live on whereas we'd previously lived on advances and gig revenue. With the money drying up I felt that maybe it was time to go out on a high. I was starting to get asked to produce albums and I produced the first New Model Army album. So that was me out of the Upstarts. There was no conscious decision, but I moved back up to the North East and ended up managing Brian Johnson's (singer of AC/DC) Lynx Studio.

All the bands up in the North East wanted to work with me but, to be honest, it just wasn't the same. Sometimes the bands would come in with rubbish gear and say to me, 'We want to sound like AC/DC.' And I'd think *well that's going to be tough considering you've bought your drums at Woolworths*. I'd compare it to when we were in Abbey Road working on our own stuff and me and Decca never wanted to go home, we'd even sleep there. So recording other people's stuff which you thought was s*** was not great. I mean there were many bands I recorded like Prefab Sprout and the Kane Gang who were just fabulous, so I don't want to be too down on it. There was one band who came in and will remain nameless who asked me to record a backward hoover sound. So I miked up the hoover and then turned the tape round. It took me hours. So we listened to it and they said 'What do you think then' and I said 'It sounds like a f****** backward hoover.' And they said 'In a good way or a bad way?' I said 'Well, to be honest, I wouldn't bother with it.' So, people would waste a lot of time.

IF: Did you ever get asked to go back with the Upstarts?

Mond: Yes, constantly. Mensi would ask me every year. But I just have no interest. I put the guitar down in 1984 when I left and I have barely picked it up since. I wouldn't know how to play the songs. I did the studio work for a couple of years but after that I just didn't really like playing anymore. When I was in the band I had a guitar next to the bed and I'd get ideas in the middle of the night and pick the guitar up and work stuff out and I had a cassette recorder to record the stuff. Mensi was doing the same and would come into my bedroom in the morning and throw sheets of words at me saying 'There's another one Mond.' He was brilliant, he would come up with really meaningful songs with such ease.

IF: Do you have any regrets?

Mond: Other than not taking a camera into Abbey Road studios I don't have any at all. I just lost the passion for it all. The people who are still doing it now are loving it but I feel that was then and it was f****** great but I have no desire to do it anymore. I don't miss it at all. I still get emails telling me things like, 'Mond, your songs were the sound of my youth and they meant so much to me' and it brings a tear to my eye. And I think maybe I did some good or maybe made just a little bit of a difference.

●●●●●●●●●●●●●●●●●

I tell Mond that his attitude contrasts with most of the other people I have interviewed who have mainly continued with music in one way or another. Whereas for him it was a brief, wild and exciting time in his life. When it ended the music ended. Mond responds with a shrug, pulls up the collar on his coat and he's off out into the cold streets of South Shields, getting on with his life. Mond is a man who takes life in his stride.

1. Liddle Towers was an ex-boxer who was arrested by the police in County Durham in January 1976 outside a night club. He claimed he had been beaten up by the police and the following month died in hospital. The original inquest found his death to be 'justifiable homicide'. On appeal this verdict was later changed to 'death by misadventure'.

2. Garry Bushell is a music journalist who, in the late '70s, early '80s wrote for the music weekly *Sounds* and was credited with popularising the punk genre of Oi! also known as street punk.

3. Sham 69 are a punk rock band who began in 1975 and are led by the charismatic front man Jimmy Pursey. They had top 20 hits with singles such as "If the Kids are United", "Hurry up Harry" and "Hersham Boys" in the late 1970s. They became linked with the Oi! movement and suffered like the Upstarts with a right-wing skinhead following despite Pursey's staunch left-wing politics.

4. The Whisky A Go Go is a famous music venue on the Sunset Strip in Hollywood, California. It has hosted just about every major rock band in history from the Doors to Led Zeppelin and Fleetwood Mac to Guns N'Roses. The Angelic Upstarts played there in June 1982.

5. The National Front is a far-right fascist political movement in the UK. In the 1970s it was associated with the skinhead movement (although many skinheads were, in fact, staunchly anti-racist) and was at the centre of much politically motivated violence.

The Carpettes

Neil Thompson's Story

The Carpettes, from Houghton-le-Spring, near Sunderland, existed from 1977 to 1981 (with further reunion tours in 1996 and onwards). They released two albums for Warner Brothers on their Beggars Banquet label and appeared on the *Old Grey Whistle Test* in 1980. It could be argued that they were one of four North East Punk bands that got national exposure along with Penetration, the Angelic Upstarts and Punishment of Luxury. Neil Thompson was the band's guitarist (although he sees himself as a drummer first and foremost) and one their two singers, and one of their two songwriters. Their style of music covers urgent and raw punk, through reggae and a solid power pop style (although this description later raises Neil's ire when I mention it). I meet Neil in his Houghton-le-Spring home and am invited into his front room which has three walls with shelves from floor to ceiling, completely full of vinyl and CDs which Neil says is 'mainly Rock and Roll'. I should have asked him how many records and CDs he had, I have a feeling he'd know. As we chat, he refers to various notebooks in which he has listed every gig he played, every set list and every venue. Add to this an encyclopaedic memory and you have someone whose passion for music reaches obsessive heights. Neil makes me a cup of coffee and then it's none stop musical memories.

IF: How did you get into music as a kid? What did you listen to?

Neil Thompson: I've loved music as long as I can remember. My dad had records, my mam had records, my older brother had records. I got my first record at the age of two which was "Baby Sittin' Boogie" by Buzz Clifford. I had 15 records before my fifth birthday. By the end of the sixties I probably had 150-200 singles. I was always just mad about records and music. I was like other kids in that I liked racing cars and football but 95% of my time was spent on music. My Grandad had a shop in South Hetton which sold records, so we got loads of free 78s and 45s from him.

IF: How did you pick up an instrument?

Neil Thompson: I was no good at music at school, until much later on and we had no instruments in the class. As a kid I was a drummer. In fact I still class myself as a drummer. I had a little Chad Valley drum kit when I was four. Then I got a Ringo Starr snare drum with a cymbal when I was six. I got a little drum kit in 1971.

IF: How did you get into a band?

Neil Thompson: I auditioned for a club band as a drummer in 73/74. They were doing Wishbone Ash songs but I was just a kid. I was good but I was just too young. I didn't get in that band but I started a band called Brown Sugar. I did my first gig playing drums in November 1974 with George (Maddison, later bassist and singer from the Carpettes) on guitar. We played Rolling Stones, Chuck Berry and standard rock and roll. We played Newbottle Church Hall and for some reason we were attacked and had to be locked in the back room by the vicar. Quite a foretaste of what was to come. We were all still at school and after that did a gig about every six months.

Then I started playing guitar and started another band called

Eclipse. This was about March 1977 and we played places like the Royalty in Sunderland. Around this time George saw me play in Hetton and asked me to join his band. He was putting a punk band together.

IF: Were you listening to punk then?

Neil Thompson: Oh yes, I read about it. I got the Ramones album December 1976. We would get *NME*, *Sounds* and *Melody Maker* every week so I read about punk before I heard it. I read about the Pistols in April '76.

I used to see bands all over. I saw Led Zeppelin in 1971 in Sunderland, which was my first gig. But by around 1975 music seemed to get a bit boring. Dr Feelgood were the only band that was kicking against what was an overblown music scene. I felt we needed punk. I was in the White Lion Pub in Houghton and I hadn't seen George for a few months. The first thing he said was, 'Have you got the Ramones album?' which I had. His second question was 'Do you want to join a punk band' to which I said, 'Yes.' When we started we did half punk and half rockabilly like Gene Vincent, as we all loved fifties rock and roll. I said I'd get my drums out but George said, 'No, you're on guitar'. George realised that we needed to choose between the two styles and so we chose punk. We started doing gigs, half originals and half covers. But two or three gigs in the covers were dropped as we were writing pretty quickly. (Neil consults his notebook and confirms that they did eight of their own songs in their first gig).

IF: How did you get gigs?

Neil Thompson: It was very, very difficult. Our first gig was in a hall of residence for students. George was a student at Newcastle University. That was a great gig. The second gig was at the Lonsdale in Jesmond with a band called Moonlight Drive. After that it was really tough, we just couldn't get gigs. We didn't know what to do but we saw an advert in *Sounds* from the shop Small Wonder in London, who had also started an independent record label. They wanted bands to record for them. So we replied. Luckily we'd done a demo in Impulse Studio in Wallsend. So, we sent it down and they loved it. We went down London, after only two gigs, and recorded a 4-track EP for Small Wonder. We returned North with still no plan and no clue what to do. We got a manager called Rick who got us various gigs including supporting Penetration at Newcastle University.

IF: Was there a punk scene developing?

Neil Thompson: No. not really. When we played with Penetration, we were terrible. We were just too inexperienced, we weren't ready. We got a terrible slagging from local journalists, especially Phil Sutcliffe. Then we did a couple of gigs with Punishment of Luxury, who just blew me away. They were just fantastic. However, there wasn't really a punk scene, punk hadn't really taken off in the North East by 1977.

We weren't pushed by Small Wonder although they sent the single to John Peel who played it and liked it. But gigs in the North East were so scarce, so we sacked Rick. There was just no circuit. We would approach pubs but there were no punks about to create an audience, no one was interested. To us there was no scene and we never got paid for these gigs. We were the first punk band to play the Old 29 in Sunderland in 1978 and there were no punks there. It was all just hairies. The big bands, like the Clash, would play the Poly or the University and you couldn't get in unless you were a student, so there was nowhere for punk fans to see punk bands. It was a bit disheartening.

The next step for us was to do another single. This was March 1978. Then we did our first London gig supporting the Leyton Buzzards[1]. The single was called "Small Wonder", in honour of the label. We came back and tried to keep gigging, with people like the Vibrators. We played the Rock Garden in Middlesbrough with Penetration and by that time we had developed into a decent band and this time we went down great. But really little was happening so we moved down to London in October 1978.

IF: At age 19/20 that is a massive thing to do on your own.

Was it not daunting?

Neil Thompson: There was a chap called Colin Faver who worked at Small Wonder and he booked gigs. So we went down on a half promise of getting gigs through Colin. My mam was worried sick but I don't regret it one bit. I've lived half my life down in London. Our drummer, Kevin, quickly got homesick and came back home. Just prior to this we did a John Peel session and the engineer, Bob Sargeant, was from the North East and he loved us. Bob said if we came down he'd try and get us a deal with RCA.

IF: So, at the time did you think this is going to be my career?

Neil Thompson: I always knew it would be my career. The thing was, if you want to make it, you had to go down to London, as there was nothing happening in the North East. So we moved to Clapton in a grotty bedsit. Pete Stennett, who ran Small Wonder, helped us find the drummer. We put an advert in the *Melody Maker* and Pete had a phone. We ended up with Tim Wilder, who drummed up North with the Young Bucks. We started doing a few gigs and did another Peel session. I'd get all the gigs just by phoning up venues. We used to buy all the music weeklies and just to see who was putting on gigs. We had two singles out, had done two Peel Sessions but initially that seemed to count for nothing. We started from scratch but slowly built it up and got a following.

George then went to see Mike Stone, who was working behind the counter at one of the Beggar's Banquet record shops and gave him a tape and he took it to his bosses at Beggars Banquet (the record label) and they loved it. Beggar's Banquet let us use a PA they had and let us use their employee, Plug, to roadie for us. Gary Numan[2], who was on Beggars Banquet, became a good friend and came to every gig. He loved us. At that time Beggar's Banquet were owned by Warners Brother. We were half promised a deal but then they said, 'It's off, we've got no money' which meant we then couldn't use the PA etc. Within a couple of weeks though, Gary Numan had a hit with "Are

Friend's Electric" and all of a sudden they had money and offered us a five-year deal. It was all down to Gary Numan that we got the deal. They got us straight into the studio to do the album. Bob Sargeant was the obvious choice to produce us. We recorded it at Camden Sound Suite in two weeks. At the time we were on the dole, but when we said we were in a band we had to sign off and I got a job, which restricted the time in the studio.

IF: At that point did you think you'd made it?

Neil Thompson: Not really. We didn't get that much support from the record company. It was all down to Warner Brothers, Beggar's Banquet didn't have much of a say. The idea was to release a single to get the name known and then hype the next one to get it into the charts. It worked with the Pretenders, it worked with Gary Numan. So, with us they released the first single "I Don't Mind it" to get the name out and then really hyped the next one "Johnny Won't Hurt You" but for us it just didn't happen. "Johnny Won't Hurt You" got to 123 in the charts, I didn't know they went back that far. The next week it went up 6 places to 117. Third week it went out the charts. We didn't realise at the time, but we now think Warners lost interest that quickly.

IF: How did you get on the *Old Grey Whistle Test?*

Neil Thompson: We got seen by lady on the production team at a London gig. We did the *Whistle Test* the week we released the single but for some reason it just didn't help sales. The album got good reviews in the *NME*, and Robbi Millar from *Sounds* gave us a great review. We should have toured the album but we didn't. Instead we got a residency at the Marquee club with the Lurkers[3]. The main problem was that both Beggars and Warners didn't really like punk. When we signed the deal and were going to the pub to celebrate Nick (Austin) from Beggars said, 'Right Neil, you've now signed for us so you do exactly what we tell you. When you get as big as Santana you can do what you want'. This stopped me in my tracks. It kind of took the wind out of my sails. For some bizarre reason they tried to get us on a tour with Wishbone Ash[4].

In the Summer of 1980, we moved on to the second album. We did our one and only tour with the Inmates[5], which was fantastic. In the meantime we were going to Italy a lot. As Warners in England lost interest, Warners in Italy got interested. We recorded a third single in Virgin's studio and it was brilliant, the sound was great and we were on fire. We asked to do the album there but Warners said they could afford it.

IF: If you had a good manager pushing you would that have made a difference?

Neil Thompson: I don't think so because if a manager had gone into the Warners office they would have got the same answer I had got. At the time I was sort of the manager.

We recorded this album with Colin Thurston who later went on to do Duran Duran. We did this one in a studio in Chipping Norton. It was pushed by the record label even less that the first album. I don't think it was even advertised in the music press. Again it got a 4-star review in *Sounds* from Robbi Millar. We then did a full tour of Italy that went really well. We got back to London and did a final single called "The Last Lone Ranger" but it was not released. Then, in December 1980, we got a letter from Beggars Banquet saying they were going to stop paying us but that we were very welcome to stay with the label, which was absolute rubbish. We had had only 18 months on the label. We were so annoyed that our drummer, Tim, immediately moved back to Oxford. We didn't even contact Beggars and just took it that we were dropped. The real problem was that Warners simply weren't interested in us. Pretenders and Gary Numan were having hits and they just didn't need us.

We decided to get a new drummer and got Simon from the Merton Parkas[6]. But he then left after three gigs to join Mood Six, a psychedelic band on EMI. We still had five gigs lined up and Tim came down to finish it off. I put an ad in *Sounds* that our gig in Hammersmith in 1981 would be our last gig and it was rammed. The sad thing was the last few gigs with Tim were just fantastic and we were on fire.

Small Wonder later released a compilation which the Carpettes were on and then our albums were re-released in 1996. We were then invited on to the first Rebellion festival[7] in Blackpool and then the next one in Morecambe. We then got gigs in Germany and then, bizarrely, in Japan. We did a further album but to be honest I'm not too keen on it, it doesn't sound good. By November 2003 I had had enough. I was losing money by touring and I didn't hear from George again for years. I had formed a band called the Only Alternative right after the Carpettes and have played with them on and off right up till now.

IF: Why did you get as far as you did and others didn't?

Neil Thompson: Just desperation. We had to move down to London because nothing was happening up here. We had to start from scratch and work hard when we were in London. So, for us, it was a mixture of hard work and desperation.

•••••••••••••••••

Neil's rather downbeat memories of the late 1970s music scene in the North East contrasts with those of the other protagonists of the punk scene at the time that I have talked to. Where they describe energy and excitement, Neil remembers a rather soul sapping lack of scene and lack of gigs to the extent that he and his pals had to relocate to London to keep it going. Maybe Neil tends towards more negative reflections or maybe he has less nostalgia for a period that was so grey and drab that it spawned both punk and the divisive Margaret Thatcher. Nonetheless, if you go on the band's Facebook page you see photo after photo showing the vibrancy of the Carpettes. More pertinently, if you watch their performance on the *Old Grey Whistle Test* you can see a band that had all the ingredients that led others to fame and riches. Such are the fine lines in life. What is also so apparent is that Neil and George were so young when they went to London to seek fame and fortune and the casual disregard that the record company showed towards their young clients is a depressingly familiar theme that is repeated time and time again in this book.

1. The Leyton Buzzards were a punk band from London who had a minor hit with "Saturday Night Beneath the Plastic Palm Trees" in 1979 released on Small Wonder Records.

2. Gary Numan is an electronic music innovator who had a number one hit in the UK with "Are Friends Electric?" in the UK under the name Tubeway Army in 1979 released by Beggars Banquet. He followed this with a number one in the UK with "Cars" under his own name. "Cars" was also a Top Ten hit in the US. Gary Numan continues to do sell-out concert tours to this day.

3. The Lurkers were a punk band formed in London in 1976. They were the first band to release a record on Beggars Banquet

4. Wishbone Ash are an English heavy rock band who were very successful in the mid-1970s and known for pioneering the dual lead guitar approach to blues rock.

5. The Inmates are a British pub rock band who started in 1977 and had a top 40 hit with the cover version "The Walk" in 1979.

6. The Merton Parkas were a Mod Revival band from the mid-1970s. Their keyboard player Mick Talbot went on to achieve fame in Paul Weller's Style Council

7. The Rebellion Festival is an annual punk rock festival first staged in 1996 and normally held in Blackpool.

Neon

Tim Jones' Story

Normally when writers or reviewers discuss what a band sounds like they will reference other bands as it is easier than trying to describe the nuts and bolts of what they hear. With the Durham Punk band Neon this is actually quite difficult. There may be the merest hint of US bands Devo and Pere Ubu or the angularity of the Gang of Four but really that doesn't hit the mark. They sound different and not the punk we would normally expect to hear. It begs the question, and it's one I feel their main man, Tim Jones, may really wrestle with to this day, what would they have developed into had they not been dealt such a stinking hand by their record company? Would they have gone the intelligent post-punk route of XTC or even Talking Heads or the noise punk of Fugazi or something totally left field? Alas, we will never know but we can talk about it. In fact, that is what I do.

IF: How did you get into music and start playing in bands?

Tim Jones: I grew up in Dundee and, up until the age of 12, I was just into football. But me and my mates used go to see lots of bands at the Caird Hall in Dundee. I then saw a band called Tear Gas in an open-air concert in Dundee. They were the pre-curser to the Sensational Alex Harvey Band. They had Zal Cleminson on guitar but it was before Alex joined. They were playing on the back of a truck. We shouted out "Voodoo Chile" and Zal played it and we were just 'wow'. They blew me off my feet and after their set we went behind the stage and had a chat with them and they were great, giving us cans of coke and stuff. I was hooked. Out went the footy and in came music. I actually learned to play the guitar in the Boys Brigade and was pretty much totally self-taught, which helped later with punk stuff.

Then, when I was 14, my dad got a job in the North East and I found it all a bit difficult. My dad blagged me into the Durham Johnston Grammar School. The education system was different in England and I couldn't get my head round it and it left me a little adrift. I found refuge in bands. The guitar was something that could get me respect as academic challenges had affected me quite badly. So, at 16 I left school, I left home and went to Middlesbrough to join a band with a friend who was a year older than me. There were seven of us living in this house and we were a band called Eyes to the Sky. A year later I moved back to Durham and formed a band called Whippet and we did gigs all over the place. We even did old folks' homes.

IF: What sort of music did these two bands play?

Tim Jones: Well this was before punk and we were influenced by the prog rock scene of the time. This was about 1975/76. We liked bands like Hawkwind, Gong and Steve Hillage and our sound reflected that. However, things changed, strangely enough, with my job working at the local council and the people I met there.

My first job was in the Building Surveyor's Department in Durham and Gary Chaplin, guitarist from Penetration was also there. He said he was in a band and, knowing I was into bands, that I should come down a see them. They practised in St Margaret's Church Hall in Durham. They were just great. You could tell straight away that Pauline Murray, who was their singer, was going to be a star. It got me thinking that something was up. They had a lot of urgency to them.

Paddi (Addison), who was the drummer in the Middlesbrough band that I was in, also worked at County Hall. There were quite a few musicians working there and we all hung out together. One day Paddi brought in either the *NME* or *Sounds* and on the front page there was a big picture of John Lydon and Paddi said: 'There's more to this lad than meets the eye'. And, you know what, he was right. Punk just happened so quickly and it changed lives overnight. So we formed Neon and as Mark (Dunn), our bassist, had seen one of those punk package tours with the Damned in the Durham Students Union we soon found a direction to follow. So we decided we were punks and we got our Dads' old suits on and we entered a battle of the bands thing at Durham University and it went down really well. We started gigging all over the North East in 1976 and 1977. There were just so many places to play. We played something like 300 gigs in three years.

IF: Were you writing your own stuff from the beginning?

Tim Jones: Yes, we only did original stuff. That was always the important thing for me. I made up songs from the age of 14. I think being self-taught I used to find it difficult to play other people's stuff so I was never in club bands and never really bothered with covers.

IF: What was the scene like when you started?

Tim Jones: There was a very vibrant scene, especially in Newcastle and it was centred round a BBC Newcastle radio show called *Bedrock*, which was produced by a gentleman called Dick Godfrey. He used to play local music and that was a great outlet for us. Then you had the likes of Phil Sutcliffe and Ian Penman, who both wrote for national weekly music papers like *Sounds* or *Melody Maker*, and they interviewed bands for *Bedrock*. Then they started a magazine called *Out Now*. I can't over state how important the support of these local writers was. They started reviewing the gigs they saw in Newcastle for the national papers and there was a real buzz about.

Through these reviews, a label in Edinburgh called Sensible Records, who had the Rezillos[1], got interested. Lenny Love, who ran Sensible Records came down to see us play a couple of gigs in Newcastle. He said he wanted to release a single by us and he paid for us to go into Guardian Studios in Pity Me, Durham. So we made a record, an EP called "Bottles" as a bunch of kids. So, as kids, you make a record and you think, hang on, we must be something special and that changes everything. It all happened so fast.

IF: I have listened to Neon's songs on YouTube and with most bands you can hear quite clearly their influences. With Neon it's much more difficult to hear those influences, certainly not the Sex Pistols. It sounds more like US bands like Pere Ubu or Devo. In fact, you actually sound more like modern bands like Squid or Sports Team or Yard Act. If Marc Riley played your stuff today on 6 Music it would not sound out of place. So what influenced your sound and your writing?

Tim Jones: Well thanks for that, and you are correct. Neon was too punk for the metal heads and too metal for the punks. We forged our sound from all sorts of sources, probably because we started before Punk. We listened to a lot of German rock bands like Kraan and Nektar. We were also influenced by early XTC stuff and they weren't playing the three chord stuff that the Sex Pistols were playing. Also, things like Jeff Beck and more jazzy types of stuff. This became more marked when we added a second guitarist in Martin Holder, who was a great guitar player but quite jazzy in his approach.

IF: Were the other bands on the scene helpful, was it competitive?

Tim Jones: It was very supportive and it didn't seem competitive at all. We would play places like the Bridge Hotel in Newcastle and that was such a great place. We always seemed to go down well there. Same with the Cooperage or the Newton Park Hotel or the May Day gigs in the Guildhall in Newcastle. We played Newcastle City Hall with Penetration and Punishment of Luxury. We were really proud of this. We were just a bunch of kids and we were playing the City Hall, it really was a dream. All the colleges would also put on punk gigs.

One time we played a gig with Punishment of Luxury and

they were off straight away to a gig in London and Nev, their guitarist, burst into the dressing room and shouted, 'Has anyone got a spare pair of underpants?' as he didn't have time to go home and get some. It was that sort of camaraderie. We would all watch each other's bands and learn from them.

IF: What were the gigs like?

Tim Jones: It could vary a lot. It could be absolutely fantastic. Some gigs were about coming off covered in sweat and it would be all about the energy. It could be quite electric. But it could also be violent. When we played in the Guildhall in Newcastle with Punishment of Luxury and the Angelic Upstarts it was literally a blood bath. You could see chairs coming off the people's heads. I saw Mark, our bassist, pulling a girl out of the audience covered in blood. We had, for some reason, bikers from Durham following us and the Upstarts fans were like an army from South Shields. So it ended up as a pitched battle between those two factions. It was an absolute riot. The police were outside but they just contained it and allowed the fighting to die out before coming in and making any arrests.

Another time we were playing at Sunderland Poly and some of the crowd tried to turn our van over. We ended up barricaded in our dressing room. You see at that time just the mention of the name punk would arouse passions both ways. Punk was a great time to be part of music but it was also very volatile. There was a lot of violence. We played a gig in the Coach and Eight in Durham and our soundman, Wevans, was knocked out by a pint mug. When played in the Nashville in London I had someone come up to me before we've played a note and poured a full pint of beer over my head while on stage. So I had to play this gig with all my strings sticky and whatnot. So it was great but it was also quite frightening at times.

IF: You had the three-song single "Bottles" out and people liked it. What happened from there?

Tim Jones: We did the single and Lenny, who ran the label, sent the record out all over. He sent it to John Peel and he liked it and played it. That was massive for us. You can't overplay the importance of John Peel at the time. The single got to number eight in the Independent Chart in the *NME* which was quite a big thing in terms of exposure. Martin Rushent heard us on John Peel and liked us. Martin was a big producer at the time and had produced the Stranglers and Buzzcocks and later produced *Dare* for Human League, which was massive. He was a very big name in music at this point. United Artists, one of the major labels, who had signed Punishment of Luxury were also interested in us. However, Martin was forming Genetic Records (part of Radar Records, home of Elvis Costello), which was basically a subsidiary of Warner Brothers and said, 'Come with us, you'd be much better off and get more attention with a smaller label to look after you.' At the time we were rehearsing in crumby old Kibblesworth Church Hall and Martin Rushent came down from London to see us rehearse there of all places! He decided which songs he wanted to produce from those rehearsals. Looking back its quite surreal.

So he took us down to Manor Studios in Oxfordshire. This was costing £1000 a day. Bear in mind I was 18 at the time. It had an actual go-kart track and we were sleeping in four poster beds. It was in beautiful countryside. It was great but all the costs ultimately went to us. We had to pay it all back, ideally through sales. In hindsight it makes you wonder why we did that, why not just stick us back in Guardian studios in Durham? I guess it's because he was a top producer and that's what top producers did. But anyway, we signed up with Radar Records for more than one single but we ended up just doing the one which was "Don't Eat Bricks" (backed by the excellent "Hanging off an O"). It was played on John Peel again and things again looked really good.

IF: If thing were going so well, why did it fall apart?

Tim Jones: Through Rushent we got an agent in Asgard Promotions from London who got us gigs up and down the country. Our PA was dropping to bits as was our van. It began to take its toll and we were getting into so much debt and we realised that we were getting into a hole we couldn't get out of. Phil Sutcliffe, the journalist, actually lent us money to fix the PA because he believed in the band.

I can explain the demise quite easily in retrospect. Record companies can make young bands and young musicians feel very special, like they are your friend. They take you out for meals and there's all this camaraderie but as soon as there's a problem they are no longer your friend. We were 18 or 19 and we were fooled by it all. I went down to see Martin with Paul, our manager, expecting that he could help us fix our various issues. He was at Advision Studios mixing "Are You Receiving Me" by XTC. I remember that quite clearly. So we told him about the problems with the van and the PA and about the impossible itinerary where we were expected to go here, there and everywhere with no money and he said, 'Don't give me your problems.' Effectively, just get on with it, it's nothing to do with me. We came back down to earth with a crash. We realised in that moment that they weren't our friends and that we didn't mean anything to them. It's just a product. If you don't make money then they're just not interested. You have to be very tough to succeed in that world and we were just kids. People are disposable much more than in other industries.

It was very demoralising. We had formed a limited company to manage the debt and thank God we did or we would have really struggled to pay off the debt. We split the debt. And we split the band.

In reality we were led down the garden path by a pipe dream. We were led down the path and dropped from a great height. We were completely disillusioned and that causes harm to young people. We weren't old enough or equipped to deal with it. It has caused damage and that's not the right way to treat young people. I have a son now who is 19 and I look at him and I can't believe that people could be so callous with kids his age.

IF: If you had a more supportive record label how would the sound have developed?

Top: The Alan Price R&B Combo just before being re-named The Animals. Left: John Steel and Eric Burdon at a hop in a church hall in Byker, 1959. Photos courtesy of John Steel. Bottom: The Chosen Few (left to right) Alan Hull, Tommy Jackman, Mick Gallagher, Alan Brown and Rod Hudd.

Top: The Unthanks. Left: Lindisfarne, playing in Sydney (photo courtesy of Ray Laidlaw). Bottom Left: Kathryn Williams. Below: Richard Dawson at the Cumberland Arms, Byker.

Above: The Carpettes outside a carpet shop. Below: White Heat on the Newcastle Quayside, c1979.

Photo credit: Janette Beckman

Photo credit: Rik Walton

Photo credit: Paul Taylor

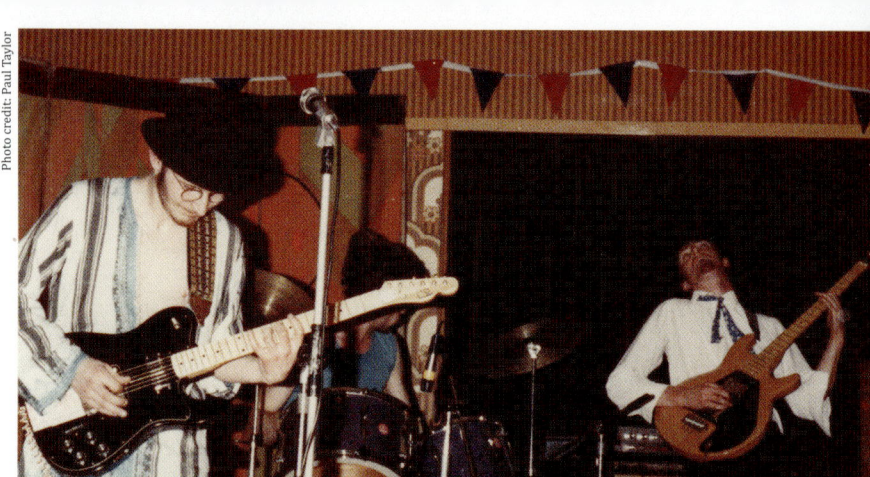

Neon at the Newton Park Hotel in 1978. Below: Pauline Murray and Gary Chaplin of Penetration at Newcastle City Hall in 1978.

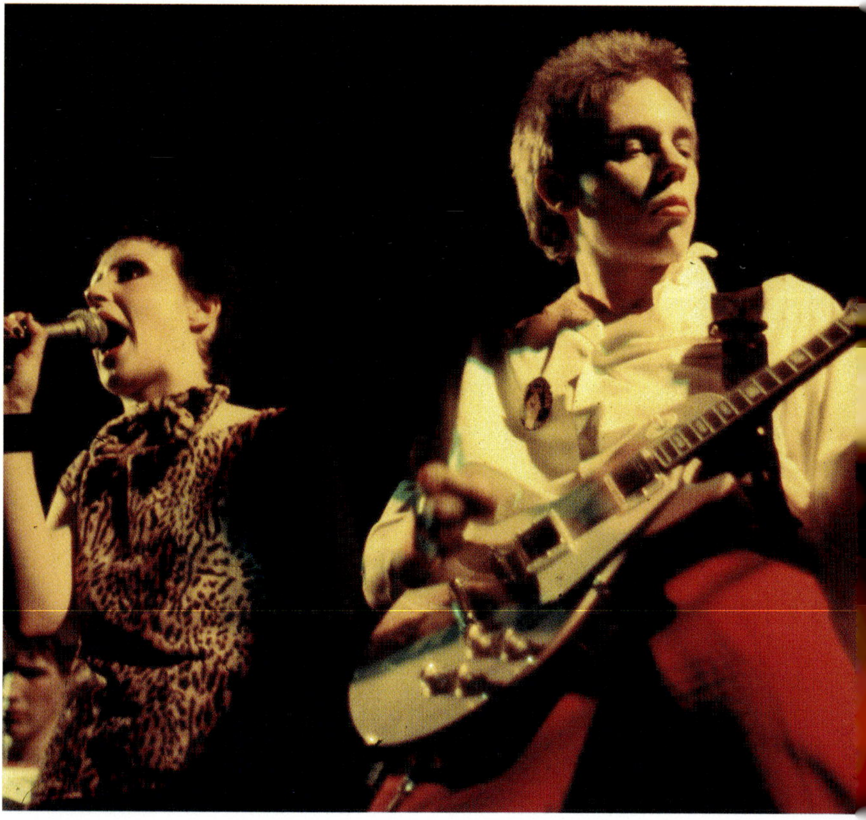

Photo credit: Rik Walton

Angelic Upstarts at the Rex Hotel, Whitley Bay in 1978. Below: Punishment of Luxury. Photos credit: Rik Walton

Photo courtesy of Keith Armstrong

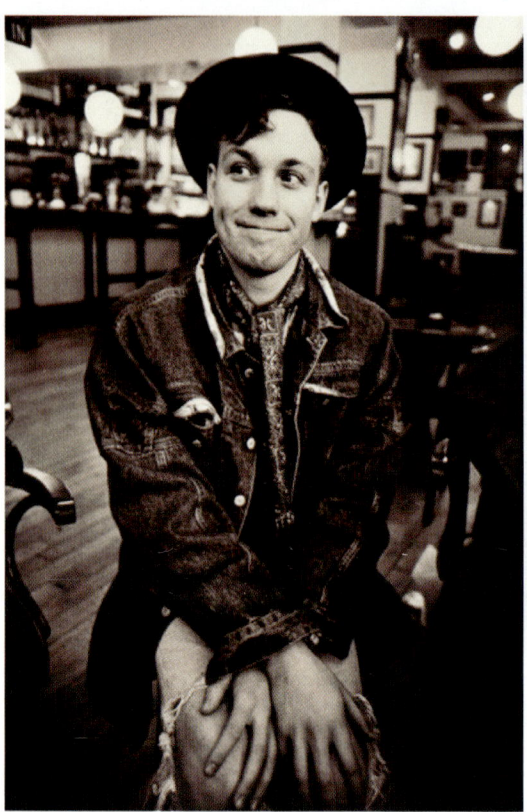

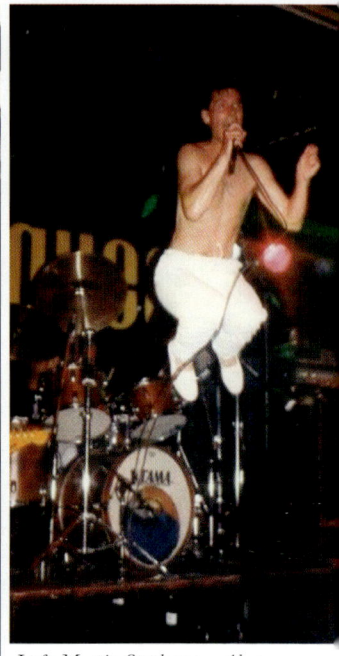

Left: Martin Stephenson. Above: Robert Kane of Showbiz kids at the Marquee, 1979. Below: Tygers of Pan Tang at the Reading Festival in 1980.

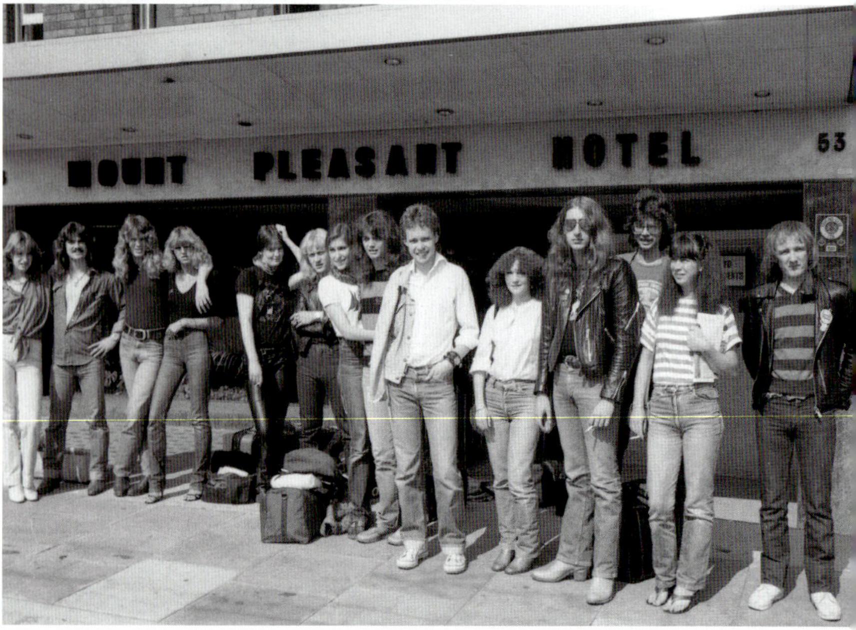

Photo credit: Rik Walton

Hurrah! upstairs at the Handyside Arcade, Newcastle (Photo courtesy of Keith Armstrong).
Below: Raven at Newcastle's Think Tank in March 2023

Photo credit: Ian Winston Coult

A sign of things to come as Field Music's David (left) and Peter Brewis play together on Christmas Day, 199
Below: Frankie & The Heartstrings on the roof of the original Pop Recs, Sunderland.

Tim Jones: If we'd gone with United Artists we would have done more. We recorded an album worth of music and I think with UA we would have got that out and then hopefully really built on what we were doing artistically.

Later on there was a programme on Channel 4 called *Famous for 15 Minutes* by Geoff Wonfor, who started *The Tube*. So I put in for it years later and was successful. It was amazing. They had parties for the show. I was at the London show and I met Annie Roseberry, who I knew as Martin Rushent's secretary but became head of A&R for Island and actually signed U2. She walks in and she sees me and she says 'what are you doing here?' It was like, 'You're history, you're not supposed to be here'. You would meet household names at things like that and they were god awful people.

IF: What did you do after Neon finished?

Tim Jones: I have basically bounced around within music for the rest of my life. I was in a band called Treatment Room and we did OK. We got gigs round Newcastle. Then I joined Punching Holes, which was Brian from Punishment of Luxury's band. We played quite a bit down London and then after I left them I joined Punishment of Luxury and that was the only time I played the old Marquee before it was knocked down. I had to wear a ski hat, a pair of dark glasses and an umbrella hat and I couldn't see a thing.

I started doing my own stuff and eventually got a deal with a company called Prism and they employed me to write songs, which was great. Then I did various records and more live work in a band called Somebody Famous. We played round the North East for three years and we did a CD. Also when the Consett Steel Works shut down a bunch of ex-steel workers got together and opened a studio in the local miners hall to encourage local artists. They employed local musicians to work with local kids and we worked with schools and choirs. It got European funding. That was fantastic.

I then got together with my then partner Terri-B and we

started our own record label called Stone Premonitions. The first band we signed was a space rock band from Sunderland called Mr Quimby's Beard. There was loads of people involved and it was a co-operative. We actually set up a studio in the house. We released over 100 albums. Barry Lamb from Falling A records got interested and he took the catalogue. We provide the music and he will release it. We still do this to this day. It's primarily bands from the North East. I now also do radio shows called the *Reverend Rabbit Show*. It goes through various stations from River Gibbs FM in England as we well as a 'pirate ship' in the Harwich Harbour and stations in the US.

So, as you can see, I have had a pretty varied life in music. Looking back, it's easy to be bitter about music but in many ways it saved my life, it gave me a direction and it's given me so much. It's like a drug you can't give up.

•••••••••••••••••

Tim was a fantastic interviewee who maintains an amazing enthusiasm for all things musical and has sustained a life in music to this day. However, I can't help think that Tim, rightly, feels let down badly throughout his early life, whether it be an unsupportive educational system in the 70s or the uncaring and exploitative experiences he had dealing with the recording industry. The scars remain and are very close to the surface when talking to him. That he has remained involved in music is testament to his abiding love for the medium of music. Neon were short lived and in the history of north east music were a flicker but if you seek out their music on YouTube you will hear fiercely intelligent music that, as I discussed with Tim, would be right on point on various 6 Music shows today. It's a case, more than many others I have talked to, of what might have been. However, although this is a cautionary tale Tim remains amazingly positive. Keep on Rocking, Tim.

1. Rezillos were a punk/new wave band formed in 1976. They had a hit record with their song "Top of the Pops" which got to number 17 in the UK Charts in 1978. They continue to play and release records to this day.

The Toy Dolls

Olga's Story

For many people the Toy Dolls mean only the novelty hit "Nellie the Elephant". In reality this is not even a fraction of their story. They have released 16 albums and continue to tour around the world. I speak to their main man, guitarist and singer Michael 'Olga' Algar via Zoom a few days after three sell-out gigs in Spain. Whisper it, but Olga has just turned 60. I was lucky enough to see him in September 2022 in a triumphant hometown gig in the Hedworth Hall in South Shields and it is not an exaggeration to say that he looked under 30 years old and jumped about the stage like a 20-year-old. The Toy Dolls mix high-velocity punk guitar with fun-filled lyrics and snappy song titles such as "She Goes to Finos" (about a sticky-floored nightclub in Sunderland), "Tommy Kowey's Car" (about Olga's love object getting into the car of local businessman and Sunderland football club owner, Tom Cowie) and "Fisticuffs in Frederick Street". Look on YouTube and you will see videos of the band playing one particular song, "Dougy Giro" in Argentina and Brazil. The fans belt out the words to the song:

You can guess what life for Dougy
is like, he wakes up in the street,
No home, no bed, he says he's lucky,

That he can smile and be happy

Dougy, Dougy, Giro,
Dougy, Dougy, Giro.

There is no way they will know where the word 'Giro' comes from but scream the chorus out anyway (for younger readers a 'Giro' was the a cheque people received weekly when unemployed, which was a very common thing when the song was written in the early 1980s). The contradictions and confusions that this happy scene describe are maybe the secret to Olga's enduring success.

About six months earlier I had popped round to Pete 'Zulu' Robson's house for a very pleasant chat in his garden. Pete was bassist with the Toy Dolls for a couple of short periods. He is a very affable chap and is also known in these parts as a TV Chef and restaurateur. As luck would have it my chat with Pete filled in some blanks found in the call with Olga. Thanks Pete!

IF: How did you get into music?

Olga: I got into music because I was bullied at school. I wanted to find a way out to prove I could do something. Anyway, I was a massive fan of Suzi Quatro so I decided to buy a bass guitar. To do that I started to deliver newspapers to earn the money to buy it. I saw one in Woolworths and it took me about a year to save up. Unfortunately, when I went back to Woolworths the bass I wanted had gone up by about a pound but I couldn't be bothered to do any more of the papers so I bought a guitar instead of the bass. So all my life the bass has been where my heart is because of Suzi Quatro but I taught myself the guitar. I saw Dr Feelgood and Wilko Johnson and that inspired me on the guitar along with the Jam and then all the rest of the punk bands.

IF: How did you move on to a band?

Olga: We started a band at school called Exit. Later that changed into the Straw Dogs. I started pretty much straight away to write songs for this band. Then I met a girl, who sadly died just last year, and she inspired all my early songs like "She goes to Fino's" and "Tommy Kowey's Car". I had the songs written before the Toy Dolls started and I had all the image stuff worked out as well.

Pete Zulu: In July 1976 I went up to my cousins and there was a kid sitting in the kitchen. He was playing a Les Paul copy guitar and a Selmer amp. He played "The Last Time" by the Stones. He played it perfectly all the way through and even got the sound right. It was Olga. His hair was really long and he was shy. This pretty much changed the world for me. I decided to form a band. We called it the Straw Dogs. I was 21 and he was just a kid of 17. He had the ability and I had the attitude and the want. We started rehearsing in a community centre in Ashbrooke. We knew instantly that Olga was a star.

IF: Was it easy for you to write songs at that age (15 or 16)?

Olga: Yes, well most of them are crap though, as they are now. In between a handful of enduring songs you get loads of rejects. I now have a studio in London where I work and I have been trying to do lyrics for the new album I am recording and its really hard work. People say 'you can't force songs out' but that's actually what you have to do or you'll never get them written. You have to prise it out of yourself and now and again you'll get a good one but most of the time they're crap to be honest.

IF: What inspired the comedic lyrics against punk guitars style songs?

Olga: Well, there were plenty of bands already singing about the political side so I intentionally went the other way to write about real people and real situations. We're not comedy as we write about depressing situations but I look at the light-hearted side of it. For me it's nice for to offer an hour and half of escapism on stage.

IF: When did you start playing?

Olga: In those days in the North East of England you had to play in the working men's clubs. It was horrible but it's what you've got to do. We'd mainly do rock and roll cover versions of the likes of Chuck Berry as well as a couple of your own things. Then, slowly, places like the Old 29 in Sunderland and the Bird's Nest in Hartlepool would allow us to play and do a set of our own stuff. This was excellent. It wasn't like the clubs where you had to do two sets with the bingo or a stripper in the middle. That's what it was like in 1975 and 1976.

Pete Zulu: We would play a set of fast rock and roll. We tore places apart. Whether we played in pubs or working men's clubs we wouldn't compromise. This was just before the Toy Dolls when we were called the Straw Dogs.

IF: Which other bands did you rub shoulders with?

Olga: In the working men's clubs it was bands like Geordie and the Showbiz Kids. Later when punk came in it was bands like Red Alert, Red London and the Angelic Upstarts.

IF: When you started the Toy Dolls, what were your ambitions?

Olga: Definitely not to make any money. I just wanted to prove to myself that I could do something after years of being bullied at school. That scarred me, and it's still there now. So it was great for me that people liked the music I was writing rather than having to change my music to suit what was being demanded. We used to play at the Marquee Club in London every month and we were supported by what became Spandau Ballet who changed their direction every month until they hit on the new romantic idea as their vehicle for success. We just wanted to be what we were.

IF: You have a fantastic stage persona. Did this come naturally?

Olga: Yes, but you have to keep working at it. I've just come back from Holland and I put on an usherette's uniform and I hand out sun glasses to the audience. But you can't do that every time, you have to keep it fresh.

Pete Zulu: Really early on Olga used have a table with 30 pairs of kid's sunglasses on, all different colours. He used long leads and he'd get out in the audience. Flip, the bassist, was dead still with an unlit cigarette in his mouth and people would come up and try and light it. Olga would be playing whip off his sunglasses and throw them into the audience and then put another pair on. It was dead gimmicky but it went down great.

IF: How did you put out the first single – "Tommy Kowey's Car/She goes to Fino's"?

Olga: We put it out ourselves because no one else was interested. A gentleman called Ian who owned Harvey's Restaurant in Sunderland stumped up £500 for us to do it. It hardly sold any. We supported a band called The Executives, who later became Dance Class, at the Empire in Sunderland and at the end I was walking round with three copies of the single saying 'Does anyone want a free copy of our single "Tommy Kowey's Car"?' but I got no takers. We only pressed 500 and it's now worth £500 a single on the internet and yet I couldn't give it away.

IF: How did you move from not being able to give away a single to getting on *Top of the Pops* with Nellie the Elephant?

Olga: I already had the idea for the 'Ooooohhhhh' bit but couldn't think of a song to put it on. Then I saw that kids show 'Handful of Songs' and the lady was singing 'Nellie the Elephant' and I thought it 'that's it'. We got a deal with Volume Records in the North East who were brilliant and they released it. They let us do what we wanted. It sold about 3,000. We re-recorded it later and then it took off. It was really just kids who bought it. In fact, it's been pretty detrimental for us in the UK as people saw it as a sell out even though we'd been playing it live for three or four years. We lost our credibility in England but this didn't happen abroad. In England it's like being the Baron Knights or the Worzels whereas abroad we're thought of as a punk band. It's a little frustrating.

IF: What was it like playing *Top of the Pops*?

Olga: We played it a couple of times. It's tiny, there were only about 25 to 30 people in the audience and the play-back was really quiet so when you're jumping about it drowned out the sound of the playback. I was in a bit of a dream world at the time, I was just 19. It happened very quickly and then we were straight off on tour in Germany after that. But really for us touring has always been what it is about.

Pete Zulu: *Top of the Pops* was daft but I remember after we'd done our bit, I put my arm around Olga's shoulder. We had Madonna on one side and Wham on the other side and I said 'well, Olga, you've achieved exactly what you set out to do'. Olga was such a talent and he deserved all this.

IF: How does it feel to be playing all round the world 40 years later?

Olga: I think about this question all the time. We've just done three sold-out shows in Spain in venues that hold 1500 people so not exactly Wembley Arena but everyone is singing along to every song. I think 'how can that happen?' It's absolutely priceless. I'd rather be doing this than anything.

IF: How much do you plan your career?

Olga: All the time. It's planning things for three or four years ahead. The album I'm working on now won't come out till the end of next year. You have to keep updating your routine or people will get bored. You have to be thinking about things all the time. Its quite draining.

IF: Why do you think you appeal to worldwide audiences? When you are in Argentina playing "Dougy Giro" and they cannot know what a giro is yet they are singing along passionately. How does that happen?

Olga: Well, the most important thing when you're writing songs is the melody, as this is international. So you can be in Osaka in Japan with a thousand people singing your songs. Most may be just mouthing the sounds, while some will understand them. So melody is paramount while it's still important to have nice words as well.

IF: Which countries are you most popular in?

Olga: Probably in South America. We play in Chile, Argentina, Brazil, Uruguay where we would typically play in 1,500 to 2,000 capacity venues. It used to be Japan but that's died down a little. It goes well in Europe as well in places like Spain, Germany, Poland and the Czech Republic.

IF: Do you get nervous before you go on stage?

Olga: Yes, all the time. I even get nervous for the support bands. We do lots of gigs with the Exploited. Every time they go on first I get dead nervous for them. Its never gone away. Its probably because of the singing which I hate. I only started singing, because I lost the toss of a coin before a gig. I said I'd do one gig and that was 43 years ago. I love playing the guitar but I'm not keen on singing and, to be honest, I can't sing.

IF: So, when you first sang were you surprised you had a voice?

Olga: No, I just copied from Jilted John and Clare Grogan from Altered Images. I put on that squeaky voice (Olga says 'hello' in a voice that sounds like Norman Wisdom to make the point). After the first gig, there was a second at Seaburn I think. We auditioned other singers but eventually I said, 'Oh, I'll just do it then.' I wasn't keen and I'm still not keen on singing. I'm not keen on three-piece bands to be honest (The Toy Dolls are a three piece!!), I prefer a four piece with a singer out front.

IF: Having seen you recently you have a symmetry with you and the bassist at the front forming a triangle with the drummer, especially with the choreographed Pete Townsend-esque jumps. Does the jumping about play havoc with your knee?

Olga: Yes, it does! I was running all the time as I live near Regent's Park in London and my knees were knackered but I thought it helped the gigs. I went to the doctor's and he said that I've got torn ligaments in the knees. And I said 'Well, I've been jumping up and down on stage for years.' And he said, 'well, exactly'. So, he said get a bike. So I got a bike and now the knees are 99% better. Also, we wear Dr Marten boots and we stuff them with hiking socks to give us a bit more cushioning.

IF: What is the future for you?

Olga: Same old things. I'm busy writing another album and that will probably come out towards the end of next year. I think this year and next year will be mainly festivals. So I am planning two and three years ahead. What makes it difficult is that we had a great, great manager for 35 years (Dave Chumbley, who also acted as Kylie Minogue's agent) and then he unfortunately died about four or years ago. So, I'm like a fish out of water without him.

IF: What inspires a new album?

Olga: Being stuck in a studio doesn't help. I get inspired by meeting people, reading books, going to the theatre and listening to other bands or things like your girlfriend or other people's girlfriends or people you meet.

IF: Looking back, do you have any regrets?

Olga: Not many. In the early days I was eager for success and that led to us signing for EMI and that was not a happy experience. That was the worst thing we ever did because they tried to change everything. They put us in a studio and the producer was saying things like, 'Turn the guitar down, make it cleaner' and he said, 'Change your voice, just sing in a normal voice' and that was the worst period of my life because I was doing exactly what I didn't want to do. So, I regret that. But after that we signed to Volume Records and they just let us do what we wanted. You will never be happy until you are doing what you want to do. If you aren't doing that you will never be creative. Apart from that I enjoy every second of it, oh except waiting around in airports.

IF: Why have you had such enduring success?

Olga: (Laughing) Call this success? Well everything is relative. I remember being interviewed along with a lad from the band The Little Angels about 35 years ago. And we were both asked where would we like to be in 30 years' time. He said, 'I'd like to be playing stadiums' and I said, 'I'd be completely happy if, in 30 years, we are playing in front of the 800 or 900 that we have now when we play'. So, I suppose that is success for me. One secret from us is not leaving it too long between playing in places so we aren't forgotten but also not too often so people get sick of us. I think also the audience knows if you aren't happy and you're not enjoying it. Also, you need to keep things it fresh.

For us it is an advantage that we are never on the telly so people need to got to the gigs. Another is that we are not fashionable so we can't go out of fashion. But to be honest we see people bringing their grandchildren to the gigs, which is ridiculous and probably means I have to admit we have been a little successful.

••••••••••••••••••

Olga is a breath of fresh air. He is humble, self-depreciating and great company. Talking to others for this book you also hear the repeated goodwill towards him. You can't help but be happy for his success and the fact that he is someone who has such a love of life. This doesn't hide his capacity for hard work as well as his acknowledgement that scars from the past are what drive him forward. What is also recognised by many of his peers is that he is a unique talent and, despite his protests, it's not really luck that has sustained his career.

White Heat

Bob Smeaton's Story

Benwell is in the west end of Newcastle and it was first mentioned in the *History of St Cuthbert* in 1050. More recently it has fallen on hard times, in common with many places in the North East. When you look at the Wikipedia page for Benwell it lists a number of famous people associated with the place like Joseph Swan, the inventor of the light bulb, who, although born in Sunderland, opened a factory in Benwell in 1881. Lindisfarne's Alan Hull was born in Benwell. One glaring omission is Bob Smeaton, who is also from Benwell. You may not have heard of Bob, but he is one of the few people from Newcastle who have won a Grammy[1]. In fact, he has won two Grammys as film maker for *The Beatles Anthology* and a subsequent documentary on Jimi Hendrix. He has also made music documentaries on the likes of The Who, Elton John, Roxy Music and the Spice Girls, along with series like *Classic Albums*. In the music documentary world this son of Benwell is at the top of the tree. However, when I catch up with the affable Bob all he wants to talk about is his time as singer of the North East top band at the time, White Heat. It is the classic story of *nearly did, should have but didn't quite succeed*.

IF: How did you get into music?
Bob Smeaton: The first music I heard was my dad's record

collection and he was really into singers, that was his thing. So, it was people like Slim Whitman and singers who told stories like Tom Jones and "The Green, Green Grass of Home". The big revelation for me was when my dad brought an Elvis Presley album back and I thought he looked the best thing ever. He was so handsome and he had a fantastic voice. The first song I got into by Elvis was "Do the Clam" which was one of his worst songs. (Bob then sings me "Do the Clam,"). It was a story song with a great voice.

IF: How did you move into performing?

Bob Smeaton: When I got to 14, 15 all my mates started getting into rock music, Free, Led Zeppelin. Everything was about guitars and everyone wanted one. At the time I had zero money and guitars were an expensive piece of kit. My mates got guitars but I couldn't play them because I was left handed and picking up their right handed guitars felt really alien. I realised that I would never be guitarist but that I could be a singer in a band because all a singer needed was a microphone, which I could buy from Jeavons Music Store in Newcastle for £30. So, I bought a red microphone. The guy who sold it to me, a guy called Colin Rowell who later worked on *The Tube*, told me that microphone would make me sound like Robert Plant. And I believed him!

IF: Did you discover that you had a voice? How did you get the confidence to stand out front?

Bob Smeaton: Well, when I was at school my mates might have been good footballers or good looking or good fighters and I was none of those things. What I could do was make people laugh. One day I got in front of the class and I sang what I think was "Delilah" by Tom Jones (Bob sings me "Delilah"). I suddenly realised that everyone stopped and looked at me and I liked it. To be honest I was never a great singer but I had confidence and I loved performing. So, we got a band together and when I heard myself singing "Jean Genie" by David Bowie through a PA I thought this is it! As I say I wasn't the best singer and I had a problem singing in tune. However, at the time, back in Benwell, there weren't many singers. There were any amount of guitarist, bassists but no singers. So I was in demand even though I wasn't great. I had the confidence and I jumped around but me singing "Stairway to Heaven" or "Highway Star" by Deep Purple was never going to be great. The jumping about and performing could hide the bum notes. I was in a load of bands with names like Wild Honey, Pony and Roadrunner but barely did any gigs. These bands were never going to go anywhere but I met a guy in the Man in the Moon pub in Newcastle called Bryan Younger and he was a mind blowingly good guitarist. He could play anything. We got talking and I said I was a singer so he asked me if I wanted to try out for his band. So, I went down to his house and along with a bass player called Colin Roberts. We played all of Led Zep I, II and III. I was just stunned by Bryan's playing. We formed a band called Hartbreaker, named after the Free album but with slightly different spelling.

We started gigging but we didn't play the working men's clubs, partly because I wasn't a great vocalist so we couldn't play the sort of songs you had to play in the clubs. There was a fledgling pub rock scene in Newcastle at the Bridge Hotel, the Newton Park Hotel and the Gosforth pub. We would be doing Led Zep and Free but we started to write our own stuff and I realised I could sing my songs better than Led Zep songs. There was band called The Scratch Band and they had a residency at the Bridge Hotel and our bassist knew their drummer and we asked if we could support them. They said, 'Yes, if you bring along 20 people with you.' We got all our mates along and it was the best thing ever. So, we asked to play with them again and each time we played we brought more people. Eventually more people wanted to see us than the main band. People were coming along to see Bryan who was great. We had a brilliant drummer called John Miller and Colin was a good bass player and I was the bloke who jumped about.

So, we got a following and we had a residency at the Bridge, then at the Newton Park Hotel and we started to fill the places out. But we were never going to be anything other than a pub band. Then two things happened. Firstly, we became a five piece with a guitarist called Alan Fish, who looked great but, most importantly, was a really good song writer. So, we started writing good songs but with my voice we were never going to make that step up. Then the second thing that happened was punk rock. Suddenly, being a singer was all about attitude and performance rather than being note perfect. We also realised we had to change from blues rock to what was happening. Being 18 or 19 we were the same age as the likes of the Pistols and the Clash. Me and Alan decided to sit down to write songs in the new style but to suit my voice. I couldn't be like Robert Plant but I could be like Elvis Costello (Bob sings me some of Elvis Costello's "Oliver's Army" – it sounds good!). We started writing songs that were faster and shorter. We changed the name to White Heat and we moved into the Graham Parker and Elvis Costello territory. Then we wrote "Nervous Breakdown" and it was the best song we had written by a country mile. We would play that three times in our set it was so good. This led to a record deal with Rubber Records, which was run by Brian Mawson who ran Windows Music in Newcastle. Brian liked what we were doing so he got us into Impulse Studio in Wallsend. We recorded "Nervous Breakdown" and "Sammy Sez" for the B Side. And, as luck would have it, John Peel started playing it and he liked it. Now we were contenders and with that the audience started to grow.

IF: At the time you were an apprentice welder in Swan Hunter's shipyard. Did you begin to imagine leaving that job to follow pop stardom?

Bob Smeaton: That was always the plan. I wasn't a big fan of the shipyards. I spent a lot of time sleeping and I could sneak out to get to Impulse Studio to do some recording. Another big thing was that Mond Cowie from the Angelic Upstarts worked in the same shipyard as me and we would chat about our bands and music and he said, 'That's it, I'm leaving.' And I said, 'What do you mean?' He said, 'We've been signed, the Angelic Upstarts.'

I was nearly in tears, I was so jealous. That turned into a real motivation to get out of the yards and be a rock star. No word of a lie, I thought we were going to be as big as the Rolling Stones.

By then I had become a really good front man and something I haven't mentioned is how much a singer called Robert Coyle (now called Robert Kane, singer of Dr Feelgood) influenced me and showed me what a front man can be. This would have been when I was about 17, pre-punk, and when I was a floor waiter at the Scotswood Social Club. They would have bands on Thursday, Friday, Saturday. The bands were generally rubbish but one night a local band called the Showbiz Kids were playing and it was life changing for me and all down to Rob Coyle the singer. This guy was brilliant and was the first singer I'd seen who you just couldn't take your eyes off. He was like the North East's Mick Jagger. He had his shirt off and had the audience in his hand. I have seen him since and told him, 'Everything you did I copied.' He was in a working men's club and it was like he was in Wembley Arena. So, I owe a lot to Rob.

IF: How did you make the move to being a full-time band?

Bob Smeaton: Well, I said let's get down to London and do some gigs to get seen. Brian Mawson said no we will get the A&R men to come up here. He said, 'You don't want to go down to London and play to 10 people.' By now we were a great live band and could pull the crowds in up in Newcastle and could really get them going. Brian had the record shop and all the music reps would come in and ask what was selling and what was hot and Brian would tell them that White Heat were what was selling and that they were the next big thing. They would go back and tell the A&R men and that resulted in every record label from CBS to EMI coming up to see us. Sometimes we'd have three or four record companies at one gig and we would blow the place apart. Eventually we signed to Virgin Records. It was for five albums but they would have an option after each album depending on sales. To be honest I had no interest in the business side. All I wanted was to be signed to a major record label and get out of the yards. I was the first from White Heat to pack my job in. As soon as it looked like something was happening I was out of the yards.

IF: Working in the shipyards was a good, reliable trade. What did your parents think of you packing in?

Bob Smeaton: My dad wasn't at home a lot so he wasn't interested. My mam, though, would be at the gigs and was my biggest fan. She loved it and would say, 'Eeh our Bobby, you're better than Mick Jagger mind.'

IF: You released an album with Virgin, what was that like?

Bob Smeaton: Well, we signed a publishing deal first and we were desperate to get into the studio before actually signing the record deal. So, we recorded the album and then got signed by Richard Branson at Virgin but this was the biggest mistake we made. The debt from making the album stayed with us at Virgin Publishing after being dropped by Virgin Records. If we'd signed to CBS, for example, and been dropped after one album the debt would have been written off. We were unlucky that Virgin at the time had some difficulty financially and they had a big cull of their bands and we were one of the victims. We actually bought the master tapes before Virgin put it out and we thought we'd put it out via someone else. Unfortunately by then we were damaged goods. The album did well but we realised that time was running out. We still sold out gigs and we were, in fact, supported by the likes of the Tygers of Pan Tang and Raven, even though we were far from being a heavy metal band.

IF: Why did it not take off like you wanted? Your sound certainly fitted in with the likes of Elvis Costello or Joe Jackson who were big at the time.

Bob Smeaton: The bands that make it tended to have really strong management, they all had a record label who 100% believed in them and they all moved to London. I was keen to move to London but the others weren't up for it. I also have to admit I wasn't the best singer and that held us back a bit. Now when I record I am a much better singer. I think we were in too much of a rush. Six months later we were writing better songs that suited my voice better.

IF: How did the band finish?

Bob Smeaton: Well we wanted White Heat to be a Champions League band not a Northern League band and it just wasn't going to happen. So we decided to go out in a blaze of glory. Brian Mawson suggested we did a final gig at the Mayfair. Where we were really lucky was that Geoff Wonfor, who was at Tyne Tees Television, was a massive fan of the band. Geoff suggested we make a documentary about the band finishing to be broadcast on Tyne Tees. So Geoff did that and filmed a gig at the Gulbenkian Theatre in Newcastle and that was shown on telly a week before our final gig at the Mayfair. And everyone thought what a great band, let's go and see them but unfortunately we were splitting up. The last gig was a sell out and it was absolutely bouncing. It was amazing, everyone knew all the words to our songs and for that gig we were the best band in Newcastle even in the UK. If we'd had record labels there they would have thought why are they splitting up?

The next morning I woke up and I had no band. Everything I'd done for the last five years was based around the band. It was 100% my life. When the euphoria of that gig wore off it was like what am I going to do now? I certainly wouldn't be going back into the shipyards. So, I did what the band should have done and that was move to London. Within four weeks I joined another band called Agent Orange, which was basically two of the lads from a band called the Chords who had had a bit of chart success. When they split up Chris Pope, their songwriter, approached me. I joined a band with Chris, who was writing all these great songs and before we'd even done a gig we had an offer from Polydor records. But it dawned on me that I was down in London and this could be a really great band but they weren't my mates like White Heat or Hartbreaker were. So, I turned round to Chris and said, 'Sorry, Chris, I'm leaving the band. I'm going back home.' I realised I wanted to make it but with my mates.

IF: You then went into television. You certainly landed on your feet. How did that happen?

Bob Smeaton: I've been really lucky throughout my life, meeting the right people at the right time. Geoff Wonfor, who very sadly died just last year, was so important for me and my career. He had done the documentary on White Heat. We got really close and he was like a father figure to me.

Geoff set up his own production company called 'Strictly the Business' and he said, 'Come and work for us and maybe do treatments and scripts for pop videos.' I just grabbed this opportunity with both hands and, as I always have done, I grafted really hard to make it work and learn the business. We made a series for Channel Four called *Famous for 15 Minutes*. Geoff was really good, he was getting more and more jobs and then he landed the *Beatles Anthology* and he brought me on board. And from there I just learned on the job. I learned by observing professionals. What I found was that I really liked the editing process. That was like writing songs or telling stories. Effectively, in making these films I realised that you had a limited amount of time to tell a story. Things like the shot composition came with experience and watching the experts but the story telling element seem to come more naturally. My strength was to take all the interviews and elements and put them in an order that told a story. And today this is still my strength. It became second nature to work out how to tell the story. And I learned from great people like the editor Andy Matthew, also unfortunately now passed as well, and, of course, Geoff Wonfor. And, you know, I learned on the job with the *Beatles Anthology*, which took five years of my life. So, I didn't start with some two-bit band and everything from then on has been downhill! Somehow I won a Grammy for the *Beatles Anthology*. Wow, that was lucky. My next job was directing a film on Jimi Hendrix and ... I won a Grammy for that. And I am on stage thinking collecting my Grammy in the US thinking this is a piece of piss. My dream was to play at Maddison Square Gardens as a rock star not as a film maker.

IF: So, when you are trying to strike up a rapport with the Beatles, you don't say to them 'I used to be in a band you know?'

Bob Smeaton: Too right I do. I knew the Beatles hadn't really done this type of extended documentary before and I knew I had to get the information directly from them. And I am a friendly sort of person and I hope there's no bullshit with me. So, early on the likes of the Beatles suss out whether you knew your stuff. So, I could talk to Paul McCartney about why he chose a Hofner bass over a Rickenbaker bass. Most filmmakers hadn't been in bands. So that was an advantage for me. After the Beatles and then Jimi Hendrix I could come up against some really difficult people like, for example, Lou Reed. So, whenever I was interviewing these people within five minutes I'd mention the Grammy for the Beatles, the Grammy for Hendrix and I'd say, 'I was in a band once.' Straight away they think that this guy knows his stuff. Of course, you are not on their level but they know that maybe you know your stuff. Equally important is that, to this day, I give 100% on each job.

IF: How were the Beatles?

Bob Smeaton: Whatever their differences that might be talked about, when they were in the room together it was like three lads from Liverpool. I was the last person to interview Paul, George and Ringo together collectively and when they were together they became the Beatles and there was love in the room.

IF: Do you have any regrets?

Bob Smeaton: Well, I do have one. I was invited to George Harrison's 50th birthday party. Jools Holland's band was there and George sat in and played with them. George and I got on really well and George asked me if I was going to get up and sing. Anyway Jools said to George, 'sing Roll over Beethoven' and George said, 'No, I'm not going to sing that.' And George shouts, 'Bob, you come and sing it.' And I turned it down and Geoff Wonfor sang it instead of me. Why did I do that?

IF: Who was the best person to work with?

Bob Smeaton: Well, the Beatles obviously as they were so generous but outside them I would say Pete Townsend. I love The Who and getting the chance to do the Classic Album film on Who's Next was the chance to work with a hero of mine. So, when I was chatting to him, he was everything I wanted a rock star to be. He was grumpy, he was angry but he was so generous with his time. He doesn't just turn up and chat. He'll ask what are we going to talk about and he'll prepare properly. And Pete said that he loved working with me because he recognised I am also a really hard worker.

In the back of my mind I think *remember Bob you could be back in the yards in Wallsend*. Sometimes you have to pinch yourself to think where you have come from to maybe being sat in Malibu interviewing Ringo Starr. But anything I have achieved has all come from being in a band. Without seeing Rob Coyle in Scotswood Club or meeting Brian Younger or Alan Fish or Geoff Wonfor none of this would have happened. On stage is my natural habitat and comes in to play now when I am on stage introducing a band for a film I may be doing. Sit me in front of Paul McCartney or Elton John and I am on stage again. It's all about that moment and not worrying about anything else and that comes from being in a band.

....

Bob tells me that he has a new album coming out and tells me to check out The Ballad of White Heat video on YouTube and I can tell you, it's great. Having heard his tale I'm sure you will agree that someone needs to update Benwell's Wikipedia page as soon as possible. Equally, go on to YouTube and listen to "Nervous Breakdown" by White Heat and scratch your head and wonder why they didn't make it.

---

1. The Grammys are annual awards presented by the Recording Academy of the United States to recognize "outstanding" achievements in the music industry. They are regarded by many as the most prestigious, significant awards in the music industry worldwide.

The Showbiz Kids

Robert Kane's Story

I am going to meet Robert Kane and I am distracted. On a snowy March day I arrive at the thankfully warm Pop Recs café in Sunderland, Robert's home town. I was introduced to Robert by Linda Valentine, wife of the late Hilton Valentine with whom Robert had sung in the 1990s version of the Animals. Bob Smeaton, of the band White Heat and the *Beatles Anthology* fame, has described Robert as the best front man the North East has ever produced. Bob modelled his act on Robert, when Robert fronted the new wave band the Showbiz Kids in the late 1970s. I became aware of Robert after seeing the highly touted band Well, Well, Well on Channel 4's programme *The Tube* when they were set to be the next big thing. So, my quandary is where do I fit Robert Kane into the strict structure of this book. Where do I fit Robert? is bouncing round my brain when in bounds the dapper 68-year-old singer that I am due to meet. He greets me with a friendly smile and a firm handshake. I get him a black coffee and we are off. We chat for two hours with no distractions. He tells me a tale that is similar to many others but also wildly different. When we finish, I realise it doesn't matter where he fits because his tale is a hell of a good one.

IF: How did you get into music?

Robert Kane: It was pretty much in me right from the start, from as far back as I remember. When I was a kid I got into my mam and dad's Al Jolson[1] records. Al Jolson was my first idol when I was a small boy. That was along with Bing Crosby and Slim Whitman. I was able mimic them quite easily. I didn't realise but I was getting singing lessons from listening. So Slim Whitman taught me how to go from full voice to falsetto quite easily. We also had a Lonnie Donegan record and I absolutely adored him. The music was great but his performances were intense and they would build as the song went along. Again I was getting a lesson in singing by listening. I didn't realise by listening to Lonnie I was listening to Leadbelly songs or Woody Guthrie songs. He was the punk music of the time because anyone could do it.

I got taken to see *The Al Jolson Story* at the local cinema and I was transfixed. This was in about 1961 or 1962. I loved the story of a young kid going from town to town on a train earning his keep through singing. Soon after, the Beatles came along and I thought that's what I wanted do but had no clue how to go about it.

Most people get into bands in their mid-teens with mates from school but I was a bit of a loner and I was very shy so I didn't get into a band until I was 19. I was working in the DHSS in Longbenton and I was talking to a lad who said his mates were looking for a singer. I had only sung in the bedroom but I said, 'I can sing.' And that was it. We were called Mania and we were pretty good. We did our first gig in the Londonderry in Sunderland. This was about 1973. We did some Alice Cooper, New York Dolls, some Led Zeppelin. We soon fell apart but the bass player, Phil, said he knew a few people who wanted to get into a band. He introduced me to Pat McMahon and Bob Kent and that was the beginning of the Showbiz Kids.

IF: What was the plan with the Showbiz Kids?

Robert Kane: Well, we played songs we liked but gradually started introducing originals. We took the name from the Steely

Dan song and it was a bit ironic as we were the opposite of Showbiz kids. We started to get a bit of a buzz as a good live band. I have always been a performer and could get a crowd going. To digress, my Dad lived until he was 96 and only started telling me important things towards the end of his life. He told me that he sang when he was younger, my Auntie Myra was a dancer at the Sunderland Empire, my uncle Tommy was a dancer, my Uncle Amis was a boxer, my Auntie Doreen played the piano. So, I had heritage in entertainment but I never knew this until later in life.

Anyway, the band was starting to get this buzz as a live band. I would do things like step off the stage when we were playing the Lieber and Stoller song "Framed" and stare intensely at audience members and stuff like that got us a reputation round the North East and people loved it. So, we got picked up by well-known local promoter Geoff Docherty[2] who offered to manage us. He saw something in us and our performances. He had loads of contacts in the business and started getting us gigs in London. At this point all we wanted was a record deal so we started developing our song writing. In those days you couldn't succeed from the North East so we would do three weeks of intensive gigging in the working men's clubs to get enough money to spend a week gigging in London. We played many of the famous venues in London like the Marquee and the Hope and Anchor. This was about 1978 and I think you would describe us as New Wave. Geoff Docherty would tell record companies we were like a cross between the Jam and Teardrop Explodes, which wasn't really too accurate but it was what record companies were interested in at the time.

At home we were getting very big and wanted to make a dent down South. I found out that when we sold out the Mecca in Sunderland, the biggest audiences they had had were the Bay City Rollers, Led Zeppelin and us. But we were big fish in a small pond. We were getting better at songwriting but being honest we probably didn't have good enough songs. Olga joined the band

and we released a single with "She Goes to Fino's" on one side and a song written by me and Pat on the other side called "I Don't Want to Discuss That". (Writer note: You can listen to "I Don't Want to Discuss That" on YouTube and it's a cracking power pop song quite close to what the Boomtown Rats were doing at the time). Olga started singing in songs like "Tommy Kowey's Car" and I felt I couldn't sing them so he went off and formed the Toy Dolls. We played a song called "Maybe" on the Tyne Tees programme *Alright Now* while Olga was in the band. Unfortunately, the band just petered out as it just wasn't happening, which was a big shame.

IF: How did you move on to Well, Well, Well?

Robert Kane: Geoff Docherty introduced me to Steve Clifford, who had been in bands with Dave Taggart and Tony McAnaney, who were later in Dance Class. Geoff had also bumped into a guitarist in the Isle of Man called Colin McGuiness. Now Colin looked like a rock star even when he was in a café drinking tea and he still does to this day. Colin came across here and that started Well, Well, Well. We were on the dole but we worked really hard at the song writing. We had a portable studio and recorded the songs to send off. Occasionally, a record company would pay us to record proper demos. We got turned down by every major record company. We got most interest from Warner Brothers, so we invited Warner Brothers to a sold out gig at the Marquee in London. Their UK arm was really keen on us and they invited across a US bigwig. We did a storming gig and we came off and thought that's it we've done it. All the British Warner Brothers staff came in to congratulate us but the US guy said no. We were devastated.

Then Arista records came in and, because they were interested, others made offers. We almost signed with Mickie Most but Arista offered more money and we went with them. Maybe that was a mistake but we'll never know. Mickie had great contacts and was a pop genius.

Anyway, we recorded an album for Arista in 1987, which we

thought was great. We record it at Langer and Winstanley's studio. Madness and Dexy's had recorded there.

However, it turned out that Well, Well, Well were the unluckiest band ever. I came up with the name from the John Lennon song, we thought well that's a good name. While we recording the album Wet, Wet, Wet had their first hit. We hoped they'd be a one hit wonder but unfortunately they turned out to be the biggest band of the next few years. We had all these discussions and meetings with the record label but in the end stuck with name. We were signed on the strength of two songs "A Thousand Years" and "Set me Free". The record company was convinced these would be worldwide songs. For some reason the demos sent to our producer, an American guy, didn't include those two songs and he was adamant he wouldn't record them. He said, 'Keep it for the next album.' Another big mistake. Then I got pneumonia, which put me out of action for six months. The album was finished and we couldn't promote our first single. Then finally for the second single the record company said they would chuck a load of money at the video. They spent something like £35K on it. This was a lot of money in 1987. We decided to do it on an oil rig. So they flew us up there and spent a fortune on things like a helicopter for over-head shots. When the single came out it was the exact week of the Piper Alpha oil rig disaster and so no one played the video at all. That was the kind of luck we had. Obviously, that was a terrible tragedy and our problems were dwarfed by that but we were just so unlucky. It simply wasn't meant to be.

We played a couple of times on *The Tube* and Malcolm Gerrie, *The Tube* producer loved us. We played all those programmes like *Alright Now* and *Get it Together* but it just wasn't meant to be. We were dogged with awful luck. And maybe expectedly we were dropped after one album.

IF: How did you feel at that point?

Robert Kane: Absolutely devastated. I was the oldest in the band at 33 and it felt like it was my one chance to be a pop star and it was gone. I had two small children and I said to my wife, 'I feel like I'm in the middle of a desert and no matter where I look I can't see anything on the horizon.' I felt completely lost. I didn't know what I was going to do. Singing was all I knew. I am useless in the real world, I don't even drive, so I couldn't even get a job even driving a van. I didn't know how I was going to provide for my family as I had no money coming in.

Out of the blue I had a knock on the door and it was a drummer called Dave Dodsworth, known as 'The Dod'. He asked me if I wanted to get a band together to play round a few pubs. And I thought well, it will get me out of the house. That was the beginning of the Alligators, which later morphed into the Animals II and a band that toured round the world. We were basically a rhythm and blues band playing songs by the likes of the Stones, Chuck Berry, Muddy Waters, Little Walter. The Dod knew Hilton Valentine from the Animals and knew he was at a loose end, so he joined the band. We had George Fearon on guitar, Bruce MacDonald on harmonica and Dave Coulson on bass. Hilton was the last to join. We didn't even think about money to begin with as we just wanted to play. Then we started playing the clubs and started making money and getting a reputation as a top live band. We were having a party on stage every night. The audiences loved that. As with past bands, we started introducing some original stuff. There was no ambition beyond enjoying ourselves but Chas Chandler liked us and he got us in the studio.

This went on for four or five years. Then Hilton was approached and asked if he wanted to do a version of the Animals. We discussed it and thought why not? For a while we did the Alligators and the Animals II in tandem and then it became more the Animals as the bookings came in. The line up changed over time and John Steel joined the band. We toured the world. We played Australia, New Zealand, South East Asia, America and all over Europe. It was great. Apparently, Eric Burdon grizzled a little bit about us using the Animals' name but we just got on with it.

After a while and for various reasons I was tiring of being in the Animals II. At about this time we were on the same bill as Dr Feelgood in Sicily. They were looking for a singer and I was looking for new band. When I left the Animals I don't think they were too surprised. The Feelgoods felt that I'd be a good fit and 24 years later I'm still with them playing gigs week in, week out. Anyway, I went down for an audition and we did a few songs and it went well as I'd learnt them. After a few songs one of them said, 'Did you bring a harmonica then?' as Lee Brilleaux[3] used to play that. I said, 'I don't play the harmonica but I can learn.' They said, 'Well can you learn by next week?' So that's what I did, I learned to play harmonica in a week.

IF: Joining Dr Feelgood following on from Lee Brilleaux must be a daunting prospect. Did you get any grief from the fans?

Robert Kane: Well, before Lee died, he told Kevin, the drummer, to keep the band going even without him. So, after a mourning period that's what they did. But when I first joined I got loads of grief because I don't sing like Lee. He was a gruff, growly sort of singer and I'm not. Obviously I did the same sort of phrasing as Lee but bit by bit my own style and tone came in. I had just stepped out of Eric Burdon's shoes so I was used to it. The thing is to retain the spirit but do it your own way. Don't be a copy. We now have a new album out called *Damn Right* and it's the first ever album by Dr Feelgood with 100% original songs.

For me I haven't had a career as such. I've just stumbled from one thing to the next, but it's kept me busy for nearly 50 years.

• • • • • • • • • • • • • • • • • •

As we are leaving, Robert tells me he's off on a ten-date tour of Spain next month with Dr Feelgood. He says the Spanish audiences are very lively. He doesn't get nervous as this is what he is, a singer. At 68 it's probably too late to learn to drive and get a job driving a van. He strikes me as a very contented fellow and with good reason.

1. Al Jolson was US vaudeville star who rose to fame before WW2. A film about his life called *The Al Jolson Story* was made in 1946.

2. Geoff Docherty is a North East music promoter who put on gigs by Led Zeppelin, The Who, David Bowie, Pink Floyd, Rod Stewart and many others. He wrote a book on his experiences called *A Promoter's Tale*.

3. Lee Brilleaux was the charismatic original singer of Rhythm and Blues legends Dr Feelgood. Lee died from cancer in 1994 aged 41.

4. New Wave of British Heavy Metal

Heavy Metal came to prominence in the late 1960s and early 1970s with bands like Black Sabbath, Led Zeppelin, Deep Purple and Judas Priest. It tended toward loud, often distorted guitars, heavy beats, extended guitar solos and powerful (male!) vocals. It sold in its millions. According to Michael Hann, author of the book *Denim and Leather: The Rise and Fall of the New Wave of Heavy Metal,* the second wave of Heavy Metal, NWOBHM, began in 1979 with an article in the music weekly *Sounds* and it ended in 1983 with the release of Def Leppard's album *Pyromania,* with its heavily US, softer oriented sound and that went on to sell over 10 million records in the US alone. If this album pointed the way to success for UK bands, it also meant removing the very Britishness from which they were defined.

In its heyday NWOBHM was a very dispersed scene with bands from the North East prominent along with bands from places as diverse as Sheffield, London and Stourbridge. Although the bands were numerous, there was not necessarily awareness of what was going on round the country so that bands in the North East were not necessarily aware of the likes of Iron Maiden in London or Def Leppard in Sheffield. It meant that while they all sat within the broad definition of Heavy Metal they often had very distinct styles from the Thrash or Black Metal, of Venom to the Athletic Rock of Raven.

The timeline of the scene came soon after punk and the

major record labels saw quickly that the next big thing after punk would be NWOBHM and were all in a rush to hoover up the talent. The record label MCA signed up three North East NWOBHM bands in very quick succession in Fist from South Shields, Tygers of Pan Tang from Wallsend and White Spirit from Hartlepool. That two of the bands were dropped after one album shows perhaps both the record industry's short termism but also their lack of understanding of the genre.

The North East had a distinct twofold advantage. Firstly, there was the existence of a record label in Neat, based in Newcastle, with a studio that could churn out what became era-defining records. Secondly, it boasted a circuit of gigs in working men's clubs, where the bands could learn and hone their craft as well as see the competition up close. Working men's clubs and heavy metal may seem an incongruous pairing but it worked! The audience developed a grass roots knowledge of who was playing where, ensuring that the places were packed out. The competition between the bands that played this circuit was, seemingly, friendly, but competitive nonetheless.

While the North East bands may not have sold records in the numbers that Def Leppard or Iron Maiden did, it is fair to say they had global influence. Venom had genres named after their records, namely Black Metal. Both Venom and Raven helped launch the careers of global megastars like Metallica and Anthrax, by taking them out as support bands on their first tours of the US. Both bands are still namechecked by these and other bands as important to their careers.

However, when meeting these rockers, what is most arresting is their absolute enthusiasm and passion for the music that they make. All bar one of bands I talk to are still playing 40 years later, often touring Europe, the US and Asia and selling out such gigs. They are also releasing albums, which to these ears have vitality, energy and a desire to keep breaking new ground. And they are such great company! It is quite apparent that heavy metal is not tied up with fashion and it will never really be fashionable. That doesn't matter to either the bands or their fans. It is more a case of a life-time devotion to a very particular style of music and a sense of community that never seems to die.

Raven

John Gallagher's Story

Raven came to prominence in 1980 with their first single "Don't Need Your Money". It is a high-energy rock song with powerful, sometimes high-pitched, soaring vocals. They were given the epithet 'Athletic Rock'. Following this they have sustained a career that has led to major label releases and popularity in the UK, the US, Europe and the Far East. It is a career of pronounced highs and lows, but also one that is characterised by an unstinting self-belief that is as strong today as when they started in 1975.

Reading back this chat I had with bassist and vocalist John Gallagher it easy to see where their energy comes from. When I speak to John it appears that he barely takes a breath and its almost exhausting to read. It's now 2023 and John and his brother, guitarist Mark, are about to release their 15th studio album and take it on tour in the UK, Europe and the US. The energy levels aren't reducing. If anything they are on the rise.

IF: How did you get into music?

John Gallagher: I always had a good ear and could figure out what was going on. Music was always interesting to me. I heard Hendrix, Deep Purple, Free, Fleetwood Mac on the radio and I thought this is really cool. However, it really started when we went for a holiday in Spain about 1971 or 1972 and the hotel had entertainment on at night time. They had a band on and there was a guy playing a Fender Strat with a tremolo arm on it. He was doing the whole Hendrix trip, playing the guitar with his teeth and stuff. Mark, my brother, and I were shouting, 'I wanna do that'. Mark got a classical guitar in Spain and we fought over it. When we got back a few months later, Mark and a lad from down the street, Paul Bowden, said, 'We're going to form a band and you are going to play bass.' We formed a band before we could play or even had proper instruments and figured it out from there.

The first band we saw play live was Slade supported by the Sensational Alex Harvey Band. This was another pivotal moment for us. Both bands were tremendous and we got a master class in how to perform. We'd never heard Alex Harvey before and had no interest in him and just wanted to see Slade. But Alex won everyone over. He was a totally charismatic performer. Then Slade came on and, as always, they were amazing. So, right from the start, we studied bands to see what got the audience going. We took it seriously.

IF: Did you start off as a covers band?

John Gallagher: We were writing right from the start, so we always did three or four originals. Our first show was Slatyford Comprehensive in December 1975. Both me and our drummer fell off the stage when the lights went down because we couldn't see the edge. We played some Uriah Heep and some Sweet and "Roll Over Lay Down" by Status Quo. We were called Raven from the get go and that was the start. We then went through drummers like toilet paper until we ended up with Mike Kenworthy, who was older than us. He was a student, and he got us playing in pubs and working men's clubs. He moved on and we got Shaun Taylor in and we really started doing the work.

There was a real rock scene in the social clubs in the North East. You might not think of those clubs like that but there was a real scene and a lot of places to play. Even the likes of Judas Priest would come up and play the working men's clubs. There is a DVD released by Judas Priest called *Metal Works* and it has footage of them playing at Easington Colliery Club. Saxon also played the same clubs.

We had an agent called Ivan Birchall and he would send us round all the clubs. With the exception of Ashington, all the clubs would be south of the Tyne like the Boilermakers in Sunderland or the British Legion Club at South Shields. The last club we ever played like that was Westerhope Comrades with the Tygers of Pan Tang and we got paid off[1]. The place was jumping and the committee weren't happy so they pulled the gig and paid us without performing. But my mam and dad had gone to the same club to see John Miles[2] and he'd been paid off so we thought we'd made if we were in the same company as John Miles.

IF: At what point did you say 'this is the job I'm going to do'?

John Gallagher: We were always deadly serious about it, right from the start. We never had any doubts. We realised that we had something that other people didn't have. We had fire and attitude and we knew that graft paid off. All the bands we played with in the pubs wanted to be the next Eagles. There were bands like Moonlight Drive who were known as 'the Blue Oyster Cult of Lower Benwell' because they had three guitars but they would play soft rock. We were the hooligans and stood out like a sore thumb.

IF: How did you get the deal with Neat Records?

John Gallagher: We played Balmbra's in Newcastle and we now had Rob Hunter playing drums. Tom Noble, who managed the Tygers of Pan Tang, came up to us and said 'would you like to record a single with Neat?' and we said 'let me think about it .... yes'. We recorded the single, "Don't Need Your Money", at Impulse in Wallsend.

IF: You've been known as trailblazers within heavy rock, was it your intention to be so fresh and original from your first single?

John Gallagher: Yes, when we became a three-piece band everything changed and went up a notch. Before that we'd always had two guitarists. Instantly we became more mean and lean and crazy. Mark, my brother, had so much more space to play and blossomed as a guitar player within days. The first article in *Sounds* written by Ian Penman/Ravendale said 'the highs, the lows and the lows and the highs, the needle in the haystack.' Mark had the space and he used it and it was like sparks coming out of the record. We revved everything up and certainly played faster than anyone else, but we had both structure and chaos. Without structure it would be jazz fusion and that was not us. We had pulled from lots of influences but by then we had our own recipe. We took from all the bands we saw from Slade and Alex Harvey to Status Quo, Budgie, Deep Purple, Led Zeppelin. We tried to see everybody and when we did we watched closely. This was our education. We would think *why is this band going down well?* or conversely, *why is this band going down badly?* We would see bands lose their audience when, for example, the guitarist's amp went off and he showed a bad attitude. If he'd put a smile on and laughed it off then the audience would go with them. Once you lose an audience you won't get them back. So we learnt from every band we saw and would take the good and avoid the bad.

IF: The single got great reviews so were you keen to do an album?

John Gallagher: Yes, we moved straight on to the album again on Neat. It was done piecemeal – a day here and then a couple of days there. Some of that was because as the producer, Steve Thompson, said we were just too intense. He said it would have done his head in being stuck in the studio with us for a week. It's weird listening back because you can hear the band growing and developing from song to song. We were developing at such a pace.

IF: Were you doing other jobs to supplement what you were earning from the band?

John Gallagher: Well Mark and Rob were getting five pounds, a couple of lumps of sugar, a mint drop and a shirt button from Neat and I was working as a clerk at the Health and Safety Executive office in town.

IF: How did you move from being a local club band to being a touring band?

John Gallagher: The club gigs ended round about 1981. Tom Noble and Graham Thompson, who by now jointly managed the Tygers of Pan Tang, were really helpful, they would put us up for things like supporting Iron Maiden at the Marquee club in London. Then Ozzy Osbourne got in touch as he'd heard "Don't Need Your Money" on the radio and he wanted us, so we did four shows with the Blizzard of Ozz[3]. Then we did two dates with Whitesnake after Gary Moore had quit the tour. We did a date opening for Motorhead. Basically, we were getting a reputation but also we wouldn't say no. At the time we didn't have a manager so it really happened through word of mouth. We then started headlining a bit ourselves. In 1982 we got offered the Girlschool[4] tour, which was 27 dates up and down the country. We went to Italy and Holland in 1981 and must have gone to Holland about five or six times, then Germany.

Take-off really came when we were contacted by Jon Z (Jon Zazula) from the US[5] and he said: 'I've got the biggest import record store on the Eastern Seaboard of America and I want to bring you over to do some dates and a festival'. He'd heard the records, liked them and was selling them quite well.

IF: Where would Jon Z have found out about you?

John Gallagher: Well *Sounds* and *Kerrang*[6] were really influential in the US and they loved us. We played with Anvil and Riot at the St Georges Theatre in Staten Island to about 3500 people. It was crazy, unbelievable. So next year it was let's do it bigger and better. So we came across the next year to do a headline tour. Jon Z said, 'I've got the biggest band in San Francisco to open for you.' We said, 'Yeah? Who is that? Journey? Y&T? Sammy Hagar?' And he said 'no. its Metallica.' And we got a tape to listen to and we thought is this on at the right speed? It was like Motorhead on 78 rpm. But we also thought yeah, these guys will be fine. We did about 26 or 27 dates with Metallica as support.

IF: What were Metallica like?

John Gallagher: They were just crazy kids. The only one with his head screwed on his shoulders was Cliff Burton, he had an old head on young shoulders. It's funny to look back because in 2021 we were recording at our drummer, Mike Heller's studio in the US and we went up to Metallica HQ and sat down with James Hetfield (guitarist and vocalist of Metallica) for an hour and talked about that tour. We said to James, 'You seemed to be drunk all the time on that tour, do you remember anything?' He said, 'I hardly remember anything from those days but I remember everything about that tour because that was the start and we learned everything from you guys.'

IF: You were called 'Athletic Rock' what did you think about that?

John Gallagher: That was Dave Wood from Neat's idea and he put it on the first single. We thought as long as you spell our name right you can call us anything you want. We were wearing running togs and we were jumping around so maybe it fit.

IF: How did you move on to your major label deal with Atlantic?

John Gallagher: We developed a rather contentious relationship with Neat. We were saying, 'When are we going to do something?' as nothing was happening. After our third album with Neat, *All for One* and then the 'Kill 'em All For One' tour with Metallica, we thought, right in 1984 we're going back over to the States and we will tour until we get a major agency and major record deal and that's what we did. But we had to get away from Neat. Problem was we stored all our equipment at Neat. So we found somewhere else to store the gear, got a truck and said, 'We've got a gig at the weekend.' We distracted the secretary and took all our photos and stuff. We didn't want them to release a greatest hits record after we'd left. Then we left the rest to the lawyers and Neat ended up getting a slice of the next record.

So then it was over to the States and pretty soon we were living there. We were staying in New Jersey, then when we recorded the *Stay Hard* album we recorded in Ithaca, which is upstate New York. We stayed in a little place called Cortland in New York State when we weren't touring. It was nice and it was dirt cheap.

IF: How was it being on a major label?

John Gallagher: Well it's the classic 'be careful what you wish for'. We were on the same label as Led Zeppelin and AC/DC but we were signed by the 'disco' guy because the 'rock' guy was in rehab. It was pretty awful. There was certainly some money but there were many people getting their slice before we touched it. We famously got $3000 each and thought we were rich. When we did our second album on Atlantic, *The Pack is Back*, it cost the thick end of $200K and we didn't see a cent of that. We were in the studio for six weeks, then mixed for four weeks. It was produced by Eddie Kramer, who had worked with Led Zeppelin, Jimi Hendrix, Kiss amongst many others and it all cost crazy money.

IF: Did you choose the producer?

John Gallagher: Well one of those mentioned was Gene Simmons from Kiss. We heard the phone call where he said, 'Yes, well these guys can't write their way out of a paper bag but luckily I've got a load of great songs and I need $100k to start with'. So Eddie, with his track record, was a no brainer. The idea was that we'd make a high-tech heavy metal album, which would be highly commercial and Rob would be playing to a click track. It was all antithetical to what we do and what we were about. But such is the joy of being on a major label. Basically it was bound to fail.

We did produce a third album with Atlantic Records, our sixth overall, *Life's a Bitch,* but we were really tiring of it all. That was Rob Hunter's last album with us. We had done what they wanted by being more commercial but then they wouldn't stump up the money to do a video. It just became a battle. We had problems with our agencies and although we toured with W.A.S.P. and Slayer we just seemed to be fighting against the system. We chose to leave Atlantic. We could have done another album but they were offering less money and we said, 'Let us go' and we signed with an indie label called Combat Records.

It was at a time when music was changing. In the heavy rock genre it was either Glam Metal or Thrash Metal and we were neither. But, as always, we just rolled our sleeves up and got on with it. Our belief in ourselves never wavered and we knew whatever the trend was in music it would be a passing thing. We knew we were good. We just moved on and focussed on Europe. We got ourselves a European manager and toured the UK and Europe in the early '90s. Then we got a record deal in Japan and ended up going there and doing a live album. So it just goes on and on.

IF: At each point did you sit down and plan the next angle?

John Gallagher: Well, we'd obviously been burned by the major label experience and we knew it would take time to get back up. In many ways it's taken till now to get back to the level where we were. When we were playing in the clubs, punk music was coming in and that was a battle for us, so nowt really changes.

IF: Does it make a difference that the band is family?

John Gallagher: It helps obviously. I get asked if I fight with Mark. I say, no we used to fight before the band and now we just take it out on the guitars. We are very different people but we have a common goal and a common understanding of what the band is and what the band should do. We can be quite wary of managers promising the world and not really working for their dollars.

IF: Who released your records after leaving Atlantic?

John Gallagher: We were with SPV from 2009 to about 2021. They did well for us, but we needed to push forward in the US and they didn't quite have the coverage for that. So we signed for Silver Lining records who have Uriah Heep, Saxon and Diamond Head and they are very good for us. We now have a new album in the can, ready to go, with them. That is due for release August/September 2023.

We currently record at our drummer, Mike Heller's studio. He had replaced Joe Hasselvander who had been with us for 30 years but had got sick of going on the road and unfortunately had a heart attack. That was just before a string of dates. We got Mike and we talked for 30 minutes before the gig then we went on stage and he nailed it. He joined in June 2017 and we did 150 dates in six months. We did festivals, a 40-date tour in the US, 70 dates in Europe.

IF: How do you maintain your voice given how demanding your singing style is?

John Gallagher: I don't smoke, I don't drink, I don't do any of the funny stuff and I get plenty of sleep. As long as you look after yourself and get your rest, the voice gets stronger and stronger as time goes on. We have just done 47 dates in the US with three days off and these were brutal drives of 500 or 600 miles a day to get to the next gig. We like to do it like that.

IF: Is there ever a point where you get up and think 'I can't be bothered today'?

John Gallagher: No, we love it. We recently did the *Wipe Out* album in its entirety, which we hadn't done before. We had no rehearsals and re-learnt all the parts on our own. Then we got on stage and jumped in at the deep end. There were no train wrecks and we loved it. To be honest our career has had ups and downs but at the moment it's on a real upturn. We have a great rapport with our fans but this recent tour was another level. Quite often we had fans coming up to us and saying things like 'you helped me through the worst parts of my life. I had your music to help me through and I love you guys for it'. It was really emotional and we were getting it over and over. It felt like we'd pushed into another level with that sort of feedback.

Mark had a terrible accident in 2001 where a building fell on him, crushed his legs and he nearly died. Both his feet came off. I was told he might not make it and they were going to have to cut his legs off. And Mark was saying, 'No, you're not amputating my legs.' So they said. 'Well we'll have to take your right leg off' and Mark said, 'No, you're not doing that'. He was told he'd never walk again. Mark said, 'Yeah right, just watch me.' Three years later he was doing shows in a leg brace. A year later he was on stage jumping about like an idiot. He proved them all wrong. That's our attitude and that's inspirational for me too. That sums it up. We returned with the *Walk Through Fire* album and it planted the flag for us saying, 'look out we're back' after the hiatus of seven or eight years.

IF: What is the future for you?

John Gallagher: Well, we've got the new album coming out next year which we think is great, we've got the new label and it's all push, push, push with that. We've got a UK tour then we are touring Japan, Australia and then Europe to coincide with the record release.

IF: Was there a kinship with other bands in the North East in the early days?

John Gallagher: It was friendly competition. We respected Axe who became Fist. They were the real deal. But there was such talent about at the time. There were people like Davey Patton, a great guitar player. Keith Satchfield, a great guitarist and song writer. A lot of it was the general characteristics of the Geordies. They are people who don't whine, they just roll their sleeves up and get on with it. When times get tough, they get tougher. In the darkest times in the US, when we didn't have a label and couldn't play, I would do guitar lessons to make ends meet. But we never lost faith. We said to ourselves look at where we've been and look at where we can go. All we need to do is write some more songs, record another album and that's what we did. In some ways we were naïve but in other ways we'd done our research. It was a case of 'the record companies are going to screw you'. It was great when we got our first record out with

Neat but we totally knew at that time that Neat was not forever and was just the start. There is always luck and happenstance and that was true with having Neat on our doorstep but you realise that if you keep pushing then you make your own luck.

Just at the moment we feel that we are now on a wave and it's a very exciting time for us. We've been there two or three times before and so we feel it and its both exhilarating and scary. It's all about enjoying what we do. Everything else is just gravy. When I'm sitting in a room coming up with a new riff that is what really excites. Getting it recorded and playing it live is great but taking the germ and making it into a song is what really makes it enjoyable.

IF: When you look back do you have any regrets?

John Gallagher: Not really. I don't play the 'what if game' I get asked this a lot from the perspective of 'hey, Metallica opened for you and look where they are and look where you are'. And I think *well they're a one off. Why should I complain?* We played again with Metallica this year in Florida. It was fantastic, probably about 7,000 fans. James and Lars came and said, 'Here they are the boys from Raven and they are going to play "Don't Need Your Money" about 12 times in a row, ha, ha.' We walked on and Mark's guitar didn't work. It was like 25 seconds but it felt like a year. Someone had turned the volume off on his guitar. But then he just went waarrggghhhh and we were off. But going back, James and Lars studied everything that we did and leaned from it. They said, 'You took a chance on us and we'll never forget that' and true to their word they never did. It was the same with Saxon, who we knew from the early days, and they came back recently and asked us to play with them. Again, just great people.

IF: Is that loyalty and decency more typical in your genre of music?

John Gallagher: We have lots of friends. We took Anthrax out on their first tour and they are mates to this day. We played with Pantera and they said they were big fans of ours. We met the Michael Schenker people and they were great. All these people have been through the wars like us. There are so many people we meet who are so cool and so few of them are arseholes. Japanese promoters have told us in the past that generally people in the rock genre are down to earth, nice people whereas as in other genres people can be quite awful, demanding and egocentric. We learned early on that you need to treat people like you expect to be treated. But we also knew from the start that you need to put in the graft or you get nowhere. With every song we always look to see where we can get 10% more out of it. We will never stop that pursuit of excellence. We feel we owe it to the fans. I have always been like this. When I was a kid working at the Health and Safety Executive I took my bass to work every day and practised through my breaks. I've been an obsessive from the start. It's never ending though, you can always get better.

....

And breathe. John is fantastic company. On March 3rd 2023 I go to see Raven playing a hometown show in Newcastle. It is part of the UK leg of their tour celebrating the 40th anniversary of the release of their third album *All for One*. The venue is packed and it is a sweaty, noisy event that has everything. It is full of long hair, short hair, no hair, rickety old people and headbanging young people. There is humour in the show, 'Anyone here from Darras Hall? Well, it could be worse, you could be from Sunderland.' However, what is clear is that there is telepathy between the brothers and they play a speeding brand of heavy rock that is as tight as a banjo string. Whatever your taste in music you couldn't help but enjoy their show and we were all bouncing as we got the Metro back home. The next morning my ears were ringing but I still had a smile on my face.

1. Gettting paid off is where you are asked not to play your set but still get paid.

2. John Miles was a successful rock star from Jarrow, Tyne and Wear most famous for the UK number three hit in 1976 "Music".

3. Blizzard of Ozz was Ozzy Osbourne's band after leaving Black Sabbath.

4. Girlschool are a four-piece all-girl heavy rock band who scored a UK number five hit with a joint single with Motorhead called "Please Don't Touch" in 1981.

5. Jon Zazula was a record store owner, rock promoter, record label owner and producer from New Jersey, US who was highly influential in the heavy metal genre in the 1980s and 1990s

6. *Kerrang* is a heavy metal magazine that began as an offshoot from the weekly music magazine *Sounds* in 1981.

Venom/Venom Inc.

Jeff 'Mantas' Dunn's and Tony 'Demolition Man' Dolan's Story

In the UK the heavy metal guru of music writing, Geoff Barton from *Sounds* and *Kerrang*, described Venom's first album, *Welcome to Hell* released in 1981 as 'possibly the heaviest record ever allowed in the shops for public consumption'. Their second album, *Black Metal* released in 1982 inspired a musical genre of the same name. In fact, Barton opined in 2005 that 'The reason why Venom remain such an important band is because they invented and defined at least one, and probably several, all-new musical styles. They certainly created thrash metal, the genre that spawned bands such as Metallica, Megadeth, Anthrax, Exodus, Death, Possessed and many more in the US'. Their story is one of satanic lyrics, musical excess and a convoluted tale of fallings out and unresolved conflict. They have now split into two incarnations, as will be explained very powerfully in my chat below, Venom and Venom Inc. Today Venom Inc. have a phenomenal 92,000 followers on Facebook while Venom have 74,000 followers. Similarly, Venom have 234,000 monthly listeners on Spotify. Heavy Metal, or whatever sub-genre is applied, is an often derided music form with bands and their fans sneered at but it is an incredibly popular form of music. Jeff and Tony from Venom Inc. have a vitality and enthusiasm that would put many musicians half their ages to shame. What is also apparent is that this lust for life is appreciated and reflected in the loyalty of their fans and the incredible longevity of their careers. You can laugh all you want at such bands but they will undoubtedly have the last laugh.

I talk to Mantas aka Jeff Dunn and Tony 'Demolition Man' Dolan over Zoom as Jeff lives in Portugal and Tony lives in London, quite a long way from their native Newcastle. Jeff was guitarist and founder of Venom and now Venom Inc. and Tony began in Newcastle with a speed metal band called Atomkraft but subsequently joined Venom in the late 1980s and is currently bassist and vocalist with Venom Inc. Throughout the chat they will refer to Cronos aka Conrad Lant and Abaddon aka Tony Bray and I will get an explanation of where these monikers came from as well as where the conflict that has dogged their career emanated from . And that conflict crops up throughout the chat. Venom are led by Cronos and Venom Inc. are led by Mantas. To say there is no love lost between the two is an understatement.

Venom have released 15 studio albums and a number of live albums. Venom Inc. have just released their second album, *There is Only Black*, to rapturous reviews. It was described in the heavy metal bible that is *Kerrang* as follows: 'It's a proudly heavy, relentlessly aggressive work from a band with a reputation to uphold. Deadly sharp and always on the attack, the studio door probably felt under threat the whole time they were recording. Rightly so.'

I begin my chat with Jeff and Tony by congratulating them on releasing such a brilliant album and ask what inspired such a fresh and hungry record forty years after the first Venom album.

Jeff Dunn: We had a degree of success with the first Venom Inc. album, *Avé*, and the reviews were great. When we got together to do the second album it was essentially a pandemic album because we couldn't get together to record. So Jeramie (King, who is the Venom Inc. drummer) recorded all his parts in Tampa where he lives, Tony recorded bass and vocals in

London where he is and I recorded my guitar parts and mixed and mastered it all here in my studio in Portugal. I wrote the song "It's only black" and sent it Tony and he understood it straight away and said, 'That's it the album title'.

The title song is inspired by my experience in 2018 when I had a heart attack and technically died for five minutes and was brought back from the dead by the doctors. While dead I saw no lights only black. There were no chats with God or the Devil, which is a line out of the song. So that inspired the album rather than the satanic and demonic s*** we have used in the past.

After the heart attack I was completely changed. It happened five years ago on April 30th, 2018, and I've since spoken to a number of people who have had the same sort of death experience as me. People have described how they were technically dead but could see exactly what was going on below them as if they were above the medical scene with a panoramic view. With me I was lucky that a doctor was on call in the next street and I had him work on me in the ambulance. Anita, my girlfriend came to me in the ambulance and asked, 'How you feeling?' and I said, 'Actually the pain's gone' and that was after feeling excruciating pain. At that moment everything went black. The doctor then kicked everyone out, shut the doors and for the next five minutes Anita said that the ambulance rocked from side to side while they gave me CPR, the electric pads and adrenalin shots direct to the heart. When I came round I had horrendous pain where the needle went through my ribs. I was then kept alive artificially for two weeks until they could do the double bypass.

The weird stuff happened after I came back. I said I was screaming, 'You better not f***** give up, you better keep fighting' and Anita said, 'No, that didn't happen, you never said a word.' But I know I heard that in what I would say is my angry voice. And that's another line in one of the songs 'fight, don't give in'. It's been traumatic, I'm suffering from a form of PTSD.

IF: Was the album a form of therapy for you?

Jeff Dunn: Well, sort of. Certainly that particular song. But

I've had a load of people say to me, 'Jeff, we're glad you're here' and I say, 'Not as glad as me'.

IF: Was it difficult to get a coherent sound for the album when you are all recording your parts remotely?

Tony Dolan: It can be a risk but with us we never rehearse. When we have live shows we rehearse our own bits at home. We fly in, do a soundcheck and then we're off. Our principle is that we are playing some songs which are 40 years old so if we don't know them by now then we are in trouble. We play hundreds of shows so we know each other really well. It keeps it fresh for us and fresh for the audience. Some bands are accused of 'dialling it in' but not us. Doing the recording we did as much stuff analogue and live and then transfer it digitally so that we can keep the energy in the playing.

IF: Does the fact you don't rehearse give you nerves?

Tony Dolan: No, the reverse, it gives us a freedom. We don't want to be rubbish but we trust each other and we all give 100%. Jeff would say, 'If you f*** up just pull a great shape.' Jeff listens to every live recording to pick up how we can improve it whereas I just want to live the experience. We constantly vary the set to keep it exciting.

IF: Going back to the start, how did you get into music?

Jeff Dunn: It actually started at a Taekwondo club in the Lifghtfoot Sports Centre in Walker near Newcastle. I was bang into my martial arts from the age of 10. Funnily enough I have had two life changing events and both happened at the City Hall in Newcastle. One was seeing Judas Priest on May 24th, 1979, and the other was a Taekwondo demonstration by a gentleman called Albert Maloney who became a mentor of mine and I became his top student in the North East. He had a massive effect on me, just as KK Downing from Priest had on me. I then met a lad at the Taekwondo called Dave Rutherford who was into Deep Purple and asked if I wanted to be in a band. I said yes but he didn't realise I had no musical ability whatsoever. I don't think I could even tune up the guitar. Anyway, we started a band. The first song we ever jammed out was "Hotel California". The drummer then left and I put a note in the local music shop, Rock City, for a new drummer. We got a call from a couple of people and we went down to meet them and the first one to turn up was Abaddon (aka Tony Bray) and we got on great so we didn't bother meeting the other one. So whoever you were I'm sorry! And at the aforementioned Judas Priest gig Abaddon was there with a lad called Clive Archer, who was a Priest fanatic, and he joined the band as the singer. So we were up and running.

I learned to play the guitar through a paperback book I bought in about 1979 with a flexi disc in it by an amazing guitarist called Pat Thrall. That taught me how to play power chords and the pentatonic scale on the guitar and that was the extent of my knowledge. As soon as I had that I started writing songs.

IF: Were you playing covers at the start?

Jeff Dunn: No, not at all. I was writing stuff right from the off, some of which appeared on the first album like "Angel Dust", "Buried Alive" and "Red Light Fever". Dave wasn't really into this style of music and he left so we needed another rhythm guitarist. Fast forward a little bit and I was at a party with my girlfriend Anita, who I lost touch with for 30 years, but who I got back together with after both of our divorces and am with now 14 years later. Anyway, at this party there was a lad there with one of Anita's friends. I said, 'Hallo, I'm Jeff' and he said, 'Alreet mate, I'm Conrad'. He had long hair and was into his metal. He said, 'I play guitar' and I said, 'We are looking for a rhythm guitarist, why don't you come to one of our rehearsals'. We used to rehearse in a big church at the top of Westgate Road in Newcastle. Anyway, Conrad (Cronos) turned up and Abbadon, the drummer, turned to me and said, 'Who's she?' because he always looked a bit funny. Cronos joined the band straight away. It's important to say a lot of the stuff was already written. He did not change the face of the band as he claims now. We were not a Judas Priest covers band as he claims. We played one Priest song and that was "Green Manalishi" and that's actually a Fleetwood Mac song.

Anyway, the bass player left just before our first gig. People say that was at Westgate Church Hall but it wasn't. It was at Anita's 16th birthday party at a social club in Wallsend and boy did we upset the committee. We were so loud. At that gig Conrad had taken over on the bass. We then played Westgate Church Hall, then Wallsend Methodist Church Hall where there was a bit of a youth club.

IF: What was the gigging scene like at that time?

Jeff Dunn: From about 1979 to the mid 80s the rock scene in Newcastle was second to none. It was a brilliant scene. I saw everyone at the Mayfair from Bon Jovi to AC/DC with Bon Scott. Every NWOBHM band played the Mayfair. I saw Judas Priest there supported by the first line-up of Iron Maiden.

IF: Why were there so many successful heavy rock bands coming up at the time in the North East?

Tony Dolan: It was an attitude thing. There was a hardness and hardiness about the North East. We struggled to get journalists up here so we had to try twice as hard or do it ourselves and we created our own scene. All the musicians hung out in the same bars so it was a really friendly scene. We all supported each other. My original band Atomkraft had done loads of local shows. Then we did a European tour with Venom and it just rolled on.

IF: At that time, before you got your record deal with Neat Records, what were your aspirations?

Jeff Dunn: When I met Conrad that night one thing he said made my ears prick up and that was that he was working at Impluse Studios. In fact, he was on a Youth Opportunity scheme, like a glorified tea boy at Impulse. We'd already been down to Impulse to ask how much a demo would cost, not that we knew what a demo was, but we actually couldn't afford the £40 they were quoting. So, credit to Conrad, he got us some downtime at the studio for free. After recording the first demo we bugged the studio owner and Neat Records owner, Dave Wood, to put a single out for us. To this day I think he pressed maybe 1,000 copies of "In league with Satan" our first single and expected it to flop just to get rid of us because in reality we just couldn't play. But what happened was the opposite. It went mental with that first single and so Dave Wood popped his head round the door next time we were in and said, 'Have you got enough material for an album'. So he said 'right, you've got three days, get it done' and that was *Welcome to Hell*.

I had a vision but I had no plan and haven't got a clue how it happened. I believe the stars aligned above Newcastle and they said, 'Right those three idiots will be the next big thing'. I think it was simply right place, right time. Yes, we went out to shock people but there was simply no plan. Every other band on Neat Records were far harder working than us, far better musicians, far more driven and yet we went from zero to hero overnight. We went from being three fools in Newcastle to playing America and being supported by Metallica or playing Stadiums in Europe with Metallica supporting, then back to America with Slayer supporting us. All the other bands around us just couldn't believe it. I firmly believe that the world was ready for something different. It was coming off the back of the punk thing. We were anti-everything. I remember doing our first interview with Garry Bushell in *Sounds* and they were inundated with letters the next week with both love and hate.

IF: You are often credited with inventing Thrash Metal or with your second album Black Metal, did you set out to do something different or innovative?

Jeff Dunn: There was no magical formula to it. A lot of the stuff on those first two albums is simple blues progressions because that was all that I had. I was very limited in my ability. If I wrote those songs now I'd put them in the bin. It was so simple and naïve. There was no real quality control. I sometimes wish I could get back to that simplicity. I wrote 80-90% of the first two albums and I believe it was the inexperience and inability to play that created the sound that went on to send us round the world. My Dad financed my first amp and guitar. I got a copy Flying V, a horrible old blue fuzz pedal and a Marshall amp and that's what I used on the first album. Conrad had a horrible bass and then borrowed one from our roadie. Abaddon had an old Viking drum kit and that was rubbish. Add to that that Abaddon couldn't keep time in a bucket. So we were poor players, we had crap gear and this album ended up selling millions. If you listen to the "Welcome to Hell" track on vinyl and put the needle down at the start then lift it up and put it towards the end you'll hear it has totally sped up. I was into Status Quo and listen to "Teacher's Pet" and you will hear that we are the only band in the world to play 13-bar blues, I kid you not. There's a section in that song where, if we came out of it all at the same time, we'd look at each other and shout, 'Yes'. I believe the success came from what us three, inexperienced muppets did to those songs. We just bludgeoned our way through the songs.

In the early days of Venom we were just story-tellers and we had a lot of Geordie humour about us. We had an album called *Welcome to Hell* and everyone thought 'oh spooky, spooky satanism' with the album having a pentangle on the front and what have you but we had our tongues in our cheeks a lot of the time. On the second album, which created a genre that is still going on today called Black Metal we had a song on it called "Teacher's Pet", which is about fancying my RE teacher at school. So it wasn't quite the satanic vision that some would claim.

We did our first UK national gig in 1984 at the Hammersmith Odeon and the stage show was totally homemade. We were almost making it up as we went along.

IF: What was it like going across to America and taking Metallica or Slayer out on the road with you?

Jeff Dunn: We so cocksure of ourselves that we just didn't care. It came about because we did a video for two tracks at the People's Theatre in Newcastle. We cobbled the stage together, with old fashioned dry ice machines. That video was seen worldwide and Jon Zazula, who was a record importer in New Jersey, saw it and said, 'Oh, we need these guys in America'. And so we went off to the US. Then we were the first band to take Metallica to Europe. The last time they supported us was at the Lorelei Festival in Germany in 1985 and that was the night Metallica wiped the floor with us. Recently, when we played in San Francisco with Venom Inc., James Hetfield from Metallica came to see us and afterwards I talked about the Lorelei show where I was offstage and I saw them playing 'Search and Destroy' and I realised they were going to be massive. What they did and what Slayer and Exodus did was they worked hard. I think maybe we took things for granted a little bit because it happened so quickly for us. We didn't have to slog it in the clubs for years like other bands did. For us it was release a single, release an album and then it was immediately playing stadiums. We thought *oh, this is what happens* but it's not what happens and we were very, very lucky. It was right place, right time.

IF: Soon after this you left Venom. Why was that?

Jeff Dunn: Well, that's a difficult one. All I can say there was an incident that happened at the festival I was talking about and then another worse incident in the hotel afterwards. It was a horrible thing to see but I can't really say more than that. What it really comes down to is that bands like us were really a dysfunctional family and bands can be the biggest destroyer of friendships. I go back with Conrad right back to the martial arts training. He would come to my house and talk about the band and my mam would make him tea. So there was a massive camaraderie. We had a real 'us against the world' attitude. As soon as success and fame and the notoriety came personalities changed drastically. I was always seen as the quiet one. I'm not into drugs and the rock and roll lifestyle. My drinking actually stopped before the band took off. So, I was called the boring one. My party was always on stage.

IF: So you left Venom in 1986 and then you went back in

the mid-90s. How was that?

Jeff Dunn: Well, of course I needed an income and my girlfriend at the time was a nurse and she told me that the Freeman Hospital in Newcastle wanted orderlies. So I ended up working in the operating theatres in amongst all the blood and guts, transporting amputated limbs about and suchlike. I wouldn't change that two-and-a-half-year experience for the world. It gave me great respect for NHS workers. Anyway, I was at work and I got a call from Venom's manager and I thought oh here we go. He said, 'I've got a weird one for you' and I said 'if it's a Venom reunion you can f*** off' and that was that. There were more calls and I wasn't keen but I agreed to meet Abaddon at the KFC on Northumberland Street in Newcastle. I walked in and he was stood there with a briefcase full of money and I was still stinking of blood and gore. I just walked away and told him I didn't want to do it. I had done *Winds of Change* with my band, Mantas, and that was just fluffy haired '80s party rock and that's what I wanted to do. It was a breath of fresh air, actually. However, allegedly Eric Cook, our manager, and Abaddon had signed with the record label Music for Nations as Venom but without even having a band or any songs. This was at a point where Conrad left and went to America to do his thing (Jeff stresses the point that Conrad left and was not sacked). They needed someone to write songs. Eventually we said yes and so did Tony Dolan and so we recorded *Prime Evil* in 1989 and that was a great record. It harked back to classic Venom. It was looking good but yet again it all fell apart.

IF: Tony, how did you end up joining Venom?

Tony Dolan: I'd see them around all the time and their music was everything I wanted. Venom's management was also managing Atomkraft and by the end of 1986 we'd just done a big tour through the eastern bloc. At the time we played a Venom number, "Welcome to Hell" in our set and it went well. A couple of weeks later I got a phone call to meet in a pub. Cronos was relocating to America and would I be interested in replacing him?

I said I would as long as Mantas would be part of it and he agreed. The response to the album was great but for me this was just my mates. This lasted until 1995 when Cronos returned. That then fell apart a few years later due to the old conflicts resurfacing.

IF: Skipping forward how did Venom Inc. come about?

Jeff Dunn: Well, I had a martial arts gym in Newcastle for 19 years but I kept my hand in with various music ventures. I even played session guitarist for the German Techno band Scooter, playing live with them for a year, and that was great and every gig was a stadium. Anyway, I'd been asked to do a charity gig at a local rock pub called Trillians for something called Jeff Fest (which was in honour of Little Jeff, a well-known local Rock DJ). We pulled together Antton, Conrad's brother, Mike Hickey, who had been in Venom, and Tony Dolan and did the gig. It was good and we decided to keep going but not as Venom.

We called the band M-Pire of Evil but later changed it to Venom Inc. There was then an offer of 22 dates in the US but Antton didn't fancy it so we got another drummer. Later on from that we got the offer to play the Keep it True festival in Germany in 2015 and Tony Dolan persuaded me to ask Abaddon to play with us again, despite my reluctance. We finished that set and the phone rang off the wall and we then went off to Canada, China, Singapore, Japan. When we called it Venom Inc. we got a letter from Conrad's lawyers saying we couldn't do it. I replied, but that went nowhere and we didn't hear from him again.

Now to be clear, Conrad is doing Venom because I gave him verbal permission over the telephone in 2005, at a time that my mother was very ill. She later passed away. At that point I didn't care but I did say I will not recognise a Venom without Conrad and me. Venom Inc. ok but not Venom.

IF: How would you get on with Conrad if you bumped into him in a festival for example?

Jeff Dunn: I honestly don't know. I'll never retract anything I've said about him as everything I said about him is true.

Recently, when the 40 years anniversary of *Black Metal* was coming up Venom Inc. were invited to play the album at a special show but not Conrad. So I invited all past members to come and play it onstage together and we all play some songs from each line up. Who replied? Nobody.

IF: Looking back, do you have any regrets?

Jeff Dunn: No, you play the cards you are dealt. We could have done things differently but everything happens for a reason. I am going to Japan in March 2023 to play a load of Venom songs with some Japanese musicians. Without Venom nobody would be interested in Jeff Dunn, so I have to be grateful for it all.

IF: Your audience seems very loyal.

Tony Dolan: Yes, but we get people coming up to us and saying 'your songs helped me through cancer' or 'your songs helped me get through a break up' and that's very special.

IF: What's it like playing live these days?

Tony Dolan: It works like this. Before we get on stage we're 50 or 60, when we get on stage we're 25 and when we get off stage we are 95. Eleven weeks after Jeff's heart attack we were back playing a festival in Finland. When we got on stage I looked round at him and he looks about 20 and that is just the music filling his cheeks with colour.

IF: Can I finish on a really superficial question? Where did the names come from Mantas, Cronos and Abaddon?

Jeff Dunn: We probably had an old battered copy of the Satanic Bible. We had things when we started like 'we're going to be faster than Motorhead or have a better stage show than Kiss' and all that type of aspiration but really all the satanic imagery was just for shock value. For a long time no one knew our real names and it gave us a bit of mystique. I remember reading a letter in *Kerrang* where I had shattered someone's illusions when they saw me, Mantas, walking out of Marks and Spencer's with a carrier bag. I had the same view of Judas Priest when they came on the stage in 1979, they weren't human to me.

They were like Gods to me. I knew we were just regular, normal lads. We might have been creating a mystique but really we were just full of s*** spouting out nonsense. Later on there were stories of parents destroying our albums as we were a danger to their kids. Our view was 'if you love us great, if you run away screaming even better'. Back in those days there were no grey areas with Venom. No-one said 'yeah, Venom's alright' it was either they loved us or they thought we were s***.

••••••••••••••••••

Using a modern idiom 'pick the bones out of that.' You can say that the Venom story is one of conflict, amazing highs and some crushing lows. It's all twists, turns, break ups and reformations. It is difficult to really explain their immense success but it is a story that has gone on for 40 years plus and shows no sign of slowing down. Maybe its best summed up in Jeff's words as three idiots from Newcastle who changed the world of heavy metal for ever.

Tygers of Pan Tang

Robb Weir's Story

The Tygers of Pan Tang released four albums in the 1980s on the major label MCA. The first album, *Wild Cats*, reached number 18 on the UK charts and their fourth and final album on MCA, *The Cage* reached an even more impressive number 12 on the UK Charts. This was a peak time for record sales so these represent big numbers. It is quite appropriate then that I meet their founding guitarist, Robb Weir, along with their manager, Tom Noble. Although it is not discussed overtly, it is quite apparent that then having an astute manager helped them have a successful run at a time when many bands were cast off after one album or two if they were lucky. It's also notable that the band themselves were savvy enough right from the start to be aware of the importance of a good manager. They are back with Tom after a long break and together they are adapting to the new, streaming and downloading music world with aplomb. They have just released their 13th album, *Bloodlines*, to great reviews. Robb's tale, like so many, is one of highs, lows, betrayals, renaissance and maximum rock and roll.

IF: Tell me how it started.
Robb Weir: It started with an advert in the *Evening Chronicle*

saying 'Guitarist seeks bassist to jam songs of the day and write rock songs.' This was in 1977. Within an hour of the advert appearing, I got a phone call and it was Richard Laws, aka Rocky. He was on a course at Newcastle Polytechnic and he played bass. He lived half a mile from where I lived. He was into Thin Lizzy, Rush and Uriah Heep and that was what I liked. He knew a lad on his course who played drums, and that was Brian Dick. We hired a church hall in Whitley Bay and we jammed AC/DC and Motorhead. I also had a few song ideas and they actually appeared on the first album, songs like "Slave to Freedom" and "Euthanasia". Rocky, it turned out, was a lyricist and so it all came together very quickly. We got a singer in from Blyth called Mark Butcher. About 25 gigs in Mark said he'd got a good offer in from a blues cover band in Newcastle called The R&B Spitfires so off he went.

IF: When you started what was your ambition?

Robb Weir: We wanted to be the next Kiss or whatever the biggest band at the time was. We were a bit of an anomaly at the time because we didn't just play covers, we always played our own stuff. That was a bit of a risk. We played anywhere we could, pubs, clubs, birthday parties, people's back rooms. We'd fly post our own posters and were really working hard at it. When Mark left, we advertised for a singer in the *Evening Chronicle* again. We got two applicants and one had a PA and so he got the job, and that was Jess Cox. This re-energised us again and it wasn't long after that we got a residency at a bar called Mingles in Whitley Bay.

IF: Were you called the Tygers of Pan Tang from the start?

Robb Weir: Yes, we were, and the name came from Rocky who had a real interest in fantasy writing. When we were thinking about, it I came up with Achilles Heel, which I thought was good, and Rocky said Tygers of Pan Tang, which blew me away. It came from a Michael Moorcock book, the fantasy writer. I thought if people don't remember the first part they'll remember the last bit.

Around the time we got the residency at Mingles. I knocked on Tom's door to ask him to manage us.

Tom Noble: At the time I was moonlighting as a writer for the *NME* as well as doing a local music show called *Bedrock* on Radio Newcastle. Robb thought that he could use me to get some publicity. Little did he know that the *NME* would never write about heavy rock bands like the Tygers. Robb said, 'Come down and see us.' I said no, but he was persistent and I went to see them at Mingles. It wasn't my sort of music at all, but these four guys made an interesting racket. What struck me was the four people. I met them and they were forceful characters, very sure of themselves and already with a vision of where they wanted to go. I found that really impressive.

We realised that they needed to make some money, so we went to Ivan Birchall's agency in Newcastle and he got us on at a working men's club circuit at places like Sunderland Boilermaker's Club. We thought it was a risk just playing original songs but they were adamant and the audience loved it.

Robb Weir: They were very different times as there was still heavy industry up here with the shipyards, the steel works, the mines still operating. So, people really valued their free time and they seemed to really appreciate loud, heavy rock on a Friday and Saturday night. The clubs were packed out. It was a great time to play these shows.

The music scene, though, was quite segregated and we didn't really go outside the North East. So, we weren't really aware of what was stirring with Def Leppard and Iron Maiden. But the North East was really vibrant at the time.

IF: How did you move on to getting a record out?

Tom Noble: There was a studio in Wallsend called Impulse, where Lindisfarne did all their early recording and it was owned by David Wood. His son went to Whitley Bay High School and as coincidence would have it the Tygers were going to play that school after hours. So he asked his dad to come along and watch. Dave went along and was impressed enough to offer to make a single with them, which we said yes to straight away. Dave had this studio and had put out a couple of singles by Janie McKenzie, who sang in the clubs and then a power pop band called Motorway. They were the first two singles on the Neat label. The Tygers with "Don't Touch me There" became Neat 03. The first two singles maybe sold 100 each but when the Tygers' single came out it started selling like hot cakes and we couldn't get them re-pressed quickly enough. I had a friend called Ian Penman/Ravendale[1] and I asked him to write about the Tygers' release in the music press and he did. Again, he wasn't necessarily a heavy metal fan, but he really liked the guys and we took him on tour with us. He did a piece in the *Evening Chronicle* and then *Sounds*. He saw the Tygers in Spennymoor and I think the title of the piece in *Sounds* was 'The Tygers of Spennymoor'. We also sent it to John Peel and he played it and that again boosted the sales of the single. John Peel liked the rawness of the song, even though it may not have been his usual sort of music. So, Ian had a major influence on the sales as did John Peel but Neat itself did very little marketing. All the singles at the time were sent out mail order, it wasn't even in the shops. So, the Neat release and re-print sold about 5,000 but when it was later released by MCA we had no idea how many they sold.

IF: From there how quickly did it move on to a major record label contract with MCA? That must have been a step change for you.

Tom Noble: Well, the band also won a battle of the bands competition for a PA company called Vitavox. The final was at the Westerhope Excelsior Club. After that we set up a gig at Sunderland Mecca Ballroom and invited all the top record companies up who had shown interest. The guy from EMI who had signed Iron Maiden turned up and said, 'not for me thanks.' The guy from Chrysalis came and said, 'No, thanks.' And anyone else who came passed on us and the band were really down hearted. The following week we had a gig at Newcastle Mayfair and MCA sent someone up to see us. But he didn't talk to us and we had no idea what he thought. That night I was doing the *Bedrock* radio show on Radio Newcastle and just before I went on air I was told there was someone on the phone for me from MCA and when I picked up the phone he said, 'We want to sign the band.' It turned out to be a huge record deal for us.

IF: You had a deal with MCA and you recorded your first album. It seems the choice of producer is vital for your first album. How did you choose your producer?

Tom Noble: Well, Neat still wanted to be involved with the band and Dave said they could record at Impulse at really good rates. MCA suggested Chris Tsangerides who, as he had produced Gary Moore, the band were really keen on. So, Chris came up from London to look at Impulse and he looked at the equipment and facilities and said, 'I can't record there guys, it's not a proper studio.' He suggested Morgan Studio where the likes of Yes and David Bowie had recorded.

IF: It seems like MCA were a good fit for you.

Tom Noble: Yes, they were but another key factor for us was that we got a really good lawyer on the advice of our agent. We were lucky to sign with the biggest agency, ITB, International Talent Booking agency run by a guy called Rod MacSween. They had the likes of Def Leppard, Iron Maiden, Fleetwood Mac. Rod gave advised us to get a top lawyer and he helped us to do that. As soon as we got a lawyer we made sure we got a good publishing deal, separate to the record contract and a long record deal which was at least four albums. I am guessing that other bands signed from our region didn't have the benefit of a good lawyer to look after their interests. He was a young guy and became a friend of the band. He was young enough to understand music but in a top London law firm.

Robb Weir: MCA were certainly good for us and they made us feel very welcome.

IF: The first album, *Wildcat*, reached number 18 on the UK charts which was amazing. How did you cope with such a rapid rise?

Robb Weir: Well, we played the Wildcat tour round the UK at Mecca Ballrooms, all about 2,000 capacity and it was a sell-out tour. That was a realisation of how far we'd come to have that many people come to see us play songs I'd written or had a hand in writing. It was quite amazing. When the album charted we were bookended in the chart by Michael Jackson and David Bowie and it was almost surreal.

Tom Noble: You could say they got big headed but that wasn't really true. Right from the start the band were always sure of themselves and in control of their career. It didn't change them but accelerated what they were which was four very self-confident individuals.

IF: By the time the album came out you had John Sykes, who later played with Thin Lizzy and Whitesnake, in the band. How did that come about?

Robb Weir: Around 1980 we did tours with Magnum, Scorpions, Saxon and some shows with Iron Maiden and Def Leppard. Tom and Rod, our agent, came up with the idea that we had been playing with bands with two guitars or in Magnum's case they had a guitar and keyboard and that a second guitarist would help to fill out the sound for the Tygers. It was decided I was to have a friend, so to speak, and I wasn't completely on board with the idea.

Tom Noble: He was completely hacked off with it to be honest. When they played with the Scorpions they had such a massive sound with two guitars. Although the Tygers went down well we felt there just something missing.

Robb Weir: To be honest comparing us with the Scorpions at the time was like comparing a Mercedes and a Mini with a hole in the exhaust. So, we put an advert in the *Melody Maker* and held auditions at Tower Bridge Studios in London and we saw something like 80 guitarists in two days. There were only two who were any good. One was John Sykes and the other was Steve Mann, who is now in the Michael Schenker group. I possibly favoured Steve as he played keyboards and sax and was a real all-rounder but the others went for John, who had the additional benefit of looking great. I was still a little unsure about a second guitarist but I later roomed with John as we travelled round the world and we got on great. If anything I had to up my game. John was an incredible guitar player with blond hair down to his waist. And at the start he didn't realise how good he was. John was an innovator on the guitar at the time. Now such players are ten a penny but he was unusual at the time.

IF: You were doing exceptionally well with MCA putting out four albums, all charting and the last one, *The Cage* got to number 12 in the UK Album Charts. Why did you fall out with them?

Robb Weir: Well, it started with the making of the fourth album where the label got us to use outside song writers.

Tom Noble: With the third album, *Crazy Nights*, the band was rushed into it and the songs weren't as good and the production is dreadful. Then John left and we got in Fred Purser, who used to be in the punk band Penetration. He was brought in temporarily to play in France but all the band gelled with him really well. Fred also wrote a few songs for the band and they were pretty good.

MCA weren't too impressed with *Crazy Nights* so they brought in a producer called Peter Collins, who had actually produced a hit single for the Tygers earlier with the cover, "Love Potion Number 9". As it turned out Peter Collins' manager was Pete Waterman of Stock, Aitken and Waterman fame. Pete Waterman had chosen "Love Potion Number 9" and so he said, 'I've got some great covers for the band to record and also some written by Steve Thompson,' the producer of the first single for Neat and coincidentally brother of my partner in managing the Tygers, Graham Thompson. I felt the band, having written all their songs to date, wouldn't be happy with this but Pete Waterman was a force of nature and we'd been happy with 'Love Potion Number 9' so we all kind of went along with it. He sucked me in and sucked the band in.

The producer then came up to the North East to hear the

songs the band had written and took me for a coffee and said, 'They're crap. I can't work with those.' He liked three songs written by Fred and I said, 'What about the songs written by Robb and Rocky?' And he said, 'I'm not recording those.' I asked the band and apart from Robb they all said, 'Ok, we'll do what the producer wants.' So, we were kind of bulldozed into it. Despite all their reservations it turned out to be their biggest selling album.

After the release of *The Cage* I met with MCA and wanted to persuade them to get the band to America. Def Leppard and Iron Maiden were doing well there and I wanted the Tygers to get across and give it a go. They refused and said, 'We'll take them across when *The Cage* is a hit and I said, 'Take them across there and it will be a hit.' They didn't get our logic. I went to see the band at the Edinburgh Playhouse on The Cage Tour where they were absolutely on fire and I said, 'I can't do this anymore, the label simply won't listen to me.' As a manager I should have been able to influence the label.

Robb Weir: We were completely gutted as Tom had been with us from the start. We were annoyed with Tom as well.

Tom Noble: The band then went off to Japan and their agent warned me that when they came back from Japan they will think they are megastars. They were selling out 5,000 seaters in Japan and he said, 'They will be so difficult to deal with when they get back.' And boy was he right.

Robb Weir: Japan was insane. We were literally mobbed by fans, riding round in stretch limos. What was strange was that there was an early curfew in Japan so you would play at 6:00 pm and finish at 8:30 and then back to the hotel.

Tom Noble: I talked to Ian Gillan's[2] manager, Phil Banfield, and told him I wasn't going to be the Tyger's manager anymore and would he take them over as he'd been doing a great job with Gillan. He said he'd love to. So, when they got back from Japan I said, ', I've got a new manager lined up for you.' And the band told me where to go. If I wasn't going to do it they would choose who they would get in not me. Their agent suggested Beiny and Dolan, who managed high-profile acts like the Eurythmics. They went to MCA and said they were now the Tygers' managers and they wanted $1m for their next album.

Robb Weir: We'd done these demos, for the next album. We played it to MCA and they weren't keen as they wanted us to use outside writers. We gave it to Beiny and Dolan and they said, 'Leave it with us. We'll get you your next record deal' as the four-album deal had been completed and we were expecting to re-negotiate. MCA were actually keen for us to sign up for four more, but with outside song writers, which really went against the grain, particularly with me as I'd written albums that had charted. So, we had a meeting with MCA and in this meeting I stood up and said, 'I am not doing this. I am not playing other people's songs.' And I walked out. Was it brave or stupid, I don't know. Everyone kind of followed. And that was the end of it. As we walked out we were told, 'Walk out the room and there is no more record contract, we won't sign you.' There was bravado and some arrogance but that was us.

Our new managers had the new album and were apparently taking it to Chrysalis Records. So, I remember calling the managers from a pay phone in Whitley Bay to ask them about this new deal and they said, 'Leave it with us, it's nearly there.' So, I phoned up a week later and got the same response. Same again a week later. So, I rang Chrysalis and got through to the A&R Department. I said, 'Apparently, you've got our new album and are considering signing us.' And they said, 'No we've never heard anything from your managers and don't have your album to listen to.' And so we rang the managers and confronted them and basically said 'Goodbye' without even hearing any explanation and that was it. So, we now had no record deal, no management company and with that the band fell to bits, from being on top of the world to nothing.

IF: How did it feel going from headlining in front of 5,000 fans in Japan to nothing?

Robb Weir: I couldn't have felt lower. It felt doubly bad as I just couldn't fix it. I was furious as we'd been lied to and so badly let down. They could have said we've talked to everyone and they aren't interested, go and write a bunch of new songs.

We were in limbo. So, I went on holiday in early 1983 and when I returned I phoned Rocky. And he said, 'Well, we've had a meeting with our agent and you and Brian aren't in the band anymore.' There wasn't any logic to it and I didn't believe him, I thought he was joking. But he wasn't. This wasn't really the band's idea but the agent's and that was that. So, Brian and I decided to carry on with a new band called Sergeant that we put together. I had a pal called Colin Rowell and he was stage manager at the Newcastle City Hall and then for *The Tube* TV programme and he agreed to manage us. We had a singer called Tony Liddle who was really good and a bassist called Anthony Curran. We recorded four songs at Brian Johnson's studio. Colin and I went down to London with the tapes and CBS wanted to sign us for a £60K. Dave Novak from CBS came up to see us rehearse and they loved what we were doing. We wanted to be a sort of Bad Company type of band. The songs sounded great. The band had a meeting at the Rose and Crown pub in Newcastle to discuss it. Anyway, one of the band said, 'Before we start we are really sorry but we don't want Robb to be in the band anymore because he's not good enough.' So, we got up and turned to go and they said, 'Colin, you're still going to manage us aren't you?' and he told them where to go. I think they did five or six shows and then they folded. At that point I was totally sickened by it and I just walked away from that world. It was 1987 and I sold all my guitars and my amps and was done with it. I didn't want anything more to do with the music industry. And that was me done with music from 1987 to 1999.

IF: So, what dragged you back in?

Robb Weir: A phone call dragged me back in. It was a phone call from Jess Cox, our first singer, to say that the Wacken Music Festival in Germany wanted the Tygers to reform and play a 20th anniversary show. It took me a nano-second to say yes. I was ready to return. There was only me and Jess up for it and I had to go out and get guitars and amps. We hired three local musicians including Gav Gray who later joined the band full time. On the plane over Jess told me we were headlining.

IF: You were a confident band originally, all these years later were you nervous headlining this festival?

Robb Weir: I had bicycle clips on my trousers but after about 30 seconds of playing it all came back. The show went well and I had re-caught the disease called Rock and Roll.

IF: Jumping ahead, listening to your new record its sounds vibrant and quite in your face. How do you keep it all fresh?

Robb Weir: Well, thank you but, to be honest, that has never left. We have always had a hunger to produce great music.

IF: What are your ambitions now, 47 years after starting the band?

Robb Weir: More albums, more touring. It's never been better. We sell records, we tour Europe and we control it all ourselves.

Tom Noble: We may have been given an advance of £100K by MCA, which we thought was amazing in the early 1980s but we didn't realise that had to pay for the studio and all costs and had to be paid back. It took ten years after the band first split to pay MCA back. We get better royalties on the old records now because there is no debt. Now we run it like a cottage industry where we make our own videos, our own merchandise, our own sleeves. We have a great record company in Denmark but we are in total control. We obviously make more money from touring than anything else whereas back in the day touring was the loser. We sell more records at shows and loads from merchandise.

Robb Weir: In the old days I would have a guitar roadie for myself and I was getting paid £100 a week and the roadie was getting £250 a week so touring was an expensive business. Now we cut our cloth to suit our means.

(At this point the new Tygers of Pan Tang single, "Back for

Good" comes on the speakers of the pub. I tell Robb and Tom, in all sincerity, that it sounds great. And it does!)

IF: Do you have any regrets?

Robb Weir: Simply put no. The only thing I would have changed was that we didn't talk Tom out of walking away in the '80s.

●●●●●●●●●●●●●●●●●

The Tygers of Pan Tang have had, according to Wikipedia, 23 members over a period of 46 years. Robb Weir was there right at the start and is now banging out the riffs in 2023. The band's line up now seems a happy bunch and Robb can look back on the ups and downs with wry satisfaction. The band is characterised by an almost arrogant self-belief and that has, at their admission, led to mistakes and fallings out. But they are still at it, selling out concerts and doing it their way. When we meet Robb is happy for their manager, Tom, to describe large parts of their story and this is a tacit acknowledgement that a good manager is worth their weight in gold in the unforgiving and cut-throat world that is rock and roll.

---

1. Ian Penman was a music journalist who was based in the North East. He wrote for the weekly rock paper *Sounds* under the name of Ian Ravendale as there was another Ian Penman who wrote at the *NME* at the same time. He also worked on Radio Newcastle's *Bedrock* show along with Tom Noble, Rik Walton, Phil Sutcliffe and Dick Godfey, which supported local music.

2. Ian Gillan is the singer of the Heavy Rock legends Deep Purple.

Neat Records

Steve Thompson's Story

In heavy metal circles Neat Records are somewhat revered. They are known as the home of the New Wave of British Heavy Metal (NWOBHM) and were responsible for launching the careers of highly influential bands such as the Tygers of Pan Tang, Raven, Venom, Fist, Blitzkrieg and White Spirit amongst others. A key figure in Neat's story was their house producer Steve Thompson, a proud son of Consett, County Durham. Although Steve acknowledges the importance of the work he did with the bands mentioned, he primarily sees himself as a songwriter. And having written a top 20 hit for the band Wavelength, having had his songs recorded by artists such as Celine Dion, Sheena Easton, the Searchers, Elkie Brooks and the Tyger of Pan Tang, he has good right to do so. His story starts in Consett and ends in ... Consett.

IF: You started as an apprentice at Consett Steel Works. How did you escape that world for a life in music?

Steve Thompson: Well I ended up in the Steel Works, like everyone. Recently I found my old school reports and they are terrible with comments like, 'Stephen must try harder', but they all end up with the comment, 'Stephen shows a keen interest in art and music', so, of course, I ended up as an apprentice at the Steel Works. But I was really interested in music and wanted to put a band together but my interest was in how they put that sound together. I got a guitar but I was more interested in making music, in writing songs and in the production. I listened to *Pet Sounds* by the Beach Boys and was fascinated by Brian Wilson's production.

I was in the training centre for a year and then out into the plant. There was a lad who had been to my school and was in the year above at the Steel Works and we got talking about music and he said, 'I'll give you a bass guitar if you join my band.' This band was Bullfrog. Anyway, he came to my house with a drummer and he asked me to play some songs I'd written and he listened and said to the drummer, 'See, I told you he was talented. You're in the band.'

IF: How easy was song writing for you?

Steve Thompson: For me, life was easier if you made your own tunes up rather than play other people's. To be honest I was probably a strange kid. I would buy music books like '*Easy to play Classical Music*'. It didn't seem strange to me to want to write songs. With the band we'd do the classics of the day like Deep Purple and Hendrix but also played our own. We used to do pubs, village halls, working men's clubs.

I lost all interest in the Steel Works. I finished the apprenticeship and was now a time-served fitter but I wasn't long out of my time and I quit. I was making so much money from the job and the band that I didn't know what to do with it. The crunch came when I booked a Mediterranean Cruise on my own with this money.

The band was doing really well. We had a big following in the North East and we had got a record deal with a label called Cube Records. I used to send all the letters out to all the record companies along with cassettes. We had won a recording audition with EMI but Cube came to see us play at a club in Wingate and the punters were swinging from the rafters. Cube said, 'Come with us as you'll be a small fish in a big pond at EMI.' They were independent but had the likes of Joe Cocker, T-Rex and Joan Armatrading. We had a studio date and I had the cruise to go on just before that. I went to see the foreman and said, 'I want the third week in June off.' And he said, 'No, no you're not an apprentice anymore you need to get a slot on the rota.' And I said, 'Ok, well I quit then.' I had the cruise to go on and I was going to be a rock star when I got back so it was obvious to me to quit. The foreman couldn't believe what I was doing. The cruise was fabulous.

We went down to the Basing Studio in London and we had Roger Bain to produce us. Roger had produced Black Sabbath and we loved Sabbath. He brought along Gus Dudgeon[1] who was his mate. I worked a lot with Gus later on. I came up with quite an intricate but interesting riff and we played it to the singer who said, 'Riddly, tiddly tum' and that became a song and we stupidly sent it to the record company who then wanted to put it out as the first single. It sounded like a novelty song to us. We changed the name to "Glancy" but we weren't into it. To be honest we blew it. We got a slot on Tyne Tees Television and we played the B-side not the A-side. We had a record deal, a publishing deal and a management deal. There was another band on Cube from the North East called Kestrel and they were our mates. Then the management decided that the guitarist from Kestrel, Dave Black, later of Goldie[2], and our singer Pete MacDonald, would go forward with the Spiders from Mars with Trevor Boulder and Woody Woodmansy, after David Bowie and Mick Ronson had gone. And just like that we were done.

It was at that point I decided I was going to be a song writer. As I said I was a strange kid. I was sat in Consett in about 1975 and I thought I could make a life as a songwriter. I didn't lack self-belief. I had a friend in the village who would help me make little demos of the songs I was writing. In the meantime I got a job at Fenwick department store in Newcastle packing the glass and china. Every spare moment I got I was recording my songs.

I learned to record sound on sound with two recorders. Occasionally I would hire a village hall and get a load of guys to help record my songs. I was learning the art of recording or even production. Using these musicians meant I was learning the psychology of how to get the best performances out of people. I would send the tapes out and go and visit record companies and publishers in London. I actually started by sending manuscripts out, which was really stupid but I was thinking of Tin Pan Alley. I got rejection after rejection. Sometimes I got feedback, which was helpful.

Occasionally, I would branch out and book time in local studios and one of the places was Impulse in Wallsend. Dave Wood, who owned the studio, liked what I was doing but he said it was a bit sloppy and that I needed session musicians to help me. He asked me how much I was earning at Fenwick and he said he could pay me that to work there as a record producer and promoter. He also wanted me to write songs, run the publishing company and generally be creative. It was a young lad's dream. So in about 1977 I became the house producer at Impulse Studio at the age of about 25.

IF: Were you daunted to become a house producer with so little formal experience?

Steve Thompson: No, I didn't give it a second thought. I was determined to do it. I was on a mission and saw this as a tremendous opportunity. I think Dave picked up on my obsessive nature. He realised I would work round the clock for next to nothing.

The first thing I recorded was by someone who was a warden on Hadrian's Wall and he'd written a song on the accordion. So, I got my mate from Consett, Barry, on drums and I helped with guitar and we recorded his song. We put it out on Rubber Records, which was Impulse's label in partnership with Brian Mawson from Windows music shop in Newcastle. I then made a record with Frank Wappat's[3] Big Band and that put me on the map. I was producing all sorts, including the comedian Bobby

Thompson[4] whose LP was a real hit for Rubber Records. I also did a single with Bobby Thompson "When I Was a Lad". He was a nice fella.

IF: What is the job of a producer?

Steve Thompson: Firstly, bring in the recording on budget. Secondly, get the songs to sound their best. We had a great engineer at Impulse in Micky Sweeney but I had to make sure the songs came out as good as they could, so that could include arranging. The Tygers of Pan Tang, for example, were very raw but they were also very open to what I suggested. I would suggest things from a songwriter's point of view. John Gallagher, from Raven, showed me a video documentary about Raven where he talked about how I helped make their songs more solid. You may spot the hook that they don't spot. You also have to get the best performance from them. There's also a lot of psychology in the job and often you would relax them by getting them to laugh.

IF: How did Neat Records start?

Steve Thompson: I think Impulse may have wanted to be a totally independent record company. So, Dave set up Neat Records and Neat Publishing but we had no product. I was sharing a flat in Earsdon with some musicians and asked them if they wanted to record a song and that became Neat 01. It was called "All I Wanna be is Your Romeo" by Motorway. (This is a real power pop song like Graham Parker or The Boomtown Rats and worth checking out on YouTube). The lead singer, Malcolm Lilley, was a good songwriter. Andy Taylor, later of Duran Duran, had been in the band earlier but not on this song. The song did okay but didn't sell that well. Neat 02 was an 11-year-old girl who was doing great in the clubs and that was Jeanie McKenzie and she recorded two of my songs with Andy Taylor on guitar.

It was Neat 03 that was the take-off. Dave had heard about Tygers of Pan Tang, after they had played at his son's school. They were making a bit of a splash in the North East. Anyway, they came into the studio and I listened to them play their heavy metal and I thought *this went out of fashion years ago*. What was big at the time was the new wave and power pop of Elvis Costello and the like. Dave said it was making a splash so I gave it a go. They were really raw and I talked to them a lot about song construction and we moved things about. We recorded three songs but I didn't know what to make of it. They certainly had energy and they certainly listened to what I said, they showed me that respect. I was really unsure and I had to be pushed by Dave to get the final mix done. Me and Micky Sweeney realised we couldn't polish it so we emphasised the rawness of it. We had a thousand pressed and they flew out so we needed to get another thousand pressed. And they flew out. We actually used a husband and wife's pressing plant up in Wooler in Northumberland. We struggled to keep up with the pressings. Then Tommy Vance played it on his Radio 1 show and it went ballistic. We became aware that we wouldn't keep up with the demand and so we struck a licencing deal with MCA and off went the Tygers. To be fair to them it put Neat on the map.

IF: Who came next?

Steve Thompson: Well, I went off to work with a great band called the Caffreys[5] and when I came back Dave had signed two or three more heavy metal bands and now it was a heavy metal label. It was all due to the Tygers' success that heavy metal bands beat a path to Impulse and Neat. The next two we had were Fist and White Spirit, they were both great. Dave then played me a rehearsal tape from a band and it was heavy metal but it was quite different with interesting arrangements and great playing. That was Raven and I thought they really had something. Dave said we'd do something we hadn't done so far and that was putting an album out with Raven. He also told me to look in the office and find a box full of tapes that had been sent. He told me to listen to the tapes and so I became the A&R man. I was really wary of turning bands down in case I missed a real gem. I was told nobody got turned down. Some were cut just to sell at gigs while some were cut because we saw real potential.

Raven were genuinely crazy. They were full on, all the time. I went to see them at Mingles in Whitley Bay. It's a low stage and at one point John Gallagher came at me with his bass pointing out like a lance and charged towards me and he stopped about six inches from my head. I didn't flinch and he slightly smiled and went back on stage. I was checking them out and they were checking me out. They had so much energy that I had to gaffer tape their microphones to their heads because they were bouncing all over the studio. They did their full act in the studio. I booked three days at a time, like shifts in the Steel Works, because I couldn't have done it none stop as it was too full on. They were so talented and open to every suggestion. I didn't realise that this album *Rock Until you Drop,* would become so influential but the energy of it rubbed off on me. There was one track where Mark was doing a guitar solo and we did several takes that weren't quite right. With some bands they need TLC. Raven never needed TLC, they needed a push every now and then. So, I said to Micky, 'Get ready to press record' and pushed the talk back button and said, 'If you don't get it next take, I'm coming in to do it for you.' Mark went berserk, throwing himself against the wall and going mad and that's the take we used.

IF: Who came after Raven?

Steve Thompson: Well there was a bit of an interlude. I did some great stuff with a band called Southbound that I really thought should have made it. Unfortunately, it didn't go anywhere but years later the record label, Cherry Red, contacted me about putting out the Bullfrog stuff. They are going to put out my recordings with Southbound which I am delighted about as they are the one band that should have made it but didn't. They were like the North East's version of Little Feet. They were really special.

IF: Tell me about recording Venom.

Steve Thompson: Ok, well I'll tell you the true story of Venom as I was there. At the time Conrad, or Cronos as he is known, was the band's singer and he was a nice lad at the time. He was a tea boy and a tape operator on the Government's Employment Training Scheme. He was really keen and helpful and kept going on about his band. He would tell me the stories about how they were on the dole and they'd saved money for months to buy enough pyrotechnics to blow a village hall up. Then they would go and play and the pyros would be all he was interested in. He kept going on and on about this band of his and he wanted an opportunity in the studio so I said, 'Okay.' I told them to come in for an afternoon with his two mates. I had to lend him my bass, from my Bullfrog days, because he wasn't a bass player at the time and he wasn't really a singer. He'd stepped up as they'd recently lost their singer. So he put the bass through a Marshall stack and they let rip and I thought Jesus, it was all about Satan.

IF: When you heard them did you spot their potential?

Steve Thompson: It was certainly different. Tony Bray, their drummer (aka Abaddon), said to me a few years ago, 'You know those first sessions we did, I hadn't actually learned to play the drums yet.' It was beyond punk. They were raw as hell and really naïve and I got the best out of them that I could.

IF: How did it proceed from there?

Steve Thompson: Well, I felt at that this was the time to go. A lot of the bands were being licensed to MCA and I felt like I was part of a nursery ground. The label was becoming very successful and I was not really feeling any benefit.

IF: Neat Records is known as a real driver of the New Wave of British Heavy Metal movement. Did you sense that there was a real scene developing and you were at the centre of it?

Steve Thompson: No, it was just happening. If I'd sensed it, I may have capitalised on it and stayed with it. I walked off the job at age 26 to pursue my aim of being a successful songwriter. I was penniless, but I was young and daft enough not to care. I didn't take a production royalty on Venom as I didn't realise that it was even going to be released.

I did a bunch of demos at a studio in Newcastle called Morton Sound. It wasn't as good as Impulse but I needed a change. At that session I wrote and recorded songs that were hits. They were "Hurry Home," which was a top 20 hit for the band Wavelength, "Please Don't Sympathise," which was recorded by Sheena Easton and later covered by Celine Dion.

IF: Do you write songs specifically for artists?

Steve Thompson: No, although sometimes you hear that acts are looking for songs so you write with that in mind. I try to write songs which can be sung by males or females. One I wrote for Elkie Brooks specifically. She liked a song I wrote and wanted to record it for her album. She said it was a good song but it didn't sound like a single. She asked if I could write a song suitable to be released as a single. So, that is what I did. It was a tough assignment but I got there.

For a while I signed a song writing deal with Bruce Welch of the Shadows, who had been involved in Neat Publishing. When that came to an end, the Tygers, who were still with MCA, were recording their fourth album with Peter Collins as producer. Peter Collins was managed by Pete Waterman, of Stock, Aitken and Waterman fame. My brother was co-managing the Tygers and he gave Pete Waterman a cassette of my songs and Pete was dead keen to sign me and use some of my songs on the Tygers' album. Pete was saying anything to get a cut of the money. A lot of my songs were getting picked up, especially on records produced by Peter Collins, like the Searchers. At this time John Sykes, the guitarist from the Tygers, walked out and this left a big hole in the song writing. So, I suggested they send the singer, Jon Deverill, to me and we would co-write. So, we wrote a few songs including "Paris by Air" and "Lonely at the Top". So, that's a snapshot of my career, writing for people as diverse as Celine Dion to the Tygers of Pan Tang. I guess in the end it's all about writing good songs. And, you know, the royalties still come in, albeit at a lower level.

IF: What are your ambitions now?

Steve Thompson: I think it's just to stay alive. As my school reports said Stephen must try harder. Stephen has a keen interest in music and art.

••••••••••••••••

Steve Initially greeted me by telling me that he was a rock star. We had met at Harbourmaster Productions, which is a studio in South Shields where Steve is recording his latest solo album. He has contributions on this album from people like John Gallagher from Raven and, having listened to it, is sounding great. He is a rock star, a producer and a song writer but he is also that strange little, obsessive kid from Consett, County Durham. And although his ambition is just to stay alive, I feel he has a lot more creative activity to come. Don't bet against a future Eurovision entry featuring the song writing credits of S. Thompson. Watch this space.

1. Gus Dudgeon was a record producer who produced hits for Elton John, David Bowie, Joan Armatrading and Elkie Brooks.

2. Goldie were a North East band featuring Dave Black and Pete MacDonald who had a number seven UK hit in 1978 with "Making up Again".

3. Frank Wappat was a local radio personality and big band leader.

4. Bobby Thompson was a North East Comedian know as 'The Little Waster' who played the clubs and had a hit album with recordings of his club act.

5. The Caffreys are a soft rock group from North Tyneside who feature top class vocal harmonies from the three Caffrey brothers.

Fist

Harry 'Hiroshima' Hill's Story

In the late 1970s while punk rock was raging there was also a surge of interest in the new wave of British heavy rock groups. Like punk, heavy rock was a genre that was under scrutiny from major record labels. Like bees around honey the majors could sniff profits. For some reason, the North East of England was a hotbed for this type of music. Fist, or Axe as they were originally known, were one of the first and most influential of the new wave of heavy rock groups in this area. They wrote catchy rock songs that attracted the record labels, most notably MCA, who they signed with. For local fans and the bands that they inspired it was the stand out musicianship of their lead guitarist, Keith Satchfield and their drummer, the charismatic Harry 'Hiroshima' Hill, that was the main appeal.

So, one damp autumn morning, I find myself having a cup of tea in a café in the pretty Victorian Marine Park in Fist's home town of South Shields to find out from Harry what all the fuss was about.

IF: Tell me about the start, how did you get into music?

Harry Hill: Just lucky I guess. When I was about 12, I was interested in music and I wanted a trombone. Unfortunately, my father had just died so we didn't have a lot of money. My mother went to Saville's Record Shop in South Shields. She came back with a small box and I thought, *well that can't be a trombone*. It turned out to be a recorder as she couldn't afford a trombone. I tried it but all I could get out of it was a bit of squeaking. So, I started using it to bang on things and that got me thinking I may be a drummer. So, what I did was I sold my mother's piano. She kept it in the front room but nobody played it as it was my Dad's. It was a beautiful thing. So, I thought I'd sell it and I got £45 for it and bought a set of drums for that. It was probably worth far, far more. With my warped logic I put the drums in the place where the piano had been and thought no one would notice that the piano had gone as people never really went in the front room. Well, my mam did notice, and I got the hiding of my life. So that's how it started.

I was listening to Deep Purple, Led Zep, Wishbone Ash, Pink Floyd, all heavy rock. This was the early 1970s. I would borrow and buy music and was totally obsessed. I got into a rock band called Fixer. My mate, Geoff Bell, was the guitarist and he was excellent. We were about 16. Actually, Geoff and I went down to London in about 1976 to audition for David Coverdale's new band at the time, Whitesnake. We were auditioned by Deep Purple's manager, Tony Edwards and Martin Birch, the rock producer, having sent down some tapes we'd done with Fixer. We actually did really well in the audition and we got a phone call later saying we were both going to be in the band. We were cock-a-hoop. Unfortunately, that dream soon died as Coverdale married a German girl, moved there, and picked up a German band to play for him instead.

We played all over with Fixer, places like the Newcastle City Hall and Redcar Coatham Bowl. We were doing all originals. We had a singer called Idris Amin and he sounded just like Paul Rodgers. But then I was offered the job in Keith Satchfield's band. Now Keith was a local hero and one of hell of a guitarist. The band was called Axe, who later became Fist. The scene was fantastic. Keith had a big following as he was a real one off. We started off playing in working men's clubs. This was a great rock scene in the late seventies. We were playing six or seven nights a week, mainly in social clubs, right round the North East. We went through Ivan Birchall's agency.

IF: What were your aspirations?

Harry Hill: At the time the only ambition I had was to be a drummer in a proper rock band which Axe was. We had developed a real following but then, out of the blue, we split up. We had recorded a song called "SS Giro" but it was never released while we were Axe.

I can't even remember why we split up but anyway Keith and I formed a band called Hawkmoon. The bass player was Martin Bland, who is now singer with the Animals. Our first gig was at the Mayfair in Newcastle and it went great. But then along came this thing called the New Wave of British Heavy Metal and Dave Wood from Impulse Studios in Wallsend asked us if we wanted to put Axe back together. So we did, but it was a much heavier sound and we called it Fist. There was a band in Canada called Axe, hence the name change. Probably mistakenly, we tried to match the heaviness of the likes of Motorhead. Anyway we recorded the single "Name, Rank and Serial Number," which came out on Neat Records. We had two guitars in Keith and Dave Urwin, John Wiley on bass and me on the drums. Keith was the singer. The single became popular very quickly. I didn't know anything about any contract and I wasn't bothered. The big exuberance was running home to your mam to tell her you had a single in your hand by your band.

IF: How did the single do so well?

Harry Hill: The main thing that happened was *Sounds* magazine. Geoff Barton at *Sounds* had it as his heavy rock single of the week. From that we then supported Iron Maiden at the Marquee Club in London. The audience actually knew the words of the song, which was quite bizarre. It was all a bit of a dream to be honest.

IF: How did you sign the major deal with MCA?

Harry Hill: MCA just jumped on the New Wave of Heavy Metal bandwagon. EMI had Iron Maiden so MCA wanted a band like that. So MCA signed the Tygers of Pan Tang, us and White Spirit[1]. The problem was that they didn't really know how to handle hard rock bands. We recorded the album in De Lane

Lea Studios in London, which was a fantastic studio. You had Queen in Studio One, Emerson, Lake and Palmer in Studio Two, Wishbone Ash in Studio Three and Fist in Studio Four. The problem was we didn't give it enough thought. The attitude of the band was right we've signed to a major label, we don't have to work as hard, it's all just going to happen. Of course, it didn't happen like that. The first thing that went completely wrong was the production on the first album. The producer was Derek Lawrence, who worked a lot with Wishbone Ash. The rough mix sounded phenomenal on studio speakers. Keith stayed down for the final mix. When this came back it sounded so weak. The lighter tracks sounded okay but for the punchier tracks the power wasn't there and the thing about Fist was the actual power we generated. It was disappointing.

We toured with Samson, who had Bruce Dickinson on vocals before he joined Iron Maiden. Then we did two tours with UFO in 1980 and 1981, which was a great experience. We were then dropped by MCA, possibly down to lack of album sales. With MCA we had an excellent opportunity, but we mucked it up by trusting others to do things we should have kept an eye on. We also needed a strong manager, which we didn't have. So, I can really only blame us. We should have requested someone like Martin Birch to produce the album, who we'd already met.

We then split with Keith, who was really chasing a hit single. Dave and I wanted to stay with the rock stuff so we recorded an album up here in the North East and released it on Neat Records. Again, the production wasn't great but there were some good songs on it. By 1985, though, it just fizzled out. I'd got my first pub. I was 25 and I thought *Jesus I'm too old to be a drummer in a rock band*, I was married with my daughter on the way and, to be honest, wages of £25 a week wasn't going to cut it.

IF: With so many heavy rock bands in the North East of England did you feel part of a scene?

Harry Hill: Not really. To me there was competition between us all. But all the players at the time had both character and heart. We all had a sheer desire to succeed and that is why so many of the bands did well and got major record deals. Some are still doing really well to this day.

IF: When you got back together in 2014 how did it come about?

Harry Hill: We just started to rehearse and we sounded good and started doing festivals in Europe. The first gig back was at Brofest in Newcastle. When I arrived, I had all my drum accessories in a carrier bag. I saw this other drummer who had all this expensive stuff and I said, 'Alright mate' but he blanked me, captain nobody with my carrier bag. He didn't know we were topping the bill. Anyway, when we came off, the other drummer came up to me and wanted to be my best mate then and he said, 'How do you manage to do that at your age', I was 58 at the time, and I said, 'Simple really, if I played as shit as you I'd pack in.' He didn't see the funny side. He was one of these blokes who took himself too seriously. Sometimes if it wasn't for the mistakes, it wouldn't be live music. You don't need to be perfect, but you will never be any good if you don't play with feeling. Unfortunately, I had to leave a couple of years ago due to ill health. I can still be dynamite for one minute 32 seconds but then I run out of breath.

IF: You are known for the double bass drum sound. What inspired you to play like that?

Harry Hill: I would put that down to Cozy Powell. I heard the absolute power he would generate on things like "Kill the King" by Rainbow. It was also made more popular by Motorhead on things like "Overkill." The double bass drum requires a totally different technique to a single bass drum. So I spent two weeks locked away in my flat in South Shields until I mastered it. I'm not sure if my neighbours were deaf but I got no complaints. I was fortunate that I picked it up quite quickly. But I realised that you had to be fit to play the double bass drums so I started running up and down the coast every day. It was also important that you didn't use that technique on every single song. It did make us stand out as a band though. We used to do a lot of gigs with Raven and Rob Hunter, their drummer, was left-handed like me and also used the double bass drum so that was great. I actually played one 26-inch bass drum and a 24-inch bass drum, so that it gave an alternating sound between the two drums.

IF: Where did your nickname Harry 'Hiroshima' Hill come from?

Harry Hill: We were playing at South Shields Legion Club and we did a song called "You'll Never Get Me Up in One of Those," which had the double bass drum sound. We started off the show with this song and this fella walked past the PA with six pints of beer on one of those metal trays and just as I started the drums he got such a shock that he hoyed the tray up in the air with all the pints on and he said, 'F*****g hell that was like Hiroshima going off.'

IF: Do you ever think what would happen if your Mam had got you a trombone as you seem like a natural drummer?

Harry Hill: To be honest I think it's still 80% hard work and 20% ability. So, although the drumming was great, I may have ended up in a brass band if she'd got a trombone. You just never know.

IF: Looking back are there any regrets or would you do anything differently?

Harry Hill: To be honest no. The only thing I wish was that I had the knowledge of the music industry that I have now. At the time I just assumed everything would be fine. I was probably thinking *how big is my swimming pool going to be in LA*. But, to be honest, at the time nobody could tell me what to do because I knew best, or so I thought.

•••••••••••••••••

As we get up to go, Harry tells me that he's thinking of getting his drums out of the loft to give them a go again, maybe inspired by our chat. If he did, I can only apologise to his next-door neighbours who, if they weren't before, may now be half deaf after getting the full 'Hiroshima' treatment.

---

1. White Spirit were a NWOBHM band from Hartlepool who signed to MCA at similar time to Fist. Their guitarist, Janick Gers, later joined Iron Maiden and remains a member of the heavy metal superstars to this day.

Mythra

John Roach's Story

John Roach is guitarist with Mythra, a heavy rock band from South Shields formed in 1976. Today they play around the world and have enduring popularity abroad in places like Germany, Belgium and the US to a greater extent than they do at home. This is a feature of all of the heavy rock and heavy metal bands I talk to. Other similar features that crop up in my chats are their ambivalence towards the name of the genre they are often linked with, that is the New Wave of British Heavy Metal or NWOBHM. It becomes apparent that, although their music is very different to punk that was prevalent when they formed, the attitude and the energy of punk played a part in what they were doing. John is one of the few people featured in this book that I knew through work. He was the Head of the South Shields Marine School until recently. It was quite incongruous to see him wandering around the college with important guests in a suit but also sporting a very impressive ponytail, albeit one that was completely grey. Such is the life of a rocker.

We meet at Fausto's Café in Roker, Sunderland, which has a fantastic view of the North Sea and Roker Pier. After catching up on news of old colleagues we get down to chatting about John's life in rock music.

IF: What were your earliest memories of music?

John Roach: My mam, in particular, was a huge Beatles fan. My dad was into skiffle and big band jazz. I became indoctrinated by my Mam into the three-minute pop song of the Beatles, the Kinks, the Rolling Stones. When I started discovering music on my own, the act that I loved the most was Rick Wakeman and his album *Journey to the Centre of the Earth*, which I heard through a mate's older brother. Also I learned about bands through *Top of the Pops* and Radio 1 and that got me into all the glam bands like Slade and Sweet. The guitarist in the band was always the person I would look to. Then I got into the rock thing with bands like Humble Pie and Free. The song that really resonated with me was "Wishing Well" by Free. From there it went to Led Zeppelin, then Black Sabbath.

IF: How did you pick up an instrument?

John Roach: I started playing guitar when I was 12. At that time, I wanted to be John Lennon. I saw the Beatles films and had Beatles Jigsaw puzzles. I had a very rough acoustic guitar. When I was 14, I got an £11 Audition Guitar from Woolworths and a 5 watt amplifier. Then when I was 15, I got an Antoria Les Paul Copy.

When I left school, I got an apprenticeship as an engineer at Swan Hunters shipyard and all my money went on equipment. I was in a band called Zarathustra, which was a forerunner of Mythra. We started at 15 and by the time we were 16 we were playing in pubs and clubs. It was all covers. We played everything from Humble Pie to Budgie, Led Zep, Black Sabbath. Anything that had a guitar in the charts we'd give it a go. We were quite ambitious and fearless. We'd play "Show me the Way"[1] and "You Ain't Seen nothing Yet"[2]. We were decent musicians and had the arrogance of youth, so we'd try anything. We played in pubs and clubs but because we were only 16, we needed my dad and Maurice's dad (Maurice was the singer at the time) to ferry us about and take us into the pubs. Everything was stuffed into two cars. We played mainly South Shields to begin with.

Eventually we got an agent from Newcastle called Ivan Birchall, who was a really big name in the North East. This allowed us to start and play all round the North East.

IF: How did you get such a prestigious agent given your age?

John Roach: We went and knocked on his door in the Cloth Market in Newcastle and he liked our brass neck. We would do any gigs offered. If anyone pulled out, we would step up at zero notice. We started getting loads of work through Ivan.

IF: At 16 did you have an aspiration?

John Roach: It's funny because we genuinely believed we were going to be as big as Led Zeppelin. We had no plan but also no doubts. We were all apprentices. So we put all our spare money into the band, buying equipment. Maurice passed his driving test in December 1976 and I passed mine in January 1977 so we bought a van at the age of 17.

The game changer was seeing bands at the Mayfair, in particular UFO with Michael Schenker on guitar. They were promoting the *Lights Out* album. Then we saw Judas Priest, with a two-guitar sound, and they really pulled it off live.

We also started seeing rock bands locally playing original songs. We saw a band called Warbeck at the Legion Club in South Shields and they played a mix of covers and originals but the originals were so good that I thought they were covers. Then three weeks later we saw a band called Axe at the Legion, who played one of the same songs we'd heard played by Warbeck that was an original. Axe were a great band with Harry Hill on drums and Keith Satchfield and Dave Irwin on guitar. When we got there it was full of 'hairies' and they had a mixing desk and soundman, which blew us away. This was in 1977, on a Tuesday night. It turned out this song was written by Keith Satchfield, who was originally in Warbeck. The songs were "Big Rig" and "Name, Rank and Serial Number". So we asked if we could play them and Dave Irwin showed us the chords and Keith wrote out the lyrics for us. From that point we realised we could do our own stuff and I wrote about five songs straight away. Maurice was also writing. We just started putting our own songs into our set.

We were working Thursday, Friday, Saturday and Sunday nights and sometimes a Saturday afternoon. We would gig all over the North East. We had a van and two PAs. There was a circuit to play. It was mainly working men's clubs. In the late 70s it was the norm for rock bands to play the clubs. So, there were gigs as far as Shildon and Hartlepool and we got a following in these places.

Then we started to promote our own gigs, firstly in youth clubs and we could make money as there were kids hanging from the roof when we played. We wanted to play the Bolingbroke Hall in South Shields, where there had been an infamous Angelic Upstarts' gig where a pig's head was kicked about and that involved police action. We were there and it was bloody great. We had to go to the Town Hall but they weren't keen after the Upstarts played. So we put on our gigs at the Boldon Lane Community Centre and hired big equipment and played with local band Hellenbach. It was getting a real buzz.

IF: At a time when punk was popular why were there so many heavy metal bands in the North East?

John Roach: For us we identified with competent musicians which maybe punk didn't. However, the punk bands I knew just pretended they couldn't play when, in fact, they were very competent. We aspired to be respected by our peers as musicians.

IF: When did you move towards recording?

John Roach: We saw a small advert in the back of *Sounds* for a single called "Get Your Rocks Off" by Def Leppard. It turned out this was on Def Leppard's own label, Bludgeon Riffola. The next week it was reviewed in *Sounds*. We thought, well that's what we need to do, get a record out and get a record deal. So we thought we needed to get a demo tape and put it on record label desks. As we were quite well off due to being in work, we had about £260 that we could use to record a demo. We went to Impulse Studios in Wallsend. We got the price but the place smelled of sweat and damp as they used mattresses to deaden the sound and they got damp.

Maurice found another studio in Pity Me, Durham called Guardian Studios and it was brand new. We talked to Terry Gavaghan, who owned the studio and engineered all the recordings, and said we wanted to make a demo and he said 'Well, how much money have you got?' and we naively told him. He said for that we could record a vinyl record, which would make us stand out compared to the cassettes that arrive on the desk of record companies.

We made an appointment for a Saturday to record an EP, turned up only to be told we were a week early. So we used two Saturdays instead of one. We recorded four of the songs that we played live. Terry mixed it then he returned a few weeks later with 200 singles. We then went back for another 200 as we sold all the first batch at our gigs. We sent about a dozen away. Then we went back for more singles and Terry Gavaghan got us a distribution deal which got it into the shops. The lead track was "Death and Destiny" and it was backed by three other songs, "UFO", "Overlord" and "Killer".

We sent it to Geoff Barton, from the national music weekly paper *Sounds,* who reviewed it and billed it as 'this year's "Get Your Rocks Off"'. A few weeks later there was a full article on North East bands as part of NWOBHM and we were in the front cover of *Sounds*. Us, Raven, Fist and White Spirit all featured. We always said that we weren't the best but that after Def Leppard we were the first of the NWOBHM bands to release our own stuff. (there follows a discussion on the origins and suitability of NWOBHM as a moniker, which John is far from sure about). Recently I was interviewed by a Polish journalist, and he asked us if we were influenced by Iron Maiden and I had to say that, no, I hadn't heard of them. I listed a load of local North East bands that he'd never heard of but that who I was influenced and inspired by.

We sent the single all over the place including Tommy Vance, who played it on his 'Rock Show' on Radio 1. Fluff Freeman played us. It was through Tommy Vance that we got signed to ITB Promotions, who represented the likes of Judas Priest and Iron Maiden.

By this time, however, I was beginning to get sick of the whole 'jam tomorrow' scenario. Terry Gavaghan promised us lots, including record contracts. We felt that he was holding back for a big score. We couldn't understand why things weren't happening as we felt they should. We didn't have a manager and relied on Terry. I felt I was as far as I could go and my enthusiasm was waning. We were being promised slots on the *Old Grey Whistle Test*[3] but it was all empty promises. By that time, I was at Sunderland Poly doing a degree in Mechanical Engineering while an apprentice with Swan's and I just couldn't afford the time. So I left the band at this point, a little disillusioned that my big dreams weren't going anywhere.

I later joined Fist. This was at the back end of 1982. We released an album *Back with a Vengeance*. They had been on MCA but were dropped but we were able to release this on Neat Records. I was in Fist for three and half years and we did five gigs in that time. Even though the album had been well received we just couldn't get gigs. It seemed like the time had passed quite quickly for heavy rock bands.

While I was in Fist, I was also in a covers band called Centre Fold with me, Glenn Coates (singer of Fist), Harry Hill (drummer of Fist) and a bassist called Peter Scott. We were making a lot of money in the clubs. We'd get dressed up as Laurel and Hardy, I'd take my clothes off and then we'd finish with a couple of AC/DC songs, it was all a show. Peter the bassist started acting clumsy and we thought it was drinking but it turned out to be a brain tumour and he died. I was 22 and it was my first experience of death and although the band wanted to carry on, I just couldn't take it. So I packed in and sold all my gear. I was devastated when he died, he was a great friend. This was about 1982.

IF: So how did the Mythra reunion come about?

John Roach: This happened in 2014. We'd been approached by Stewart Bartlett, who organised a festival in Newcastle called Brofest. So we agreed to have a rehearsal and if it was any good we'd play. We missed that year as I fell off my bike and broke my collar bone. The original bassist, Peter Melsom, flat out didn't want to do it and the drummer, Barry, was in Azerbajhan as a coded welder so making big bucks. But Maurice and Vince, the singer, were happy to give it a go. We rehearsed at Downcast Studios in Gateshead and the owner said he'd play drums. Alex Perry, who'd been in the band at the end of the first stint was also up for it. So we did our first gig in 2015. The day after Brofest we got a call from Keep It True Festival in Germany asking us to play there. We got a manager and a record deal and recorded and released an album called *Still Burning*. That year, 2017, we played Athens, Belgium and Holland. We played in California and it turned out we had a big following in the US. In the US they don't differentiate between punk rock and the New Wave of British Heavy Metal. They see it as independent bands who haven't got deals releasing records.

IF: Was there a north east heavy rock scene?

John Roach: Yes, there was a lot of bands who were similar and were very supportive of each other and this spilled over into the pubs and some of the clubs in the late '70s. The '70s was a strange time. We were coming out of a three-day week[4], strikes and industrial action by the bin men and the utilities. There was not much money about but watching *Top of the Pops* you could see a way out. What we didn't realise was that it was a business and you, as a musician, were just a tool. It's very rare that you make money as a musician. You can make money as a promoter or studio owner but not as a musician. The punk rockers told us we could do it on our own even if we didn't really get their music.

IF: What is the North East scene like now? Can you get gigs?

John Roach: No, there's only one venue in the North East and that's Trillians. There isn't really a scene in the UK. We play predominantly in Europe. The crowds are far bigger in Europe. But we now play because we enjoy it. I am now 62 and I'm not going to make it! We don't have a deal yet. We recorded a new album but are awaiting a deal. It will come out. We recorded it just before the Pandemic.

IF: Many local bands like yourselves, Raven and Venom have been name checked by Lars Ulrich of Metallica. How did the US hear about you?

John Roach: It was through reading the magazine *Kerrang,* which was started by Geoff Barton of *Sounds*. In fact, Raven have been asked to support Metallica on an upcoming benefit concert.

My only concern is that the NWOBHM is talked of as a genre and it isn't. It comprises so many different styles of bands from proto-punk to Doom Metal to Blues-based bands. We were similar in that we played heavy rock but linking us all to that spurious moniker is a bit restricting in my view.

....

I saw Mythra in 2018 at Think Tank in Newcastle and they were amazing. They were tight as a band, very loud and all really accomplished musicians. To be seen as accomplished on their instruments was a driver for them right from the start in 1976 and this is something they have achieved in spades. While we are at that gig, they were supporting their friends Blitzkrieg, who were launching an album, scattered about were a handful of what appeared to be original Mythra fans judging by the fact that they knew all the words to their songs from their first EP "Death and Destiny" as well as songs from *Still Burning*, released in 2017.

John tells me that they have just returned from a heavy rock festival in Germany called Keep It True, where they played to a packed hall. You can see that gig on YouTube and the place is absolutely jumping. It is remarkable that they struggle to get gigs at home but can fill out venues in Germany, Poland and the US.

When John was 18, he was on the front page of *Sounds* as an example of the future of heavy rock. He believed he'd be part of the next Led Zeppelin. He didn't achieve that but at 62 he's still playing fast, urgent heavy rock to literally adoring fans. John doesn't complain.

1. "Show Me The Way" was a hit for Peter Frampton who rose to fame as guitarist from Humble Pie. The album from which it came, the live album *Frampton Comes Alive* was released in 1976 and was on the US album chart for 97 weeks and sold 11 million records worldwide.

2. "You Ain't Seen Nothing Yet" was a hit for the Canadian band Bachman-Turner Overdrive. It was number 2 in the UK and number 1 in the US in 1974.

3. *Old Grey Whistle Test* was a highly influential rock music programme broadcast at nighttime on the BBC. It ran from 1970 to 1986. Bands would generally play live, and it was a more serious concept than *Top of the Pops*. Bands from Bob Marley to Roxy Music and the New York Dolls all made famous appearances on the show. Its successor could be seen as *Later ... with Jools Holland*.

4. The three-day Week was part of a highly volatile period of politics in the mid-1970s. As a response to strikes by the mine workers Ted Heath's Conservative Government restricted the use of electricity by commercial companies to three days per week to conserve coal stocks. This ran from January 1974 to March 1974.

5. Kitchenware Records

Kitchenware Records was an independent record label set up in Newcastle in 1982 by three pals, Keith Armstrong, Paul Ludford and Phil Mitchell. It began as an attempt to get gigs in Newcastle for the bands that the three friends liked. It soon developed into a record label that was responsible for the release of some of the best music in the 1980s. Whether by luck or design they signed up four fantastic bands in Prefab Sprout, the Kane Gang, Martin Stephenson and the Daintees and Hurrah! They secured beneficial licensing deals with major record companies - CBS, Arista and London Records, that ultimately saw the release of 10 albums by Prefab Sprout, four from Martin Stephenson and the Daintees, two by each of the Kane Gang and Hurrah! As Keith Armstrong will state when I meet him, there was no 'Kitchenware Sound' and no 'sound of Newcastle' as each of the bands was stubbornly individualistic. However, they were all purveyors of thoughtful and intelligent music that sat nicely within the 1980s zeitgeist.

There is an argument to be made that Keith Armstrong was, or even is, the Tony Wilson (joint owner of Manchester's Factory Records) of Newcastle. Keith may be both appalled and delighted by such an analogy. Tony Wilson, or Anthony H Wilson as he later re-branded himself, was a bag of contradictions, an intellectual who revelled in lower brow media and a bon viveur who was obsessively guarded regarding his privacy. Tony Wilson relentlessly drove and promoted Manchester and its cultural renaissance, Keith, and his fellow Kitchenware colleagues, had the same civic pride and a desire to shout from the roof tops that Newcastle, and the North East, is great and no one needs to leave this region to make a dent in the UK's musical landscape. Where Tony Wilson used pseudo-Situationist sloganeering and aesthetics, Kitchenware used the equally subversive *Viz* Magazine team to get their message across with the record companies. The parallels are numerous.

However, I would suggest that Kitchenware were a long way ahead of Factory Records regarding business savvy. Famously, Wilson's Factory Records had a socialist principle that inserted a key clause into all their group's contracts *The musicians own everything, the company owns nothing, all our groups have the right to f*** off.* This is all very nice and quotable but when Factory Records was heading towards bankruptcy and they attempted to sell the company to London Records they discovered that in fact they did not own the recordings of their assets such as Joy Division, New Order and the Happy Mondays. Factory Records duly went bankrupt. Kitchenware Records, in contrast, sought and succeeded in getting the best deals for their bands and helped them sell as many records as possible. It is quite a coincidence that London Records was the company that signed up both the Daintees and the Kane Gang.

By the 1990s, for various reasons, the Kane Gang, Hurrah! and Martin Stephenson and the Daintees were either no longer entities or were on a completely different path. However, a decade later, as if to prove those shining lights were no fluke, Kitchenware did it all again with the massively successful band the Editors. Although Kitchenware ceased to be in 2017, Keith Armstrong currently runs Soul Kitchen Recordings which, as well as managing the prodigiously talented and successful Jake Bugg, also signs and promotes young North East acts such as

Kay Greyson, Sweets and Luke Royalty. The late Tony Wilson is rightly lauded as an important and inspirational character in the UK's illustrious pop history. When assessing the North East's pop music story, you should never underestimate the significance of figures like Keith Armstrong and his record label Kitchenware Records.

Of course, there is a glaring absence in this chapter of any direct voices from Prefab Sprout. They are notoriously private. However, because their story weaves throughout the other bands' stories and especially that of Keith and Kitchenware itself, means they are far from ignored. This is a relief as their cool detachment and sweet songs resonate today and will tomorrow. And they, along with the Kane Gang, Martin Stephenson and the Daintees and Hurrah!, for a period in the mid-1980s, were releasing the best records around and were recognised as such by an adoring music press. It was a time when the North East music scene was the coolest in the UK, in my totally unbiased opinion!

Kitchenware Records

Keith Armstrong's Story

If we look at the rise of musical scenes historically, we can sometimes see that a record label is pivotal in driving their creation and development. In Manchester there was Factory Records, which launched Joy Division, New Order and the Happy Mondays. In Glasgow there was Postcard Records, which launched Orange Juice and Aztec Camera. In the North East there was the Heavy Metal label Neat and then there was Kitchenware. Factory, Postcard and Kitchenware reflected a certain civic pride and a desire to promote bands that would reflect well on their region. They were also led by charismatic characters in Tony Wilson, Alan Horne and, in Kitchenware's case, Keith Armstrong. To my ears Kitchenware, especially in the 1980s, represented a high water mark for North East music and North East creativity. I sit down with Keith at Newcastle's upmarket Malmaison Hotel and listen to a real North-East musical trailblazer.

IF: How did Kitchenware evolve?

Keith Armstrong: At the start of the '80s there were a few people round Newcastle who were the same age doing similar things with similar values, not necessarily just involved in music.

There were three main players at the time. There was us, at what became Kitchenware, myself, Paul Ludford and Phil Mitchell. We originally started because there were loads of bands around at the time that we liked but they didn't play Newcastle, so we decided to start our own club to put them on, which we called The Soul Kitchen. Then there was Tommy Caulker, who had the Trent House Soul Bar. We had similar values to him, with an awareness of the civil rights movement and things like that. We tended to be influenced by the same music such as Marvin Gaye and David Bowie. Tommy was quite pioneering, especially when it came to championing black music. The third group of people on the scene were Simon and Chris Donald, who were just starting *Viz* Magazine. I knew them because, at the time, I was managing the HMV shop on Northumberland Street and we happened to have a big stapler. They used to bring their comics in as we were the only people they'd heard of who had a big enough stapler to staple them. So, we asked them to design our posters for the Soul Kitchen, which they did. Then we'd stick them up in Tommy Caulker's pub or in HMV and this was how we built up what became the scene. All of our slogans were things like *You're an idiot if you miss out on this*.

We started the club at the Casablanca club in the Haymarket. It was the only gay club in Newcastle at the time and it was the only club that would let us use their venue. This was the forerunner for things like Rockshots. We had tried everywhere else and got nowhere and got no help from the promoters. Casablanca said we could have Tuesday nights as that was the slowest and they stipulated we had to let their members in free.

The first band we put on were the Fire Engines from Edinburgh. Paul and I did the records. Phil got involved with the club. We also had a film maker and a poet. It was a real collective. We had Jenny, who designed and made clothes. Anything that came from the people involved with the Soul Kitchen would be called Kitchenware, whether it was clothes or records or anything else. We would try and do things differently. So, for example, when we put on Aztec Camera the support was a photography exhibition from the rock photographer Derek Ridgers. Or we'd show films by our friend Mark, who was a student film maker, before a band went on. Paul and I would DJ but we'd ask the bands to DJ after they played their set. It was an eclectic mix. And there was a mix of people attending from students to the gay community, which was quite underground at the time. The vibe in the room would always be great. We felt like we were doing something that nobody else was doing. It was underground but popular.

IF: The original aim was to put on bands that you liked. How did this progress into putting out records?

Keith Armstrong: We had a local band called The Green Eyed Children asking if they could play the club. We went to see them rehearse and thought they were brilliant so we got them to support Aztec Camera. We said to them, 'You're great but you can't be going round called The Green Eyed Children. I'd seen a propaganda poster from the 1930s called Hurrah for Youth. So, we suggested that name and it was then shortened to Hurrah! They became the first band that we got involved with. At the time we were really inspired by Postcard Records, from Glasgow and we got a lot of their bands down to play.

By this time, we had decided that the Soul Kitchen could move around so we could use bigger venues. We really wanted to put New Order on so I rang up their manager, Rob Gretton, from a pay phone in the Egypt Cottage pub. This was around 1982. We'd already put on A Certain Ratio, who were on Factory Records along with New Order, and they gave us Rob's number. I called Rob and explained what we were about and he said, 'It'll cost you £2000 and you have to pay us up front.' So I said, 'Can I have a week to sell the tickets?' Then the pips went on the phone and I frantically had to find another 10p. Rob said, 'Are you on a f****** pay phone? Right, you've got ten days to sell the tickets and we want paying up front or we're not coming.' There were no contracts, they would just turn up, collect the money, then play. I had no money, so I borrowed £50 to get posters and tickets printed. *Viz* did the posters. We hired the Mayfair in Newcastle and the tickets sold out just like that. New Order were amazing.

Anyway, we made something like £2000 out of this and we thought I know let's start a record label with this money. We didn't have a clue what to do but we thought we'd get Hurrah! to record a single but didn't know where to do it. At the time there was a single by Scritti Politti called "The Sweetest Girl" and I loved it. I found out where it was recorded, in London, and off we went to do the first single. The day before we went down, Martin Stephenson and his band were busking outside my HMV shop, and he was getting grief from some of the people in the street. So, I went outside and asked him if he wanted to come in and play in the shop. We thought they were pretty good, so we said, 'We are off down to London to make a record. Do you want to come too'. And they said, 'Yeah, Ok.' We had the studio, in Bury Street, London, for 24 hours so we just stayed up and did the first Hurrah single and the first Daintees single. So, really, we had New Order to thank for starting our record label.

I used to listen to loads of records that came in the shop. One day I put on this record called "Lions in my Own Garden" by Prefab Sprout. I thought it was amazing and I asked where it came from and one of the lads in the shop said, 'Oh, someone just came in and dropped them off to see if we could sell them.' So we contacted Prefab Sprout and asked them if they wanted us to put the record out for them, which they were more than happy with.

Around the same time, we got a tape from the Kane Gang of "Brother, Brother". We thought that each of these acts sounded a bit like our favourite artists. So, Prefab Sprout sounded a bit like Steely Dan, Martin Stephenson sounded a bit like Ry Cooder, the Kane Gang sounded a bit like Gil Scott Heron.

IF: They were four fantastic bands. How much was it talent spotting by you and how much of was these bands falling on your lap?'

Keith Armstrong: There were a lot of other bands sending us tapes and a lot of bands around trying to play the Soul Kitchen, but those four were the ones who stood out. None of them looked like typical bands. We weren't looking for a Kitchenware sound but for bands who were like our favourite artists and our tastes were quite diverse so the bands we signed were all different. When you look at equivalents like Factory Records, they sort of had a sound but that was because they mainly used one producer, so it was Martin Hannett sound, rather than a Factory Sound. We never chased that and were quite happy that our acts were diverse.

IF: How important was the music press to you?

Keith Armstrong: It occurs to me that we didn't have a recognised scene around here because we didn't have the strong media support that they had in Manchester or London. The one thing we didn't find was a great writer. However, what we wanted was credibility and you can't buy that. So, I only sent the early records out to writers who I thought could give us some credibility. I sent them to Julie Burchill, Dave McCullough from *Sounds* and Adrian Thrills from the *NME*. I got a letter back from Julie Burchill who said, 'How dare you suggest I write about music as I don't do that anymore but if I did write about music I'd write about Prefab Sprout.' Dave McCullough came up and we took him out for a pint and showed him around Newcastle. He said, 'Listen, I can't be your mate because I need to be impartial' and I thought that was really cool. And from that he wrote a three-page article about us in *Sounds*. We felt we were on a mission to save the world from new romantic music, which I hated. We started to get support from the music press like Dave McCullough and Barney Hoskyns, who championed Prefab Sprout. But there was never anyone up here to help fan the flames.

It was really important for me to show you could do all this from Newcastle and that you didn't have to go down to London.

And I think we proved that. A weird thing happened, while we were doing this, the Channel 4 programme *The Tube* started up right on our doorstep. So, I rang them up and I said to the producer, Malcolm Gerrie, 'You're a phoney. You've set up in Newcastle and you've done nothing about Newcastle.' So, he said, 'Come in and tell us all about it.' He suggested they put Prefab Sprout on and I would be interviewed. I said, 'a. If you're putting one band on you need to put all four on and they need equal time or we're not doing it and b. I'm not doing an interview because it's not about me, it's about the bands.' And so they acquiesced and did what we wanted. We scripted it all, as we didn't trust anyone to get it right. But, in the end, it was that slot on *The Tube* that really launched the label. That introduced us to London Records and put us on to what I called the world's first Dependent Record Label.

IF: Did you always set out to link with a major label?

Keith Armstrong: We just didn't have any money. The first thing I did was I went to Rough Trade to try to distribute Prefab Sprout's first single. They said, 'How many do you expect to sell?' and I said, 'Well, everyone should have this record but maybe 5,000.' And they said, 'Anything over 5,000 is just not cool.' I thought I'm not in that business. I'm not in a business that doesn't aim to get as many people as possible to hear your records. So, I borrowed £5,000 to make Prefab Sprout's first album, *Swoon*, and I thought it was just too good to go out on an independent label and I said to Paddy, (McAloon, singer and songwriter) 'I am going to get you a £100K record deal,' I was just so confident about how good the record was. I had three meetings with the Head of Warner Brothers, the Head of London Records and the Head of CBS. Muff Winwood of CBS records got halfway through the record and pressed the pause button and said, 'What do you want?' and I said, '£100K'. He went off to check and then came back and said, 'Yes, you've got a deal.'

IF: Was that figure plucked out of the air?

Keith Armstrong: Yes, pretty much. I don't know where I got it from. We said all the records would be on Kitchenware label and we would do the art work and that was for a seven-album deal.

IF: Was CBS the most amenable of the record labels?

Keith Armstrong: No, they all bought into what we were doing. London signed the Kane Gang and Martin Stephenson and we had our first hit with the Kane Gang in "Closest Thing to Heaven". There's no way we could have made records of that sort of quality on our own. These people could market you round the world, they could get you on the radio. We didn't know about any of that. These companies had massive marketing teams.

IF: You had a steep trajectory from the start. How did it feel?

Keith Armstrong: Well, I was only 23 or 24 at the time so it was bonkers to be honest. For some reason we expected it all. We just jumped on the ride and enjoyed it. For me, I wanted all the acts we had to be the biggest acts in the world. Hurrah! were the hardest to get going. Everyone loved them but it wasn't until Arista stumped up some money that we got them going.

We certainly had the press interest, but we needed to get the songs on the radio. With Martin we did the first album with a producer called Gil Norton who has gone on to do great things. After that, in an attempt to get him on radio, London Records suggested we use a guy called Russ Kunkel[1] to record a song called "Wholly Humble Heart" on the radio and we sent Martin across to Los Angeles to do it. But Martin just didn't fancy it at all. He turned his back on it eventually. But I loved him, he was like a little brother to me. I could see Tom Waits in him, I could see Charles Bukowski in him, all these characters that I love.

Looking back at the Kane Gang I wish we had done more gigs with them. We only really did a handful of gigs but the gigs they did were great. Their musical director was Wix, who plays with Paul McCartney now. They were a great band. Martin (Brammer, one of two singers in the Kane Gang), of course, went on to have a great career as a songwriter, starting it off with the Lighthouse Family, who we managed.

IF: Are Prefab Sprout still an entity?

Keith Armstrong: No .... and yes. Paddy makes music all the time and anything he wanted to put out he could. But the real answer is no, but they could be. I was down at a music industry awards ceremony a little while ago and took Paddy down with me. I was talking to Simon Moran of SJM concert promoters and he said, 'Do you mind if I have a chat with Paddy to see if he'll do a tour?' I said, 'He just won't do it. Not for all the tea in China.' Simon asked Paddy, 'How much?' and Paddy said, 'It's not about the money. I just hate touring and I have all these problems with my ears.' Anyway, I thought about it and I thought let's bring the tour to him and book the Sage in Gateshead out for five or ten nights. I thought it would be like what Kate Bush did. I said to Paddy we could sort out the sound to compensate for his hearing problems but, in the end, it just wasn't for him.

Then, of course, there is the Spike Lee[2] story. Spike phoned me up one day and said, 'Hi, this is Spike Lee' and I thought yeah right, Spike Lee phoning me up. And it was Spike Lee and he said he wanted to talk to me about Prefab Sprout. Apparently, his brother is a massive Prefab Sprout fan and his brother had done a whole script for a film based on Prefab Sprout songs. They wanted to meet us in London to discuss doing this film. So, me and Paddy went down to London to meet Spike and his brother. This was probably a few years before the lockdown. We met them and they had the script and it all looked great. A little later I was in New York and I got a call from Spike saying he wouldn't be doing the film because he'd fallen out with his brother. I asked Spike if he minded if I had a chat with his brother and I managed to talk his brother round and it was back on. Paddy reckoned he could write better versions of the songs having read the script. We met up with Spike again in London to go through the script and song revisions. Then he fell out with his brother again. His brother wanted it to be animated and Spike wanted it to be like the Wiz (the Wizard of Oz remake with Michael Jackson). It was a Christmas story. But they just couldn't agree and so it's just lying there in abeyance probably never to see the light of day. Paddy, of course, had written and demoed a whole album of new songs for it based on the script. He videoed him performing the songs and sent them, with notes, to Spike but no one other than me, Spike and one other have seen these songs. Its brilliant stuff.

IF: This was a golden period and represented very much the first chapter of Kitchenware. Were there any regrets relating to that period?

Keith Armstrong: I wish we had got a better record out of Hurrah! We got some money to make *Tell God I'm here*. We were all massive Rolling Stones fans and we found out their legendary producer, Jimmy Miller, was available so we got him and booked some studio time with him but we couldn't get the album out of him that we hoped for.

The Kane Gang wrote lots of great songs and had some really strong hits. Martin Stephenson obviously turned out to be a great songwriter. So, no regrets. And with Prefab Sprout we did some really pioneering stuff. I know everyone thinks Steve McQueen is the one but, for me, Swoon was their masterpiece. Paddy just hated touring but really with all four bands things seem to come to a natural end.

IF: Does Paddy realise how good a songwriter he is?

Keith Armstrong: I think he realises he's good but he will look at Rod Temperton, who wrote some of Michael Jackson's hits, and think he's on a different plane, which isn't really true. In truth Paddy writes for himself. Paddy has such a romantic view of life and that makes him just different. He is the best lyricist I have ever come across, he never spills a drop. So, for me, it's quite sad that he doesn't make records anymore. He's still got a deal at Sony AND they will pay for anything he wants to put out. They ring me every three months or so to see if he'll put anything out. I went across to his studio a while ago and he has boxes and boxes of stuff he's recorded. It's a massive treasure trove of artistic endeavour.

IF: How did the second Kitchenware chapter with the Editors come about?

Keith Armstrong: Well, in between that I was managing the Lighthouse Family. So, apart from Prefab Sprout, the first stage came to an end. We were going through a bit of a fallow period. We signed a band called the Fatima Mansions who were brilliant. We had a modern classical artist called Nichola Walker-Smith. We started a club called Resurrection. Then Lighthouse Family took off like a rocket. When that imploded, we decided to relaunch Kitchenware on a less altruistic, more sound business front. I borrowed a load of venture capital money. The first band we signed were an all-girl hip hop band from Newcastle called Sirens. And strangely that took off in Japan and we ended up doing a deal with JVC for them in Japan. They then had a number one dance hit in the US.

Then I signed the Editors. At the time they were called Snow Field and one of my mates heard them and told me about them. I went to see them in Birmingham and it was one of those times where I thought the first song is great, the second song is great, by the third song I was going to sign them and then by the fifth song I was urrgghh what happened? I talked to the singer afterwards to see what he was like and he had a real intensity to him. So, I got them to play the Cluny in Newcastle and there were only about 10 people in the room, and they were all involved with Kitchenware. They played an absolutely blinding set and we signed them on the strength of that. We said they needed to change their name as it sounded too much like Snow Patrol. I thought they sounded like Interpol, who I loved and who were really happening at the time.

IF: As a talent spotter what are you looking for?

Keith Armstrong: With the Editors we acted quickly, which was important and what appealed was the sound, the songs and the intensity of the singer. The guitarist had all the hooks and he made a big impression. Sometimes it looks more complicated than it is. We put the song "Bullets" out and it got Zane Lowe's song of the week and their first two singles were hits. It was like we put all our money on red and it came up. We were set up as an independent record label and Rob Stringer, head of Sony came to us and said they wanted to sign them. We were unsure and Rob asked us how many albums we expected to sell so we said 40K. He said he'd give us the money for 40K records up front and, to be honest, it was an offer we just couldn't refuse. We signed a distribution deal with them. You also have to think of the band at that point. Sony could take them worldwide and we couldn't.

Around about the time of the Editors' third album I had a friend from Nottingham who had a demo studio and he said he'd had a kid come in to do some demos and he said, 'He's really young but he's really good would you mind having a listen to him as I think he's got something.' He sent a song called "It's true" by Jake Bugg and I thought it was amazing. So, he said, 'Would you come and meet as I don't really trust anyone to look after him right.' I went down to see him and signed him up. As the Editors were coming to an end for us, we got Jake Bugg and again that went off like a rocket.

The label came to an end after 30 years but we carried on managing Jake Bugg and also ran the publishing. We now use that to develop new things.

IF: So now Kitchenware doesn't exist but you have Soul Kitchen Recordings. Tell me about that?

Keith Armstrong: Well, during the lockdown there was nothing we could do. We had a record waiting to go with Jake Bugg. So, we thought we'd start a 'son of Kitchenware'. We'd find young talent who wanted to put records out and see if we could help them develop. They are mainly local to the North East. We have Sweets from Newcastle, Kay Greyson from Newcastle, Luke Royalty from Darlington, but we also have Girl

Band from Nottingham. We try, where possible, to get young managers to act for each artist, to develop music management talent as well.

IF: What is success for you now?

Keith Armstrong: I have always thought that success is making a living from what you love doing. For the acts we want them to be in a better place than where we found them, whatever that may mean.

IF: Are you as passionate now as when you started?

Keith Armstrong: Yes, but probably not as mad. I listen to new music all the time.

IF: Looking back is there anyone you worked with that didn't make it, that you thought should have?

Keith Armstrong: Somebody said to me everyone rises to the level they deserve and I think that is true of all the acts I've been involved with. I would hope no one who has been involved with us regretted that involvement. We have always done our absolute best for all our acts.

....

As I am editing this piece I hear an interview with Rob Dickens, a legendary record label executive who, while running Warner Brothers, was instrumental in launching the careers of Prince and Madonna and the re-launch of Cher. In his spare time, he lectures students in the skills of A&R or talent spotting and talent launching in the music business. He explains that actually this is an ability that you are either born with or not. It really can't be taught, which must be a little demoralising for his students to hear. However, reflecting on Keith Armstrong's career, this natural ability is something that Keith has in spades. Prefab Sprout, the Kane Gang, Martin Stephenson, Hurrah!, the Lighthouse Family, the Editors and Jake Bugg is such a rich abundance of talent and success, all spotted by Keith. It may appear to be luck but it almost certainly isn't. Whatever Keith is looking at is worth checking out.

A founding principle of Kitchenware was, and is in its current guise of Soul Kitchen Recordings, that we are great up here and you don't have to leave the North East to get success. It's quite clear that the North East needs people like the Kitchenware collective and that is a challenge laid down to all aspiring cultural leaders in the region. The talent is there but it needs nurturing and then it will fly.

---

1. Russ Kunkel is an American drummer who has played with everyone from Neil Young to BB King. He has produced acts like Carly Simon and Aaron Neville.

2. Spike Lee is an Oscar winning American film maker best known for *Do the Right Thing* and *BlacKkKlansman*.

Martin Stephenson and the Daintees

Martin Stephenson's Story

After spending about an hour and half in Martin's company it is apparent that he is on a spiritual journey as much as a musical one. He rose to fame in the 1980s when, as part of the Kitchenware stable of bands and signed to London Records, he made four highly acclaimed albums with his band the Daintees. However, fame was the last thing he wanted. This is a man with no ego in an industry that gorges on ego. He tells me that for his last album on a major label, the brilliant *Salutation Road*, he was given a budget of £150,000 and was staying in the fabled Chateau Marmont Hotel in Los Angeles. He hated every second of it. For Martin this was a meaningless life and he literally chose poverty. He walked away from his record label, his band, his manager and even his marriage and went back to a life of busking that he had started with at the age of 16. He was 31 years old.

Fast forward 30 years to today and Martin feels he has it cracked. He has just recorded an album with a musical hero of his, John Perry, guitarist from the new wave greats the Only Ones, and is in the middle of a sell-out tour. He is beloved as a great song writer and a man oozing sincere bonhomie. Most importantly he is a contented man. He is a proud father of two girls, he is back with Gary and Anth Dunn of the Daintees and is living a sustainable existence in the Highlands of Scotland. How he got there starts with his love of table tennis. I kid you not. Be warned though, keeping Martin on track in any conversation is like riding a wild horse without a saddle, he is apt to go off on a tangent at any point.

IF: How did you get started on your musical journey?

Martin Stephenson: I won a football penalty competition when I was a kid, I was 11. I wasn't very good at footy but this big lad, who we called Lurch and was a goalkeeper, thought I'd be good at penalties and he asked me to be in his team. Somehow I won the penalty shoot-out. He then told me about the Scouts and from there I got into table tennis.

It was in the table tennis club that I met a coach, Jim Sixsmith, who turned out to be a bit of guru for me. He was 27 and when he put a table tennis bat in my hand my life changed. He basically mentored me to become a county level table tennis player. He lavished attention on me that I didn't get at home. This journey took me out of my council house and all over the North East and I had a bit of a gift. I was beating players who were 30 years old. Also, though, Jim would lend me all these amazing albums such as the Doors and Frank Zappa. Before that music had pretty much passed me by. He used to go to places like the Club a'Gogo and used to tell me about that scene. I got a real education through music.

When I was 15 punk came along and it made me feel like I was re-born. Jim thought punk was shite but I loved it. And like Joe Strummer you annihilated your previous life and you got embarrassed about liking Crosby, Stills and Nash. You sort of re-birthed as a punk. That's when I started to try to make music. Up to that point I thought only geniuses made music. Before that I was totally focused on sport but I was coming to the point where I didn't have the funding or support to get past county level. I had the drive but not the intelligence to get past that point. Also, my guru maybe resented me a little as I'd got past him as a player. Maybe his ego got in the way and he rejected me and sent me into the abyss at the age of 15. So I retired from table tennis at 15 and I dove into punk and I rejected everything before punk except Syd Barrett.

IF: Was there a point where you found you had a voice?

Martin Stephenson: Well, no, because our heroes were the likes of Lou Reed and Jonathan Richman and it was like it was all about not having a particularly good voice. That was better than having a good voice. It was all about doing it with your mates rather than being good. I loved the lads out of the Kane Gang but they were like aliens. They were pop hunters. They had a career plan and were buying houses in 1982 while I was just a punk at heart. Same with Prefab Sprout. When I met Paddy (McAloon) there was something that bonded us together as we both were lyricists. But he was like a jeweller as he planned everything but I was more into making mistakes and connecting with people. I was like a fool rather than a master. I was into community and the cargo that the Daintees carried was goodwill. We recognised that goodwill was more powerful than money or fame. Even now I am proud to be a Daintee. We're in our 60s and still playing even though I have no management at all. The miracles keep happening, like selling out the Sage.

IF: How did you progress to your first band?

Martin Stephenson: In the new wave era I heard "Another Girl, Another Planet," by the Only Ones. I saw them live in 1978 at the Mayfair and John Perry was playing a white Stratocaster. Anyway, I've just done an album with him and I went across to Dublin to see him and went up to his flat and there was that same white Stratocaster sat in the corner of the room. So that takes me from the age of 17 to the age of 61 and that's the power of the musical universe.

My cousin Jamie got a job with Maurice Summerfield, who used to fix guitars in Newcastle. He lived in Newcastle but his best mate was George Benson[1]. The job he got was a trainee guitar technician and he would come home with these ragtime music books and in one of them there was a photo of Etta Baker in 1954. She was a black blues player and she was pictured playing a Gibson guitar. I learned her rag in 1979. And in the year 2000 I was sat in her house playing music with her and she had the same guitar from that picture. Again, this is the power of music. She was 87 and I was 40. That's what I have discovered from playing music. For me, it's nothing to do with playing *Top of the Pops* or meeting someone famous; it's the little things that matter. If you have faith in what you love it will show you great things. It's not about me, it's about me, you and everybody.

The first band I was in was called the Cosmic Outbursts and I learnt "Another Girl, Another Planet" with my cousin. There were a bunch of lads from Washington who were about 20 and they heard us playing so we were able to join their band. So I was a new wave guitarist first of all and not a singer.

IF: What were your aspirations at the start?

Martin Stephenson: I connected to the punk ethos. I wanted to be an awake person who wasn't cocooned by the industry. I wanted to be an independent writer. But I started as a guitarist. I had no idea I was going to be a songwriter or a singer. I never, ever saw it as a career to let me social climb. I see buskers the same age as me and I tell them they are alright. They mean as much as I do, no more, no less. Even if you have never made a record you are totally important to the universe. The universe has a totally different perspective to the industry. So I can't really connect to industry heads. They are still fooled by that dream of being famous. It's a sad, narcissistic trait.

So anyway, I was in the new wave band and then I got sacked because I had a flanger[2] which wasn't very punk and I was into the Cure. They were all older than me. I was sacked at Christmas 1979 and it was the first time I'd had my heart broken. I started hanging around with a band called the MPs in Newcastle and their singer, Tim Reed, was from Manchester. I was moping about and wounded and he sat with me and he was so kind and he said, 'Why don't you write your own songs'. Within eight months I'd written all these songs and the old punks were back in my band and I was the band leader. And that became the Daintees around 1980. And we started busking, we were a busking band.

IF: Did you find your voice then?

Martin Stephenson: Well, I don't really think I'm a singer. I have a go. You need to show all your mistakes and your vulnerability and then people can relate to you. The likes of Elvis and Roy Orbison were naturally gifted but Lou Reed gave us hope. If you heard Pavarotti sing Perfect Day it would be awful but if you hear Lou Reed sing it, it's pretty perfect.

IF: How did you go from being a busking band to a Kitchenware signed band?

Martin Stephenson: Early 1982 we'd play in the Market Square in Sunderland and the only reason I became the singer was because I could work an audience. I could crack a few jokes and connect with the people watching. The rest of the band saw that. I only really wanted to be a guitarist but I got pushed to the front. We'd heard about Kitchenware but we got them mixed up with a guy called Andy Kitchen who was social secretary of the University. So we went to the University and asked for a gig and got told where to go, in less pleasant terms. At the same time Keith, who set up Kitchenware, was managing the HMV shop in Newcastle. He was knackered because he was doing two jobs. He'd turned up with a Mancunian DJ called Phil Mitchell and Keith's school friend, Paul Ludford, who was good with figures, and they set up this label. Keith had been manager of a few HMVs round the country so he'd studied the business. Anyway, when he saw us busking he asked us to come into the shop and do some busking there. At the time we were doing stuff a bit like early Josef K because we were big Postcard Records[3] fans, as were Kitcheware. At the time nice was the new nasty. The Who had done the nasty as had the Pistols. But now we were part of a movement along with the Bluebells, Orange Juice, Aztec Camera, who were just a bit nicer. It annoyed people because we didn't want to be Bruce Willis, we wanted to be

Michael Crawford. The likes of Edwyn Collins could laugh at himself and we were like that.

IF: What was the deal with Kitchenware?

Martin Stephenson: Well we busked in Keith's shop and he loved the spirit we had. He had been inspired by Postcard Records. He'd already signed a band called the Green Eyed Children who became Hurrah! We had already gigged with them.

Now Keith was taking Hurrah! down to London to record a single. At the time he loved a single by Scritti Politti called "The Sweetest Girl" and he'd seen that it was recorded in Bury Street, London so he took Hurrah! down there. He said to us, 'Do you fancy coming down with us and if there's half an hour spare we'll get you recorded?' We went down in three cars. We really bonded going down there. When we got down there we had to sit in the coffee room for hours while Hurrah! recorded their songs. All of a sudden the engineer popped his head round the door and said, 'Right you've got thirty minutes.' They said we could use their amps and I asked the engineer if he had a shaker and he said no. So, I asked if there was a shop nearby and he said, 'Yes, over the road.' So, I went and bought some rice to make a shaker and when I got back they said, 'Right you've got 15 minutes.' I got two plastic cups and put the rice into them and sellotaped them together but it didn't work. Our bassist wanted to hit me, I'd wasted 15 minutes to make a shaker and it didn't work. And then, of course, the engineer held up a shaker and said, 'Oh, did you want something like this?' So, he said, 'Well you still only got ten minutes.' So we tuned up and played a song I'd recently written called "Roll on Summertime". We recorded, it went great and Keith came running out and stood in front of me and said, 'Right, I'm your manager.'

And so it happened just like that and he was great. He and I clashed later on in life because of my spiritual programme but he was a great manager and did a great job for us.

It then all happened very quickly. Between 1980 and 1983 I wrote all of *Boat to Bolivia*, all of *Gladsome, Humour and Blue* and probably some of *Salutation Road*. The songs were literally flowing out like magic. I met up with Anthony Dunn and his brother Gary from Sunderland and we also had John Steel playing with us. We had a drummer called Paul Smith and he was in his early thirties. Before that we had a drummer who was a rockabilly drummer and he felt he couldn't do the drumming for songs like "Crocodile Cryer" and "Colleen," which maybe had more of a jazz feel to them. So we swapped drummers with the Toy Dolls and Paul came from the Dolls to join us and he really helped us. And coincidentally, I've just finished a tour and our drummer is now the 22-year-old grandson of Paul Smith, which is yet another example of the power of the musical universe. Paul is currently in Lindisfarne.

IF: At the time of writing these songs, did you know they were special?

Martin Stephenson: Well, when you come from a council house background you lack that self-confidence so I was never sure. I could easily be crushed, I was like a flower. And you know what, it never leaves you. About ten years ago I found this little song I'd written when I was 16 called "Cherryade Rock and Roll". And as soon as I saw the words on this sheet of paper, I could remember details of day I wrote it. I remember it was sunny day and I had a cheesecloth shirt on. I was a Syd Barrett fan and I was trying to write a Syd-type song. And I could hear my little voice trying to copy Syd's voice. But I hid the song as I just had no confidence and I knew my sister would say it's rubbish. And then it turned up ten years ago and, as an elder, I said to my younger self, 'I'll sing this song now because maybe I've just a little more confident now.' I'm not so bothered if someone laughs at me now. So I recorded this song and it realigned the vulnerable child within me. We can travel down our spiritual spine and heal the child we once were.

IF: You were getting great reviews at the time from the *NME* and *Sounds*. That must have been great for your confidence.

Martin Stephenson: Well, I didn't suck on it at the time. It's lovely to get a bit of attention but part of you cringes. I don't like to be disrespected but I don't like to be above people. I've always been wary of people who want power. I was bullied at school and I used to study the bully to understand him. People from the North East either develop a bit of an attitude or we'll spend time apologising for everything. I was more of an apologiser and I turned away from the praise. Sometimes people thought I didn't appreciate it. I was very much aware of not letting it go to my head whereas I witnessed it with others where the adulation could change people. I later fell out with my manager a bit. I had a work ethic and I wanted to learn my trade. I would do a gig for £150 at the Jumpin' Hot Club[4] because I thought it was a good gig and good people. Whereas my manager would say, 'You can't play there, you're too big for that.' I felt I was not too big for anything and this brought conflict with my manager.

IF: You signed for London Records while still being managed by Kitchenware. How did that go?

Martin Stephenson: Well Kitchenware outgrew itself very quickly. It was a perfect moment in time for about two or three years but the label wanted to progress and he (Keith) realised that he had serious song writing talent on his hands so he sent Paddy (McAloon from Prefab Sprout) to Muff Winwood and CBS and put me with Roger Ames of London Records.

There were things I loved about Roger. He was a music person, he'd been a drummer, he was from Trinidad and his best mate was Eddy Grant[5]. He was like a millionaire playboy. When I signed with him he said, 'What do you want?', and I said, 'Let's have some fish and chips' and he loved that. So when we went in to see Roger my manager, Keith, would say, 'Keep your mouth shut I'm after some big publishing money.' When I got in there Roger would wink at me because he knew the score and he could read Keith. He was a brilliant guy but we would clash as he didn't understand that my band was a real brotherhood, and he just wanted me as a song writer. The record company told me to sack all the band straight away and go into the studio with Courtney Pine[6]. I was in development as a songwriter but my band was maybe a bit behind me. The record company was about having a fast track hit and making money. If I wanted to be a pop star I would have walked away from the band and done stuff with session musicians. But that just wasn't me.

IF: You did four critically very well received albums with London Records, so why did it end?

Martin Stephenson: It happened over a slow process. What I didn't realise was that when I was training as a table tennis player at the age of 15, I had been set on a spiritual programme. I didn't realise this, but these things ignite later on down the path and at the right time. I started seeing things in the industry that made my toes curl. I couldn't get away with people's behaviour, the greed, the ego on display and as the years went by, I started feeling ill on the inside. The further I went into the industry the less I felt I knew about myself. I felt I was in a cocoon and there was all these people round me feeding off me. I was fighting against it for years and saying no to lots of things and me and Keith were constantly clashing. I was feeling totally lost spiritually and I started asking lots of questions about my own self, not asking God but the collective consciousness. I knew I had to get out of this situation for my wellbeing but I had two little kids and I was married and I was totally trapped. It was then the spirit said, 'Step into the loin cloth and drop what you've got and see who sticks with you.' So that's what I did. I was recording *Salutation Road* in Los Angeles with a budget of £150K, effectively everything a boy could want and hated everything about it. All that mattered to me was the people I knew before all this happened. So I stepped away from it all and stepped into poverty. I divorced my wife and gave her the house. I let go of everything. I started busking again and went right back to start. I was 33 or 34 years old. It was like a re-birth for me and I started reconnecting with the angels which were my real friends.

IF: Nearly 30 years later you are sustaining a career via a community of sorts. You must feel good.

Martin Stephenson: After I got off the majors with their huge budgets I did an album called *The Incredible Shrinking Band* and I kid you not the budget was £10 and I sold one record and

I broke even, so who is the idiot? Then I moved to the Highlands of Scotland and I started observing crafts people and they would do 10 pictures to get by. It's the opposite of trying to take the world over. So recently I did a re-recording of *Salutation Road* at a studio in Airdrie and it was well recorded but on a budget of £1200 and I could pay the band. I did vinyl and CDs which cost £1000. So I did 300 CDs and I stopped. The record company would have wanted me to do another 300 CDs but I knew that was enough to sustain me. Looking back, my manager would have said, 'There you go again, you've got no drive'. But with the sales I could pay all my bills for a good period. I have learned how to do things in a way that suits me and makes me happy.

IF: Do you have any regrets looking back?

Martin Stephenson: Nah and you know what? I may have had fallings out at the time, but I don't bear any bitterness. I love Keith, my old manager, and I think if he hadn't done all the good work in the early days I wouldn't have the bit of profile I have now that enables me to carry on doing what I'm doing. So I feel grateful to him and I feel a bit sorry that it must have been difficult to understand where my head was. He was a very good manager and in many ways I didn't deserve him as a manager because I was kicking against him from really early on.

Also, in my late 20s I put a lot of work into my guitar playing. I studied Chet Atkins and Merle Travis and I went to North Carolina and played with some of the best guitar pickers in the world. And that gave me a confidence in my guitar playing, which has fed into my music. So, all in all I have no place in my life for regrets.

•••••••••••••••••

You may hear the phrase 'stream of consciousness' from time to time and talking to Martin is very much a case of that. Sometimes it is difficult to follow the narrative thread but for Martin all the dots join up and his path has taken him to where he is now and that is a very contented place. In the North East we may call him crackers but when I tell Martin the story below that Dave Brewis from The Kane Gang told me, Martin lets out a hearty laugh and I get the impression he thinks if that's crackers that suits me just fine. I think it benefits us all to be in the midst of someone who has been brave enough to go his own way, in a manner that is generous of spirit and full of compassion and is still producing passionate and thoughtful music.

Dave Brewis: I did some producing with the Daintees in London. They would go to the pub during the recording of "Comes a Time", "Nancy" and "Wholly Humble Heart" and tell me to do the bass and they'd do vocals when they came back from the pub. So when they get back, Martin says, 'Turn the lights off to get the vibe right.' So, we turn the lights off and I pressed play and waited for the vocals and nothing came. I tried again and there was still no sound coming from Martin so I said, 'Martin, are you ready, can you hear the song?' He said, 'Sorry, I can't see the lyrics.'

---

1. George Benson is a legendary American jazz and soul guitarist and singer who has scored many hits and won ten Grammys.

2. A Flanger is a guitar pedal that makes the guitar produce an oscillating, wave type sound. It does not fit into punk rock!

3. Postcard Records is an independent record label that began in 1979 in Glasgow and signed many 'jangly' and sometimes rather fey indie acts such as Orange Juice, Aztec Camera, Josef K and The Go-Betweens. It is viewed historically as both a music scene and a particular sound.

4. Jumpin' Hot Club is a multi-venue club that has brought authentic country, reggae, soul and rockabilly music to the North East of England for nearly 40 years. It is still going strong.

5. Eddy Grant is a Guyanese-British reggae artist who had hits with the Equals in the 1960s, particularly with the single "Baby Come Back," which got to number one in 1968. He later scored UK and US top ten hits as a solo artist in the 1970s and '80s with "Do You Feel My Love", "I Don't Want to Dance" and "Electric Avenue".

6. Courtney Pine is a British jazz musician primarily known as a saxophonist.

The Kane Gang

Dave Brewis' and Paul Woods' Story

The Kane Gang had a very 1980's sound. It was soulful, melodic and produced with clean, sharp pop sensibilities. They were right for the time, the early to mid-1980s. Accordingly, they scored hits with the yearning pop gem that is "The Closest Thing to Heaven" which reached number 12 in 1984 and a cover of Aretha Franklin's "Respect Yourself". Their song "Brother, Brother" was later re-fashioned by the band as a jingle for Radio One DJ Gary Davies (as in 'Ooh Gary Davies, Ooh Gary Davies) and the theme tune to the TV programme Byker Grove. In 1987 they had hits in the US with "Motortown", their cautionary welcome to the new shiny Nissan car plant, which had just been built in Sunderland and where some of their mates were getting jobs, and another cover of "Don't Look Any Further" which got to number one in the US Dance Chart. Their sound was right for the 1980s but maybe a surprise for a band that came out of the tough County Durham town of Seaham.

Soon after these hits, the band slipped out of the public view and disbanded. I meet their multi-instrumentalist, Dave Brewis, and one of their two singers, Paul Woods, in the Black Horse Pub in West Boldon. The pub is run by owner and chef Pete Zulu, who appeared in this book earlier as erstwhile 'bassist' of the Toy Dolls. Pete, quite the polymath, pops out to see the lads mid-chat to talk about doing some photos for their new venture, Autoleisureland. The North East of England is a small pond and talent clearly attracts talent.

IF: How did you first get into music?

Dave Brewis: The first memory I had was of listening to the radio and listening to a song in the early 60s called "Singing the Blues". I went mental for it. It was a country type song and I just loved it. I kept asking my mam to put it on but she explained that she couldn't do that and we would have to wait to hear it when it came on the radio again. On the back of that I asked for a guitar at the age of about four. I was obsessed straight away. Strangely the song doesn't have guitar on it. First of all, my parents borrowed a plastic guitar with a picture of Elvis on it, although I didn't have a clue who he was. He had a checky shirt on and I thought he was a joiner. Then they borrowed my cousin Ian's plywood cello guitar from the fifties.

Paul Woods: I listened to the radio obsessively. I loved the Stones and I also loved Motown. My mam used to go to Jacky White's market in Sunderland and get Juke Box singles. She used to buy them indiscriminately but there was one, "Little Red Rooster" by the Rolling Stones and it was like something from another planet. Later I was on holiday down south at my auntie's and I heard "I Was Made to Love Her" by Stevie Wonder and I felt a rush of happiness. It was the first time I realised the power of music. From then on, I was hooked.

IF: When did you know you had a voice?

Paul Woods: I learned guitar and learned to sing along to the likes of Bob Dylan and Neil Young. I went along to a folk club in Seaham, the Dun Cow Folk Club, when I was about 15 and sang there. From there I gravitated towards Dave and Martin's band.

David Brewis: When I was at school in Seaham, I formed a band with my mate Martin and a couple of others. There were about four or five bands at school and they were all pretty good. We played a showcase night and although I was dead nervous, it went down really well. We would play Glam Rock stuff, Roxy Music and even a little bit of Yes. We used to practise a lot and then go down the pub. We started writing songs pretty immediately and started playing the local folk clubs and pubs. Right from the start we never had aspirations to be just a local band. We always wanted to write songs and write songs good enough to get us on *Top of the Pops*. It wasn't till "Young Americans" by Bowie came out that we found a way to go. We kept writing and writing.

What helped was that I went to Music College in Newcastle when I realised sixth form was going nowhere for me. Playing with musicians there who had played in soul bands and jazz bands taught me a hell of a lot. I got a job with Ray Chester's Big Band and I played bass for him in about 1976. It was basically the players from Last Exit, Sting's first band. It was a great learning curve. I thought if Sting can do it maybe I could do it. It gave me a massive boost of confidence. I was still in a band with Martin at the time.

IF: With Martin was it just for fun?

Dave Brewis: No, no we always wanted to make a record and have a hit. We were never going to give it up until we'd made a record.

Paul Woods: I would see them at the local pubs and sat in sometimes. However, what differentiated us was we wanted to record much more than just gigging.

Dave Brewis: Martin and I did also have a band called the Motivators that played at places like Balmbra's in Newcastle and various hotels doing covers. We'd always have a few originals in with the covers as we never just wanted to be a covers band.

IF: How did the Kane Gang come about?

Paul Woods: I bumped into the others at a Springsteen gig at the City Hall, around 1981. I had just returned from working in St Helens and got a job on the *Sunderland Echo*. The three of us then formed a band called the Reptile House. Then we became the Kings of Cotton. We wrote new material with each new name. It really started though with the song "Brother, Brother," which we just kept writing and re-writing.

IF: Were you starting to stand out?

Dave Brewis: Yes, we were using tapes and drum machines.

IF: When you became the Kane Gang what were your aspirations? Was it a career?

Dave Brewis: It was absolutely a career. I think we realised that this was the vehicle that was going to do that. We felt this is it. We knew we had some good songs coming on. Well certainly Martin and myself didn't want to stay on the pub/club circuit. Martin actually said 'We're not going on tour until we can headline. We've got to be big and we're not going to be a local band. We're going to be a national band.'

Paul Woods: "Brother, Brother" really moulded our sound. It happened pretty quickly. We played a gig in the Vestry in Sunderland and we were playing "Brother, Brother" and the DJ pulled the plug while we were playing. It was a sign to move on.

Dave Brewis: We actually said, 'Right we are not going to do another gig until we have played *Top of the Pops*', which we ended up doing with "Closest Thing to Heaven" and 'Respect Yourself' in 1984.

IF: How did you start to progress towards these lofty aims?

Dave Brewis: Well, we were really motivated after seeing Prefab Sprout. We saw them at Domefest in Durham in 1981 and they blew us away. Anyway, they told us they were playing the next week at the Brewers Arms in Durham and told everyone to come along from the stage. So we went and they blew us away again. They were streets ahead of anyone else.

Paul Woods: They were totally naïve. They thought they needed two times 45 minutes sets, like a club band, even though they played originals. They had just so much great material. We had a handshake agreement with them that whoever got a single out, the other one would release a single with the same people.

Dave Brewis: They (Prefab Sprout) had recorded a record independently and they went into HMV records in Newcastle to see if they could sell them there. Keith Armstrong was the manager of that HMV but was also starting up a record label called Kitchenware. He really loved it and asked them if they wanted to be part of the label he had started. Through that they mentioned us. He asked to hear us. Keith didn't really get us but Phil Mitchell, his partner, really liked us. Phil was a DJ at Julie's and Walkers in Newcastle and he was more into the soul direction. We said we had a single that we wanted to put out. We had recorded it at a mate's house with a four-track recorder and a couple of borrowed synths, a vocoder, a bass and a guitar. We did "Brother, Brother" and "This is it". We were dead confident. Keith, on Phil's suggestion, asked us to re-mix it for the clubs. We couldn't really do that as it was all just a tape. So we worked out a thumpier bassline and some four on the floor drums. We planned to play along to the tape and record it all together but then realised it worked better without all the synths. So we recorded it built from the drums and bass in a small studio in Edinburgh and that was what was released.

Paul Woods: We signed a management deal with Kitchenware. The agreement was that Kitchenware would license the band to a major record label, in our case it was London Records. It was the Kitchenware imprint but distributed by London. In the Sprout's case it was CBS, the Daintees it was London and Hurrah was Arista.

Dave Brewis: Kitchenware pressed about 1000 singles and Keith, who compiled the chart, put our single at number one of the *Evening Chronicle's* pop chart. London Records wanted to take it over nationally and do some promotion on it. It was initially a one single deal and it was a struggle to get to an album. "Brother Brother" got some airplay so they just wanted a follow-up single. That was "Small Town Creed," which was recorded with Pete Wingfield and it was nearly a hit. The next single, which was recorded in that same session, "Closest Thing to Heaven", was a hit and it all took off. But they still weren't going to put an album out. We had to persuade them. We did a lot of TV in the UK and Europe. TV and video was the name of the game at the time.

Paul Woods: The stuff we recorded was actually quite difficult to play live but we did some local gigs such as Tiffany's and it was there that we realised that something was happening. We were also liked by the *NME,* which was important.

Dave Brewis: At that point we had no plan, we were just in the slip stream

IF: How did the recording of the album go?

Dave Brewis: Well, it was a disjointed thing with the record label. We recorded the album and booked a tour for December 1984 when it was planned to release it. We had the single "Respect Yourself" out but then London pushed the album release back to Easter. So we toured with no product to sell. I think coming up to Christmas they wanted to push Bananarama[1] and their press department couldn't cope with another album to promote. So we toured on one single and when the album came out there was nothing to promote it.

IF: All the Kitchenware bands were quite disparate in their sound. Did you feel a kinship or part of a scene?

Dave Brewis: There was a scene in so far as we all went in the same office to see Keith. We used to do gigs with Prefab Sprout before either of us were signed to anything. So we felt a kinship with them, sometimes we'd support them and sometimes they'd support us but they were just pub gigs.

Paul Woods: That was as far as far as kinship went. Everyone was friendly and there wasn't a rivalry between us, probably because we were so different. Keith felt that it was a north east scene. He felt there was an ethos holding it all together.

Dave Brewis: We were all aspirational. Keith, like us, didn't want to be local. He wanted us to be international but based in Newcastle. But we were forever on the train or plane to London. It would have been easier to live in London, but it would have been horrible and we didn't want that.

IF: You were on London, as were the Daintees, Prefab Sprout were on CBS and Hurrah on Arista. Did you feel that London Records were the wrong label for you?

Paul Woods: Yes.

Dave Brewis: Yes, but we were grateful for anything. The album sold pretty well but would have done far better if we were on the road promoting it.

Paul Woods: While we were demoing the second album *Miracle* we were pretty much at loggerheads with the label. At the time there were a couple of other companies interested. So when they heard this they decided to keep us. They leased us on a deal to Capitol Records in the US.

Dave Brewis: Capitol in the US wanted an album out and wanted it by a certain date and were much more switched on to us. On the second album we made a conscious decision to make the writing three way. Previously it had just been me and Martin. He would ring up and say 'I've got a song called "Gun Law" and I'd go round to his house and we would put it together. By the time we got the Capitol deal we were professional. Prior to that I'd be on *Top of the Pops* but still working at Windows. We all had jobs and so we'd meet at Martin's house but had to be at the pub by 9:00, so if we wanted to write a song we had to be pretty sharpish. We wrote "Small Town Creed" and "Closest Thing to Heaven" and then straight up to the Dun Cow to celebrate.

IF: How did the second album go?

Dave Brewis: It went great. We had more recording experience and we had top session musicians like Wix (later a long time Paul McCartney band member) and Kamel Hines who played with us live. We produced the album with Pete Wingfield. There was an aspiration from Capitol records to make something of us. They loved the album, they loved all the songs. They were all musical people

Paul Woods: It got a bit Spinal Tapish as we would travel to the US for marketing meetings. In the UK it would be one person doing TV and one person doing radio. In the US we would go into a room for a marketing meeting and there'd be 20 people and they would stand up and applaud when we walked into the room which was just bizarre.

In the US we got TV shows, live vocals over tracks, on things like Soul Train. They were brilliant. They wanted us to tour and they lined up supports with Hall and Oates, Bruce Hornsby or Robbie Robertson. The big thing in the States is that support bands get paid whereas here you have to 'buy on' to a tour. It would have been coast to coast with Australia and Japan to follow. All they asked for was, as part of the deal with London, is that London would have to put up something in the region of £20k-£30k for the musicians' costs and London refused, saying they couldn't afford it. So it didn't happen. That's when we lost all momentum. In the US we had a hit with "Motortown" (Number 36) and a number one in the Dance Charts with "Don't Look Any Further". We shot videos out there and it was all great.

Paul Woods: In America there was this weird thing where artists had to phone record stores to thank them. I'd be ringing up a store in Hackensack, New Jersey, and I'd say 'Hi this is Paul Woods from the Kane Gang' and he says 'Who?' and I'd say, 'Paul Woods from the Kane Gang' and he'd say 'What you phoning me for?'

Dave Brewis: I rang one up in New Jersey and said 'Hi, this is Dave from the Kane Gang, you're selling our single, how's it going?' And he said 'This is New Jersey, we sell Springsteen, we sell Bon Jovi, we don't sell the Kane Gang.'

Had we signed directly with Capitol they would have had us in a rented house, on the road and really given it a go. As it happened it pretty much ended there and then.

IF: So how do you feel now? You'd got within touching distance.

Dave Brewis: Well, we got to make some good records and we did what we set out to do, which was go on *Top of the Pops*. It sounds corny but we got to see the world.

IF: How did it end?

Paul Woods: Well Miracle didn't sell as well as we hoped in the UK, although it did OK elsewhere. We got an option to do the third album.

Dave Brewis: We got a small budget to demo some new songs up at the Cluny in Newcastle but it was depressing.

IF: Did you have dialogue with London as to why things weren't happening?

Paul Woods: We did but it was difficult. Roger Ames, MD of London, was very astute but was only interested in singles. So he loved us when we sold 25000 of "Closest Thing to Heaven" in a week.

IF: Why did you make it when the likes of hotly tipped local bands Dance Class or Well, Well, Well didn't make it?

Paul Woods: We were good song writers. We had the belief we could write songs that would get us on *Top of the Pops*. I used to write a column in the local papers where I reviewed local bands and the only one I was sure would make it was Olga from the Toy Dolls. As soon as I saw him, I knew he'd make it. He had the full package, the personality, the voice and the songs with things like "She Goes to Finos".

Dave Brewis: For us it wasn't necessarily bravado, we weren't trying to blag anything, it was self-belief that we weren't going to stop until we'd written a hit. You have to have that self-belief. We didn't aspire to play the local clubs, we were interested in being like Steely Dan and Todd Rundgren.

IF: Was there a point where you said, 'That's it we're done?'

Paul Woods: We worked on the third album. Dave and I started to write separately. I didn't really like the stuff we were doing with the Kane Gang. So I left. It wasn't bitter.

Dave Brewis: By this time we were out of step with what was in the chart. So we were being asked to do much more dance oriented stuff, which wasn't really us. We were a bit lost. Martin and I had three months in New York, put up with Capitol money. It was fine but it wasn't the Kane Gang anymore. It lacked a hit record on it.

Paul Woods: We got offered a one-off single deal from CBS and we would be put on a tour with the Psychedelic Furs in Germany. By that time I was expecting my first kid and I thought *no, not for me.*

Dave Brewis: Martin moved to London as a songwriter. I was a session musician and played with Prefab Sprout and played on some of their albums. I also played with Jimmy James (I was a Vagabond) and Ben E King, all lovely people. It was great with the Sprouts. All I had to do was turn up and do the job and have no responsibility for the career path.

Paul Woods: We do get offered the Kim Wilde/Nik Kershaw nostalgia tours but they have no appeal.

....

Paul and Dave are loving what they are doing now, 30 years after finishing with the Kane Gang. From being on the cusp of serious success to the band splitting due to a lack of record company backing there is no bitterness. As with the Kane Gang, they are writing songs that have great melodies as well as having that mystery ingredient that makes the 'earworm'. They are recording them to high production values and releasing them as Autoleisureland, which is actually named after an old car accessory shop in Sunderland. It is a pleasure to spend a couple of hours in their company and it's a pleasure to listen to their new songs. I would suggest you check them out.

It is important to explain that the other singer of the band, Martin Brammer, moved to London and has sustained a very successful post-Kane Gang career as a songwriter. In addition to co-writing the hit 'Lifted' with the Lighthouse Family, which got to number 4 in 1995, he has written hits for the likes of Tina Turner, James Morrison, Olly Murs, Mel C amongst many others. Very talented boys are the Kane Gang lads.

(1) Bananarama were a very successful female pop trio who 10 top ten hits in the 1980s with the likes of "Robert De Niro's waiting" and "Love in the first degree". They were signed to London Records at the same time as the Kane Gang.

Hurrah!

Paul Handyside's Story

If you read a review or description of the 80s Kitchenware band Hurrah! it will typically call them 'indie jangle pop'. That does not do them any justice. To my ears they are one part REM, one part Go-Betweens and one part Aztec Camera. For a brief period they were touted by the *NME* and *Sounds* as the 'next big thing'. After a great run of singles that featured the aforementioned jangle along with catchy, soaring choruses, they signed to the major record label Arista and went on to release two albums with them. They also got support slots to play arenas with the likes of U2, David Bowie and the Stranglers as well as tours of the US and Europe. This is impressive stuff. I meet one of their co-singers, Paul Handyside, at a pub on Newcastle's smart Quayside and he still maintains the look of an indie rock singer. This description of him will, I expect, cause both derision and disbelief when or if he reads this. He is, without doubt, the most self-depreciating musician I have met during the process of writing this book. His story is both entertaining and illuminating but you will have a job getting him to accept that.

IF: How did music start with you?

Paul Handyside: In the early 70s I got into playing the guitar and my big thing was the Beatles, the Stones, Dylan and Hendrix. I was less interested in anything contemporary until punk came along. I met up with Taff Hughes (co-singer in Hurrah!) at college and started going to gigs. My friend from school, Dave Porthouse, played bass so we got a band together. We went through various drummers and started doing gigs. We were all based in Northumberland around Ashington, out in the sticks. We were doing gigs wherever we could, often in Newcastle in dodgy pubs like the King's Head. They tended to be the worst, roughest pubs around. Despite this, we would play our own stuff from the start. We never, ever did covers.

IF: How did you have the confidence to write songs?

Paul Handyside: I think we were just such big fans of music at the time. We were going to gigs every week and getting a lot of input, visually and audibly, and so your head starts filling up with this stuff. We were seeing all the punk bands and then the likes of Talking Heads. When we started it wasn't very good but we persevered.

IF: In the late '70s and early '80s was there any sort of scene in Newcastle?

Paul Handyside: There was a big heavy metal scene with Raven and Venom and such like but that was really a different side of music to us. We came from Ashington and Bedlington, where heavy metal was huge so we would get chased by the heavy metal fans for being punks. We didn't really mix but we used to rehearse at Spectro Arts and Venom used to rehearse there also.

IF: Could you describe your sound at that time?

Paul Handyside: I am famously one who will not listen to anything I've done. Even my own stuff now I don't listen to it once it is done so I am the last person to ask what we sounded like.

IF: In the early days did you think of music as a possible career?

Paul Handyside: You always dream, just like when you play football in the park you dream of playing in an FA Cup final. It's always there, the allure of getting somewhere else, or getting out of this place that we don't really want to be. It certainly wasn't planned and we certainly didn't have the attributes to go places. We didn't have the typical lead singer. We liked the Band, who had a few different lead singers or the Go Betweens who alternated between two lead singers. But we knew we didn't really have the right formula.

Where it really started for us was Kitchenware, or Soul Kitchen as it was known originally. They started putting on gigs and we went along to them. They used a great venue called Casablanca, which was upstairs in some building in the Haymarket in Newcastle. It was a dark and dodgy gay bar and it had great atmosphere. At the time we were called the Green Eyed Children. We saw the likes of the Fire Engines and the Bluebells[1] from Scotland and we ended up supporting the Bluebells on a later gig. It was all happenstance. Taffy started at Newcastle Poly along with a girl called Jenny, who happened to be the girlfriend of Keith Armstrong, who started Kitchenware. She was putting up a poster for a gig and Taff said 'we are in a band' and maybe passed a tape on. That's how we got the gig with the Bluebells and it just rolled on from there.

IF: How did you get signed to Kitchenware?

Paul Handyside: We did a demo and they thought it was okay. They had a bit of cash and they paid for us and the Daintees to drive down to London in a minibus to cut a single. I think we got as far as Birtley Services and stopped for a game of footy in the car park. We did three tracks for our first single in a day.

IF: Why all the way down to London?

Paul Handyside: Because that's where the best studios were. Kitchenware had ambition and there was a view at the time that maybe Newcastle wasn't quite up to scratch. To be honest it was a nice day out. The engineer was really helpful and we all felt pretty relaxed about it. At that point there was no contract, it was just get a single out and see how it goes. The Daintees got their first single out of that session as well.

We did that first record in early 1982 and we got the odd review, but we weren't doing well at all. We were struggling to get gigs. Kitchenware tried their best for us and eventually we got a support with Aztec Camera, which was a step up.

We were friends with Prefab Sprout from the early Spectro Arts days. It was actually Taffy who told the owner of Kitchenware, Keith, to check out the Sprouts. By then there were four of us, Kane Gang, the Daintees, Prefab Sprout and us and we were all very different. So we did gigs with the Sprouts and the Daintees but we always felt that we were the one that was never going to succeed. That was fine because we recognised that Martin Stephenson is a star with boatloads of charisma, Paddy McAloon, main man of Prefab Sprout, was a genius and the Kane Gang had the pop sophistication that was in vogue at the time. With us we always felt like the imposters. That was the case from 1982 till about 1985. We didn't have any money and could only afford to record one single a year with Kitchenware. We were kicking our heels for a lot of the time. It wasn't what you could call success at all.

IF: Kitchenware Records caused a stir in the music press. Did you feel that something special was happening?

Paul Handyside: We felt something was happening but not for us. The Kane Gang got chart hits, as did the Sprouts and the Daintees were known as a really great live act. We were none of that and couldn't see a way ahead for us. The major record companies would say to us, 'You're not the right sound'. Keith was trying all the time to get all of us signed by a major label.

IF: How did the deal with Arista come about?

Paul Handyside: I am not sure. It was a last-ditch effort. Kitchenware scraped some money together so we could go up to Edinburgh to record the album *Tell God I'm Here*. Keith then hawked it around and finally Arista showed interest. But then you get into bed with the devil. Be careful what you wish for. We lost our drummer, the producer we used fell through and issues just kept coming up. It just seemed to us to be issue after issue once we signed.

IF: Having signed for a major record label, did you feel this was a career for you?

Paul Handyside: I didn't really think of it like that. All you are trying to do is solve the next problem. Firstly, it was how to get gigs and how to make money and then it moves to a whole other set of opinions and problems with the major deal. So, no, I didn't see this as the start of 'making it'. We knew when you're on a major label they give you an advance but that soon runs out. It's an endless cycle of paying money back unless you're really successful. For us, it just carried on trying to get gigs etc. It is a business rather than the idea of creative benefactors. Being on a major label opens doors but it also lets in a load more s***. Unfortunately, all of our singles bombed. There was an indie chart in the *NME* and we were credited with hits on that chart but that was all faked, it was nonsense and had nothing to do with sales. We recorded the single Gloria with Jimmy Miller, the producer of the likes of the Stones. That was great but that doesn't make people buy a record. He'd just come out of rehab but he was a lovely bloke. We probably just spent the week asking for stories about the Stones.

IF: The *NME* and *Sounds* talked up your band as the next Big Country or Waterboys. How did that feel?

Paul Handyside: I can't remember that to be honest with you. We started off as Indie and we were against all that corporate nonsense. So, for us, when we were supporting the likes of U2 we may have been accused of moving away from what we stood for. But, in reality, we were just looking for gigs all the time. As for being touted as the next U2 or whatever was said we knew it wasn't going to happen because we didn't want that. The reality was that we just weren't that popular. We would do university gigs around the country and there'd be, like, three people turning up, which was pretty demoralising. There may have been the odd gig in London where all the indie kids would congregate but in the rest of the country or even Newcastle it wasn't happening. So, when you do get signed, you think 'well let's just do it' and try and play the game.

IF: You supported U2. What was that like?

Paul Handyside: We felt like fish out of water. We were used to paying tiny stages so when we got to Wembley Arena our curly guitar leads were only about 20 feet long so kept popping out of the amps if we moved to the mic. We got sorted out but that snapshot told us 'we weren't made for this stage'.

IF: How were Arista?

Paul Handyside: After two months with Arista the person who signed us left and that means you then struggle for support or focus. By the second album we realised it wasn't going to work. They were showing lack of interest and eventually they just cancelled the contract.

IF: After that was there any plan hatched up with Kitchenware who were still managing you?

Paul Handyside: No, there wasn't any plan. If I could replay those years I would plan it better. We wanted to go on, but we realised that once you're out of the major label orbit you don't get back in.

IF: How did the band come to an end?

Paul Handyside: We recorded a third album but Kitchenware weren't interested so that was that. Pretty soon after that we decided to call it a day.

IF: How did you feel?

Paul Handyside: The worst thing was that we stopped hanging about as friends as much. They are still friends but that was an intense time and that came to an end. I still wanted to do something, so I started a band called Bronze but, to be honest, it worked so well with Taffy and Dave, who were really good friends, it was hard to replicate that with other musicians. Now I produce solo albums which are more folk or acoustic. It's a mix of full band stuff, maybe a bit REM-ish or acoustic folk. I love the process of writing and pulling that together.

IF: Looking back, do you have any regrets?

Paul Handyside: Oh yeah, if we'd been a bit more switched on and had bit more of a plan it could have gone better. But then again that would mean we were different people and we may not have even done what we did. It may have been a conflict having Kitchenware as our management and our label but that's not to say they didn't do their best for us but technically maybe those two roles should have been separate.

IF: You do downplay your career or what you achieved a little bit.

Paul Handyside: It's not downplaying it. The reality was different to the outside perception. There were a few people who thought we were the bees' knees and do to this day and tell me when I meet them and this surprises me. The reality was that there were too few sales and too few gigs to make any of us think we were 'the next big thing'.

It may be a product of me not listening to anything I've done but it's like a past life that I don't think of. I think constantly about the next song I am in the process of writing but not what I did with Hurrah! Coming to see you today I am thinking 'what on earth is there to talk about?'

Maybe the problem was that me and my band mates wanted to be in music but didn't want to play the required games or be part of the industry. To illustrate the point, I could say when we played with U2 they were lovely guys but it was not our world. We didn't do the obvious things like when supporting U2 we should go and hang out at the post-gig parties but we never did. I remember playing with them there would be a rider that supplied us with drinks etc. It always had fruit on it, so after the gigs the four band members and the roadies would turn off the lights in the dressing room and get everyone sitting in a circle. Then we'd each get a piece of fruit and take in turns to shout out someone's name and throw the fruit at them. Anyway, on the last gig with U2 at the Birmingham NEC we were playing this game again with the lights off. There was a knock at the door and when it opened, we could see the silhouette of two people. They switched the light on and it was Larry Mullen and the Edge from U2 coming to thank us for the support we'd done on the tour. And we were all sat there like startled rabbits clutching our portions of fruit. In essence that summed up our relationship with the music industry. Maybe you would expect to see a band in their dressing room taking cocaine or entertaining girls and we were playing a fruit-based game. About three months later we were in Dublin doing some gigs and we went to a bar and the Edge was there in the VIP section. Really we should have gone to say hello, get him a drink but certainly ask about future support slots but we thought 'nah, let's leave him be to enjoy his night'. It wasn't shyness it was just 'let's not bother him.' To get on you need to be ruthlessly ambitious and we just weren't. I could regret it but we really preferred to knock about with each other than playing the game.

••••••••••••••••••

Paul describes his time in the music industry with complete honesty and that makes for a refreshing chat. He recognises that maybe they didn't make the most of their opportunities but more importantly that the people they were meant that it would never been any different. He steadfastly refuses to put any gloss on his story but I would suggest that you, the reader, listen to the singles 'Sweet Sanity', 'Gloria' or Who'd have thought' and you will hear songs that are a lot more to shout about than Paul would have you believe. But he certainly isn't one for changing.

---

(1) The Bluebells were a Scottish indie band who had a top 10 hit with 'Young at Heart in 1984 which later went to number one in 1993 when re-released.

6. Sunderland Scene

Sunderland can be a funny place, as are many British cities and towns. Even residents of Sunderland would agree that it can be a funny place, although, like most from the North East, they tend to be intensely proud to be from there. It has a glorious past but is in some ways unsure of where it fits in this fast-moving modern world.

Sunderland certainly has an illustrious past whether it be the birthplace of that great man the Venerable Bede (his exact birthplace is disputed but it is not disputed that he began his monastic and intellectual life as a seven year old in about 680 in the Monkwearmouth monastery) or of the inventor of the lightbulb, Joseph Swan, or being the largest shipbuilding town in the world in the nineteenth century when it had, at its peak, 65 yards along the river Wear. The last shipyard in Sunderland was closed in December 1988 as a result of a rather tawdry deal between Thatcher's government and the EU that ensured that no ships could be built on the Wear for thirty years. By this time, however, the Japanese car company opened a new factory in Sunderland which soon became recognised as one of the most efficient car plants in the world. Despite Nissan's arrival, Sunderland has seen a decline over 30 years and the city centre became a shadow of its former self. This decline was mirrored in many towns and cities throughout Britain.

However, things are stirring in Sunderland and it is reinventing itself as a city that is based on culture. That culture is a central part of Sunderland's comeback is indisputable. That music came first is almost equally indisputable. In the barren wastelands of the late 1990s came a DIY ethic from a cohort of bright, wilful and supportive musicians, who created a scene themselves and did it consciously. It started with This Aint Vegas, then came the Futureheads, the Golden Virgins and Field Music along with Maximo Park who are from Newcastle, not Sunderland! After that came Lake Poets, Slug, Frankie & The Heartstrings, Hyde and Beast. 20 years after the first stirrings we now see lots of bands coming through, such as the angular agit-rock of the Roxy Girls, the bubble gum punk and politics of Bigfatbig and the sweet indie pop of Patrick Gosling from down the road in South Shields.

Most of the original bands are still playing in one form or another and a whole infrastructure has developed that has emanated directly from the bands themselves. You now have fantastic venues like Pop Recs, opened by Frankie & The Heartstrings, the Peacock, now owned by Barry Hyde from the Futureheads, along with the Independent, the newly opened Fire Station and the Bunker. There are recording studios in the city such at the aforementioned Peacock and there is even a degree course in music industry studies, again set up with the involvement of the rather busy Mr Hyde. For the first time cranes are seen on the skyline of Sunderland building a new City Hall, hotels and office blocks. However, it was music that ploughed a lonely furrow for 20 years before the rest of the city caught on.

It is almost 25 years since the Futureheads started but the energy within the scene and its positive affect seems to be growing rather than receding. The musicians whose hunger, drive and vision started this process are still involved and need to be both recognised and applauded for what they have done for their home city. They have given it some pride back.

The Futureheads

Ross Millard's Story

A question often posed is 'name a cover version of a song that is better than the original'. It certainly makes you think. The Futureheads' version of the peerless Kate Bush's "Hounds of Love" is, in my opinion, definitely as good, which is pretty darn impressive considering the quality of the original. The key point is that it is markedly different and very much in the Futureheads' own style. They are four lads from Sunderland, brothers Barry and Dave Hyde on guitar and drums, Ross Millard on guitar and David 'Jaff' Craig on bass. Their style is post-punk of the early 2000s, possibly influenced by late '70s groups Gang of Four and Wire and possibly closest to Franz Ferdinand of their peers. What makes them stand out is that all four sing and they use their voices not only to harmonise but, as witnessed on "Hounds of Love", they use their voices in a very percussive fashion. Both on record and live they are a breath of fresh air with rousing choruses and upbeat and in your face rock with the thrill of four voices often blasted out in joyous regional accents.

To date they have released six albums from 2004 onwards, two on the major label Warner Brothers, and the remainder self-released, including the acapella *Rant,* which mixed folk and local traditional songs in what was a daring release for a so-called indie rock band. When I sit down and chat with Ross, their guitarist, it becomes apparent that their story is also the story of modern music. Their existence and career straddled the pre-streaming world when record companies were still awash with money and were willing to take risks and back young bands and the post-streaming world where careers have to be planned carefully to allow bands to survive and flourish. They may not have noticed themselves, but it appears they have navigated both worlds with some aplomb.

IF: What did you listen to when you were a kid?

Ross Millard: My mam and dad are both big music fans. My mam, who is from Sunderland, lived in London for a while and was like a first-generation skinhead and got lots of reggae records like Prince Buster. My dad was big into the likes of Free and Led Zeppelin. They don't play instruments but they loved seeing bands and listening to music. That was formative for me, listening to records like Melanie and Linda Rondstadt along with Neil Young and Bruce Springsteen, even Kate Bush. Thinking back, I was turned on by authentic music if you get what I mean. By the time I was 14, 15, 16, I was obsessional about music and spent every penny I could get on records.

I got a guitar around this time. There was me and two mates knocking around Castletown in Sunderland, making a racket in the garage. It wasn't till I went to Bede College after school that I met Jaff and the others in the band. And that was the first time that I met people who were really into music like I was.

IF: How did the Futureheads come together?

Ross Millard: Well there are practice rooms in Sunderland called the Bunker. And I heard through some lads at college that there was a youth project on there on a Saturday morning where anyone could go and they could meet other young kids who played music. Me and my mates had a little band going at the time so we thought it might be a way to get a bit of free rehearsal space. When we got there we met Barry and Dave Hyde who had been going for a couple of years. Pete and Dave Brewis, who later became Field Music, were a little older and had been going but were, maybe, just stopping at this point. But they were definitely on the scene. All of a sudden there were enough kids into it to allow you to put a gig together.

At the same time we started going to the Royalty Pub in Sunderland and we met a lad called James McMahon, who was at Sunderland University but from Doncaster, and he was putting gigs on at the Royalty. They were mainly local bands but also one or two from out of town via the fanzine scene. It was quite exciting. This was between about 1998 and 2000. Basically, there were three places that local bands would play – the Royalty, the Ropery and Ashbrooke Cricket Club. So it was a great little scene. Every Friday and Saturday there was something on. It was all the same faces but you could guarantee 60 or 70 people in a room, so it worked. By this time, I was at Newcastle University and we'd started the Futureheads as the youth project petered out.

Right from the start we felt we should do something a bit different from everyone else. So for the first few gigs we tried something different each time. Peter Brewis was on the drums at that point with us rehearsing in Barry's dad's garage. So the first gig was Ashbrooke Cricket Club and we did something like five songs, just a little intro for us. The next one we used acoustic guitars instead of electric guitars and Pete played the drums standing up. Then the third one we recorded a demo and played that and just sang vocals over the top of the demo. Then the next one we painted our faces silver and dressed as robots. I wouldn't say it was an art project, but it was something that maybe wasn't as serious as a band. After about four or five gigs we either ran out of ideas or were enjoying it that much that we were going to take it a bit more seriously.

When we started we also had rules or a manifesto, which included no effects pedals for the guitars, we would not repeat sections in songs more than once – so there would be one verse, one chorus then, maybe, a couple of further sections. There was no talking between songs. We all had to sing at the same time and in our own accents. Barry had, for a while, a no jeans rule as he favoured suit trousers but that didn't last as long as the other rules. This helped to create an identity and sound for the band. All the bands at the time in Sunderland had their own identity. The strange thing about the Sunderland scene was that no one sounded like anyone else.

IF: Did you feel interest in the band growing?

Ross Millard: Well because we'd been on this little circuit in Sunderland and we knew our mates were interested in what we were doing, we knew that, on a very low level, there was a bit of hype around us.

IF: Who were the other bands on the scene?

Ross Millard: They were all Sunderland bands. So you had a band called Brilliantine, who were originally called the Rolf and Cindy Band, and that was Lucas and Neil who eventually became the Golden Virgins. There was a great band called This Ain't Vegas. Pete and Dave Brewis had a band, before Field Music called Electronic Eye Machine and then the New Tellers. James McMahon was doing his band called Mavis. I've probably missed some out but there were some great bands about.

For us it was a matter of playing as much as we could and be part of this ever-growing DIY scene in the north east in the early 2000s.

IF: How did you get your first single out?

Ross Millard: We did a demo on Peter's reel-to-reel machine in his mam and dad's house. We burned maybe a hundred and fifty CDs and packaged them up in German Dictionary paper and sent loads off to record labels and radio stations. Anyway, there was a guy from Rough Trade Publishing, called Matt Wilkinson, and he got back to me and said, 'I like what I'm hearing.' He said he wanted to check that we weren't a far-right band because one of lyrics went 'and she fell in love when he said Seig Heil.' It was called 'The Park Inn' because that's where all the right-wing thugs went at the time. We got past that, and

Matt came up to Sunderland as he and his mate were starting a label and wanted to do an EP with us. We had started using a rehearsal room in the old Swan Street College along with Field Music. So, we recorded the songs there and they put it out. Rough Trade published it, which was our introduction to what publishing meant.

We began to play outside the region and started to get management interest. We did a tour of Europe with a band from Newcastle called Milky Wimpshake. That was basically a two-week tour of European squats and that was great. We had a guy ask us a few times if he could manage us. We thought that idea was faintly ridiculous as the band always meant to be part time. But he was persistent. He had connections with a management company in London called Big Life. So he brought them up to see us. He introduced us to Jazz Summers and Tim Parry, who became our managers. This meant things became serious as they had managed the likes of The Verve, Snow Patrol, Lisa Stansfield and Badly Drawn Boy. So that was like proper music industry types coming to Sunderland, which felt bizarre.

IF: Did all this interest shock you?

Ross Millard: Not really, we took it in our stride as we didn't really understand what was happening. I think if you were 18 now and this happened you may have more awareness as information is so much more available. Back then it was just funny having a gig in the Bridge Hotel with two blokes in fancy jackets standing at the back watching. From that Jazz and Tim said they wanted to manage us, which we agreed. That then led to loads more shows and ultimately a record deal. We signed to a label called Fantastic Plastic first, which was quite low key. But while we were in the middle of making the first album 679, which was owned by Warner Brothers, came in and bought us out of the first deal and they put the record out.

IF: The album had two different producers. How did that come about?

Ross Millard: Well to begin with we were getting produced by Andy Gill from Gang of Four. We were big fans of Gang of Four and they were a big inspiration for us. Jazz also managed Andy so that worked. In the event it didn't really work out and it wasn't a good partnership. We thought of Andy as a left-wing right-on punk. The reality was he was living in this fantastic house with a studio in Chancery Lane in London. He'd tapped out of all his rebellion and was a bit more establishment. So that was a little disappointing.

We ended up re-recording a lot of the album with Paul Epworth. Obviously he is now well known for his work with Adele and Florence and the Machine but this was the first album he had produced and he was great to work with. He had done front of house sound when we were supporting The Kills, so we knew him and got on well with him. He was class to work with. It is no surprise to me that he has gone on to do the things he has. He was a very talented chap.

When the press copies went out for review we made sure that "Hounds of Love" wasn't on it as we wanted to be judged on our own merits. We knew that song would make a stir but we didn't want it to overshadow the rest of the album and it didn't as none of the reviews mentioned it. And the reviews were really good.

IF: Why did you decide to do "Hounds of Love" as a cover?

Ross Millard: On the squat tour with Milky Wimpshake, Jaff had made a compilation for the van and it was on that. Pete and Christine from the other band were saying 'What a shame you'll never see these songs live,' as at the time Kate Bush was a bit reclusive. So we thought we'd do a version on the Newcastle gig on that tour, really as a one-off bit of fun. But it was one of those where you play it once and you know you've done something interesting with it. I don't think it's been out the set since. That gig was in the basement of the Head of Steam and there were probably only about 100 people there, but I think we knew straight away something was happening with that song.

IF: When did you discover you could all sing and it would work so well?

Ross Millard: I don't know if we did. We just had a pact from the start that we would all sing but I'm not really sure if it was any good in the early days as I have no proof. We didn't really get into the technical side of harmonising until we were doing proper recording. The idea on the first handful of songs we wrote was that everyone would sing in a different rhythm rather than harmonies. We were actually trying to mimic minimalist composers like Steve Reich[1] rather than do harmonies. None of us, at that point, had studied music. We were real amateurs just trying to be a bit different and have some fun making music.

IF: After the first album you went to the US and toured with people like the Pixies and the Foo Fighters. What were they like to tour with?

Ross Millard: It was great but again you take it as it comes. I was a massive fan of the Pixies so it's strange when something like that happens. I remember when we played at Manumission in Ibiza and Michael Stipe, from REM, came over and said, 'I'm Michael and I really like your band' and I'm thinking mate I've been obsessed with your band since I was a kid. Things like that are amazing but they are really just once in a blue moon.

IF: You put a second album out with Warner Brothers and it seems that it soured a little. Is that correct?

Ross Millard: It did really. It was a sign of the times with the record industry because we went to a farmhouse in Yorkshire to record the album and they turned it into a studio for six weeks. There was no interference from the record company. They just said 'Go and make the album you want to make.' We did this album with Ben Hillier[2]. We thought let's do everything we didn't do with the first album. So, we thought we'd do songs that were more mid-tempo and think more about the craft of song writing so that the songs are more structured. We took more time to get the sounds we wanted. Looking back on it, for our fans, it was just a bit too much, too soon. People were expecting a repeat of the first album and it was more of a departure than expected.

So, critically the reception wasn't as good.

It charted at number 11, which was pretty good, and the tour that promoted it was really good but we knew that there was something not quite right with the label. 679 were getting squeezed by Warners and this was right at the time when Napster and streaming discussions were going on. Our manager, Jazz, was very much into artists retaining their copyright and their control of their intellectual property. So he said, 'Warners will be looking to drop some artists from their roster as things were getting quite tight and it might suit us to be one and we can set up our own thing where we keep the copyright, keep the masters and put it out ourselves.' So we basically went into business with our manager. Jazz was definitely ahead of the curve. He was Chairman of the Music Manager's Forum so he was very aware of the shifting sands in the music industry at the time. In some sense we were at the tail end of people buying records which we couldn't have known at the time.

IF: How was going independent?

Ross Millard: I think it has its plusses and minuses. It's better in that, to this day, we own the masters of our songs so we can do what we want with them. But you lose the sort of manpower that Warners had. They were a massive machine and had massive marketing clout. So, we had to spend a lot of our own money promoting the next album, which was different. It's funny because when we released "The Beginning of the Twist" from the third album, it was the most played single on Radio 1 for the year of 2007, but this was just at the time when radio play was starting to be less influential on sales. Before that if you were A-listed on Radio 1 you would automatically see a massive bump in sales but from '06/'07 it became a case of diminishing returns. For our third album we went to Spain to record with Youth[3].

IF: What was Youth like?

Ross Millard: A nutcase. We really loved working with him and he actually did half the next album as well. He was very much record everything you can or throw as much mud at the wall and some of it will stick.

With Youth it was about economy and restraint. For us it felt like it had taken a bit of our personality away. It was a great experience but, for us, we felt like the ideas or the quirks of the band are what made us.

IF: You then moved on to the fourth album. Was it getting harder?

Ross Millard: Well, we had had an enormous knock in our confidence after the second one. When we made the second record, we felt utterly invincible and when we finished recording it we felt high as kites. We were just about to go on tour with the Foo Fighters and everything was perfect. We felt we'd done everything right artistically and we still stand by it and are proud of it. When it doesn't connect as the first one did, it's really tough and self-confidence took a knock. From that point on we were working to get that confidence back. By the fourth album we were really getting back in top. I guess until we made the acapella album, *Rant*, we always felt we had something to prove.

IF: When you put out *Rant* did you see it as a risk for an indie band to do?

Ross Millard: No, we never felt that because we didn't think the stakes were high enough. Basically we had heard our four voices when recording without the music behind it and thought it sounded really good. And with the guitars usually raging we felt that people maybe missed the harmonies we would do, so we thought it would be fun to concentrate on that element. At that time we felt that the four of us, never mind the world, didn't really need another Futureheads album, so let's do something different.

However this was the time when Barry started to get unwell[4]. We have always been super close mates and there has never been any tension between us but at this point real lives were starting to struggle with things like break ups. We did a tour with the *Rant* album and had a great time but with Barry getting really unwell this really was the last of the Futureheads for the time being. At the beginning of 2013 we knocked it on the head.

IF: How did you feel at that point?

Ross Millard: It seems naïve at the time but it had been building up for about 18 months. So when we had a meeting in Sunderland and Barry said, 'I just don't think I can do this for the foreseeable future,' it was no surprise. If I am honest, I think maybe I should have done more to knock it on the head sooner as we could see Barry was suffering. At that point it felt massively unlikely we would do anything again. It was disconcerting that we had done this for so many years and then it wasn't there. It took quite a bit of time to come to terms with it.

I was adamant, though, that I was a musician and was going to stay a musician. Jaff went into teaching and is still a full-time teacher. Dave went into decorating and gardening. By this time we'd been doing stuff in Sunderland like the Split Festival and the bid for the Cultural Spring and fortunately for me that sort of stuff came along at the right time. So, I've been involved with various culture-related initiatives along with musical theatre with a group called Unfolding Theatre. Things come along.

About six months after the Futureheads, I got a call from Frankie Francis asking me if I wanted to do a record with Frankie & The Heartstrings as their guitarist wasn't keen. They are good friends of mine so it was an easy decision.

IF: How did the Futureheads reunion come about in 2019?

Ross Millard: We have a really tight connection as musicians that is difficult to get elsewhere and on Jaff's stag do we chatted about that, recognising what a great go we'd had. About two years after this I got a phone call from Barry out of the blue asking if I fancied having a go again. That was the start of this last album. I feel that all the troubles Barry had are just not in him at all and he's really good now.

IF: The reviews for the comeback album, *Powers,* released in 2019, were great. That must have been heart-warming.

Ross Millard: Well, the ending had been quite unceremonious with no statement and no final tour. We had just disappeared. I guess that is a North East thing, not wanting to make a song and dance about anything. We in the North East don't bang our drum very well. So it was very nice to think we were still appreciated.

IF: How has Sunderland sustained this scene for 20 years?

Ross Millard: You are living in the cracks up here. There is not enough going on that you get trampled by other things. If you do something genuinely interesting there is enough space for it to be heard. It will be interesting to see how the city responds to having more resources in venues and recording studios and support systems. The fact that in the past there was next to nothing meant that we had to take a different approach. We couldn't wait for someone to put a gig on we had to do it ourselves. You had to create something out of nothing yourself. When we came up the thought of public funding or putting in for a PRS[5] grant or an Arts Council grant seemed bananas. Now if you don't get backed by the PRS you already have a fight on your hands.

IF: The scene is real in Sunderland but there is no 'Sunderland Sound' as there was in Glasgow with Postcard records or the trip hop scene in Bristol. Why is that?

Ross Millard: I think it's a spirit rather than a sound. Everyone seems to have the same sensibilities but a different way of expressing them. I think that makes it really interesting.

IF: What is the future for the Futureheads?

Ross Millard: I don't know but we are at the stage where we need to do another record but that is quite difficult as we all have busy lives outside the band. We do well touring or playing festivals but we make it work for us. So, all the gigs and tours have to be on weekends or school holidays as Jaff is a teacher but it works and suits us. I would love to make new music as that keeps the candle burning and I certainly wouldn't want to be a legacy band that only has a back catalogue. We have to look forward.

•••••••••••••••••

The Futureheads offer a great template for how to sustain a career in music when recording music no longer pays the rent. Barry owns the Peacock Pub in Sunderland, which puts on gigs, has a recording studio and is the base for a degree he helped set up called a BA in Modern Music Industries in partnership with Sunderland University under the banner of the of the Northern Academy of Music Education. Jaff is a teacher at a school in Sunderland. Ross is involved in various music and cultural activities such the musical theatre of the Unfolding Theatre and running the very successful annual Summer Streets Music Festival in Sunderland. Dave could be, whisper it, re-invigorating his musical partnership with Neil Bassett, erstwhile drummer of the Golden Virgins and local restaurateur, that goes by the name of Hyde and Beast. As Ross mentioned they tour in half terms to fit Jaff's teaching and everything seems to work and suit all concerned.

Everything they do is entwined in the cultural scene in Sunderland. The ethos is that no one did anything for Sunderland when the city and its traditional industries of shipbuilding and coal mining declined, so they had to do it themselves. Add in to that a very heavy dose of talent and you can see why the Futureheads continue to go from strength to strength.

1. Steve Reich is an American minimalist, modern classical composer who is known for layering his sound up and the repetition of sound.

2. Ben Hillier is a British music producer well known for producing a number of albums for Depeche Mode as well as Blur and Elbow.

3. Youth is a British music producer who began as bassist for the post punk band Killing Joke but later became a highly sought-after producer most well known for producing amongst others Paul McCartney, U2 and James

4. Barry Hyde released the album *Malody* in 2015. It is a fantastic, moving and highly musical album that documented Barry's life with bipolar disorder. At the end of the first stint with the Futureheads, Barry suffered a severe mental breakdown. The writing and recording of his solo album was part of his successful recovery. He also used its release to highlight the taboos that surround discussing mental illness especially for working class males. He rightly received many plaudits for his honesty in discussing his troubles as a way to help others.

5. PRS is a music copyright collective that helps its members collect their royalties.

Maximo Park

Paul Smith's Story

Paul Smith is both a talented lad and someone with good instincts. The same can be said of his band mates, currently Tom English and Duncan Lloyd (and former members Lukas Wooller and Archis Tiku). His band, Maximo Park, are an alternative or indie rock band who have had consistent success since the release of their first album in 2005. As Paul tells me they have released seven albums and all have reached the top 20 of the UK Album Charts, including their most recent one, *Nature Always Wins*, released in 2021. Paul is an energetic frontman and his voice is strong and certain, with a soft Teesside lilt to it, and always right out at the front in the production. Their songs are melodic, upbeat and often angular and sparse. The *NME* described their 2021 release as 'The Geordie misfits come up with joyful pop songs and introspective anthems aplenty on their seventh studio album.' They rose to prominence with the likes of the Futureheads and Bloc Party as a reaction to the more populist sound of Oasis that had dominated the previous decade. They wanted to make music that was different, challenging and thoughtful. And that is still what they are doing some 18 years later.

Where the instincts come in is both Paul's ability to recognise kindred spirits as he did when he first auditioned with the band but also his choices for a burgeoning solo career that exists alongside Maximo Park. His recent folk album made along with the haunting and beautiful voice of Rachel Unthank has garnered exceptionally good reviews but for an 'indie boy' making such a nakedly produced folk album with an established and celebrated voice was undoubtedly a risk. His guts told him their voices would work but also that self-penned songs would fit within the structure of a different genre to the one he had grown up listening to and been playing to date. And it worked splendidly. It reminds me very much of the instinctual approach of the Brewis Brothers of Field Music. Their diverse and imaginative releases similarly have the same success rate of hitting the target. It is no surprise then to find out that Tom, Maximo Park's drummer, was an early member of Field Music and that Peter Brewis produced the Smith/Unthank album in his Sunderland studio. As mentioned in this chapter's introduction Maximo Park are very much NOT a Sunderland band but their kinship, overlapping history and similar sensibilities means they fit in very nicely to this section of the book, luckily for me!

IF: When did you learn you had a singing voice?

Paul Smith: Actually, a few weeks before I joined the band, I'd sang along with the party band at a 21st birthday party. Because I played in an instrumental post-rock band called MeandthetwinS I'd been pushed on stage by friends to sing with the function band. So I sang "Hero" by Enrique Iglesias which was really awful but the people in the band, who were 40-year-old function players said to me, 'Do you know you've got a great voice?' And I said, 'What are you on about?' Before that I'd never sang in public

Even at school when I was in the choir and due to sing in a competition, I bottled out of it and the music teacher shouted at me in front of the whole class. So, I'd never really thought of singing from that point onwards.

So, a few weeks after the 21st party, I was playing pool with Tom, Maximo Park's drummer, at World Headquarters in Newcastle and it was really loud and I was singing along to Stevie Wonder's "Superstition", thinking no one could hear. Tom's girlfriend (now wife) said. 'Hey, Paul's got a really good voice.' Maximo Park had been going maybe 18 months and they didn't really feel comfortable as front people. So, they asked me to have a go and it was sold to me as having one last crack at making it as a band. They were thinking in professional terms whereas I was thinking in artistic terms. They had had local success and played in London and Manchester and felt like a proper band. They had their eyes on a different horizon whereas I just wanted to be in what I saw as the best band in Newcastle.

Even now my main role is to hold a tune. Over the years I've got more confident and can listen back to our records and not feel embarrassed. Listening to our first album still makes me squirm a little bit because I really hadn't sung that much before recording it. We'd done maybe a couple of gigs a month and that was it. So, I hadn't had much experience when we first went in the studio. It wasn't until the second album I felt that yes, I'm a singer. So, I wasn't confident when I joined the band but I was working in a call centre and I thought *yes, let's give it a go*. And it was one of the best decisions I've made in my life.

It was quite scary at the first rehearsal as, other than Tom, I didn't know them and I have Tom on the drums and these other three staring at me. I think they were also looking at other singers at the time. But we just clicked. We did songs like "Going missing" and "Graffiti", which were later on the first album. I think if the first rehearsal hadn't gone well I would have gone back into my shell and thought I can't sing and I haven't a clue what I'd be doing now. Them being a band for a few years helped me and I had a lot of ideas about performance. Having done Art History at Newcastle University I felt I'd walked in the steps of Bryan Ferry and Richard Hamilton[1] and had sort of pop-art ideas and ideas of how I wanted a band to be if I joined one and this all became part of how we developed.

IF: What was the North East scene like when you started gigging with Maximo Park?

Paul Smith: It's hard to remember too clearly but Electronic Eye Machine, who became Field Music, were out there. The Futureheads were out there. I was kind of sceptical of local bands. It's why I didn't want to be a singer of what you would call a local band as its often some egomaniac clown who thinks he's brilliant and he's not, and in those days it often was a 'he'. So, I went to see the Futureheads thinking well, they can't be that good. And I saw them and I thought *oh my word, this band is amazing*. To see a band that were that tight, and aggressive and melodic was quite affecting. Their harmonies and their arrangements were so interesting. The same could be said, minus the aggression, for Field Music. Again they were both tight and unusual. I can say the same about our band in that we were odd and eccentric. We weren't trying to be quirky but we were outside the circle and remain outsiders. Ultimately we have had some commercial success. We've had seven top 20 albums in a row but we remain outsiders and I don't feel part of any industry. I feel an alignment with the independence of the likes of Field Music. They are still breaking new ground for themselves and that is what I want to do. I don't feel a sense of competition but it does spur you on. I feel that if you put something out you should feel it's brilliant and that was what was felt by all the bands that we came up with.

There was also a lot of experimental music about. Lots of lo-fi stuff like Jazzfinger. There would be these sorts of bands playing in less traditional spaces like art galleries. There were people like Steve, later of Warm Digits, who was known as Cathode and he would use his laptop instead of instruments, which was unusual then. It was a very friendly, supportive scene where you were allowed to try new things. There was also a lot of overlap. So, you had Tom, who was in our band, was also in

Electronic Eye Machine and Field Music.

I remember going across to Sunderland to see This Aint Vegas and Richard Amundsen of the band was really supportive towards us. I'd first met Richard in the Cooperage at a post-punk night. He was maybe into more hardcore bands like Fugazi and At the Drive In but it was great to get that exposure and I would use some of that sort of aggression and try to fuse it with more melody. It felt a very creative environment where everyone influenced each other. We were trying to react against the more common themes at the time of Oasis and the more singer songwriter types. Everyone wanted to look like Liam Gallagher and we didn't.

IF: It appears that your trajectory to success was pretty steep to move from this grass roots environment to quickly being nominated for the Mercury Prize for your first album. How did that happen?

Paul Smith: It felt like every day something else would be happening. We practised for three months to start with and our first gig was to something like 500 people at Northumbria University. That felt like a baptism of fire and nothing slowed down after that. Prior to my joining I think Maximo Park were a little more psychedelic. I went for more spiky angular type of music. But it was also pop music, a kind of power pop. We were equally influenced by DIY culture and pop music. I still love George Michael and Prefab Sprout as much as Minor Threat and Wu Tang Clan.

We decided to stay in part-time jobs rather than pursue careers so we could write songs, practise and do demos. For us it wasn't a pastime. Within 18 months we were signed and once we were signed everyday was something new. It would be, book this tour, speak to Paul Epworth[2] about producing us. We had interest from loads of record companies who came to see us at places like the Cumberland Arms. We knew we wanted to be in control so signing to Warp Records[3] was a very easy decision for us even though other labels were offering more money.

Even our first record, before our Warp deal, was funded by a mate of Tom and Lukas who had got a small inheritance. He loved music and loved our band. That's how our first self-released single, on Billingham records, came about. We recorded it all in Duncan's flat in Fenham. Lukas moved to London and got the single into the independent record shops down there and then Warp got in touch on the back of that. The timeline was very quick but it felt normal. We were very excited but we felt in control.

Paul Epworth had done the Futureheads and Bloc Party so he was quite a happening producer but we were wary as we didn't just want to be 'on trend'. We tested the water with the first single on Warp but it was easy then to move on to the album with him.

IF: Is the choice of producer important?

Paul Smith: Well, on the first record we discovered what we actually were. I think the choice of producer is important. We have a lot of strong opinions in the band so having someone in the middle who can massage egos but also listen to people is important. Having an overall creative vision for what a record is going to be is important. Our last record was done in isolation to each other due to lockdown and I was concerned it would tie together and the producer was vital for this. The latest album has a seamless quality that maybe some of the earlier albums didn't have. That is fine as *Too Much Information* was intentionally all over the place but the new album is really coherent. You learn from working with different people.

IF: What is the key to your longevity?

Paul Smith: Having a genuine love of music and not falling out of love with it and feeling that there's always more to do. There is a song on our third album called "Questing not Coasting" and the first line is, 'Questing, I am not coasting. Nor will I ever.' And that's my ethos really. If you don't have a will to move forward you will come to a standstill. The evolution of the band has been subtle but I know what it is. Even if we have made a mis-step I know why we have done and its due to this questing quality we have. If you rest on your laurels that is when you start to decline. To me, to be doing this 20 years after starting is miraculous given the vast changes in fashion and tastes. With every record we still want to 'knock it out of the park'. I feel like I've only made a fraction of the music I want to make. We get to do stuff outside the band which helps a lot. I've just made a folk record with Rachel Unthank which is very different from Maximo and that helps keep the band fresh.

IF: How challenging was it moving into the folk world?

Paul Smith: Not that difficult in the end. Like starting with Maximo Park it was nerve racking being in a room with someone new singing. I didn't know if it would work. I had a hunch our voices would work well together and that first practice, after talking for a couple of hours to get comfortable, our voices clicked together. Generally if it doesn't feel natural then it is wrong. There was a risk to it all as I was out of my comfort zone. Even today I am going to try out some new songs with Maximo Park and I feel the same nervousness and excitement as I did at the start. With Rachel the traditional stuff we did felt right but writing my own songs was definitely a risk but both of us sing in a pure and plain way which suits the songs. I was nervous when the folk record was coming out, especially how it would be received from the folk world. Fortunately, Rachel's dad, who sings with the Keelers and has been in folk music for years, gave us the thumbs up early doors. It is actually probably the best reviewed record I have ever been involved with was very nice. It gives you confidence to do other things.

IF: How much of the North East is in Maximo Park?

Paul Smith: Environment is important but the further I have travelled I realise the more universal it is. There's a song called "Meet you by the Monument," which references Grey's Monument in Newcastle, but if I am singing it in Berlin it is equally about the Brandenburg Gate. I try to make the references both specific and universal. Our lyrics are born of experience so the song "The Coast is Always Changing" could be about anywhere. People have told me they have been travelling down the coast of Portugal and that song was part of their soundtrack. The song is about the Blast Beach in Seaham, County Durham, and how the land has eroded. But the meaning is universal of how things change naturally over time.

IF: What is the future for Paul Smith and for Maximo Park?

Paul Smith: Eventual death and hopefully a lot of creativity before then.

••••••••••••••••••

With that Paul is off to meet his band mates to try out some new songs. No doubt he has a spring in his step and a mix of excitement and apprehension in his stomach. Paul puts himself out there and is that canny mix of self-belief and competing nagging self-doubt. This may be what keeps him striding forward and the energy that such tensions create can be heard in each new record, even in the tranquillity of his affecting new folk album. He could be called a renaissance man of music and, while he will, no doubt, cringe at such an epithet, it is what he has in common with his generation of musicians in the North East. They are thinkers, risk takers and people who go with their instincts. The people I have talked to in this section are all in their late 30s or early 40s and one can but hope that the next generation pick up some of their individuality and creativity for it has brought this generation success and longevity.

1. Richard Hamilton was an artist and early exponent of the pop art movement which also included such artists as David Hockney and Eduardo Paolozzi. He also taught at Newcastle University and was very influential on Bryan Ferry who was a student of his in the 1960s.

2. Paul Epworth is a highly acclaimed record producer who has worked with Adele, Rihanna and Florence and the Machine. He also produced the first albums by both Maximo Park and the Furtureheads.

3. Warp Records are an independent record label based in Sheffield. Primarily they have signed electronic artists such as Aphex Twin and Brian Eno. Duncan Lloyd, co-songwriter and guitarist from Maximo Park has also released music through Warp as a solo artist. This music is more experimental, sometimes instrumental, sometimes with other singers.

This Aint Vegas

Richard Amundsen's Story

This Aint Vegas were a Sunderland post-punk do-it-yourself band from the early 2000s. They were Adam Rose on vocals, Richard Amundsen on guitar and vocals, Jordan Hill on drums and Michael Matthews on bass. While other Sunderland bands followed a more traditional route to success This Ain't Vegas threw themselves into a DIY punk community that took them to France, Spain, Germany, Slovenia and the Czech Republic. If you listen to their two albums and their singles on Bandcamp[1] you will hear an angular guitar band something akin to the Gang of Four from the late 1970s. There is urgent, chiming guitar, which reminds me of the grunge band Afghan Whigs, along with imaginative, powerful drumming. However, what really grabs you is the almost shouting but tuneful and yearning dual vocals that often deliver the same lines simultaneously. Rather than sweet harmonies, it is like they are fighting for the same oxygen. It's an oft used cliché but the two singers sing as if their lives depended on it. Listening to it now, it sounds as fresh and in your face as it did over 20 years ago.

That the band rose like a comet and then fizzled out while their contemporaries in Sunderland such as the Futureheads and Field Music continue to soar could be a source of bitterness or even jealously. However, that is not what I hear when I talk to Richard. While there is a scintilla of regret, the overriding emotion is one of pride that they travelled such a wonderful journey and stayed true to the purity of their initial aims and their desire never to compromise. He is proud of the music they made and proud of how they moved their audiences.

They chose the name of the band after hearing a comment from the drummer's dad when talking about Sunderland and he said, 'Well, this ain't Vegas.' It was a joke to begin with, but it stuck. There is a self-deprecating and rather modest gene within many Sunderland people and despite their wide travels This Ain't Vegas were, in their hearts, a Sunderland band.

IF: How did This Aint Vegas start?

Richard Amundsen: I went through school with the lads. I have known them since we were four years old. We got into music towards the end of secondary school and decided to start a band before we had even picked up any instruments. I chose the guitar, even though I couldn't play, and Jordan chose the drums, even though he couldn't play drums, and so on. We bought the gear and learnt to play in my mate's garage. We moved quite quickly to putting on our own gigs. The first one we organised was at Ashbrooke Cricket Club in Sunderland and this was the Futureheads' first gig. They went on first and we headlined. It was basically just our mates from college. It was a real buzz and a great laugh.

IF: How did you know at the age of 16 or 17 how to put on a gig?

Richard Amundsen: At the time I realised that unless you did something yourself nothing would happen or be given to you on a plate. I had worked part time at the cricket club and my dad had been a disco DJ in the 70s at places like Roker Park and he had all the gear. I said to my dad, 'Wouldn't it be great if I used your equipment to play a few records and put a couple of bands on.' And he said, 'Go and do it son.' So I did it. It went really well so it became a monthly event for four or five years.

At the time I was reading a book by someone called Micheal Azerrad called *Our Band Could Be Your Life* about the 1980s DIY Punk scene in the US around Washington DC and bands like Fugazi, Minor Threat, Black Flag, Husker Du and Sonic Youth. It was about how these bands had the spirit of doing it all by themselves. How they created their own scene and went against the mainstream. This really got under my skin and inspired me. It became my mission.

IF: Did you read the book and then get into those bands or vice versa?

Richard Amundsen: I heard a couple of songs by these bands first but read the book pretty early and it fit into my way of thinking. I see the grassroots as being important. When you get to the grassroots you get almost the purest experience and when you are up close with the bands you get closest to the magic of it all. It is magical when the music comes about organically rather than top down. For example, you organise a gig and there's a band from Florida who are playing literally five feet from you in Sunderland, all your mates are there and the band are staying at your house that night. There is something really special about that experience.

Anyway, we started playing in Leeds and got a reputation as a good live band and then pretty soon we got the chance to release a seven-inch single (Richard shows me on Zoom his first seven-inch single). We got 2,000 pressed in 2001 and I was about 17 and still doing my A-Levels. We then started to get gigs on the back of that release and started travelling around the UK in the back of a van and sleeping on floors. We got a feeling of what we were all about and that was about being DIY.

IF: How did you get proficient and a 'happening band' so quickly?

Richard Amundsen: There was something between me and the drummer in that we shared an obsession with certain types of music and a desire to study so we could become good quickly.

We had a bit of fire in us. And we worked at it.

IF: Where did the idea of having two vocals singing together, often the same parts?

Richard Amundsen: It came from listening to early 1980s US punk music but even the likes of early post punk UK bands like Gang of Four or Wire. We were also keen on singing in our own accents. You don't hear American bands singing in British accents so that was important to us.

IF: You wanted to stick to the DIY ethic. Did it help that there was nothing happening in Sunderland at the time?

Richard Amundsen: At the time there was only the odd gig going on in the back of pubs and there wasn't much infrastructure. There wasn't really a scene until we came along, with the Futureheads and then Electronic Eye Machine, which was early Field Music. Then things started to grow. There was a lad from Sunderland Poly called James McMahon who started putting on gigs every week at the Royalty and Ropery pubs and we started gravitating towards this grassroots scene. Then we became pally with bands from Newcastle and it grew. It helped that we were all so young and didn't have jobs and so we had the time to do it. It also became a real social scene as well.

IF: Did it feel special? Did it feel like the start of something?

Richard Amundsen: I think so. I was completely absorbed by it. For me, I almost defined my identity around this scene. The internet wasn't as big then and when you aren't exposed to what is going on around the world then it felt like this place was the centre of the world. It was so exciting, in part, because you didn't have anything to compare it to. It was a bubble of excitement and it got even more exciting when we took it to places like Spain and Germany. We were exporting this little bubble abroad. We felt like we were spreading the word about our little scene.

IF: At this point what were your ambitions for the band?

Richard Amundsen: We had a tension between wanting to do well and making it bigger but we also wanted to keep it DIY.

We thrived on the buzz of a big audience. For example, we played in front of a crowd of 700 or 800 in France, supporting a German band, and that was amazing for us. We fed off this. The tension, though, was this sense of purity in our desire to do everything ourselves and follow that strict DIY path. We were booking our own gigs by email, we had our own van that we would drive, we printed our own T Shirts and sold them ourselves. We felt we were echoing what the US bands like Fugazi were doing. We felt like we wanted to hang on to that purity. So when we got approached by a few major labels, when we played London, we were probably quite arrogant and said we weren't interested. We saw the Futureheads developing in parallel and doing really well commercially and we could see some of the strain that put on them and the challenges they faced. We were really enjoying ourselves and making a bit of money and probably had a bit of kudos. The downside of doing it all ourselves was that it wore us out. We did something like six weeks of touring round Europe in places like the Czech Republic and Spain, mainly sleeping on floors and it completely exhausted us. So, yes, there was a bit of a tension between the two ambitions.

IF: How would you get gigs in places like the Czech Republic and Spain?

Richard Amundsen: It was really through the underground record scene. There was a guy in Leeds who would distribute records round Europe and he did that with our records. It was really quite beautiful because everyone in that punk DIY scene at the time would help each other. If you knew someone in Cologne, they would know someone in Leipzig who would know someone in Berlin. That would lead on to Prague, then Slovenia and so on. It was a little network round Europe and when bands were coming to the UK they would email me to see if I could help them put gigs on. So, you could arrange a tour that way.

IF: This a scene that is outside of Sunderland. Who were the contemporary bands on that scene?

Richard Amundsen: Some US bands on the label Dischord records ran by Fugazi like Q and Not U, Blue Tip. Although we really looked up to these bands, eventually we became on a level with them. It was so exciting for us because, although we played ourselves down, we were becoming just as good as these American bands who we sort of idolised.

IF: How did you get an album out?

Richard Amundsen: We were lucky. The guy we knew from Leeds called Ian Simpson who helped us get gigs and sell records, also ran a label called Subjugation Records. He helped us with all his contacts and helped with distribution. We just scraped a bit of money together to record an album that we could then put out with Ian's help. We recorded it in Stoke on Trent as we liked the sound of a band that had recorded there.

IF: Did you use a producer because the sound of the first record is so sharp and fresh and feels well produced?

Richard Amundsen: No, we just had an engineer but we went down with a good idea of how we wanted the songs to sound, so the engineer helped us achieve that. We wanted a pure drum sound and we got the sound we wanted on the guitar from an old scratchy amp I used. To be honest we were really chuffed with the results. I think it reflected what we sounded like live and that's what we wanted. It got good reviews in places like *Kerrang* and the *NME* and John Peel played us so it was all really nice.

The second album we did with Fred Purser in Newcastle. Fred was great. And that got good reviews as well. We seemed to have a really good reputation without having what you would call mainstream success.

IF: The recordings sound really raw and angry. Were you angry at the time?

Richard Amundsen: I would say so. It was like a hangover from being a teenager and going to a rough comprehensive school in Sunderland, we felt that we had something to say. I guess we were just probably angry youths.

IF: With all this positivity about the band, both live and recorded, how did it come to an end?

Richard Amundsen: We did lot of tours and the last thing we did was a single on Ross Millard's label called "Short Term, Long Term" in 2007, which was probably one of our biggest songs. We did a video for it and that was done by Frankie Francis and Pete Gofton, who was Kenickie's[2] drummer. We then played the Evolution Festival in Newcastle on the big stage and that was our last gig. We didn't really decide it was done but there were now other things going on in our lives. Sometimes things naturally come to an end. We didn't fall out but I think we'd done what we had wanted to do. We thought where next? We had toured round the UK and all round Europe and made loads of mates in the process. We had made and sold thousands of records. We had been in the back of the van for weeks on end and had the best times of our lives and we just asked ourselves how much more can be done because we've done it all. It was like going to a great party but when it comes to an end you think you know what? I am ready to go home now. So that is what we did, we went home.

IF: Do you have any regrets?

Richard Amundsen: Probably only one. I became a teacher and just before I did that Pete from Field Music asked me if I wanted to do a tour of America as their bass player. My dad said, 'There's no way you're going there son, you need to get your head down and get a job and a career.' So, I turned it down and I think I regret that. I don't think I regret anything about This Ain't Vegas. I think the kudos we got from those that knew us and heard us and saw us will outlast any commercial success we could have had.

IF: How do you feel when you get name checked as the genesis of a scene that carries on to this day?

Richard Amundsen: It's nice to be recognised. I think we probably were a catalyst for what came next. We did get a bit frustrated with the Futureheads coming along and then Maximo Park and maybe we didn't get recognised by the media. It was our own fault really. That said, it was so exciting to be near to the Futureheads and Field Music and see how well they have done. We were inspired by them because they were so great and they were our mates. It was really such an exciting time.

IF: Why has Sunderland sustained a vibrant musical scene for over 20 years?

Richard Amundsen: I've thought about this quite a lot. I think when you get people who are in the shadow of somewhere else, it creates an underdog spirit. We have to do our own thing. Things have never been given to us on a plate and because of that we have put the work in. If I had been born in Liverpool, for example, with the Cavern and all that legacy on your doorstep, it may have been a different thing. Making the scene happen adds the extra excitement. When everything is there for you you've got nothing to fight for. Sunderland can be, at times, quite apathetic and negative, but there's also a lot of people here who want to fight that. That makes me proud of the place. To see the bands being so much part of the regeneration of the city is just fantastic. You have the likes of Barry Hyde from the Futureheads with the Peacock and his studio and his music industry degree course, Field Music with so much of Sunderland in their music and their studio, Frankie and the Heartstrings with Pop Recs[3]. We were all part of setting up Split Festival in Sunderland,[4] which was again part of Sunderland's cultural journey. These things are something to be proud of.

IF: What is music for you now? How do you keep involved?

Richard Amundsen: Well, I look back fondly and I miss being part of that vibrant scene. But I've got a little boy and am doing a Psychology PhD, so times change. I have a band called White Legs, with the old drummer Jordan and Martin Longstaff who is, of course, Lake Poets. We still do some gigs now and then and probably want to do some new music but start from scratch. The itch is still there.

•••••••••••••••••

So, there it is. This Aint Vegas, one of the North East's representatives in the worldwide DIY punk scene of the early 2000s. It took them round some far-flung corners of Europe where they could sing their hearts out to crowds that stood five foot in front of them. They did not achieve Fugzai's or the Futureheads level of success but they certainly achieved the level of success they set out to achieve. That is measured in memories rather than record royalties. That gets them undying kudos in Sunderland, as well Spain, France and countless other places. And they know, in their time, they created just a little bit of magic and that is enough for them.

1. Bandcamp is digital music platform where a band's back catalogue can be bought and downloaded.

2. Kenickie were a band from Sunderland who just predated what is now known as the Sunderland scene. They released two successful albums in 1996/97 and played on *Top of the Pops*. Lauren Laverne, who was guitarist and singer of Kenickie, is the sister of Pete Gofton and now more well known as a 6 Music presenter and host of R4's *Desert Island Discs*.

3. Pop Recs is a café and music venue in Sunderland set up by Frankie and the Heartstrings in 2013 originally as a six-week pop-up venue.

4. The Split Festival was a two-day festival in Sunderland set up by members of Sunderland bands that ran from 2009 to 2014. It was held at Ashbrooke Cricket Club and later Mowbray Park and was headlined by acts such as The Charlatans, Public Image Limited and Dizzee Rascal.

Field Music

Peter Brewis' and David Brewis' Story

Field Music are brothers Peter and David Brewis along with various supporting musicians. I meet the brothers in their recording studio in a quiet part of Sunderland. It is a large space packed with guitars, a double bass and mixing and recording equipment. We settle down with a cup of tea and the brothers answer each question in a thoughtful and considered manner. Often one brother will start a sentence and the other will finish it. I make an error in likening their music to XTC and Steely Dan, as that oversimplifies what is often complex and intelligent music. When I ask them how they would describe their music, David says, 'Weird pop music,' which will have to do. Their touchstones are undoubtedly the Beach Boys, the Beatles and Prince and they will later talk of art rock, free jazz and collage music. When you listen to their work it is all that and more. Sometimes it seems like an intellectual exercise but then a sweet melody will float across and carry you off. Like their music the brothers are hard to pin down, but they are great company.

IF: How did it all start for you?
Peter Brewis: After seeing Bros and the Bangles on *Top of*

the Pops I decided I wanted to get some drums. This was about 1989.

David Brewis: I was more into Michael Jackson, but our parents loved music so that influenced us.

Peter Brewis: Our parents grew up at the right age for the Beatles, the right age for Free and they were the right age to buy *So* by Peter Gabriel in 1986. So these were all things that influenced us. At the point where the likes of Soul II Soul took over from Stock, Aiken and Waterman our parents stopped buying records and we took over. Our parents just didn't get dance music, but we did. But we had all the records to play from Bob Dylan's *Freewheelin'* up to Level 42 *Running in the Family*.

Peter Brewis: Then I went with my dad to buy some drums from a classified advert in the *Sunderland Echo* and he knocked them down from £100 to £90. It was a brown Premier Kit. This would be Xmas 1989.

David Brewis: So, I felt jealous of Peter's burgeoning musical career, so I used my pocket money to buy a guitar from Argos, which I still have and still occasionally use it live (Peter picks up a battered acoustic to illustrate what David's original Argos guitar looked like). Our mam and dad didn't play and the music tuition at our school wasn't amazing but because we could play together we could progress.

Peter Brewis: Instead of me and David playing with Lego or making *Star Wars* kits we started acting out being in bands. I would have been 12 and David would be 10 at this time.

David Brewis: We didn't have lots of friends at school who played in bands but there were a couple in Peter's year who did so we started doing youth club bands who would play crappy versions of "Sweet Child of Mine". We then started having guitar lessons with a guy called Les Cheatham who played for a time live with Venom.

Peter Brewis: We weren't with him long but he had a little four-track recorder and he encouraged us to record stuff. So he got us to make stuff up as well as play other people's songs. It was then that I realised that I can play a bit of guitar and a bit of drums but what I really liked was mixing all that together.

David Brewis: Round about 1992 we got our own four-track cassette recorder.

Peter Brewis: Also, around the same time I heard Led Zeppelin and that flicked a switch in me. I had never heard anything like it. I am still enthralled by them. Every now and then I'll have a Zeppelin binge and wish I was in a band like that.

David Brewis: At this time we were fortunate that we'd got the recorder but also fortunate that we were indulged and encouraged by our parents.

Peter Brewis: Our parents encouraged us because it was a constructive thing to do but also because it meant we played nicely with each other.

David Brewis: Around the time Peter was doing his GCSEs, me, Peter and a chap called Andy Moore, who later became Field Music's keyboardist, formed a pub band called Underfoot. We played all over the place and had to drive all the stuff about including Andy's Hammond organ. We also had a drummer called Paul Taylor. We often played two gigs a week.

Peter Brewis: We were pretty good but we got a bit bored of it. We were writing stuff that was Hendrixesque and it was all a bit anachronistic at this time. It was all bluesy rock. For being kids we were an excellent pub band, especially with the novelty of us being so young.

David Brewis: To be fair we sound out of time with what we do now but we are conscious of that these days. But, as Peter said, we were a decent pub rock band and we had our first experience of going to a recording studio with Frankie Stubbs (best known as singer of Sunderland's peerless punk band Leatherface) in the Bunker.

Peter Brewis: Frankie was great for us. He was really encouraging for us.

David Brewis: But we were slightly disappointed in what we produced. We found the crappy little demos we made on our four-track to be more interesting to us. It was better quality sound with Frankie but we were on the clock. We couldn't spend the time getting the sound of the instruments right.

IF: What were your career plans at this point?

David Brewis: Like naïve kids we probably wanted to be famous.

Peter Brewis: When I went to see a careers advisor, I said I wanted to be a recording engineer even though that wasn't really what I wanted. And all these years later that's what I am. Anyway, she said I needed an A-Level in physics and an A-Level in maths so that's what I did. I ended up with a D in physics but an A in music.

David Brewis: I guess the A-level in physics does come in handy when trying to programme a synthesiser.

Not long after the pub band started, we were drafted in by someone called Dave Murray to be peer mentors at a youth music project he was doing at the Bunker in Sunderland. We got paid £20 each Saturday. We did this for three or four years. Through this we met the likes of Barry Hyde (later of the Futureheads) and Ian Black (later of Slug and the Bubble Project) who we have made a lot of music with subsequently. We gave up the pub band due to all its limitations musically and really started to discover all different types of music, especially through Barry's dad who had a massive music collection. We discovered the likes of the Velvet Underground and obscure Beach Boys albums.

Peter Brewis: Being in the pub band was not really creative and that's what we wanted to be. It was at this time that we started synthesizing different genres together and making it our own, which is what we do to this day. We started analysing what we were doing to help us be more creative.

I then did a youth work qualification thinking I'd do youth work and David did a Maths degree.

David Brewis: I did a maths degree expecting it would lead on to a job.

Peter Brewis: I did a year at Bangor University doing a Contemporary Classical Music degree, then I came back home and completed a Community Music Degree at Northumbria University, which went in tandem with the youth work.

David Brewis: While all this was happening in 1997, there was the first round of lottery funding available and, as a totally naïve 16-year-old, I applied for some money to set up a recording studio. I was successful and we set up our first studio in Sunderland. This then became part of Peter's degree where his project was musical creativity in young adults. Also, all the people we had met in the Bunker project we could take across to our studio. We had an eight-track reel-to-reel tape machine and Peter spent his student grant on a mixing desk, which we have to this day. So, we began to learn how to record people and we used our friends to practise on.

IF: How did this streamline into what became Field Music?

Peter Brewis: Well, again we were very fortunate with timing. Firstly, meeting lots of likeminded people at the Bunker project inspired us. We were also pretty pretentious in thinking we were some sort of left-bank intellectuals, when in reality we were situated in John Street, Sunderland. But, while I was in the Futureheads (Peter was the Futureheads' first drummer, later replaced by Barry's brother Dave Hyde), we put together manifestos. For example, I couldn't cross my hands when drumming and this informed the drumming style and we always had to have coffee before we played. The other thing that influenced us was the rise of punk DIY culture. There was a bunch of very young lads who formed a band called This Aint Vegas and they would get other bands from places like Leeds to play up here. They were all influenced by the Washington DC DIY punk culture with bands like Fugazi and Minor Threat. That rubbed off on us., the idea that you could just do things yourself. We had our own studio and were in control of how we made our own music. We would send demos to record labels but were always ignored, which was a bit soul destroying.

At the time we were in separate bands like the New Tellers and Electronic Eye Machine (both bands featured the brothers and various different musicians) but we had the same ideas flowing through. It was all very conceptual and, although it may not have fit with the traditional ideas found in Sunderland, it worked with the people we knocked about with. There were about 20 of us and we were all in bands and all trying to be different and creative. Success at the time was to play a gig at the Royalty in Sunderland, get 20 of our mates in there, for them to have a good time and that was it. But we were free to try whatever we wanted.

David Brewis: After playing a show in Manchester as Electronic Eye Machine we got a manager called Dave Taylor from FON studios in Sheffield. This was a music industry showcase called 'In the City' and was our first brush with the music industry. We'd previously won as a two-piece in 1999 as the New Tellers with just synthesisers and videos almost in sync. It was called 'Charity Shop Europa' and we knew we were being provocative in a world of indie guitar bands but somehow we won. After that we got lots of phone calls from music industry people, like managers and lawyers, but after having the phone calls we didn't hear from them again. Basically this was because we are awkward.

Peter Brewis: We were especially awkward then and so bloody minded that we were going to do things our way.

David Brewis: Our focus then was really on the art of what we were doing with no regard to practicality. We were very sceptical about the music industry and this only increased over time. We were getting chased around by music industry types because we'd ticked a box and won a showcase but not because they were interested in what we were doing. From then on we would only associate with people who genuinely got what we were doing.

We had loads of meetings with music labels and they would ask 'What are you trying to do?' and we couldn't answer that. We wanted to continue our musical research, but people wouldn't fund us to do that. The only person who was the exception was Dave Taylor who said, 'I don't care if you're doing two different bands, I think what you're doing is interesting.'

Peter Brewis: He said, 'We are not going to get you a record deal, we are going to get you a publishing deal.' Basically, because we were doing so many different things it meant we could get money out of Chrysalis Records to allow us to keep doing what we were doing, and they would get the rights to whatever output we achieved. They owned the songs that we wrote for ten years. We got £40K each and this was one of the last decent publishing deals going.

David Brewis: With this we set up a proper studio along with the Futureheads and a couple of other people as a co-operative. It was a rehearsal space and a recording studio. It was a turret room of an old school building in Swan Street, Sunderland. We recorded the first Futureheads demo there, the first two Field Music albums and the first Maximo Park single there. It was called 8 Music as there were eight of us. This was 2001 and I had been accepted on a teacher training course just days before the publishing deal came through, so I was saved from a career in teaching.

Peter Brewis: We didn't know what to do next. We had 20 songs but didn't know what to do with them. We were waiting for a record label to tell us what do. The money was running out by 2003 and I had to move back in with my mam and dad. I had to force myself to get a proper job. I realised that if I was going to do something with music, I had to get organised and not wait for something to happen. So, finally we decided it was time to make an album. We stopped being in two separate bands and our mate Andy Moore was up for it. It was time to take things seriously.

David Brewis: We finished the album and we had a shortlist of people from the music industry that we liked and we sent it to them and said, 'We've made this record and we're not desperate to put it out ourselves. So if you want to release it please tell us.' The only people who get back to us were Memphis Industries, who we have been with ever since. We met them through Pete Gofton who had been in Kenickie.

IF: What were your expectations of that album?

Peter Brewis: At the time the Futureheads and Maximo Park were becoming very successful. We realised our music wasn't immediate like theirs and actually playing the songs live was very disappointing. We were shy and struggled live but we got one or two good reviews. In *Uncut* they said, 'Imagine Brian Wilson of the Beach Boys producing Wire', and that meant a lot to us.

David Brewis: We didn't realise that a little bit of critical acclaim would be so important. We weren't going to set the indie discos alight, so that acclaim was affirmation of what we could do. We were always going to be a slow-burn band.

IF: How did you develop towards the model that has sustained your career since 2005?

Peter Brewis: Well, after the first two albums we quit for a bit. It wasn't till after this that it coalesced into this current model of existence. Rightly or wrongly, we felt we were in the wrong competition. We were the right age and played the right instruments to compete with the Kaiser Chiefs and other British indie bands, but we weren't like them at all. So, at the time, when people went to indie gigs they expected to see the Kaiser Chiefs and we weren't that. We were boring, boring people and you couldn't dance to what we were doing.

David Brewis: Even now, if I felt we could sustain a career without playing live I'd be tempted to take that. However, especially then, to stay in the public consciousness and to build up to something sustainable, playing live was important. We were wrung out by this time. We did a tour supporting Maximo Park with a soundman and a guitar tech. We stayed in hotels and when we got to the end we'd lost £1,000. We felt it just wasn't what was meant by DIY, not losing money. So, from then on, we would pack up the stuff in my dad's car and tour, just the three of us and doing it all ourselves and it was just knackering.

Peter Brewis: Driving all the way to the Bath Mole Club and then playing to 10 people was not good. Basically, we ran out of money. We couldn't afford to keep Andy in the band as he had a family and needed a certain income. It just wasn't working so we packed it in and put the band on hiatus. We went back to our studio and did music that we wanted. I did The Week that Was and David did The School of Language. It was back to doing experimental bands to see how it would work.

David Brewis: Previously on a Field Music tour of the USA we had met the head of Thrill Jockey records, Bettina Richards. This was a Chicago label, which was home to some our favourite musicians such as Tortoise. They put out the kind of post rock, free jazz, angular, indie, collage music we aspired to. So they put out the School of Language record in the States. In a weird way stopping Field Music and putting out these two side project records re-started it for us. We came back pretty invigorated.

IF: You got great reviews for those two records. Was that heartening?

Peter Brewis: We got great reviews for those records. But we've had bad reviews as well over the years.

David Brewis: All we have control over is the quality of what we release.

Peter Brewis: We don't tend to think of how the records will be received. I think about what I like and then think about what David might like. Then I might think what Barry, Ross, Dave and Jaff of the Futureheads might like. And, maybe, I think what my dad might like, but after that I don't really get bothered. But we are lucky because we have each other and we really encourage each other to be as daft as possible.

IF: At some point you said, 'we are professional musicians'. When did that happen and how?

Peter Brewis: I think we figured it out around 2010. We were lucky to come up in the digital music era when the possibilities are so vast. We realised we could do a double album of stuff we wanted to do, alongside rock stuff, which we could take out live. Which is what we did and we thought we'd be a rock band.

David Brewis: We'd got better as a live band during the two solo records that we put out. Also, by the time we came out with the third Field Music album in 2010 people had discovered us a bit and were ready for another album. The touring was better. We got Ian Black in the band and he was a great laugh. For the first time, playing live didn't feel like a waste of time.

Peter Brewis: For the first time we were having fun. It was almost like being back in the pub rock band. We could rock out. We performed for the first time. We did something like 90 shows that year, which was a lot for us.

IF: Would it be fair to say that you had worked out how to create a model that would sustain a living on an on-going basis?

David Brewis: We realised we didn't need a manager and these two solo records, and the third Field Music album, created a template that worked for us. We could keep our costs low, we could record ourselves in our studio, we had our own van. If we did all these little practical things whatever we made from our records came back to us. The unsuccessful records don't cost much money and the successful records make us a bit of money. We are now at the point where almost everything we've made has been in the black not the red.

Peter Brewis: We are quite risk averse. We know that everything will make a little bit of money.

David Brewis: But it is difficult to plan. For example, if some music is used for an advert that may bring in £4K. We can't plan for that but we do know it will keep us going for a period. Everything we do makes a little money but it's not too far from hand to mouth. The tours we do don't make that much for us. Our main objective will be to make sure we pay the band.

Peter Brewis: With tours we share any profits with the band. So everyone will get a guaranteed minimum amount and then any profits on top of that will be shared. The model works to an extent because we understand not to spend too much money and be in control of our production.

IF: What inspires you to make the next album?

David Brewis: There are still things we haven't tried. So, my last album was fixated on the '60s sound of Van Morrison or Donovan.

Peter Brewis: I have been fixated on Yellow Magic Orchestra. So, I have just finished a synth album of primarily instrumental music. This will be out later this year, we are just scheduling it in.

IF: Do you feel lucky to have such freedom but also the confidence that people like and are interested in what you are doing?

Peter Brewis: To be fair people have the freedom to not ever listen to us again and that is always a possibility. But if people do decide not to listen to us me and Dave will still find a way to do things. We feel that there are still so many things we haven't done yet.

David Brewis: We have been beneficiaries of so many fortunate situations from our mam and dad supporting us to working with sympathetic people, be that a label or other musicians.

Peter Brewis: None of it is talent. We are very capable and lucky to have a facility to allow us to synthesise our influences into other things.

David Brewis: But we realised that taking our influences and using them to make something new is what everyone does anyway. We don't necessarily do this consciously but we enjoy the realisation when our influences stand out in what we do.

Peter Brewis: You could look at Stravinsky sitting down and playing the old masters and then composing. And you could say that he was nicking stuff but as long as you are conscious of it, that's fine. The Beatles were always so conscious of their influences.

IF: You constantly have new projects coming to fruition, do they ever clash?

David Brewis: We always work together even if it's titled a solo effort so it works well.

Peter Brewis: We work well with our label, Memphis Industries. For example, our keyboard player, Andy Moore, has recorded an EP of his own songs with us and we are releasing that on our label but with help from Memphis Industries.

David Brewis: When you complete an album there is always the wait for it to be released and that waiting time is horrible. So, we always have the next project on the go, as the album release process is not creative but more like business, which doesn't inspire us.

Peter Brewis: We are happier when we are making stuff. Our label actually said we do too many records and they suggested we set up our own label for all the stupid stuff we do. So, we did and we have a label called Daylight Saving Records. We put out the last Slug album on this label.

IF: What do you do if one of you introduces something new and the other one doesn't like it?

Peter Brewis: It doesn't really work like that, as I always realise that Dave's intention comes from the right place. Sometimes you hear a piece and you don't quite get it but you'll do it anyway because you trust their intentions.

David Brewis: We have a lot of faith in each other being able to do good stuff.

IF: Why has Sunderland sustained a music scene for over 20 years?

David Brewis: It has had its ups and downs. The DIY ethos that came directly from Washington DC and via This Ain't Vegas created a desire to help each other. I do think the music scene has helped with the cultural renaissance of Sunderland.

IF: If there is any of Sunderland in your music?

Peter Brewis: The lyrics are all about Sunderland. Musically, one of my biggest influences was Barry from the Futureheads. We maybe don't strictly see ourselves as a 'Sunderland band' but we love all the people in this so-called scene. I would say people are very supportive of each other and I don't think there is any competition between us. I don't think we are that bothered about success. We are more bothered about did we doing something interesting or good? And I think that runs across all the people involved in Sunderland.

IF: What is the future for Field Music?

Peter Brewis: I think we should split up.

David Brewis: Really?

Peter Brewis: Yes, just for a couple of weeks. But really, Dave has just released his solo album, I've all but finished mine and then in two weeks we will probably start the next one, which may or may not be Field Music. We have a drawer full of ideas, such as making a prog rock album or an '80s Level 42 type album. So we will try stuff like but it won't end up like that. The last one was supposed to be like Free and there is, bar one bass line, nothing at all related to Free on it.

IF: You really are in an enviable position to come in here on a daily basis and be able to do what you want or what inspires you.

David Brewis: We have swapped financial security for artistic reward. For us its how do we keep doing things that are interesting and, at the moment, we generate just enough income to scrape by. I think what happens is that we are excited about a project and we know we can make it happen.

Peter Brewis: We are in an enviable position because everyday we come in and can say, 'What do we want to do today?'

David Brewis: For us we feel that we still have our best music in front of us.

IF: Tell me about the tweet Prince did about you?

David Brewis: He tweeted a YouTube link for one of our song. Now that song was a really explicit nod to Prince. It was an explicit homage to "Parade". So, we wondered whether it was a shot across the bows before getting a legal letter. There was a lot of press about it and I got asked to do an article for the

Guardian, so I wrote about five Prince songs that we'd ripped off. It was us saying how much we loved Prince. Then he tweeted a link to that article. At that point we realised he was OK with it.

•••••••••••••••••

Field Music are in the very enviable position of being able, as they say, to go to work everyday and work on music that inspires them. They will then release their music with a good idea that it will work financially for them. They are true DIY. They have taken risks, been awkward and wilfully headstrong and no doubt frustrated some people who worked with them. Like many people I have talked to, they think that they have been fortunate and on occasions they probably have but they have made their own luck. What strikes me, and they may well dispute this, is that they have and have always had a clear vision of what they want to do and where they want to go with their music. They also have the musical and creative talent to realise that vision. It now seems like an instinctual process that works time after time after time. And, to top it all off, they are thoroughly nice chaps.

Frankie & The Heartstrings

Frankie Francis' Story

Frankie & The Heartstrings are a band from Sunderland, formed in 2008 by three friends, Frankie Francis, who sings in the band, Michael McKnight, guitarist and Dave Harper, drummer. Now, 15 years later, they are known as much for their catchy, jangly indie pop music as they are for setting up Pop Recs, a café-cum-record-shop-cum-music venue. It is rightly seen as the beating heart of Sunderland's music scene. However, the road that led to the current fantastic home for Pop Recs is one that has taken a heavy toll on them.

I recently listened to a heartfelt and raw obituary for Dave Harper, the Heartstring's drummer who died in August 2021 aged only 43, by the journalist James McMahon on his podcast. James is mentioned a lot on these pages in relation to the band nights he put on while a student in Sunderland. On this particular podcast there is a recording of Dave saying the following words: 'I knew poverty and grew up round poverty. We believe only the community will save the community.' In those few words he summed up himself, his band, Pop Recs, the café and venue that he helped set up and run, and the whole of the DIY ethos of the Sunderland music scene. To say that Dave left a 'Dave Harper shaped hole' in Sunderland when he died does not really do him justice. He was a one off and was, like so much of the North East, a bundle of contradictions. He was caustic in his wit yet caring and full of love. He was funny, antagonistic, outrageous, and someone who would literally do anything he could to help others and particularly those from his community.

His absence continues to be keenly felt by those who knew him and those who had met him. So, on 22 May 2023, when Frankie & The Heartstrings play two shows at Pop Recs to celebrate 10 years of the venue, his absence is both felt and celebrated. It is fitting that his drum stool is taken with aplomb by Peter Brewis of Field Music and that the Heartstrings include Ross Millard from the Futureheads as one of their guitarists. They are joined for their last two songs by Pete Gofton, formerly the drummer of Kenickie. That these scene stalwarts are involved is testament to the longevity and community element of the musical scene here in Sunderland. However, as I attend the matinee show, which has a higher percentage of children there, Frankie makes the point that Pop Recs was set up in the first place to help and inspire young musicians to pick up instruments and follow in the footsteps of all the bands of Sunderland. It is a fantastic and inspiring show.

Frankie Francis is the singer in the Heartstrings and is an equally charismatic face within the Sunderland music scene. Like many others, he has crafted a secondary career to the music while remaining very much rooted in the cultural community he grew up in. As well as being a singer in a band he is a commentator for the official streams of his local football team and a music DJ for Amazing Radio. I kick off our chat by referring to his rather enviable career choices.

IF: You are a pop star, a football commentator and a radio DJ. That is many a kid's dream. What did you want to be when you were at school?

Frankie Francis: I used to tell me mam when she asked me that I wanted to play football for Sunderland, have a number one single and read the news on the telly and I've sort of fallen between the gaps. So, I guess it's aim for the stars and see where you end up as you fall back down. I'm sort of in that world and very happy and privileged to do what I do.

IF: How did the band get together?

Frankie Francis: Well, I'd just graduated from doing a degree in Radio Production at Sunderland University, which is really what I wanted to do but there weren't any immediate opportunities when I left, so I was DJing and attending gigs in Sunderland and I'd always been working part time in bars. I ended up running a bar in Sunderland called the White Room, which was one of the venues used for gigs. I was working there and Dave and Michael, who were pals, used to put a night on there every month. We ended up talking about bands we had in common that we liked such as Dexy's Midnight Runners, Orange Juice and '50s kitchen sink pop from Britain. So we decided to give it a go as a band. We thought *wouldn't it be great to have a band with that mix of styles in Sunderland*. The dream was simply to get a gig in the White Room. It all happened very quickly from there.

IF: Did you know you could sing?

Frankie Francis: No, in the first place I wanted to play bass. The idea of being a front man was a million miles away. The only other time I'd sang was at a charity night at the original Independent venue which Dave put on, where lots of North East Bands dressed up as famous artists. I think Maximo Park played, Field Music played as Fleetwood Mac and I did the Doors as Jim Morrison, playing along with Field Music. That was the only time I'd ever sang in public before getting the Heartstrings together. So, after a few practices Dave and Michael suggested I'd be a better singer than bassist.

IF: It seemed to take off really quickly. You released a single, then an album. Did it appear a quick rise to you?

Frankie Francis: I'd never been in a band before so wasn't sure what to expect. There were lots of bands about but only the Futureheads and Field Music had had any success. The day we made our first demo in Pete Gofton's garage I burnt a CD of what we'd recorded. That night I was going to see the DJ Andrew Weatherall do a DJ set in Sunderland. I spent a lot of the night chatting to Andrew about music. He had a show at the time on 6 Music so I thought I'd chance it by giving him a CD. He phoned the next day and said, 'I love the demo and I'm going to play it on the radio.' So, we tuned in that Sunday night and he played not just one song but all the songs we'd recorded and proclaimed us as, 'The best new band in Britain.' We'd only done two gigs at the time, playing about six songs. Things moved pretty fast from that point. We did a gig in Newcastle the week after and there were loads of record labels up to see us at the gig. By the time we'd done five or six gigs it was pretty clear we were going to be signed by someone, it was just a matter of us selecting the right people to be around us.

IF: You toured with people like Florence and the Machine and your first album was produced by one of your heroes in Edwyn Collins from Orange Juice. Did you feel starstruck or did that wear off quickly?

Frankie Francis: It really does become normal quickly. The novelty never wore off with us because we are five working-class lads from the North East but we would end up at parties with people like Kate Moss and Pete Docherty on the Florence tour. The indie A list at the time were hanging around. On that tour it was Florence, us and another band who no one had ever heard of at the time called the XX, which was an odd mix. It was an Academy tour and was just before Florence got really big.

Every day you would get introduced to someone else so you got used to it. We shared a label, Wichita[1], with the Cribs, who were one of our indie label idols at the time and one of the best indie bands the UK has ever produced in my opinion. So, it was expected that you would hang out with all the other bands on Wichita. We did our first single with Rough Trade[2] and we met up with Geoff Travis and he tried to get us to sign but we ended up just talking about Morrissey and the Strokes and all the bands he'd worked with over the years. So, you get in this world of name dropping and its only when you come back and you maybe act a bit like that in front of your mates from school and they are like, 'Will you pack that in.' It's a very strange world that and I am glad we were always anchored to the North East.

IF: Why did you only record three albums?

Frankie Francis: We got to a point before Dave died that we recorded about 20 demos but then the pandemic slowed things down. We spoke about things towards the end of the pandemic but when Dave died everything seemed to come to a stop. We still have a record deal and people would be interested to see what we might do. It would be a big decision for us to do more as everyone is so busy with their lives. As you know it's a very unique situation these days where people can make a living just from music so we've all developed lives outside of music. But never say never but it would feel very different without Dave. I guess, also, another reason why we lost momentum a little but was Pop Recs which took a lot of everyone's time.

IF: Tell me the story of how Pop Recs came about?

Frankie Francis: We spent ages making our second record with Bernard Butler[3] and it suffered a little from taking so long. We needed something to get our momentum back and put a flag in the ground to say, 'We're back and this is how we are doing it.' We had the idea of opening a shop in our native Sunderland. In it we'd sell our new record over a two-week period and get our friends from the celebrity worlds to play this shop for free or next to nothing. Amazingly, we got people like the Vaccines, Franz Ferdinand and the Cribs to put on gigs there in those very early days. That was all we planned to do so it is testament to the project and the city that ten years later it's still here.

IF: How much are music and projects like Pop Recs drivers for the renaissance of Sunderland as a whole?

Frankie Francis: It's everything. The only people who frequent the city through the week are musicians who are rehearsing or trying to put gigs on in the city centre. That's all I can remember and it's been a constant throughout that time. Club nights have come and gone, whereas Sunderland's musicians have remained constant in trying to do things and put things on in the city. They have to be given credit for being catalysts for this huge transformation that we are seeing now. Essentially, you've had all these artists going around the world, being interviewed and giving the impression that Sunderland is really cool as it spawns this music. The reality is that we have all had to kick against a system where there was no support and it wasn't cool. It made us all more hungry to try and strive to get better. The new auditorium, the Fire Station, would not have been built if there hadn't been the bands here first and that has shown that if you build a nice new shiny venue it will drag more people into the city centre that wouldn't have really thought of coming here.

IF: Prior to all this what caused the initial explosion of bands like the Golden Virgins, This Aint Vegas, the Futureheads, Field Music and many others?

Frankie Francis: When I went to Sunderland College, I found it to be a meeting place for likeminded people from the area to get together and share music. It was people from different schools meeting up in quite a creative environment. Maybe there was more a buzz from finding out new music and new sounds. Now you don't have to save up to buy a record, so maybe there was a little more excitement back then discovering new music and sharing it with others.

IF: At the recent matinee show for ten years of Pop Recs you talked to all the little ones from the stage encouraging them to pick up the baton and be the next generation of musicians. Are you confident that this movement will continue?

Frankie Francis: I think now with the Bunker, Pop Recs, the Fire Station, the Independent, the Peacock, people have far more safe spaces to express themselves. I remember Jaff from the Futureheads getting in trouble with the *Sunderland Echo* because he'd been abroad and been interviewed and asked what Sunderland was like and he said, 'It's the sort of place where I get home and get off the bus with my guitar on my back and someone will throw a stone off me.' And he was completely right but he got stick at the time. I don't think that's the case anymore and that's great. I think schools are getting better at encouraging young people to be accepting of each other and that's what young people are like. And that is all good for culture and arts as people are more comfortable in expressing themselves. So I am confident of more music coming from the area. I think we need more rehearsal space, if we are lacking anything. We just need to ensure that places like Pop Recs stay open to give young people access to places to perform. The early ethos of Pop Recs was to create a stage that anyone could perform on. If someone said, 'I want to play at Pop Recs' the answer would be, 'Yes.' Even when we were touring there would be barriers to performing and we, in Sunderland, want to break those barriers down.

IF: For those who didn't know him how would you describe Dave Harper?

Frankie Francis: Dave was one of the beating hearts of the Sunderland music scene and will be forever remembered for how hard he worked on the establishment of Pop Recs. When I first met him he was in a band with Michael, which was called Son's of Brenda because both Dave and Michael's mam's were called Brenda. He was also a promoter, putting on gigs at the White Room where I met him. He was about 10 years older than me. He was very well read and had a really big record collection, he really educated me. If you ever met Dave you never forgot him.

He was the last man standing at Pop Recs. It got into a position where only Michael and Dave got a wage. In the end it was Dave's stubbornness that kept it going when it looked like funds weren't coming in or when the new venue was threatened. It literally killed Dave to get this place open and I can't underestimate how important he was to the music scene and to the city. He was just so determined to make the city better and put culture at the centre of it.

Everything about Pop Recs works, it's purpose built. So, for example, when you load in as a band you go straight to the stage, which is really important for bands. And it's going to keep getting better! Hopefully residential facilities will be built so bands can stay overnight after playing. It was through Dave's hard work that this exists but he would say that this is just the start and that there should more places like this in a place like Sunderland.

•••••••••••••••••

Frankie tells me that having recently played two shows at their own venue, Pop Recs, to celebrate its tenth anniversary, they have talked about making more music. However, it is such a difficult process for them to consider this without their talisman, Dave Harper. I wonder if Dave is up there in heaven urging them on and intrigued to see what they may create.

---

1. Wichita Recordings are an independent British record company who have signed the likes of Bloc Party, Waxahatchee and Bright Eyes.

2. Rough Trade Records are an independent record company who most famously signed the Smiths as well as the Strokes, the Libertines and the Sleaford Mods.

3. Bernard Butler was the guitarist for Suede and then scored hits as part of McAlmont and Butler. He is also known as a record producer who has produced amongst others the Libertines, the Pretenders and Neneh Cherry.

Nadine Shah

Nadine Shah is an opinionated person. Ask her about any issues, be it the pitiful income artists get from streaming, gender inequality, racism and immigration, mental health and anything in between and you will get her opinion fired back from both barrels. And when she talks, she tends to make a lot of sense. Sometimes her opinions may obscure her highly accomplished musical career, that has seen her release four acclaimed albums, one of which, *Holiday Destination*, was nominated for the 2018 Mercury Prize. To see Nadine at her best, check out her incredible performance of her song "Out the Way" at the Mercury Awards on YouTube. She has also recently finished a run as Titania in A *Midsummer Night's Dream,* for which the *Stage* magazine said, 'Nadine Shah's unique voice brings power and melancholy to Titania.' If I was to try and describe her music, I would refer to her low, brooding voice and her percussive music. However, if I said she had a bit of Siouxsie Sioux, in her Creatures phase, that doesn't really do her justice. Really, she just sounds like Nadine Shah. She is unique.

When talking to Nadine she is an open book, sometimes painfully so. She is aware of how she may rub some people up the wrong way. She is self-effacing and brutally honest. And she is fantastic company with her heart in the right place. She truly is a diamond and maybe one that is under-appreciated in the her native North East (she was born and brought up in Whitburn, South Tyneside). However, this may be about to change as she tells me about exciting developments in her career that will see her returning home after 20 years down south.

IF: How did music start for you?

Nadine Shah: There's no brilliant story to it, I was just good at singing and from a young age that is what I decided I was going to do. My family weren't massively musical. My dad has a beautiful singing voice but he would only sing in his own language; he is Pakistani. He'd sing sad Pakistani love songs and I hated that sort of music when I was young because I didn't understand, although I love that music now. I loved Whitney Houston and Maria Carey, singers with big voices.

One of my problems, as a young woman with a big voice, is that I was never encouraged to write my own songs. But then I got into jazz music somehow when I was about 15. My mam, who was so keen to support me, went through the *Yellow Pages* to find somewhere I could record a few jazz songs. She found this tiny recording studio in Consett, County Durham ran by two old fellas called Mick and Denny. My mam would take me there once a week for about six weeks and I did some gospel covers like "Wade in the Water" and some jazz covers like "Fever" and "Cry me a River" and this became a demo, which I still have. It sounds terrible. But it was really joyous doing it and I loved Mick and Denny, they were the nicest fellas. We got a bunch of CDs made and whenever I went down to London with my mam, we'd try and give them out. I just wanted to be a singer and my mam was intent on helping me with that aim.

I was into jazz so we would go to the Pizza Express Jazz Club in Dean Street in Soho. One time we were there my mam passed the CD onto a waiter, saying 'My daughter is a great singer'. Quite amazingly we got a phone call a week later, when I was back in Whitburn. The waiter had passed on the CD to his boss, a gent called Leo and he said, 'Yes, I want to work with Nadine.' He had the idea to work with a few young artists and start his own label. That never came to fruition, but it gave me a start. So, a month later, I moved to London, aged 16, to sing jazz songs in Pizza Express. My older brother lived in London and I moved in with him, which he hated. Before moving to London I had never done a gig in my life, I had only recorded this CD of covers. I would sing in different Pizza Express restaurants round London and I'd get £50 and a plate of dough balls and a glass of wine.

IF: Was that daunting at such a young age?

Nadine Shah: Nah, I loved it. I had a pianist with me and he would get £50 as well. I learnt the Cole Porter songbook. Most people weren't listening as we were just background music. I found that frustrating as I wanted them to listen. Leo would ask me to come to the Jazz Club in Soho to watch the artists and learn from them. So, I spent a year and a half watching the greats and hanging about with them, people like Georgie Fame[1] and Mose Allison[2]. After the club would close I would be hanging about, so when the great Mose Allison finished his set I said to him, 'Sir, you didn't play "Parchman Farm"' and he said, (Nadine effects a convincing Southern American accent as Mose was from Mississippi) 'Well, I don't play that song', and I said, 'But it's class' and he said, 'Well, I'll play it for you.' The club was closed and he played that song just for me. At the time I didn't realise how magnificent or significant that was. Looking back that time as a 16 or 17-year-old in Soho, I can't believe it happened.

I didn't really have any friends my age in London, even though I pretended to my brother that I did, so the average age of my friends would be 60, all old jazz fellas. It was really the best time of my life. It was great time, I met Amy Winehouse and became friends with her as she was around the same scene and circuit.

IF: Did you have specific aspirations?

Nadine Shah: Well, they changed when I went down to London and sang jazz. When I was younger I was certain I'd be famous, I'd sit and practise autographs. I just wanted to be famous but spending all this time with all these old Jazz fellas changed my whole view of music and my approach. I lost my interest in fame and was only interested in music as an art form. I saw people doing things they loved for nothing and the desire for fame just evaporated. I felt part of a new gang, which I loved, and felt like a proper artist or musician. However, I did eventually tire of just doing jazz standards and felt the need to write my own stuff.

IF: How difficult was it moving from singing standards to creating your own songs and finding your own voice?

Nadine Shah: Even when I was singing jazz songs I'd sing them in my own accent. Even to this day I get grief for my accent. I'm from Whitburn but my parents had foreign accents so mine is difficult to place sometimes. I also loved Nina Simone, who was the first female artist who used this lower singing range, which is what I have always had. Before that I was trying to sing in a higher range as people are always pushing sound pretty, sing high. You know, you hit the high notes and you get the applause. So, hearing Nina Simone changed everything for me, and it really inspired me to write my own songs.

I was not really trained in playing the piano, but I had a keyboard and once you realise where the notes are and how you form a chord it was quite easy to use that to give me the platform to write songs. I found it easy to get nice sounds out of the keyboard and I had a collection of poems to lay across the sounds I was making. A friend of mine had died and this led to me writing poems for him and then "Dreary Town," which was the first song I ever wrote.

IF: How did this lead on to a record deal?

Nadine Shah: Well, actually, I had a brief period where I'd come back to Newcastle and was in a band called Kinevil with

Mike Porter (now in Smoove and Turrell) and Kristian Atkinson. Kristian introduced me to lots of new music, stuff like The Fall, which I loved. It was after this that I started writing my own stuff. I then put a video of me playing "Dreary Town" on Facebook and a mate of mine passed this on to Steven Braines, also from Newcastle, and he said, 'I want to manage you.' He lived in London and I went to see him. He asked, 'Have you brought all your songs with you?' and I said, 'Oh, me laptop broke.' He said, 'How many songs have you got?' and I said, 'Ten.' I was lying because I only had the one song. He asked me to come back next week so I had to write another nine songs. I went back down and met his management team and we started looking for producers to record an album with. We met a load of producers and I hated them all. They all wanted to put my vocals really far forward in the mix which I didn't want and put loads of strings on the songs. In hindsight, I wish I had as I might have made a load more money. So, I met all these high profile, hot shot producers and didn't like any of them, so my manager said look at your record collection, see who you like as a producer and Ben Hillier's name kept coming up. So we met up for a coffee, he liked my songs and Ben and I have been collaborators ever since.

IF: You must have had innate confidence to say no to all these top producers?

Nadine Shah: Success to me at that point, and still to this day to an extent, was to master an instrument so I can write some songs and then record those songs. I wasn't chasing anything beyond that. So achieving that and being able to hold vinyl with my songs on was enough. Anything I have achieved after that has been a beautiful bonus. If it all finished tomorrow, then fine because I have loads of nice stories and I've had a really nice time. People might say that is not aiming high enough, but I don't care as I've had a really nice time. But, yes to answer your question, I was a pretty confident kid.

IF: Moving on with your career, how much difference did a Mercury nomination make for you?

Nadine Shah: Personally, for me it meant loads. Lots of cool people would say they don't care but I was obsessed with the Mercury Awards and followed them every year. So, I always dreamed of being nominated. When I was nominated I was so chuffed and honoured to be there and it was probably the best night of my life. I was the bookies' favourite to win, and the favourite never wins but it introduced me to a new audience, so my popularity went up and my fees went up but more than that my confidence grew. After that I felt like a proper artist, as I've always felt a bit of an outsider. I've never been in a gang or a scene as such. With that album, *Holiday Destination*, I was invited into the punk fold with the likes of Idles, Life, Heavy Lungs and we became a bit of a gang.

IF: Your performance at the Mercury Awards was so powerful and emotional. How did you feel before and after that performance?

Nadine Shah: I remember it all very vividly. It's weird doing a performance like that partly because it's recorded live for television but also just doing the one song. The song we did "Out the Way" is normally our last song so we build up to it. Essentially for the Mercury performance you are going in for a sprint cold. Backstage I was screaming loads and punching things trying to psych myself up for it. I knew where my mam and dad were sitting and saw I my brown dad and my white blonde mam and that was why I wrote the song and seeing them put the fire in my belly. I didn't care at all about being live on the telly. We were also shoved to the side of the stage, unlike some of the acts but I wasn't bothered. I just felt you've got to do your job. I can't remember too much about afterwards. I just went backstage then out to hug my mam and dad. My table, which was my label, were convinced we were going to win so when they announced Wolf Alice as the winner they were just heads down, gutted. I looked over to my mam and she just shot me an L for loser sign which was really funny. But the night also resonates a lot because my mam wasn't herself that night. She was dressed so glamorously and beautiful that night and I was in an old pair of jeans and an old shirt. Afterwards though she was too tired to party with us and she wasn't herself. It turns out she had stage four lung cancer, although we didn't know that at the time, and this was something she didn't recover from. So, I think about that night a lot but the fact that she got to see that night means so much for me. For her, that night was sort of *my little girl is going to be okay.*

IF: Your first two albums were quite personal and then your second two albums were more political covering immigration and racism and female roles in society. Why did you change tack after your second album?

Nadine Shah: The big change was because my elder brother, Karim, is a documentary maker and he works for companies like Al Jazeera and Panorama. He goes to the frontline to report on issues round the world. I was living in London and when he'd return, we'd go out for breakfast to catch up. One time he came back, and I was asking how his trip had gone and he could hardly speak and I didn't really recognise him. He'd come back from Syria at a time when it wasn't quite front-page news. I was asking him what was going on and he said, 'Nadine, there's a civil war going on there. Why don't you know?' And he was a bit angry with me. He was understandably in a bad mood that day and he said, 'You know what? Maybe you should write some songs about things that really matter.' With that he left breakfast, and it really got me thinking. So, I rang him and said, 'Right, tell me more and I'll write about it.' As I was writing, the news started filtering through about the plight of people fleeing from Syria and there was a harrowing picture of a man holding his dead child on a beach. At the same time there were stories about refugees and immigrants ruining people's holidays. It was impossible to write about anything else. My rubbish love life certainly paled in comparison at that point. I'm glad I did it but understand that a lot of people don't like me because I did it. I understand that some people don't like me because I came across as virtuous and righteous and I get that. I didn't mean to be, I just wanted to do a job.

IF: Can musicians effect change through their music?

Nadine Shah: I have said before that it's an artist's duty to document the times we live in. But I also said there needs to be a space for artists to soundtrack their heartache.

IF: You talk about other issues in your music like mental health and gender equality. Are things improving in those areas in the music industry?

Nadine Shah: It depends who you ask. My experience hasn't been too harrowing. I've been lucky. I've always been surrounded by good men. Ben Hillier is a good man. He has never stifled me and always encouraged me. The men in my band are good men. My manager Ros Earls has been in the industry for a long time and she could tell awful stories. Music hasn't had its Me Too moment but I know of stories that could make your blood boil. There are still things happening that are quite heinous, but people are getting away with it. I get called outspoken. I am not a brave person but because I speak out people, maybe, don't target me as much.

I haven't been in the industry so much since 2018 when my mam took ill. I also became ill and spent time in rehab after a suicide attempt, so I've been outside the music industry. I did speak out regarding the streaming enquiry and that was because during the covid lockdown musicians' livelihood and ability to make a living through live work was taken away. Then we started looking at the streaming platforms. We are still being streamed so why aren't we getting paid? I joined in that fight but the toll it took on my mental health was bad. I had so many of my peers saying they would stand by me but when push came to shove, I went over the top out of the trenches to fight the music industry. I looked back and it seemed like no one had followed me. At the time I was very angry with them, but I am not now because I understand why because this is such a volatile industry. So many people want a career, so I understand why those who had one didn't want to jeopardize that. We are the creative spark for the industry, but we are treated like bottom feeders.

Very ironically, on the back of this fight I got signed by EMI, arguably one of the evil big beasts. I rang David Joseph, Chairman of EMI UK (Universal UK who effectively bought EMI). I said to him, 'If you want to be artist friendly, sign me and prove to me that you are artist friendly.' And so he did. I have now moved to EMI North, which was set up to nurture talent in the North of the UK and I am actually moving back to Newcastle, so it is all very exciting for me after having such a tough time of it. So, as with others, David Joseph is a good man in that he backed up his words, so despite him maybe getting grief for leading one of the big record labels, he gets respect from me, and I hope EMI North can be a real boost for Northern artists. He actually wants to effect change for the good. EMI North is based in Leeds and it's the first time a major label in the UK has been based outside of London. My friends in Pit Pony, from Newcastle, will be releasing music via EMI North and it is also working with Generator, the Arts support agency in Newcastle, so it is all really exciting. That's why I am with them.

With regard to females in the industry, more people are speaking up and it is changing. I knew I was getting paid less than male acts. I would ask men playing at festivals, who were playing the same stage as me at the same time but the next day, how much they were getting paid. They would say, 'Nadine, I can't tell you' and I would say, 'Oh, yes you can.' And I was getting paid 25% of what they were getting paid for exactly the same slot. I spoke to my booking agent, who also represented the male artist I talked to. It was important to try to hold people accountable. So, I think things are starting to change.

IF: Is it changing with streaming? I believe you get about £3,000 for a million streams.

Nadine Shah: It will only change when streaming is considered a rental and not a sale. I have now signed to a major label and that is part of a cartel effectively. I did tell them when I signed that I would be shutting up. There is simply no transparency in streaming. If we had the strength to stand together as artists and say that's all you are getting, then things may change but that isn't going to happen. But I think I need to stop talking about this as I need to protect my own mental health.

IF: Why in the North East has there been a lack of female artists and a lack of politically focusssed artists?

Nadine Shah: Well I had to leave the North East to get successful. I used to get angry when I got a bit of fame and then the North East wanted to take ownership and I'd think you did nothing for me. There is not a huge lineage in the North East for female artists. There was a lack of role models. There was sort of a Maths Rock scene in Newcastle when I was growing up and I was obsessed with that with bands like Obi Got Ludo, who were an amazing band fronted by Dave Turnbull and Joe Stringer. And I would go to all these gigs at places like the Tyne Bar or the World Headquarters. I'd go on my own and there was an assumption that I wanted to get off with the band members which I had no intention of at all. I'd chat to them after about what they were up to and what equipment they used but no one ever asked me to join their band. However, Kinevil did, and even though now they are apologetic that I was only a backing singer. They now say they should have had me up front. I was desperately searching for other females to form a band with, but I just couldn't find them and I couldn't really say why that was.

Years later I am mates with the likes of The Futureheads and Maximo Park and they will say 'Oh, Nadine, we didn't know you wanted in on the scene' and I would say, 'Yes, you did.' But, to be fair on them, The Golden Virgins were very supportive of me, The Futureheads have been really supportive and Maximo Park have been super supportive of me. But at the time I felt excluded and very much an outsider to the scene. It was like being a kid and you were wanting to be asked to play and I never was, even though I was desperate to be in a band. And I felt it was because I was a girl. That is changing now, I think.

IF: How much of the North East is in the music you write?

Nadine Shah: Well, my accent is pretty present. I've lived away from the North East for 20 years but I am never away from it. My parents have been there, my best friends are from there. I am moving back in three weeks. The first album was written at home so there are a lot of references to the sea. I wrote the fourth album, *Kitchen Sink* predominantly at home in Whitburn as my mam was dying. My mam knew she was dying but she had a gallows humour, as only a mother from South Shields could. Her sense of humour made me write *Kitchen Sink*.

IF: How did you transition into acting? Was it nerve racking?

Nadine Shah: As I mentioned I unfortunately had a suicide attempt 18 months ago due to PTSD and related to losing someone during covid. I had got really poorly so after this I went to rehab. I was due to go there for four weeks, and I didn't want to go but once there I opted to stay for three months and it was the best thing I ever did in my life. I came out and my manager asked if I wanted to go through all the work emails. She said, 'I'll start with the funniest one first' and she read, 'Would Nadine Shah like to be the Queen of the Fairies, Titania in *The Midsummer Night's Dream*?' And I said, 'Yes!' And Ros said, 'But the pay's rubbish.' I did that for four months and it gave me the structure that I needed after Rehab, and it was the best thing I could have done. And I got to spend six weeks back in the North East doing the play which was great. I now have a bit of bug for it. With singers we are often performers whereas people want it to be real and raw. If it was always real and raw it would drive you to distraction. But I am a performer and that's in my bones and, even though I have Northern humility, I can say I'm good at acting. With theatre there is a kinetic energy that is similar to gigging.

IF: Does performing come from your mam or your dad?

Nadine Shah: No, neither of them. My mam sometimes would say, 'When you're on stage I sometimes can't even look in case you make a fool of yourself' and I'd be, 'Thanks, mam!' As I said my dad has a lovely voice but would never sing in public. I guess I'm a people pleaser and I get a kick out of it. And I've now had two decades of performing.

It's been a funny journey over the last 20 years, and I've had a bit of break but now I am moving back to my beloved North East. It's so exciting!

•••••••••••••••••

It feels appropriate to finish this book with Nadine Shah as, in some ways, she points the way forward. She is mixed-heritage and a strong woman who has fought for everything she has got. As you can see she is so incredibly honest to the point where it is painful. She is a blunt and straightforward in a manner that can take you by surprise. She has been very open about her mental struggles and that is a force for good. At her core she is a compassionate, caring individual who certainly wants to give back to the region from which she sprang. She is a good woman. Welcome back Nadine.

1. Georgie Fame is a British Jazz musician who had top ten hits in the UK with songs like "Yeh, Yeh" and "The Ballad of Bonny and Clyde".

2. Mose Allison was an American Jazz and Blues musician, singer and songwriter. He has been described as 'one of the best greatest blues songwriters of the twentieth century.'

Conclusion

This book began with the question, 'Why has there been no nationally recognised music scene from the North East of England?' What follows has been a journey through the musical decades of this region. It has led me to meeting a bunch of the most weird, wonderful, talented, humble and friendly people. For almost all of them the passion for music that got them started on their musical paths is undimmed with age. The answer to the initial question really is, 'Who cares?' There have been undeniably influential scenes, such as the heavy metal scenes, and there have been scenes that lit up the region, such as the initial 1960s scene. However, I have learned more about the individual artists than the so-called scenes, such as, what drove them, what held them back, why some people 'make it' or are widely recognised and others are not and latterly how artists now structure their business to survive and sustain a musical career. The most consistent feeling I got when meeting these people is that they tend to be very down to earth and friendly, but you invariably get a glimpse into a natural talent that is far from the norm. It is not by chance that these people achieve what they do. They were born with innate talent. Equally, though, and this may be a

Northern trait, there is often a conflicting lack of self-confidence that competes with an inner drive. For those featured on these pages the inner drive has tended to triumph.

If we look at each period in turn, certain themes emerge that illustrate both the failings and advantages of this region in supporting the scenes as they came along. Apart from not having the Beatles, there are a number of reasons why the North East didn't emulate Liverpool in the 1960s. Firstly, the role models for the '60s up here were the Animals, who had hits with inspired choices of cover songs. Unlike Lennon and McCartney, they did not write their own hits and so, for the bands with whom they rubbed shoulders, it really didn't occur to them to write their own songs, why should they? This meant the choice of which song they recorded was crucial and for the bands up here it was invariably the wrong choice. The one person of note writing songs at the time was the talented and charismatic Alan Hull and while this didn't result in success for The Chosen Few it certainly did for his next band, Lindisfarne. In London, the Rolling Stones' manager, Andrew Loog-Oldman, intuitively spotted what the bands up here didn't, and that was the need to emulate Lennon and McCartney in writing your own songs or your time in the limelight may be short. That hints at another reason why the North East has sometimes not fulfilled its potential, a lack of visionary managers.

Over the years there have been a succession of managers in the pop world whose reputation for hit making is the equal of the artists. Starting with Brian Epstein and the Beatles and the rest of the Mersey Beat groups, an astute manager can be the difference between success and failure, almost regardless of talent. Then you had Loog-Oldman with the Stones, Lambert and Stamp with the Who, the gangsterish Don Arden. Later on you see the importance of Alan McGee for the careers of Oasis, Primal Scream, Jesus and Mary Chain and Kathryn Williams! In 1960s Newcastle there was Mike Jeffrey. Mike hailed from London but did a degree in Newcastle. After that he opened and ran clubs, such as, the Downbeat Jazz club and later the influential Club a'Gogo. Jeffrey was instrumental in getting the Animals down to London and later for helping Chas Chandler manage Jimi Hendrix. However, his reputation is somewhat shady and accusations of siphoning off money from his acts persist. He was undoubtedly an important figure for the music scene in the North East, but as a music manager, he was nowhere near the same league as Brian Epstein or Alan McGee for vision and instinct.

Throughout this book, the lack of management or the unsuitability of the management that the acts secured is a consistent theme. However, 20 years after the Animals rose, we saw the emergence of a management team in Keith Armstrong and the Kitchenware team. They showed exactly what management should be and how crucial it can be in helping bands achieve their potential. Keith is a talent spotter par excellence and that is evident even today as he spots and nurtures local talent for Soul Kitchen Recordings. However, what was most important was the label's drive to firstly promote local talent and say to the world, 'We are great up here and we don't need to go to London to prove it.' Secondly, what Keith wanted to do was secure the best deal for his acts, so they could be heard by the most people, surely the raison d'etre for all good management. No doubt people as talented as Paddy McAloon and Prefab Sprout and The Kane Gang would have achieved success regardless, but Keith and his colleague's part in this should never underplayed. The equally talented Martin Stephenson turned his back on what he saw as the greed and ruthlessness that was needed to play the music industry's game. This set him at odds with his manager, Keith. However, 40 years later Martin enjoys a happy and successful (on his terms) career and fully acknowledges that it was Keith and Kitchenware who gave him the profile in the 1980s that allows him to play to full houses around the country all these years later.

I began the folk section talking to Lindisfarne, who are one of the best loved, best-selling and best songwriting groups this region has ever produced. It raised the question of whether Lindisfarne are indeed a folk band as their roots were equally blues rock. As you delve further into this question, it becomes apparent that folk in its purest form is an area of music and culture that the North East has long been at the forefront of, but it is one that is somewhat hidden away from the general public. The folk clubs of Stockton, Birtley, the Bridge Hotel in Newcastle or the Dun Cow in Seaham and others have existed for over 60 years in some cases. If you visit those folk clubs, you will hear songs written as long as 150 years ago, often sung in local dialect, and songs written by North Easterners about the North East. They survive in no small part due to the dutiful efforts of the people who play in those clubs and those people who have transcended the clubs to national and international fame such the Unthanks, The Young 'Uns and Alistair Anderson. Obviously, there are numerous others who deserve mentioning but that would take another book dedicated to this most dedicated of musical scenes.

One element that I have been very aware of is that this region has not produced many successful female artists, or maybe failed to recognise the female talent within its midst. One field of music where female artists have been more appreciated and acknowledged is in folk music and the singer songwriter scene as described by Kathryn Williams. This is to those scenes' credit. However, talking to Keith Armstrong about his current label, Soul Kitchen Recordings, it appears that the balance is shifting far more towards recognising female talent. As well as the acts that Keith is promoting, there are lots of singers and acts coming through in this region, such as Bigfatbig, Komparrison, Beth Macari and many, many others. Let's hope this is a trend that continues.

Punk rock and the New Wave of Heavy Metal flourished in the region at roughly the same time but had very different vibes and very different trajectories. Both scenes had bands that followed the DIY ethic that later fired up the bands mentioned in the Sunderland section but where it took them was very different. In the punk scene, the violence that was witnessed at the gigs was described in shocking detail. It was an edgy time and the violence at gigs is something that people attending gigs today would not recognise at all. Many of the bands who took up their instruments after being inspired by the Sex Pistols had to up sticks and trudge down to London, as there was no infrastructure in the North East to support their development. However, once down there, a lot of the bands experienced a very uncaring, unsupportive and, in some cases, a quite devastating music industry.

Despite notable exceptions, like the Toy Dolls, most of the bands' careers were quite short lived and those involved often left with a feeling of disappointment.

Heavy Metal bands who rose to prominence in the late '70s and early '80s had a completely different experience. They had a circuit of gigs to play, in the working men's clubs, where violence was not the norm and would not be tolerated. They had Neat Records, which offered them the apparatus to get recording experience with the assistance of Mickey Sweeney and Steve Thompson. They could get vinyl out to their fans and had the interest of the music press. This was also replicated on a slightly smaller scale at Guardian recording studio in Pity Me in Durham. This infrastructure was a launchpad for some of the bands, especially Venom and Raven, to enjoy worldwide careers that amazingly persist to this day. The vibe that comes from these sexagenarian musicians who are still touring the world is one of excitement, positivity and passion. They are an absolute breath of fresh air.

When talking to the heavy metal and punk bands it raised the issue of the importance of journalists in supporting local bands and promoting them nationally. For both genres there were local journalists such as Phil Sutcliffe, Ian Ravensdale/Penman, Tom Noble and the photographer Rik Walton shouting out loud to anyone who would listen about acts from the North East. They, along with Dick Godfrey, did a show on Radio Newcastle called *Bedrock* which was dedicated to local music and some of them wrote for music weeklies such as the *NME* and *Sounds*. I hear tales of these journalists going beyond what could be expected to help the musicians of the region but, for some unknown reason, they just didn't have the national clout to raise the region to the mythical stature that Paul Morley did with Manchester. It is equally interesting to see the absolute power the *NME*, *Sounds* and *Melody Maker* had in the 1970s to the '90s. One sentence in the *NME* was enough for Kathryn Williams to get on the ladder of success. That such publications no longer exist is a worry for any band trying to get national exposure and the ear of record company A&R people. How do record companies based in London hear about acts from up here today?

The book ends with the Sunderland scene, which is possibly the most coherent and enduring of all of the scenes I have looked at. Its musicians have remained in the local area and developed careers that have not been restricted by their desire to remain local. The musicians and their music came first and what has followed as a direct result are music venues, recording studios and, as a result of efforts from the Futurehead's Barry Hyde, a music industry degree. The bands continue to support each other, also support the next generation of artists and continue to play and help out in each other's bands.

Talking to Maximo Park and Sunderland bands illustrates how the music industry has changed. Within the period of this book, we have seen the full arc of the industry. In the 1960s the music industry was in its infancy, but by the time Lindisfarne signed their deal and released their music, it had reached a golden age, where record companies were rich and a select few of the artists shared in that wealth. By the time of punk, heavy metal and even Kitchenware, the labels were rich enough to take risks. However, for many bands and artists this meant that they were given a glimpse of what was possible, only to have that unceremoniously snatched away when they were dropped by the labels with precious little explanation. Ross Millard of the Futureheads is very aware that his band was at an inflection point for the music industry, where initially they were signed to Warner Brothers and enjoyed worldwide tours and the support of an extensive record company machine. They were fortunate to have had an experienced and far-sighted manager who foresaw the effect of the change from people buying physical product to the murky world of streaming. From this point onwards, artists began to realise that being in a band or being a singer alone would not sustain a living or pay the mortgage. Many of the bands and acts I have talked to have sustained a creative career by careful planning and diversifying. Without doubt many of these acts, whether it's Field Music, Kathryn Williams or Raven, point the way forward in creating a business model that works for them.

What the Sunderland scene espouses is the DIY ethic, a sense of community and an awareness of what culture can do for a community. This was seen with Kitchenware in the '80s and is now being seen more than ever. There are many other people in this region who are following the same path. Matt Baty, singer of Pigs x 7 runs an independent record label in Newcastle called Box Records, and works at a music publishing company based in Newcastle called Wipe Out Music which boasts, amongst others, Sleaford Mods on their roster. Lee Allcock in Stockton runs the NE Volume Bar, a fantastic supporter of local original music, along with the NE Volume Magazine, which equally promotes local talent. There will be many others who I don't know about who equally deserve mentioning. DIY and community is what the North East Music scene is now about, and maybe always has been.

We appear to have come full circle. In the '60s the Junco Partners, the Elcort and the Chosen Few, and so many other great bands, were playing to packed houses in the North East of England. It was a joyous, happy and self-sustaining scene until the record industry hinted at riches available beyond this region. Between then and now, there have been tales of riches and poverty, mayhem and disappointment and everything in between. We have now come back to a time where self-sustainability and community are the drivers and creativity is flourishing. The chances of making millions are now far less possible than ever before, but that is acknowledged and factored in. Maybe, just maybe, we are on the cusp of the next golden generation for North East music where artists can thrive in a supportive and business-savvy community that puts creativity above profit.

Too Far North – Thanks

Thanks to my beautiful wife Ruth for her sub-editing and constant encouragement, to my kids, James, Jessica and Joseph, for their inspiration. Thanks to my friend Neil Saint for his advice, help and guidance and to my friend, Aidan McCann, for being a willing sounding board. Thanks to all my bandmates in Cactusman and The Red Stars.